THE VARIOUS HAUNTS
OF MEN

Susan Hill has won the John Llewelyn Rhys Prize, and the Whitbread and the Somerset Maugham Awards, and has been shortlisted for the Booker Prize. Her novels include *I'm the King of the Castle*, *Strange Meeting*, *The Bird of Night*, *A Bit of Singing and Dancing*, *In the Springtime of the Year*, *Air and Angels* and *The Service of Clouds*. She is the author of *Mrs de Winter*, the acclaimed sequel to *Rebecca*, and two ghost stories, *The Woman in Black* and *The Mist in the Mirror*. Her most recent book is the much praised collection of short stories, *The Boy Who Taught the Beekeeper to Read*.

Susan Hill has also written non-fiction, including the bestselling *The Magic Apple Tree*, and children's books, including *Can It Be True?*. The play based on *The Woman in Black* has been running in the West End for more than fifteen years.

Susan Hill was born in Scarborough and educated at King's College, London. She is married to the Shakespeare scholar, Stanley Wells, and they have two daughters. She lives in a Gloucestershire farmhouse from which she runs her own small publishing company, Long Barn Books. Susan Hill's website is www.susan-hill.com.

Susan Hill

THE VARIOUS HAUNTS OF MEN

A Simon Serrailler crime novel

VINTAGE

Published by Vintage 2005

12 14 16 18 20 19 17 15 13

Copyright © Susan Hill 2004

Susan Hill has asserted her right under the Copyright, Designs and
Patents Act 1988 to be identified as the author of this work

First published in Great Britain in 2004 by
Chatto & Windus

Vintage
Random House, 20 Vauxhall Bridge Road,
London SW1V 2SA

Random House Australia (Pty) Limited
20 Alfred Street, Milsons Point, Sydney,
New South Wales 2061, Australia

Random House New Zealand Limited
18 Poland Road, Glenfield,
Auckland 10, New Zealand

Random House (Pty) Limited
Isle of Houghton, Corner of Boundary Road & Carse O'Gowrie,
Houghton 2198, South Africa

The Random House Group Limited Reg. No. 954009
www.randomhouse.co.uk/vintage

A CIP catalogue record for this book
is available from the British Library

ISBN 9780099462095 (from Jan 2007)
ISBN 0099462095

Papers used by Random House are natural, recyclable
products made from wood grown in sustainable
forests. The manufacturing processes conform to the
environmental regulations of the country of origin

Typeset by Palimpsest Book Production Ltd,
Polmont, Stirlingshire

Printed and bound in Great Britain by
Bookmarque Ltd, Croydon, Surrey

The various haunts of men
Require the pencil, they defy the pen.

George Crabbe, *The Borough*

For
My dearly loved Ghost

The Tape

Last week I found a letter from you. I didn't think I had kept any of them. I thought I had destroyed everything from you. But this one had somehow been overlooked. I found it among some tax returns which were more than seven years old and so could be thrown away. I wasn't going to read it. As soon as I saw your handwriting, I felt revulsion. I threw it in the bin. But later I retrieved it and read it. You complained several times that I never told you anything. 'You haven't told me anything at all since you were a little boy,' you wrote.

If only you knew how little I had told you even then. You never knew one quarter of it.

Once I had read your letter, I began to think and to realise that now I can tell you things. I need to tell you. It will be good to make some confessions at last. I have held on to some secrets for far too long.

After all, you cannot do anything about them now.

Since I found your letter, I have spent a good deal

of time sitting quietly, remembering, and making notes. It feels as if I am about to tell a story.

So let me begin.

The first thing I must tell you is that very early on I learned how to lie. There may have been other things I lied about but the first I remember is that I lied about the pier. I went there, when I told you that I had not, and not just once. I went often. I saved money, or else I found it in the gutter. I was always looking in gutters, just in case. A few times, if there was no other way, I stole the money; a pocket, a purse, a handbag – they were generally lying about. I am still ashamed of having done that. There are few things more despicable than stealing money.

But, you see, I had to keep going back to watch the Execution. I couldn't keep away for long. When I had watched it, I was satisfied for a few days, but then the need to see it began again, like an itch.

You remember that peep show, don't you? The coin went into the slot and rolled down until it hit the hidden shutter that made the whole thing start. First, the light went on. Then, the three little figures came jerking into the execution chamber: the parson with his surplice and book, the hangman and, between them, the condemned man. They stopped. The parson's book jerked up and his head nodded up and down, and, after that, the noose dropped down and the executioner jerked forward; his arms went up and took the noose and put it round the man's neck. Then the trapdoor opened beneath his feet and he dropped and swung there for a few seconds, before the light snapped off and it was over.

I have no idea how many times I went to watch it, but if I did know, I would tell you, because I mean to tell you everything now.

It only stopped when they took the machine away. One day I went down to the pier and it just wasn't there. I want to explain how I felt. Angry – yes, I was certainly angry. But I also felt a sort of desperate frustration, which went on boiling inside me for a long time. I didn't know how to get rid of it.

It has taken me all these years to find out.

Does it seem strange to you that I have never seen the point of money, since then, never had much use for it beyond what is merely necessary? I earn quite a lot but I don't care for it. I give much of it away. Perhaps you knew all along that I disobeyed and went down to the pier, because you once said, 'I know everything.' I hated that. I needed secrets, things that were mine only and never yours.

But now, I like talking to you. I want you to know things and if I still have secrets – and I do – I want to share them, just with you. And now, I can choose to tell you and how much I tell you and when. Now, I am the one who decides.

One

A Thursday morning in December. Six thirty. Still dark. Foggy. It had been that sort of autumn, mild, damp, lowering to the spirit.

Angela Randall was not afraid of the dark, but driving home at this dreich hour and at the end of a difficult shift, she found the ectoplasmic fog unnerving. In the town centre people were already about but what lights there were seemed distant, small furred islands of amber whose glow gave neither illumination nor comfort.

She drove slowly. It was the cyclists she feared most, appearing suddenly in front of her, out of the darkness and fog, usually without any reflective strips or clothing, quite often even without lights. She was a competent but not a confident driver. The dread, not of crashing into another car, but of running over a cyclist or a pedestrian, was always with her. She had had to steel herself to learn to drive at all. Sometimes, she thought it was the bravest thing she would ever be called upon to do. She knew what horror and shock and grief death in a road accident brought to those still living. She could still hear the sound of the knock on the front door, still see the outline of police helmets through the frosted pane of glass.

She had been fifteen. Now, she was fifty-three. She found it hard to remember her mother alive, well and happy, because those images had been blotted out for ever by that other – of the so loved face, bruised and stitched, and the small, flat body beneath the sheet, in the cold blue-white mortuary light. There had been no one else to identify Elsa Randall. Angela was the next of kin. They had been a close unit and everything to each other. Her father had died before she was a year old. She had no photographs of him. No memories.

At fifteen, she had been left entirely, devastatingly alone, but through the following forty years, she had come to make the best of it. No parents, siblings, aunts or cousins. The idea of an extended family was unimaginable to her.

Until the last couple of years, she thought she had not only made a pretty good fist of living alone, but that she would never, now, want to do anything else. It was her natural state. She had a few friends, she enjoyed her job, she had taken one Open University degree and had just embarked on a second. Above all, she blessed the day, twelve years ago, that she had at last been able to move out of Bevham, having saved enough to add to the sale of her flat there and buy the small house some twenty miles away in Lafferton.

Lafferton suited her perfectly. It was small, but not too small, had wide, leafy avenues and some pretty Victorian terraces and, in Cathedral Close, fine Georgian houses. The cathedral itself was magnificent – she attended services there from time to time – and there were quality shops, pleasant cafés. Her mother would also have said, with that funny, prim little smile, that Lafferton had 'a nice class of resident'.

Angela Randall felt comfortable in Lafferton, settled, at home. Safe. When she had fallen in love earlier in the year, she had at first been bewildered, a stranger to this forceful, all-consuming emotion, but quickly come to believe that her move to Lafferton had been part of a plan leading up to this culmination. Angela Randall loved with an absorption and a dedication that had taken over her life. Before long, she knew, it would also take over the life of the other. When he accepted her feelings for him, when she was ready to disclose them, when the moment was right.

Until meeting him, her life had begun to seem slightly hollow. Anxiety about future illness, infirmity, old age, had crept up to the edges of her consciousness, grinned at her. It had shocked her when she had arrived at an age her mother had never been. She felt that she had no right to it. But since that meeting in April, the hollowness had been replaced by an intense and passionate certainty, a conviction of destiny. She no longer gave loneliness, old age and illness a thought. She had been rescued. And after all, fifty-three was not sixty-three or seventy-three, it was the prime of life. At fifty, her mother had been on the edge of old age. Everyone was younger now.

As she left the protecting walls of the town centre, the fog and darkness closed in around the car. She turned down the road oddly called simply Domesday, and left into Devonshire Drive. A few lights were on in the bedroom windows of the large detached houses, but she could only just make them out through the fog. She slowed to twenty and then down to fifteen miles an hour.

Impossible to see in such weather that this was one

of the most attractive and sought-after parts of Lafferton. She knew how lucky she had been to find the small house in Barn Close, one of only five houses there, at a price she could just afford. It had been empty for over a year, following the death of the elderly couple who had lived in it for over sixty years. It had not been a close then, and very few of the imposing houses on Devonshire Drive had existed either.

The house had been completely unmodernised and in a state of some disrepair, but as soon as she had stepped inside it for the first time, behind the young estate agent, Angela Randall had wanted to live there.

'I'm afraid it needs an awful lot doing to it.'

But none of that had mattered at all, because the house had embraced her at once, in a very particular way.

'People have been happy here,' she had said.

The girl had given her an odd look.

'I want to make an offer for it.'

She had walked into the chilly little eau-de-nil-painted kitchen, with its cream gas cooker and brown varnished cupboards, and seen past them, out of the window to the field over the hedge and, rising behind it, the Hill. The clouds had been chasing the sun across it, teasing, making the green slopes now bright, now dark, like children playing.

For the first time since the knock on the door had come all those years ago, Angela Randall had felt what she recognised after a moment as happiness.

Her eyes were sore, with tiredness and the strain of peering through the windscreen into the streaming fog. It had been a difficult night. Sometimes the old people were quite settled and peaceful and there was rarely a call. They just checked round every couple of hours, and did any linen sorting and other routine jobs that were left for them by the day staff. She had been able to do a lot of her degree coursework in the staffroom of the care home, on nights like that. But on this last her books had scarcely been opened. Five of the residents, including some of the frailest and most vulnerable, had gone down with an acute sickness virus, and at two o'clock they had had to call out Dr Deerbon, who had sent one old lady straight into hospital. Mr Gantley's tablets had had to be changed, and the new prescription gave him nightmares, wild, terrifying, screaming nightmares which woke those in the rooms on either side of him in fright. Miss Parkinson had walked in her sleep again and managed to reach the front door, unlock and unbolt it and get halfway down the path before any of them, frantic with sickness everywhere else, had realised. Dementia was not pretty. The best anyone could do was damage limitation and safe confinement, as well, of course, as provide clean, bright surroundings, decent food and friendly care. She wondered how she would have coped if her mother had lived to suffer with an illness that robbed people of their very selves – personality, memory, spirit, dignity, the ability to relate to others – everything that made life worth living, rich and valuable. 'You'll take me in here, won't you,' she had more than once joked to Carol Ashton, who ran the Four Ways Home, 'if I ever get that way?' They had laughed it off and talked of something else, but Angela's questioning had been like that of a child seeking reassurance and protection. Well, she had no need to worry about any of that now. She would not grow old alone, whatever her condition. She knew that.

As she reached the end of Devonshire Drive, the fog thinned and changed from a dense bank to thinner skeins and veils which wound themselves about in front of the car. There were now patches of darkness through which house and street lights shone out clear orange and gold. Turning into Barn Close, Angela Randall could make out her own white-painted gate at the far end. She let out a long sigh, releasing the tension in her neck and shoulders. Her hands were damp on the steering wheel. But she was home. She had a long sleep and a four-day break ahead.

Outside the car she could taste the fog like damp cobwebs across her skin but from the Hill a slight breeze was blowing towards her. Perhaps by the time it broke light and she was ready to go out again, it would have dispersed the last of the fog. She was tireder than usual, after the bad night and such an unpleasant drive, but it would not have occurred to her to change her routine. Angela Randall was an orderly woman, of regular habit. Only one thing had happened recently to break into the safe cocoon she had built around herself and threaten disorder and chaos, but the potential disorder and the chaos were sweet and, to her own surprise, she had welcomed them.

Nevertheless, for the present she kept to her routine, and in any case, if she missed her run even for a day she noticed the difference the next time she went out, felt just a little less supple, breathed slightly less easily. The doctor had told her that she should take up a sport, and she trusted him completely. If he had told her to hang upside down from the branch of a tree for a week, she would have done so. But no sport appealed to her, so she had started running – walking at first, followed by

9

jogging, working up in speed and distance to a daily three-mile run.

'A balanced life,' he had said when she had told him that she was also starting her next Open University degree. 'Take care of both mind and body. Old-fashioned advice but none the worse for that.'

She went into her tidy, spotless house. The carpets, an indulgence for which she had saved carefully, were thick and close-fitted. When she shut the front door, there was the silence she so enjoyed, a soft, deep silence, padded, comforting.

Nothing was out of place. In a sense, this house had been her life and more to her, until recently, than any family, any human being or pet could ever have been. It was reassuringly as she had left it the previous evening. There was no one to rearrange anything. Angela Randall relied on 4 Barn Close and it had never failed her.

During the next hour, she ate a banana chopped into a small bowl of muesli and drank a single cup of tea. An egg on toast, with a rasher of lean bacon, tomatoes and more tea would come later, after her run. Now, she set out the food under a cover, the pan, loaf and butter, refilled the kettle, and emptied and rinsed the teapot. Everything was set ready for later, after the run and her shower.

She listened to the news on the radio and read the front page of the newspaper the boy had just delivered, then went upstairs to her pale blue bedroom, changed out of her uniform and dropped it into the laundry basket and put on a clean, freshly ironed white T-shirt and pale grey tracksuit, white socks and running shoes. Her hair was brushed and pulled off her face in a white elastic headband. She put three wrapped glucose sweets into her pocket and the spare front-door key on a ribbon round her neck underneath her tracksuit top.

As she closed the front door behind her, more lights were coming on in the houses and a thin, sour, bleak dawn was breaking over the Hill. The fog still hung about, wreathing among the trees and bushes on the slopes, swirling, thickening, then shifting and clearing again.

But curtains were not yet drawn. No one looked out, keen to begin the day, to see what was going on or who was about. It was not that sort of morning. At the corner of Barn Close, a few yards from her own house, and at the beginning of the path leading to the field, Angela Randall broke into a light jog. A few minutes later, she was running, steadily, purposefully and quite unobserved, across the open green and on to the Hill and, after only a few yards, into a sudden bolster of muffling, dense, clammy fog.

Two

Sunday morning at a quarter past five and a gale blowing. Cat Deerbon lifted the phone on the second ring.

'Dr Deerbon here.'

'Oh dear . . .' an elderly woman's voice faltered. 'I'm sorry, I don't like disturbing you in the middle of the night, Doctor, I am sorry . . .'

'It's what I'm here for. Who is it?'

'Iris Chater, Doctor. It's Harry – I heard him. I came down and he was making such a funny noise with his breathing. And he looks . . . you know . . . he isn't right, Doctor.'

'I'll come.'

The call was not unexpected. Harry Chater was eighty. He had had two severe strokes, was diabetic with a poor heart, and recently Cat had diagnosed a slow-growing carcinoma in the bowel. He should probably have been in hospital but he and his wife had insisted that he would be better at home. Which, she thought, letting herself quietly out of the house, he almost certainly was. He was also happier in the bed they had arranged for him downstairs in the front room with his two budgerigars for company.

She reversed the car out into the lane. The trees around the paddock were tossing wildly, caught for a moment in her headlamps, but the horses were safely stabled, her family sound asleep.

Not many people kept budgerigars now, apart from the competitive bird-fanciers. Caged birds were out of fashion, like poodles. She tried to remember, swerving slightly to avoid a fallen branch, when she had last seen anyone with a poodle, clipped to look like the woolly pompons Sam and Hannah had made in their playgroup days. What other handmade things had they brought so proudly home? She began to make a mental list. It was eight miles from the village of Atch Sedby into Lafferton, it was pitch dark and raining and there was no one else on the road; for years, to exercise her brain and keep herself awake on these night calls, Cat had forced herself to recite poems aloud – the ones she had learned by heart at school . . . 'The Owl and the Pussy-Cat', 'This is the weather the cuckoo likes', 'I had a silver penny and an apricot tree', and, from the exam years, choruses from *Henry V* and soliloquies from *Hamlet*, the set plays. Listening to the car radio seemed to make her more sleepy, but poetry, or chemical formulae, or mental arithmetic kept her going. Or lists. Woolly pompons, she thought, and pasta pictures, and binoculars made out of the insides of toilet rolls; Mother's Day cards with yellow-tissue daffodils, crooked coil pots, papier mâché animals, mosaics from little slivers of coloured sticky paper.

The moon came out from behind the fast-scudding

clouds just as she turned into Lafferton and saw the cathedral rising up ahead, the great tower silvered, the windows mysteriously gleaming.

> 'Slowly, silently now the moon
> Walks the night in her silver shoon . . .'

She struggled to remember what came next.

Nelson Street was one of a grid of twelve terraces known as The Apostles. At 37, two-thirds of the way down, the lights were on.

Harry Chater was going to die, probably within the next hour. Cat knew that as she walked into the stuffy, crowded little front room, where the gas fire was turned to high and the smell was the half-antiseptic, half-fetid one of illness. He was a man who had been heavy but who was now shrunken and slipped down pathetically into himself, all his strength and much of his life force gone.

Iris Chater went back to the chair beside his bed and took his hand, chafing it gently between her own, her eyes flicking from his crumpled, grey face to Cat's, full of fear.

'Come on now, perk up, Harry, here's Dr Deerbon to see you, Dr Cat . . . you'll be pleased it's her.'

Cat knelt beside the low bed and felt the heat from the gas fire burning into her back. The budgerigar cage was covered in a gold velour cloth with a fringe and the little birds were silent.

There was not a great deal she could do for Harry Chater, but what she would not do was call an ambulance and send him off to die, probably on a hard trolley in a corridor at Bevham General. She could make him as comfortable as possible, bringing in the oxygen cylinder from her car to ease his breathing, and she could stay with them both, unless she was called elsewhere.

Cat Deerbon was thirty-four, a young GP, but one who, from a family of doctors going back four generations, had inherited the conviction that some old ways were still the best, when it came to individual patient care.

'Come on, Harry love.' When Cat came back with the oxygen, Iris Chater was stroking her husband's hollow cheek and talking softly to him. His pulse was weak, his breathing uneven, his hands very cold. 'You can do something for him, can't you, Doctor?'

'I can make him more comfortable. Just help me lift him up on the pillows, Mrs Chater.'

Outside, the gale was hurling itself at the windows. The gas fire sputtered. If Harry lasted longer than the next hour or so, Cat would call in the district nurses.

'He isn't suffering, is he?' Iris Chater still held her husband's hand. 'It isn't very nice, is it, that mask over his poor face?'

'It's the best way of easing things for him. I think he's quite comfortable, you know.'

The woman looked at Cat. Her own face was grey too and creased with strain, her eyes deep-set, the skin beneath them pouched and bruise-coloured with tiredness. She was nine years her husband's junior, a neat, energetic woman, but now she looked as old and ill as he did.

'It's been no life for him, not since the spring.'

'I know.'

'He's hated this . . . being dependent, being weak. He hasn't been eating. I've had a job to get a spoonful of anything down him.'

Cat adjusted the oxygen mask on Harry's face. His nose was beaked and jutted out, as the flesh had fallen away on either side of it. The skull showed clear beneath the almost-transparent skin. Even with the help of the oxygen, his breathing was difficult.

'Harry love . . .' his wife stroked his brow.

How many are there like this now, Cat thought, married over fifty years and still contentedly together? How many of her own generation would stick it out, taking everything as it came because that was what you did, what you had promised to do?

She got up. 'I think we could both do with some tea. Do you mind me rooting about in your kitchen?'

Iris Chater started from the chair. 'Goodness, I can't have you doing that, Doctor, I'll get it.'

'No,' Cat said gently, 'you stay with Harry. He knows you're there, you know. He'll want you to stay beside him.'

She went out to the small kitchen. Every shelf, every flat surface was crowded not only with the usual china and utensils but with decorative objects, ornaments, calendars, figurines, pictures, framed words of wisdom, honey pots shaped like beehives, eggcups with smiley faces, thermometers set in brass holders and clocks like floral plates. On the window ledge a plastic bird bobbed down to drink from a glass of water when Cat touched its head. She could imagine how much Hannah would adore that – almost as much as she would covet the pink crochet doll whose skirt covered the sugar basin.

She lit the gas and filled the kettle. Outside, the wind

slammed a gate. This house fitted its occupants and they the house – like hands fitted gloves. How could others sneer at sets of royal family mugs and tea towels printed with 'Home Sweet Home' and 'Desiderata'?

She prayed that her phone would not ring. Spending some time now with a dying patient – doing something so ordinary as making tea in this kitchen, helping an ordinary couple through the most momentous and distressing parting of all – put the hassle and increasing administrative burden of general practice in its place. Medicine was changing, or being changed, by the grey men who managed but did not understand it. A lot of Cat and Chris Deerbon's colleagues were becoming cynical, burned out and demoralised. It would be easy to give in, to process people through the surgery like cans on a conveyor belt and palm the out-of-hours stuff on to locums. That way you got a good night's sleep – and precious little job satisfaction. Cat was having none of it. What she was doing now was not cost-effective and no one could put a price on it. Helping Harry Chater through his dying, and looking after his wife as well as she could, were the jobs that mattered and as important to her as to them.

She filled the teapot and picked up the tray.

Half an hour later, his wife holding one hand and his doctor the other, Harry took a last, uncertain breath, and died.

The silence in the stifling room was immense, a silence which had the particular quality Cat always noticed at a death, as though the earth had momentarily stopped turning and the world was drained of triviality and urgency about anything at all.

'Thank you for staying, Doctor. I'm glad you were here.'

'So am I.'

'There's everything to do now, isn't there? I don't know where I should start.'

Cat took the woman's hand. 'There is no hurry at all. Sit with him for as long as you need to. Talk to him. Say goodbye in your own way. That's the important thing now. The rest can wait.'

When she left, the gale had died down. It was just beginning to break light. Cat stood by the car cooling her face after the heat of the Chaters' sitting room. The undertaker was on his way now and Iris Chater's neighbour was with her. The peace had been broken into and all the dreary, necessary business that attends on death was under way.

Her own job was done.

From Nelson Street at this hour on a Sunday morning it was a two-minute drive to Cathedral Close. There was a seven o'clock service of Communion which Cat decided to slip into, after checking home.

'Hi. You're awake.'

'Ha ha.' Chris Deerbon held the receiver away from him so that Cat could hear the familiar sound of her children fighting.

'You?'

'OK. Harry Chater died. I stayed with them. If it's all right with you, I'll go to the seven o'clock, and then take a coffee off my brother.'

'Simon's back?'

'He should have flown in last night.'

'You go. I'll take these two out on the ponies. You need to catch up with Si.'

'Yes, there's the subject of Dad's seventieth birthday . . .'

'You'll need some spiritual top-up first then.' Chris was an unbeliever, generally respectful of Cat's beliefs but not above the occasional sharp remark. 'I'm sorry about old Harry Chater. Salt of the earth, those two.'

'Yes, but he'd had enough. I'm just glad I was there.'

'You're a good doctor, did you know that?

Cat smiled. Chris was her husband but he was also her medical partner and, she thought, a better clinician than she would ever be. Professional praise from him meant something.

The side door of the Cathedral Church of St Michael and All Angels closed almost soundlessly. Much of the great building was in shadow, but the lights were on, and candles lit, in the side chapel. Cat paused and looked up into the space that seemed to billow out up to the fan-vaulted roof. Being inside the body of the cathedral in this semi-dark was like being Jonah inside the belly of the whale. How different from the last time she had been here, when it had been packed full of civic dignitaries and a congregation dressed in its finery for a royal service. Then, it had echoed with music and been bright with banners and ceremonial vestments. This quiet, private time early in the morning suited her better.

She took her place among the couple of dozen people already kneeling as the verger led the priest up to the altar.

She would have found it impossible to function as a doctor without the strength she derived from her belief. Most of the others she knew and worked with seemed to manage perfectly well and she was the odd one out in her family – though Simon, she thought, came close to sharing her conviction.

As she went up to the Communion rail, there came vividly into her mind the last time she and her brother had been here side by side. It had been at the funeral of three young brothers murdered by their uncle. Simon had been in the cathedral officially, as the officer in charge of the police investigation, Cat as the family GP. It had been a heart-breaking service. On her other side had been Paula Osgood, forensic pathologist at the murder scene and at the post-mortem, and who had later confided to Cat that she was pregnant with her second child. How had she coped, Cat still wondered, with professional detachment and calm when examining those three small bodies, killed with an axe and a butcher's knife? People like that, policemen like Simon – they were the ones who needed all the strength and support they could get. Beside their jobs, that of a GP in a pleasant town like Lafferton was a doddle.

The short service ended and the ribbon of smoke from the snuffed-out candles drifted down to her . . . She stood. A woman already making her way down the aisle caught Cat's eye, and immediately after her so did another. Both smiled.

Cat stayed back for a few seconds, letting them get ahead, before slipping out and making quickly for the door on the other side of the centre aisle. From here, she could make a getaway across Cathedral Green and down the path that led into the close before anyone managed to waylay her for an apologetic, unofficial consultation.

*

Apart from some cathedral clergy, few people now lived in the fine Georgian houses of the small close, most of which had long ago become offices.

Simon Serrailler's building was at the far end, with windows both on to the close and, at the back, over-looking the River Gleen, a quiet stretch of which flowed through this part of Lafferton. The entrance to 6 St Michael's was here beside a curved iron bridge leading to the opposite towpath. A posse of mallards was swirling about beneath it. Higher up, a swan trod water. In the spring it was possible to sit at Simon's window and watch kingfishers flash between the banks.

> *Case and Chaundy. Solicitors*
> *Diocesan Outreach*
> *Parker, Phipps, Burns. Chartered Accountants*
> *Davies, Davies, Coop. Solicitors.*

Cat pressed the bell at the top of the stepping stones of brass plates, beside a narrow wood strip elegantly lettered. *Serrailler*.

Knowing her brother as she did – as well as anyone could be said to know Simon – she had never been surprised at his choosing to live alone at the top of a building surrounded by offices which were empty for most of the time he was at home and with only the ducks, the dark water slipping below the windows and the cathedral bells for company.

Si was different – different from either of his triplet siblings, Cat and Ivo, even more different from their parents and the extended Serrailler family. He had been the odd one out from as early in their childhood as Cat could remember, never fitting easily into a family of

21

loudly argumentative, practical-joking medics. How such a quiet, self-contained man fitted, and fitted extremely well, into the police force was another mystery.

The building was dim and silent. Cat's footsteps echoed on the wooden stairs, up and up, four narrow flights. At each landing she pushed the timed light switch, which always clicked off just before she made it to the next. *Serrailler*. The same lettering on the plate beside the bell.

'Cat, Hi!' Her brother bent from his six feet four to envelop her in a bear hug.

'I had an early call and then went to the seven o'clock service.'

'So you're here for breakfast.'

'Coffee anyway. I shouldn't think you've got any food in. How was Italy?'

Simon went into the kitchen but Cat did not follow, not yet, she wanted to luxuriate in this room. It ran the length of the house and had long windows. From the kitchen there was a glimpse of the Hill.

The white-painted wooden shutters were folded back. The polished old elm floorboards had two large good rugs. Light poured in, on to Simon's pictures and his few carefully chosen pieces of furniture which mixed antiques and contemporary classics with confident success. Beyond this one huge room, he had a small bedroom and bathroom tucked out of the way, and then the galley kitchen. Everything centred here, in this one calm room, where Cat came, she thought, for almost the same reasons she went to church – peace, quiet, beauty and spiritual and visual recharging of her batteries. Nothing about her brother's flat bore any relation to her own hugger-mugger farmhouse, always noisy and untidy, spilling over with children, dogs, wellington boots, bridles and medical journals. She loved it, that was where her heart was, where she had deep roots. But a small, vital nugget of herself belonged here, in this sanctuary of light and tranquillity. She thought it was probably what kept Simon sane and able to do his often stressful and distressing job as well as he did.

He brought in a tray with the cafetière of coffee and took it over to the beechwood table in the window that overlooked the close and the back of the cathedral. Cat sat cupping her hands round the warm pottery mug, listening to her brother describe Siena, Verona and Florence, in each of which he had just spent four days.

'Was it still warmish?'

'Golden days, chilly nights. Perfect for working outside every day.'

'Can I see anything?'

'Still packed.'

'OK.'

She knew better than to push Simon into showing her any of his drawings before he had selected what he considered the best and fit to be looked at by anyone else.

When he had finished school, Simon had gone to art college, against the wishes, advice and above all the ambitions of their parents. He had never shown the slightest interest in medicine, unlike every other Serrailler for generations, and no amount of pressure had persuaded him even to continue sciences beyond O level. He had drawn. He had always drawn. He had gone to art school to draw – not to take photographs, design clothes or do computer graphics, and certainly not to study installation or conceptual art. He drew beautifully, people, animals, plants, buildings and odd corners of

23

everyday life, in streets, markets, all manner of public places. Cat loved his inspired line and cross-hatching, his rapid sketches, the wonderfully observed and executed detail. Twice a year and for some snatched weekends in between, he went to Italy, Spain, France, Greece or further afield to draw. He had spent weeks in Russia, a month in Latin America.

But he had not completed his art school course. He had been disappointed and disillusioned. No one, he said, wanted him to draw or was in the slightest bit interested in teaching or promoting drawing. He had gone instead to King's College, London, and read law, got a first and immediately joined the police force, his other passion since childhood. He had been fast-tracked into the CID and up the ranks to become a DCI, aged thirty-two.

In the force, the artist who signed his work Simon Osler – Osler was his middle name – was unknown, as was DCI Simon Serrailler to those who went to his sellout exhibitions in places far from Bevham and Lafferton.

Cat refilled her mug. They had caught up with Simon's holiday, her family and oddments of local gossip. The next bit would be more difficult.

'Si – there is one thing.'

He glanced up, catching her tone, his face wary. How strange it is, Cat thought, that he and Ivo are two men of triplets and yet so unlike they might not even be brothers. Simon was the only one for generations to have fair hair, though his eyes were the Serrailler eyes, and dark as sloes. She herself was recognisably Ivo's sister, though none of them saw much of him now. Ivo had worked as a flying doctor in the Australian outback, happy as Larry, for the past six years. Cat doubted if he would ever come back home.

'It's Dad's birthday next Sunday.'

Simon looked out at the shifting cloudscape above the cathedral. He said nothing.

'Mum's doing lunch. You will come, won't you?'

'Yes.' His voice gave away nothing.

'It'll mean a lot to him.'

'I doubt it.'

'Don't be childish. Let it go. You know you can get lost in the throng – God knows there'll be enough of us.'

She went to rinse her coffee mug in the steel sink. Simon's kitchen, in which little more than coffee and toast were ever made, had cost a lot of trouble and a small fortune. Cat often wondered why.

'I must get back and relieve Chris from pony duty. Work tomorrow then?'

Simon's face relaxed. They were on safe ground again. Fifteen days abroad, completely cut off from home and his job, was more than enough for him, Cat knew. Her brother lived for his work and his drawing, and then for his life here in the flat. She accepted everything about him completely, and only occasionally wished that there was more. She knew of one thing, but it was a subject they only discussed if he raised it. He rarely did.

She gave him another hug and left quickly. 'See you next Sunday.'

'You will.'

When his sister had gone Simon Serrailler showered, dressed and made a second pot of coffee. In a moment, he would unpack and go through the work he had done in Italy, but first, he put in a call to Bevham CID. Work might not begin again officially until the following day but he could not wait until then to catch up, check which cases, if any, had been closed in his absence and more importantly find out what was new.

Two and a half weeks was a long time.

The Tape

I wonder if you ever realised how much I hated the dog? We had never had a pet of any kind. Then, when I came home from school one afternoon, it was there. I can see you, sitting in your chair with the brown leather pouffe under your feet and your spectacles and library book on the table beside you. For a second, I didn't notice it. I went over to kiss you as usual, and then I saw it – the dog. It was a very small dog, but not a puppy.

'What is that?'

'My pet.'

'Why has it come?'

'I've always wanted a pet.'

The dog's eyes, bright as beads, gleamed out at me from between long strands of silky hair. I hated it.

'Don't you love her?' you said.

I can tell you now how much I hated the dog, hated it because it was your pet and you loved it but also hated it just for itself. The dog sat on your lap. The dog licked your face with a lilac-pink tongue. The dog took titbits from your hand. The dog slept on your bed. The dog hated me as much as I hated it. I knew that.

But strangely enough, if it had not been for the dog, I might never have discovered what I wanted to become, what my destiny was.

I know you remember the day. I was lying on the hearthrug teasing the dog by waving my fingers under its nose until it snapped, then whipping them away. I became very good at timing it to the split second and I know I would never have been caught if I had just continued in the same way, doing the same thing over and over again. But I made one mistake. Afterwards I was angry with myself for my own stupidity. It taught me to make a plan and then stick to it. I learned a lot that day, didn't I, from a single mistake? Instead of waving my fingers under the dog's nose I leaned over it and made a growling noise, thinking I would confuse it and that it would be frightened of me. I wanted it to be frightened of me. Instead, it sprang up and bit my face, tearing a piece of flesh out of my upper lip.

I was sure you would have to take the dog to be destroyed, for doing that to me, but you told me that it was my own fault.

'Perhaps that will teach you not to tease her,' you said. Can you understand how hurt I was by that? Can you?

I had never been to a hospital. You took me there on the bus, with a clean handkerchief pressed to my lip. I did not know what a hospital would be like. I had no idea that it would be an exciting place, and beautiful, and dangerous, and yet also a place of the greatest comfort and safety. I wanted to stay for ever among the white beds and shining trolleys and powerful people.

What they did to me hurt. They bathed my lip in antiseptic. I loved its smell. Then they stitched my upper lip. The pain was indescribable yet I loved the doctor who did it, and the nurse in the shining white cap who held my hand. You had stayed outside.

So, you see, the fact that you loved the dog more than you loved me and that you betrayed me with it, did not matter in the end because I had found my way. I can even forgive you for the betrayal because yours was not the worst. That came later. I got over your betrayal but the other never, because I was betrayed by what I had to love. I did not love you.

I have never told you that. But now I am telling you everything. We are agreed on that, aren't we?

Three

Thursday morning and the dawn just coming up through a dove-grey mist. Mild air.

On the Hill, a velvet green island emerging out of a vaporous sea, the trees are all but bare, but the patches of scrub and bramble which lie like body hair in the hollows and folds are still berried and have the last of their leaves. Halfway up the Hill are the Wern Stones, ancient standing stones like three witches squatting round an invisible cauldron. In daylight, children run in and out of them, daring one another to touch the pock-marked surfaces and at midsummer, robed figures gather to dance and chant. But they are laughed at and known to be harmless.

At this hour in the morning a few runners are making their way up and down and round the Hill, pounding intently, always alone, noticing nothing. Two are out this morning, men running seriously in silent shoes. No woman. After a time, as the light strengthens and the quilt of mist rolls back upon itself, three young men on mountain bikes race up the sandy track to the summit, straining, panting, aching, but never dismounting.

An old man walks a Yorkshire terrier and a woman two Dobermanns, around the Wern Stones and briskly back down to the path.

At night there may be people on the Hill, though not the runners and cyclists.

Later the sun rises, blood red over the scrubby bushes and brambles and mossy grass, touching the Wern Stones, picking out scraps of blown paper, the white scut of a fleeing rabbit, a dead crow.

No one sees anything unusual out on the Hill. People walk, run, ride there but find nothing, report nothing to alarm them. It is just the same as always, with its standing stones and crown of trees, yielding no secrets. Vehicles keep to the paved paths, and in any case it has rained; any tyre marks have been washed away.

Four

Debbie Parker lay in bed, curled tight, knees drawn up. Outside her window the sun shone, bright for a December morning, but her curtains were dark blue and closed.

She heard Sandy's alarm, Sandy's shower water, Sandy's Radio BEV, but none of what she heard meant anything to her. When Sandy had gone to work Debbie could sleep again, sleep her way through a silent morning, shutting out the sun, the day, life.

There was always a split second when she woke and felt OK, felt normal, 'Hey, it's day, here we go,' before the crushing, blackening misery crawled across her brain like a stain seeping across absorbent paper. Mornings were bad and since she had lost her job were getting worse. She woke to headaches that fogged her mind and dragged her down, lasting half the day. If she made a mighty effort, went out and walked around the town – did anything – the pain got slowly better. Mid-afternoon and she felt she could cope. Evenings were often quite good. Nights were not, even if she had had a few drinks and fallen into bed if not cheerful then at least not caring. She woke around three with a start, heart beating too hard, sweating with fear.

'Debbie . . .'

Go away. Don't come in here.

'Ten to eight.'

The door opened, shooting light across the wall.

'Cup of tea?'

Debbie did not move, did not speak. Go away.

'Come on . . .'

The curtains were rasped open. The noise was like having her teeth pulled. Sandy Marsh, bouncy, bubbly, bright – and concerned. She sat on Debbie's bed.

'I said I've brought you some tea.'

'I'm OK.'

'You're not OK.'

'Am.'

'Tell me I'm right out of order here, but I think you need to go and see the doctor.'

'I'm not ill,' Debbie mumbled into the yeasty hollow of bedclothes.

'You're not well either. Look at you. Maybe you've got that thing called SAD . . . it is December. It's a fact that more people top themselves in December and February than the rest of the year.'

Debbie sat up, throwing off the duvet in one fierce thrust. 'Oh great. Thanks.'

Sandy's bright, cheerfully made-up face was creased with concern. 'I'm sorry. Kick me. Sorry. Oh God.'

Debbie was crying leaning forward on her arms. Sandy reached out to hug her.

'You'll be late,' Debbie said.

'Stuff late. You're more important. Come on.'

In the end, Debbie got up and trailed to the shower. But before the shower came the mirror.

The acne was worse. Her whole face was scarred and blemished by the angry, infected rash. It spread down her neck and on to her shoulders. She had been to the doctor about it once, months ago. He had given her foul-smelling yellow ointment to spread on twice a day. It had greased her clothes and made the bedclothes stink and done her spots no good at all. She hadn't bothered to finish the pot and hadn't been back to the surgery. 'I hate doctors,' she said to Sandy, sitting in their kitchen, full of cheap DIY units whose doors kept falling off. Sandy had made toast and two more mugs of tea.

They had known each other since primary school, grown up in the same street, and rented the flat together eight months ago when Sandy's mother had remarried and living at home had become difficult. But what should have been good fun somehow never had been. Debbie had lost her job when the building society closed its Lafferton branch and then the blackness had started to creep up on her.

'All the doctor will give me is a load of pills that'll space me out.'

Sandy dipped her teaspoon into her mug of tea and tipped the liquid back, dipped and tipped again.

'OK. Well, maybe there's someone else you could see.'

'Like who?'

'Those sort of people who advertise in the health shop.'

'What? Like that creepy acupuncturist? Healers and herbal people? Bit cranky.'

'Well, a lot of people swear by all that. Just take down some names.'

*

Doing something made her feel better. There was a flicker of cheerfulness as she went into the newsagent and bought a notebook and biro, walked down the Perrott to the health shop, looked up at the Hill beyond the rooftops, its crown touched by lemon-coloured sunlight.

The health shop was in Alms Street, near to the cathedral. I might be OK, Debbie thought. I could get fit, lose two stone, find something to clear my skin. A new life.

The cards were pinned on top of one another, crammed together anyhow on the cork board; she had to lift and unpin several to start getting at the names and numbers. Alexander technique, reflexology, Brandon healing, acupuncture, chiropractic. It took ages to work her way through. In the end she took down the details of four – aromatherapist, reflexologist, acupuncturist and herbalist – and, after dithering a moment, one other . . . the address and phone number of someone called Dava. She felt drawn to the card, a deep, intense blue dusted with a swirl of tiny stars. DAVA. SPIRITUAL HEALING. CRYSTALS. INNER HARMONY. LIGHT. WHOLE-PERSON THERAPY.

She stared at it, felt herself being pulled into the depths of the blue card. It did something to her, there was no doubt. When she came out of the health shop, she felt – different. Better. The blue card stayed in her mind and now and then, when she thought of it during the day, she seemed to be able to draw something from it. At any rate, the blackness shrank back like a cowering creature right to the far edges of her mind, and stayed there.

Five

'I would like to see someone in higher authority, please. A CID officer.'

Running a care home for fifteen elderly people in all stages of dementia had trained Carol Ashton to be patient and firm, in the way of a teacher of small children – the two jobs, she often thought, had much in common. She was also skilled in getting even the most recalcitrant to do as she asked eventually. All of which the desk sergeant recognised.

'You mustn't think we take reports of missing persons lightly.'

'I'm sure. But I also know that a name goes down, together with a very brief description, on a list which is circulated to various agencies after which – unless the missing person is a child or in some other way especially vulnerable – that is that.'

She was not wrong.

'The real problem is, Mrs Ashton, that a surprisingly large number of people go missing.'

'I know. I also know that a good many of them turn

up safe and well. I am also more than familiar with the word "resources". All the same, I would still like to see someone who will take the matter further. And as I said, I am not trying to belittle the uniformed police when I say that I would like to talk to a detective.'

She turned away from the desk and went to sit down on the bench seat against the wall. There were small tears and splits in the upholstery here and there, through which grey stuffing was escaping.

Knowing that she might have to wait for some time, Carol Ashton had brought a book, but in fact she had barely time to read one paragraph. The desk sergeant had recognised a woman who would get out of his hair when and only when she had what she came for.

'Mrs Ashton? I'm DS Graffham. Will you come through?'

Daft, Carol thought, to be surprised that it was a woman, but somehow in her mind, though there were plenty of WPCs, detectives were always men. Just as nurses were women.

The room she was ushered into was no surprise of course – a dingy little featureless box with a metal table and two chairs, beige paint. You'd confess to anything just to be let out of it.

'I understand you are very concerned about an employee who has not been into work for a few days?'

She was pretty – elfin haircut, sharp features, big eyes.

'Angela – Angela Randall. Only that sounds wrong – *employee*.'

DS Graffham glanced down at the sheet of paper in front of her. 'I'm sorry, I've only just seen the information . . .'

'Oh yes, she *is* an employee. She works for me, it just

37

sounded a bit bleak. I have a good relationship with all my staff.'

'I understand – official forms. OK, let's start again. Tell me everything about Angela Randall . . . but before you do, can I get you a hot drink? I'm afraid it will have to come out of the dreaded machine.'

She will go far, Carol Ashton thought, stirring the tea round with the plastic stick that bore no resemblance to a spoon. At least I hope she will. I hope someone doesn't see her as too concerned and too relaxed . . . too – yes, too interested. DS Graffham leaned back in her chair, arms folded, looking straight at her, waiting. She did indeed seem genuinely interested.

'I run a care home for the elderly demented.'

'Alzheimer's disease?'

'That pretty much covers it.'

'I hope you know how needed you are. My grand-mother died with it last year. The care she received was disgraceful. Where is the home?'

'Fountain Avenue. The Four Ways.'

'And Mrs Randall works there with you?'

'Miss Randall. Angela. Yes. She's been with us for nearly six years and on permanent night duty for the last four. She's the sort of person you only dream of, frankly – hard-working, caring, reliable, almost never been off sick or for any other reason, and being single without any dependants she's been quite happy to do nights all the time. That's rare.'

'When did you last see her?'

'Well, I don't always of course . . . different shifts and days off for everyone, we could easily go a week without seeing each other. But of course I'd always know she'd been on duty. There's the report book and another member of staff on with her. But actually, I did see her the last time she was at work. She'd rung me in the middle of the night and I came in. I only live four doors down. Some of the patients got a nasty sickness bug and I was needed. Angela was there then.'

'How did she seem?'

'Rushed off her feet of course, we all were that night . . . we didn't have much time to chat. But she was much the same as ever . . . very calm and dependable.'

'So you noticed nothing unusual about her?'

'Oh no. And I would have noticed.'

'And she didn't come in the next night?'

'No, she wasn't due. She had a weekend and then four days off. It goes like that, so every member of staff gets a good long break occasionally. They need it. So Angela wasn't due in for a week and then I was off for a couple of days. When I got back there was a report that she hadn't been into work for four nights and hadn't rung in sick either. That was just completely out of character. I've had staff who would just not turn up and not let me know and I've got rid of them. We simply can't function like that. Our residents don't deserve it. But Angela Randall would never behave like that.'

'So what did you do?'

'Rang her – several times. I kept on ringing. There was never a reply and she hasn't an answering machine.'

'Did you go round to her house?'

'No. No, I didn't.'

'Why ever not?' DS Graffham looked at her sharply.

Carol Ashton felt uneasy – guilty in fact, though she was sure she was not. But the young woman had such a clear, steady look, searching her out, getting to her. She wondered how long a criminal would hold out against it.

'Mrs Ashton – I can't help you – and I want to – if you don't help me.'

Carol stirred and stirred the tea dregs. 'I don't want to . . . to make it sound wrong.'

The detective waited.

'Angela is very private . . . a self-contained sort of person. She is unmarried but I have no idea if she is widowed or divorced – or just single. It may sound strange that I've never discovered that in six years but she simply isn't the sort of person you could ask and she never talks about herself. She's perfectly friendly but she doesn't give anything away and you can easily overstep the mark with her. You might ask a question or make a remark anyone else would respond to without a thought, but she can just – close up, you know? You can see it in her eyes . . . a warning. Don't go there. A sort of portcullis seems to come down. So I've never been to her house and as far as I know nor have any of the other staff. And – well, I just wouldn't call on her. Telephoning was as far as I liked to go really. That sounds ridiculous.'

'It doesn't actually. There are people like that. In my experience they make life very lonely for themselves. They also give the impression that they're hiding something – maybe some dark secret, but they very rarely are, it's all a smokescreen. Do you know of any family she may have?'

'No. She's never mentioned any at all.'

'Had she a history of illness . . . of depression?'

'No. She'd certainly never been ill – maybe a bad cold a couple of times. I encourage staff to stay at home then. Our residents are very vulnerable.'

'Nothing that would cause her to be taken ill suddenly – diabetes or a heart condition?'

'No. I'd know that because of her work. There's nothing.'

'How old is she?'

'Fifty-three.'

'You'll already have gone over this in your mind, but is there anything you can think of that was different or strange about Miss Randall in the last few weeks . . . couple of months, say?'

Carol hesitated. There was something. Or was there? Something and nothing. The room was very quiet. DS Graffham did not fidget or write anything, she simply sat, looking steadily, unnervingly at Carol.

'It's really hard to explain . . .'

'Go on.'

'Nothing was ever said . . . you have to know that . . . This is just . . . just a hunch. An impression I got.'

'Those are often very important.'

'I don't want to make too much of it . . . it's so vague. But once or twice I've thought she just seemed a little bit . . . distant? Distracted? I don't know . . . as if she was miles away. I'd never noticed it about her in the past. She's always very on the ball. Look, please don't make too much of this . . . it was just once or twice, I'm not implying she was behaving strangely, of course not.'

'You think something was worrying her?'

'No. It wasn't that, or I don't think it was . . . Oh, I don't know. Forget I said it. It doesn't make sense.'

'I think it does.'

'I should have gone to her house, shouldn't I? What if she's been taken ill?'

'Well, presumably she has neighbours. You're not to blame.'

'What will happen now?'

'We'll get someone round there to check.' She stood up. 'But don't worry . . . missing people have usually gone somewhere of their own free will for all sorts of personal reasons. They either turn up again as if nothing had happened, or they get in touch. There are very, very few who have come to any sort of harm. Especially not sensible middle-aged ladies.'

'Thank you for that.'

'It's the truth.' The young woman touched her arm. 'And . . .' she smiled suddenly, so that Carol Ashton saw that she was not merely pretty, she was striking – and beautiful. 'You came here. You did exactly the right thing.'

'You have sixty seconds to explain why we should take this one beyond the routine, Freya.'

DI Billy Cameron splayed himself back in his chair, hands held behind his head, and swivelled round and round, a hairy, overweight, sweating bear of a man. Impress me, his stance said, convince me.

Freya Graffham was not intimidated. She had been at Lafferton CID for only a few weeks, but recognised the DI for the sort of policeman the Met had had an abundance of when she had first joined – large and tough-talking with soft centres. By the time she left, most of them had retired and had not been replaced by their like. The new ones were a very different breed. She knew she would not find it easy to twist DI Cameron round her little finger but there would be ways of getting round him.

For his part Cameron saw a young woman who was tougher than she looked. But Freya Graffham had left the Met voluntarily after twelve years, for a cathedral town, and he wondered why she had lost her nerve.

For now, though, she was setting out to prove herself.

'Angela Randall, aged fifty-three, a woman who lives as predictable, orderly and methodical a life as you could imagine, no family, no close friends . . . has never let her employer down once. She's not ill and as far as we know has never been depressed. Uniform found the house neat as a pin, car in the garage, table laid for breakfast, eggs in the saucepan, bread in the toaster. She had made a pot of tea and drunk a cup and there was a banana skin in the otherwise empty pedal bin. The laundry basket had her uniform in it.'

'But no Miss Randall, ill, well or otherwise.'

'No.'

'Neighbours?'

'Don't know much. Hardly saw her. Always passed the time of day but kept herself to herself. No visitors. There's something odd though, guv. Uniform said the house felt . . . peculiar.'

Cameron raised an eyebrow. 'Not like them to go spooky on us.'

'I'd like to go round there.'

Cameron looked at her. She had it – the extra instinct, flair, the nose for something . . . whatever you called it, Freya Graffham had it and it set her apart, as it always did. She would go to the top if she managed to retain that, along with the attention to detail and a capacity for hard work which would keep her pinned to the ground. The combination was rare enough for him to know he had to hang on to it when it came his way.

'You know as well as I do that if you don't come up with anything straight away and there are no further developments, we have to drop it into the missing persons file.'

'Low priority . . . no danger to the public at large or,

43

so far as we can judge, to the missing person . . . whose right to go missing at all we have to respect. Yeah, yeah.'

'There'll be a secret lover somewhere, and they've gone off on holiday . . . or she's topped herself.'

'OK, but neither of those suggestions cuts any ice with her employer.'

Cameron looked at his watch. 'More like three minutes,' he said.

'I take it that's a yes?'

'One thing, Freya . . . ninety-nine out of a hundred missing persons are a waste of police time . . . bear that in mind before you go getting carried away.'

'Thanks, guv. I'll keep it simple.'

Freya drove straight to Barn Close, taking young DC Nathan Coates with her, and, when they arrived, sending him first to check the garage and garden shed, and then to go round the neighbours. Freya wanted Angela Randall's house to herself.

'Weird,' one of the uniform patrol who had first been there had said, and as Freya closed the door softly behind her and stood in the small front hall she sensed at once what they meant. But there was nothing sinister here, she was sure immediately, it was just extraordinarily silent, with a quality and a depth to the silence she had rarely known in a house before, almost like a heavy, dense textile surrounding her, impenetrable and tightly packed.

What kind of woman was it who lived – or perhaps had lived – here? She went from room to room slowly, trying to build up a picture of her. Clearly she was tidy, clean, careful and organised. This was a bleak little house, and almost anonymous, like an out-of-date show home in which no one had ever lived. The furnishings were not ugly but they were unmemorable and might have been chosen by anyone. There was no sense of a personal taste behind the selection or the arrangement. The style was neither antique nor very contemporary, the colour scheme was pale bland. Freya opened drawers and cupboards; crockery, cutlery, linen, a charity catalogue; the small bureau contained some papers, clipped together in an orderly manner – bank statements, payslips, a building society book in which £1,236.98 was deposited, utility bills, all paid and ticked off. On the shelves in the front room were a few unrevealing books – an atlas, a dictionary, a Delia Smith complete cookery course, a wildflower guide and a couple of Dick Francis thrillers.

'Come on, come on,' Freya muttered, 'give.'

It was what was not here that seemed significant, there was nothing personal – no photographs, letters, holiday postcards from friends. Her handbag which uniform had found on a chair in the kitchen had yielded nothing beyond a purse with some change, a wallet with two credit cards and twenty pounds, spectacles, aspirin, tissues and a stamped letter containing a cheque to a catalogue company. The address book beside the telephone listed plumber, electrician, doctor, dentist, a hairdresser, an acupuncturist, the Four Ways Nursing Home, with Carol Ashton's private line listed separately and 'C. Gabb – mowing man'. Angela Randall had apparently no relative, friend or godchild. How could anyone live such a barren life?

Freya went upstairs.

The bathroom yielded plain, basic toiletries from Boots. She picked up the utilitarian shampoo, the simple white soap. No pampering went on here. The spare bedroom was clearly never used – the bed was stripped bare and the wardrobe contained a few blankets and pillows, plus two empty suitcases. So Angela Randall had not taken off on holiday. The room was bitterly cold. The whole house was cold.

In the main bedroom, the clothes hanging in the wardrobe were scarcely more personal than everything else – beige coat, brown skirt, navy jumper, black suit, camel suit, floral-print cotton dress, white and lemon, blue and grey cotton shirts. But there were two track-suits of good quality from a sports shop, and a pair of brand new running shoes, still boxed – expensive.

So far, DS Graffham's mental picture of Angela Randall had been blank, like a jigsaw to which she had not been given any pieces. Now, they had found a couple, the first to be fitted in. A single woman in her fifties of average height and size, who wore neutral colours and clothes that would never draw anyone's attention to her, had become a serious runner who spent £150 on one pair of shoes. She wondered how the DI would react if she took the fact back as her sole piece of information.

She was about to close the doors of the wardrobe and go downstairs to meet DC Coates, when something caught her eye, a faint gleam at the very back of the cupboard. She reached in.

It was a small box wrapped in gold paper, with a gold ribbon tied on top in an elaborate bow. Attached to that was a small gold envelope. Freya opened it.

To You, with all possible love from your devoted, Me.

Freya weighed the package in her hand. It was not heavy, did not smell or rattle.

Was Angela Randall the 'You' or the 'Me'?

*

She went downstairs and let herself out of the front door as the DC was coming up the path.

'Any joy?'

'Not much. Neighbours that were in said she was always pleasant, kept herself to herself, no visitors they could think of . . . only thing was, the lady on the corner, Mrs Savage, said in the last six months or so, Angela Randall had taken up running.'

'Yes, there are tracksuits in the wardrobe and a pair of brand new very expensive running shoes . . . proper gear.'

'She went out of the house every morning at the same time, regardless of whether she had just come in from night duty or just got up.'

'Where did she go?'

'Up on the Hill usually, except when it was very wet, and then she went down the road.'

'And when did Mrs Savage last see her?'

'She is pretty sure on the morning after Mrs Ashton reported her as last having been to work . . . Mrs Savage hasn't seen her, or any sign of anyone at the house, since then. She thought she'd gone away.'

'Did she see her come back from her run that morning?'

'Doesn't remember, but says she didn't always . . . Mrs Savage goes out three mornings a week to catch an early bus to her daughter's or to go to the Tuesday market . . . so Randall may have come back without being noticed.'

'Or not. Anything else?'

'Nope.'

'OK, let's get back. I've got a present to open.'

An hour later, the golden gift stood on Freya Graffham's desk, shining like a prop for one of the three kings in a nativity play.

She had come in and checked the latest reports. Angela Randall's details were logged on to the missing persons database and her description had been circulated to hospitals.

One of the things Freya had been looking for at the house had been any relatively recent photograph, which could eventually be put up on the County Police Force's official website. There had been none and neither was there any news.

'And no body,' the DI said, stopping by her workstation.

'There will be.'

'You've got a feeling?'

'She seems to have had a lonely enough life . . . if I lived in a sterile box like that and apparently hadn't a friend or a loved one in the world, I'd jump in the cut.'

'From which she'd have been dragged days ago.'

Freya pulled the parcel towards her again.

To You, with all possible love from your devoted, Me.

'I'll leave you to open it then.'

Freya hesitated. Going into Angela Randall's house, even searching through her drawers and cupboards, had seemed a job; she had not felt like an intruder simply because there had been nothing private or personal to make her feel that she was prying. Searching for a contact name and address, or some clue as to where the missing woman might have gone, was routine. But opening this ostentatiously wrapped parcel felt like an invasion of privacy, and something Randall would have minded very much.

Freya still hesitated, smoothing her thumb over the mirrored paper, and then took a paper knife to the neatly taped edges. The gold paper sprang open, revealing a gold box. Inside it, among crisp tissue and deep in a nest of blue velvet, was a pair of gold cufflinks, set with deep blue lapis lazuli.

Not *for* Angela Randall then, but *from* her, 'To You,' an unnamed man, 'with all possible love'.

Freya looked at the cufflinks, and at the box, the silk-lined lid, the tissue . . . an intimate secret exposed on her desk. A sad secret, too, an extravagant gift from a lonely woman in late-middle age . . . to whom? Not a relative. A lover? Obviously. Yet, if so, why had there been no other indication of a man in Angela Randall's life?

She went to fetch coffee from the machine. Without any clue as to the woman's whereabouts or movements, with no reported sighting, no suicide note and no body, she knew perfectly well she could not justify spending any more time on the case . . . she had probably spent too much on it already. Angela Randall had disappeared, and until she turned up again in some form, she was merely the number she had had assigned to her . . . Missing Person BH140076/CT.

Six

The last week before Christmas and a clear, cold night, so that at dawn, the slopes of the Hill are thinly iced with frost and the Wern Stones gleam with rime like snail trails over their backs. The ground is too slippery at this hour, the runners are not out, but the mountain bikers strain up the slope, their breath pluming up white in the crackling air.

The woman with the Dobermanns is not on the Hill yet but Jim Williams with the Yorkshire terrier is out because he can't sleep. For the past week or two he has come here earlier and earlier, sometimes long before dawn, both of them bundled up into warm coats. Jim had promised his sister that he would take care of Skippy, though he knows he will never love the dog, whose breath smells fetid and who snaps at him when he puts on the lead. But Phyl could not have died comfortably unless she had been sure Skippy would not be sent to strangers or be put down.

This morning the mountain bikers whisk by, heads down. With no runners to chase and no other dogs out yet, Skippy can be let off the lead, though Phyl would never have done such a thing. She'd petted the dog too much, kept him under her eye more like a child than an animal; but that was what had made her happy.

Now, Jim Williams watches the little dog break into a quick trot, heading towards the undergrowth, and then on into the trees. It seems to him Skippy has a better life now, freer, enjoying what an animal should.

The wind is sharp as a blade on his face up here on the Hill, but as the dawn comes up, the view of Lafferton, the dark line of the river and the cathedral rising out of the frosty air, is worth the climb and the cold. Now, from somewhere on one of the paths below, Jim Williams hears the barking of the Dobermanns.

'Skippy . . . Skippy . . .' He hears his own voice ringing round in the bitter air, and his whistle that sets the Dobermanns off again. 'Here, boy . . . Skippy . . .'

But there is no sound from the little terrier and no sign of him, there are only the yelping Dobermanns coming nearer, up the slope, and the faint rumble of a vehicle going away down the road.

Seven

Cat Deerbon stood at the window of her consulting room, looking out through the slats of the blind to the surgery car park. Rain streamed down the glass. It was almost nine o'clock and still not fully light.

Monday morning – a full list of appointments, two drugs reps, calls, an afternoon antenatal clinic, and Hannah to be taken to the dentist after school . . . and she had hardly made a dent on the preparations for Christmas. But none of this troubled her very much, set beside the fact that Karin McCafferty had an appointment.

Cat let the blind slats drop back together sharply. I can't do it, she thought – and it was a feeling so rare that it alone worried her.

Karin McCafferty was forty-four, a patient who had become a friend when Cat's mother, Dr Meriel Serrailler, had engaged her to redesign the garden at Hallam House.

Cat saw her now – tall, with red hair that sprang from her head, a long, oval, creamy-skinned face. She had a face that was plain, in an oddly memorable way. Karin had given up a high-powered career in banking to become a garden designer and plantswoman, a change that had transformed her, she said. Her new career had blossomed along with her hardy plants. An upmarket garden magazine had recently featured her work and one of her gardens had been shown on television.

Karin – great company, interested in a multitude of things as well as gardens. She and Mike McCafferty – a dull man Cat thought – had been married for twenty-two years. No children. 'We went down every route and side route but no go; IVF had a much lower success rate then and I always knew that it was my known children I wanted – I couldn't have adopted.'

Sam Deerbon adored Karin, though Hannah was wary of her. 'She's bossy.'

'Too right I am,' Karin had said when told.

Karin McCafferty. The X-rays and report from the oncologist at Bevham General were on Cat's desk.

'You shouldn't let patients become friends,' Chris had said the previous evening. Perhaps he was right, but detachment was not something Cat had ever been good at. She took the problems and pain of her patients to heart, and the joys as well, and she would not like to be any different. But then came the hard confrontations, as this one with Karin was going to be.

Her desk telephone rang. 'It's nearly quarter past.' Jean in reception.

'Sorry, sorry . . . wheel them in.'

She pushed Karin's results to one side. Before that, four-teen other people needed her full attention. She turned to smile at the first of them, coming through the door.

Iris Chater had aged since her husband's death. But Cat knew, watching her walk disconsolately into the room, that the process was reversible. At the moment, the shock and stress of bereavement, the tears, lack of sleep and unaccustomed loneliness had crumpled her, drained her of all vitality. But she was not too old for time and rest to heal and restore her. Now, she sighed as she sat down. Her eyes had the flat, inwardly focused look of the recently bereaved.

'How are you coping?'

'I'm managing, Doctor, I'm not too bad. And I know Harry is best off now. I do know that.' Her sad eyes filled with tears.

'It's hard. Of course it's hard.' Cat pushed the box of tissues across her desk.

'I keep hearing him in the night . . . I wake up and I can still hear him breathing. I feel him with me in the room. I suppose that sounds daft to you.'

'No, it sounds normal. I'd be worried if you said it wasn't happening.'

'I'm not going mad then?'

'Definitely not.'

The question they never failed either to ask, or to leave in the air unspoken between them for the doctor to pick up. Iris Chater relaxed, and her face took on a little more colour.

'Apart from missing Harry, how's your own health?'

'I'm just tired really. I can't eat much either. It comes and goes.' She shifted about in her chair, picked her bag up from the floor and put it down again. Cat waited.

'Harry lost his appetite.'

'I know. He lost it because he had cancer, and he'd had a long struggle. You've lost yours because you've been bereaved. Don't worry about it at all. You say it comes and goes, so just eat when it's there. Eat what you fancy . . . Your appetite will get back to normal when it's ready.'

'I see.'

'Are you worried about being in the house on your own at night?'

'Oh no, Dr Deerbon. He's there with me, you see . . . Harry's always there.'

Like many of Cat's older patients, Iris Chater was not ill, she needed reassurance and a listening ear. Nevertheless, Cat sensed that she was holding something back, in spite of her gentle probing. She waited a moment, but nothing came.

'Well, pop in and see me again in a month. I want to know how you're getting on and in the meantime, if there's anything at all . . .'

Iris Chater made a business of getting up, gathering herself, going towards the door, then, at the very last moment, she turned.

'There is something, isn't there?' Cat said gently.

The tears filled the woman's eyes again.

'If I could just know, Doctor. If I could just be sure that he's all right. Is there any way I can be sure?'

'Aren't you sure? In your own heart? Come on . . . Harry was a good man.'

'He was, wasn't he? He really was.'

Still she did not go.

'I wondered . . .'

She glanced at Cat, then quickly away. What is it, Cat puzzled, what is it she wants to ask me, to get reassurance about?

'I get this funny breathing.'

There was nothing wrong with Iris Chater. She was afraid . . . afraid of dying as her husband had died, and vulnerable after his death. Cat examined her briefly. She had no symptoms, had had no chest pains or breathlessness and her lungs were clear.

'I don't want to prescribe you sleeping tablets or tranquillisers. I don't honestly think you need them.'

'Oh no, I wouldn't want anything like that, Doctor.'

'But you do need to relax.'

'It's just what I can't do, you see.'

'Have you ever listened to one of those relaxation tapes . . . soothing music, and exercises to do to calm your breathing?'

'Like in those Eastern religions?'

'No, these are much more straightforward – just aids to relaxing. I'm afraid I can't prescribe them but they sell them at the health shops. They're not expensive. Why don't you go and have a browse . . . ask them if there are any they recommend? If you buy one of those and try using it to help you relax every day even just for quarter of an hour, I think you'll find it will really help. But you've lost your husband of fifty years, Mrs Chater. What you're going through is normal. You're not going to feel yourself again for a while yet, you know.'

The rest of the surgery took its course through sore throats and period pains to children's ear infections and arthritic joints.

At twenty to twelve, Jean brought in a mug of coffee.

'There's just Mrs McCafferty.'

For the past busy couple of hours, Cat had been able to put it to the back of her mind.

'Give me a couple of minutes.'

Jean smiled sympathetically as she went out.

*

How often, Cat wondered half an hour later, have I been helped through a difficult consultation by the patient? Been comforted myself by people who have just been told that their illness is terminal? Even had to tell parents that their child is going to die, only to be re-assured by them that they were certain she, the doctor, had done everything she could and that they knew she was as upset as they were.

And now, Karin McCafferty had been calm, controlled – and sympathetic. 'It's rotten for you as well . . . probably worse with a patient you know as well as you know me.' Those had been her first words, as she had given Cat a hug. 'But I'm OK . . . and I liked Dr Monk very much.'

It had been three weeks since Karin had first come to the surgery about the lump in her breast, and Cat had suspected at once that it was malignant, but she had been shocked at the results of the X-rays, which had shown extensive involvement of the lymph glands. The biopsy had highlighted a particularly aggressive type of cancer.

Now, Karin had had her first consultation with the consultant oncologist, Jill Monk, whose report Cat had already seen.

'You can't begin to know how sorry I am.'

'Yes I can. And look what you've done . . . got me X-rays and an appointment lightning fast and I know what a difference that can make.'

Karin looked bright – too bright, Cat thought. 'It's early days,' she said carefully, 'it takes time for all the implications to sink in.'

'Oh, it's sunk, don't you worry.'

'Sorry, I don't mean to patronise you.'

'You're not. People are meant to agonise . . . ask "Why

me?" But why not me, Cat? It's random. After I saw Dr Monk, I got home, had a huge Scotch and howled my eyes out. But that's that. So let's talk about what's next.'

Cat glanced down at the oncologist's letter. It did not make cheerful reading.

'Surgery is the immediate way forward, as she will have told you . . . in this instance, she won't want to be too . . . conservative.'

'Full mastectomy, including the glands, yes, she said.'

'Then chemo, certainly, and radiography, possibly, depending on how she decides after the operation. There is a possibility that she might want to do a double mastectomy, you know that?'

Karin was silent.

'Bevham General is a centre of excellence for oncology and I wouldn't recommend you go privately . . . though if you want an amenity bed, by all means pay for that. I would . . . If I'm feeling rough, I like to be by myself to do it.'

I'm babbling, Cat thought. Karin was unnerving her. She sat without fidgeting, apparently quite relaxed, and for the most part she kept her eyes on Cat's face. Her wild red hair was tied back in a black velvet snood, to reveal her bony face – large nose, high cheekbones and forehead – it was an interesting, intelligent face, with the repose of a woman entirely comfortable in her own skin.

'Cat, I have thought about it . . . well, as you may imagine, I haven't done much else. I have thought very hard and very clearly and carefully. And I've talked to Mike. And now I'm telling you. I don't want to have any of this. No, hang on, let me say it all. The only suggestion of Dr Monk's I did consider seriously was the surgery. I know it's radical, but oddly enough the idea of it is still acceptable . . . I want to keep the possibility in reserve. Chemo and radiotherapy I won't go near.'

'I'm not sure I understand you.'

'I want to go down the other route . . . alternative, complementary, whatever you call it. The gentle way. I'm thinking of going to America to the Gerson Clinic. I'm absolutely sure that it's a better way, Cat . . . physically, spiritually . . . everything tells me so. I won't poison my body and destroy my immune system with toxins and I won't be subjected to overdoses of radiation. I am quite sure about it, but you're my doctor and of course I will listen to what you have to say. I'm not a fool.'

Cat got up and walked to the window. The car park was almost empty. It was still pouring with rain.

'Did you say any of this to Jill Monk?'

'No. I hadn't thought it through then. Besides, I don't think she'd have been sympathetic.'

'And you think I am?'

'Cat, whatever the outcome of this, it is my body, my illness, my decision, and I live with it. Or not, I suppose. But whatever, it isn't yours so don't worry.'

'Of course I bloody worry . . . all my training and knowledge and experience and instinct tell me to worry because you are wrong. Just plain wrong.'

'Are you washing your hands of me?'

'Look, Karin, you are my patient and it is my job to give you my professional advice and counsel. It's also my job to support you in any medical decisions you make because, ultimately, those decisions always are the patient's. And you are a good friend. And the more certain I am that you are making the wrong decision, the greater my support and help have to be. OK?'

'Sorry. I'll need you.'

'You will.'

'I didn't think that you'd be so against the alternative way.'

'I'm not – in some circumstances, quite the contrary. I send patients to Nick Haydn for osteopathy, and to Aidan Sharpe who does acupuncture. He works miracles on a few stubborn conditions. Just now I sent a bereaved lady who can't sleep and is in a generally anxious state to look through the relaxation tapes in the health shop . . . and an aromatherapy massage is a lovely thing. But none of them are cures for cancer, Karin. The *most* complementary therapies could do is help get you through the proper treatment, make you less sick maybe and relax you generally.'

'So why don't I just get a facial and have my nails done?'

Karin stood up. Cat knew that she had upset her and put her back up, and she was furious with herself. She walked with Karin towards the door.

'Promise me that at least you'll think hard about it.'

'I'll think. But I won't be changing my mind.'

'Don't burn your boats, don't close any doors. It's your life we are talking about here.'

'Exactly.'

But then Karin had turned and given Cat another warm and accepting hug, before walking, calm and confident, out of the surgery.

'You can't go along with it, for God's sake.' Chris Deerbon faced Cat across the kitchen table, as they sat drinking mugs of tea late that night. He had just come in from a call.

'You mean I should ask her to change GP?'

'No, I mean you have to try much harder to make her see why she can't go down that road . . . it's not an option, you know that . . . she hasn't the luxury of choice.'

Chris was totally opposed to any form of alternative treatment, with the exception of osteopathy for his own bad back.

'It worries me, of course it does, but she was very adamant and you know Karin.'

'She probably hasn't taken it in properly yet.'

'I think she has. If I'm going to support her I'm going to have to do some research . . . at least steer her clear of the real cranks.'

'I don't think you should encourage her even that far . . . she has got to have surgery and chemo. What's got into you?'

'Just Karin, I suppose.'

Chris got up and put the kettle back on the hob.

'There's too much of it about. All those loonies up at Starly Tor.'

'Oh, they're just New Age airheads . . . crystals and ley lines.'

'Where's the difference? Let Karin McCafferty loose and she'll be dancing round Stonehenge at dawn.'

When Chris had left on the next night call, Cat had a bath, and then got into bed, propping her laptop on her knees. *'Cancer,'* she typed into Google. *'Therapies. Alternative. Complementary. Gerson.'*

An hour and a half later, when Chris came in from dispatching a teenager with acute appendicitis to hospital, she was deep into a research article discussing the effects of a sustained programme of meditation and visualisation on cancer patients in New Jersey.

She had filled several pages of a notebook on the pillow beside her. The least she knew she could do for Karin McCafferty was take her seriously.

The Tape

When I speak to you here it is like being in the confessional. I am shriving myself by telling you everything. The difference is that I am not asking you for your forgiveness. It should be the other way round.

But I will feel better once you know everything. Some of the secrets of the past have become a tiresome burden to carry alone, though it is not guilt that has weighed me down, simply the knowledge.

What I am going to tell you today was a secret I did not carry alone. From the beginning, I shared it with Aunt Elsie. She went to her grave with it, as she had told me she would. Uncle Len knew, of course, but you know how meek he was, how he would have said nothing unless she told him to.

It happened one of those times I went to stay with them. You knew how I loved it there, how I always asked when I could go next. I wanted to live there. I loved the bungalow, because it was a bungalow, there were no stairs. I loved the breakfast she cooked for me every morning, and the small bookcase against the wall beside the telephone where I sat on the floor and read 'Your Body in Health and Sickness' by Dr Roberts. I learned so much from that book. It helped to shape my destiny.

I loved opening the door of my bedroom slightly and listening to the murmur of talk in the sitting room just along the short corridor, and the voices from the radio.

That was how I first heard of Arthur Needham. I heard his name on the radio, and then, them talking about him, so that he became a mysterious figure in my dreams.

'Who is Arthur Needham?' I asked one morning in the middle of my scrambled egg.

Aunt Elsie and Uncle Len looked at one another. I can see that look now. He frowned and I was sent to clean my teeth. But later, she said, 'You'll hear about it soon enough, so I'm going to tell you. You're quite old enough to know.'

The tone of her voice seemed to change, to go lower into her throat, though she wasn't whispering. I caught an excitement in it. She was enjoying this, behind the solemn expression.

Arthur Needham was a small draper who had married a widow with a bit of money and, a year later, murdered her. When he discovered that she had in fact left the money not to him, as she had made out, but to her only daughter, he had murdered the daughter too.

I was interested at once.

'Where is Arthur Needham now?'

'In the condemned cell.'

I wanted to know, I wanted to know everything. A

spark from her excitement had touched me and lit something inside me that would never go out.

'He's a wicked, evil man, and I'll be there, watching and waiting until I know he's been punished and justice has been done.'

'What will happen?'

'He'll be hanged by the neck until he is dead.' Her face had changed too now; her eyes were bulging slightly and her mouth was thin and tight and bloodless.

'You can come with me,' she said.

Four days later, when she was seeing me to bed, and after she had heard my prayers, she said, 'It's tomorrow morning. If you still want to come.'

'To the hanging prison?'

'You can change your mind and no shame.'

'I'm coming with you.'

'It'll do you good to see evil vanquished.'

I didn't understand, of course, but I knew that I wanted to be there.

'I'll be waking you,' she said, 'early. And now you have to make me a solemn promise.'

'I promise.'

'That you never breathe a word to a living soul about this coming with me tomorrow, where you go, what you see. Your mother'd never forgive me. So you promise. Never a word.'

'Never a word.'

'To a living soul.'

'To a living soul.'

I remember that I added, 'Amen.'

My aunt went out of the room and I lay on my back, thinking that I would never sleep for wanting to go to the hanging prison. And not wanting to. 'To a living soul,' I promised.

I kept my promise. But it's all right now, isn't it? I can tell you at last and the promise is still not broken.

It was as dark as tar when Aunt Elsie woke me before six the next morning, but there was a cup of hot, sweet tea for me before I had to set foot out of bed and then a fried egg tucked into a thick fried-bread sandwich.

If I close my eyes, I can smell the air now, the smoke from all the chimneys thick in my mouth, mingled with the sharp cold. I can still feel Aunt Elsie's hand in mine and the hardness of her rings bedded in the soft plumpness of her fingers.

We walked down Pomfrey Street and then Belmont Road, to the tram stop, and now the streets were busy with women walking to the factories, arm in arm and three or four in a row, all wearing headscarves, and the men in caps, a lot of them on bicycles. The smoke from their cigarettes merged with the chimney smoke. The tram was full and smelled of bodies. I was squeezed between large women, their rough coats pressed against my cheek. We changed, and when we boarded the second tram, I felt it at once – something was different, people were silent and still now, and I thought how big their eyes looked. We were all going to the prison. I was pushed up against more women, and stared at.

'Queer place to bring a child,' someone said.

'I don't see why. They have to learn there's evil in this world.'

People began to take sides across the tram, but my

aunt crushed my hand in hers like a bone in a mincer and said nothing at all. I felt sick, or perhaps afraid. I did not know what might happen.

The tram stopped and emptied out. I looked back at it, a fuzzily lit caterpillar. But again, what I was most aware of, what I remember most vividly, were the sounds . . . the footsteps of all the people walking up the black road towards the great dark hulk with sheer walls and turrets like a castle.

'The prison,' Aunt Elsie said, in the low, choked voice.

Footsteps – one-two, one-two, one-two. The sky behind the prison was turning grey as the dawn started to come up. The smoky air felt damp, though it was not raining,

One-two. One-two. One-two.

Nobody spoke.

We joined the crowd that was already there, ten-deep in front of the high iron gates.

'There's the clock. That's how we'll know.'

I looked up, though I didn't understand her, but all I could see were people's backs, dark coats, scarves, felt hats.

'Let's have you up then or you'll see nowt.'

And I was swung up on to the beefy shoulders of a stranger. The rough cloth of his jacket scratched the inside of my legs, but I could see over the tops of the heads now, as the sour light strengthened slowly, see the iron gates and the tower and the bone-white clock with its black fingers. As I looked the second hand jerked one point closer to eight and from behind and all around me there was a soft murmur like the sea, spreading, then dying away again.

I was afraid. I still could not imagine what was going to happen, but I was sure that they were going to bring Arthur Needham out on to the prison tower and hang him there before us all. I couldn't see how the whole crowd could go inside the prison itself to watch, as I had watched down the viewing tube at the peep show on the pier. I didn't know if I wanted to see the hanging or not. It was the condemned cell that I thought about. I wanted to see that, to be there inside it with Arthur Needham.

The clock hand jerked forward again. Then, from somewhere behind us, someone began to sing, and gradually, the crowd took it up, until everyone was singing, but quietly. The soft low swell of the hymn made me shiver.

> Abide with me
> Fast falls the eventide.
> The darkness deepens
> Lord with me abide.

They sang another verse and then the singing stopped quite suddenly, as if there had been a conductor some-where who had given the signal. And after that there was the greatest silence I had ever known.

The clock hands were at eight. The man carrying me on his shoulders gripped my legs tightly. I stared and stared at the tower. Everyone in the crowd seemed to have stopped breathing and the sky was grey and faintly shining behind the dark prison.

Nothing happened. No one came on to the tower. I screwed my eyes up in case I was not seeing prop-erly, but still there was nothing, nothing at all, for quite a long time, and still the strange and dreadful silence went on.

And then I saw a man in uniform walking across the prison yard towards the gates, holding a white piece of paper in his hand. There was a murmur at the front of the crowd, and a whisper took off and spread like a flame. The man came out of a small gate set within the great one, and pinned the piece of paper on to a board. The murmur grew. People were telling one another and passing it on, passing it on, and then the man swung me abruptly down from his shoulders, so that I felt giddy and sick.

'Say thank you,' Aunt Elsie said.

I did not know what I was to thank him for. I had seen nothing. Nothing had happened. I told my aunt.

'A wicked evil man has been hanged to death and you were here, you witnessed it, you saw justice done. Never forget it.'

Eight

Iris Chater had told Dr Deerbon that she was tired but she had not been able to find the words to convey just how tired. Every day since Harry's death had been a struggle, with an exhaustion that muddled her mind and seemed to fill her limbs with warm wet sand. When she went to the shops – and she always chose those nearby now, she had not been into the centre of Lafferton for weeks – she could have got down on the pavement and slept there.

Now, she lay on the sofa in the front room. It was the middle of December. The tiredness was worse, even though she had just slept for over two hours. The fire sputtered and the curtains were half drawn. The birds were quiet under their cover.

She could see that it had turned dark outside. That was one of the harder things about being alone at this back end of the year, the dark early and late, making the days so short and the nights never-ending.

But for the moment, warm under a rug, she felt comfortable, and oddly happy. The room seemed to hold her in a glowing embrace and the warmth eased the arthritis in her knees. Best of all, she had the feeling, which came and went so unpredictably, that Harry was in the room with her. After a moment, she spoke his name aloud, quietly, tentatively, startled by the sound of her own voice.

'Harry?'

She heard nothing but she knew he had answered her. She put out her hand.

'Oh, Harry love, it is hard, it's very hard. I know you're happy and not in pain any more and I'm glad about that, of course I am, only I do miss you so much. I never dreamed I'd find it so hard. You won't go right away from me, will you? So long as I know you're here with me like this, I can manage.'

She willed him to be sitting in the chair opposite, to be able to see him, not only sense his presence, to have him show her he was all right, and not changed.

'I want to see you, Harry.'

The gas fire flared suddenly, and the flame went blue for a second. She held her breath, willing and praying.

He was there.

'I want to see you,' she wailed aloud, and the sudden cold certainty that she would not, and the disappointment of it, were as bitter and sharp as at the beginning.

The tap on the back door made her start, until she heard Pauline Moss calling and struggled to get up from the sofa.

'I'm all right, I'm in here.'

Pauline was a good neighbour, a good friend, only just sometimes less than welcome. There were days when Iris thought she would prefer never to see or speak to another living soul again.

'I've made some drop scones. Shall I put the kettle on?'

Iris Chater wiped her eyes and replaced her spectacles, switched on the lamps. Well, I'm very lucky, she told herself. What about those who have no neighbour to keep an eye on them and share a cup of tea?

'Hello, my dear – oh, did I wake you? I'm sorry.'

'No, no, I was just lying having a think. Time I pulled myself out of it.' She followed Pauline back into the kitchen. 'You are good.'

The tray was laid, the plate of warm drop scones stood on the stove under a plate.

'I'm not, I'm selfish. I wanted drop scones that badly and you gave me the excuse. I'll never get that weight off now with Christmas coming up. I got the tins for my cake out while I was at it. Do you fancy coming up the market on Saturday while I buy the fruit?'

Christmas. Iris stared at the embroidered lupins on the tray cloth. Christmas. The word meant nothing. She couldn't imagine it, didn't want to try.

Pauline picked up the tray. 'Could you bring the pot in?'

She stood up and the pain like white-hot skewers shot through her knees so that she had to hold on to the table edge, catching her breath. Pauline glanced at her sharply but said nothing until they were sitting beside the fire, the drop scones had been eaten and they were on their second cups of tea.

'I put a pinch of bicarbonate of soda in drop scones . . . my mother always did and I don't know why but it does make them tastier, don't you think?'

Iris Chater looked affectionately across at her friend. 'I don't know what I'd have done without you these past few weeks. And all the time Harry was ill. I wish there was something I could do for you, Pauline.'

'There is.'

'You've only to ask. You know that much, I should hope.'

'Right. I want you to take those knees of yours back to the doctor, and don't start saying they're not so bad because I know they are.'

'No, I meant do something for *you*, Pauline.'

'I know you did. Now, what did Dr Deerbon say last time?'

'Oh, the old story, waiting list for an operation, only apparently knees aren't as successful as hips, she said. And tablets for the pain.'

Iris was not going to admit that her arthritic knees had not been mentioned to the doctor. Where was the point? They were a lot worse, the pain was sharper and always there, but what she had told Pauline was true, it would be a question of a waiting list for goodness knows how long and the strong painkillers that upset her stomach. She could buy aspirin for herself.

'Go back then. Tell her you're not satisfied, ask her to get you on to the urgent list.'

'There are plenty worse than me.'

'Hm.'

Iris reached forward to pour a last half-cup of tea from the pot.

'Harry's still here, you know,' she said.

Pauline smiled. 'Well, of course he is . . . he's looking after you, always will.'

'I mean here, in this room. It startles me sometimes. Only I want to . . . see him, I want to hear him . . . not just feel it. Am I going daft?'

'You?'

'It's such a comfort, Pauline. I don't want it to fade away.'

The room was warm. The lamplight caught a row of brass monkeys on the shelf, and made them glow.

'Have you ever, you know, thought of going to see someone?'

'How do you mean?'

'One of those spiritualists? A medium.'

Hearing Pauline speak aloud the idea that had been in her own mind made her flush and her heart jump.

'A lot of people do, a lot say they're really . . . well, that they do have a gift.'

'Have you ever been to one?'

'Never had occasion really. Anyway, it was only a thought.'

'I'd be afraid.'

'What of?'

'Just . . . it would upset me.' She looked down at her cup. 'My grandmother used to read the tea leaves.'

'Oh, so did mine. They all did then, didn't they? Load of rubbish.'

'Oh yes.'

Yet when Grandma Bixby had described the man Iris was to marry, before she'd ever set eyes on Harry Chater, she'd got him just right, everything about him, looks, manners, line of work, family, everything. She'd got it right that they'd have no children, years before they'd had to give up hope.

'Besides,' she said, 'how would I go about finding one? I'd want to be careful.'

'There's that spiritualist church in Passage Street. They might have a noticeboard.'

'I never like the look of that place, it's a bit of a Nissen hut.'

'Well, you wouldn't want to go to one of those that come round the hotels . . . the Deer Park sometimes has them. They put a board out . . . "An Evening of Clairvoyance and Psychic Fair" and all that. Madame Rosita, all gold earrings. They're just a joke.'

'They take people's money though.'

Pauline started putting the tea things on to the tray. 'I suppose it's like anything else . . . you need someone to recommend, don't you? I'll ask about a bit. Now, do you want to come in later and watch *The Weakest Link*?'

'I won't tonight, Pauline, I've a few bits to do.'

'Well, if you change your mind.'

'I know. You're a good friend.'

For a long time after Pauline had gone, she sat turning the idea of going to a medium over in her mind, wondering if it was wrong, whether it would be expensive, or a trick to make unhappy people better? Most of all, she found the idea frightening. But why would that be? It was either a lot of baloney, or some of them had a gift, and if she found one, they could put her in touch with Harry, and what was there to be afraid of in that? But how was it done? What exactly would happen? Would she really be able to speak to him and have him answer her so that she could actually hear his voice? And could a psychic person prove it all by telling you things only you knew, private things? Grandma Bixby had read tea leaves, her aunt had told cards. But, as Pauline said, women did then, it made a bit of entertainment, a laugh, a break in the dreary days when you had to do your washing all by hand. Sometimes it might give you a shiver, but that was not what she wanted now. She wanted nothing except to know that Harry was really there and to talk to him.

The hot little front room seemed empty tonight, as if he had withdrawn. Maybe he wasn't happy about what she had been thinking.

In the end, to stop her brain from going round, she went next door to watch Pauline's television after all.

But no quiz programme, no comedy, no thriller, no television or any other diversion, could keep her from missing Harry and now from thinking about having the chance to be in touch with him, if only she could summon up the courage. She worried about it all evening, and woke twice in the night, to worry again.

In Lafferton, the shops were in a frenzy of Christmas. On the third Saturday in December, Iris Chater wandered hopelessly in and out of them, confused by the glut of things, things, things and anxious that she ought to be buying food and presents. But there was scarcely any need. She was invited to Pauline's for Christmas Day and intended to go for lunch, but Pauline's two sons and their families would be there, all crammed into the little rooms. She didn't want to outstay her welcome. She wanted Christmas over this year, the quicker the better.

On the Sunday morning, after a bad night, she did what she had not done for years and went to a service at the cathedral, but she felt out of place among the young couples with babies and small children, singing hymns she did not recognise to unfamiliar modern tunes. The family service was not the right setting in which she could pray about Harry and whether she would be wrong to visit a medium. She sat and stood and knelt and listened to the chatter and babble around her and felt as if she had landed by accident on some quite friendly but alien planet.

As she walked home her knees gave her such pain that she was almost in tears. The rest of Sunday ran away ahead of her like a ribbon of unending road.

Pauline was at her window watching out, and when she saw her, held up a cup.

The hot sweet coffee and chocolate biscuit were comforting.

'I've got a name for you,' Pauline said.

The walls seemed to bend in and out like rubber.

'I said I'd ask around and then I remembered a girl I used to work with at Pedders telling me her mother-in-law had gone to see a medium.'

She reached behind the clock on the shelf for a folded piece of paper.

If I take it, Iris Chater thought, if I touch it at all, something will happen. She looked down at it. Once taken, she felt there could be no going back. You're a stupid woman, she thought. But the feeling was overpowering.

'I'd always come with you, you know, if you were nervous . . . just wait for you, I mean, of course, not come in the room. Well, there you are anyway.'

Pauline put the paper down on the table between them.

'Have another cup.'

She did so, and sipped it slowly, talked about the shops, Christmas, the cost of everything, the funny new hymns, spinning the time out. Because when she left Pauline's house for her own, she would have to take the piece of paper, and when she had closed her own front door, she would be alone with it and the name and address and number.

To make it easier, she glanced down quickly now at Pauline's round writing. *Sheila Innis. 20 Priam Crescent. 389113.*

The plainness of the woman's name and the address, on a road she knew, were reassuring somehow, so that she took the paper and folded it away into her handbag quite cheerfully, scoffing at herself for having been worried.

Nine

DS Freya Graffham stood in the entrance hall of the Four Ways Nursing Home, waiting to be directed to Carol Ashton's office and wanting to flee. It was the smell – polish and chrysanthemums to the fore, but with heavy notes of antiseptic and stewing meat. It took her back to the corridors of her convent school, and, more recently and distressingly, to the care home in south London where her grandmother had spent her last two miserable years. And there had not even been the disguising smells of the polish or the flowers to mask the stench. Coming into a nursing home again, however different this one might be, struck chill to her heart.

Carol Ashton's office was bright and pleasant with pictures, plants and a comfortable chair.

'Have you found Angela? Do please sit down . . .'

'I'm sorry, I'm afraid we haven't.'

'It seems so long. I'm absolutely certain something must have happened to her . . .'

'Mrs Ashton, I'm trying to build up a picture of Angela

Randall. I wonder if you'd mind going back over a couple of things again?'

'I'll do anything, of course I will.'

'You told me that just going away without saying anything to you, or as far as you know to anyone else, just wasn't in character.'

'I've been thinking about it a lot and I'm sure. I know people sometimes behave unexpectedly but I truly do not believe Angela would ever have gone away like that. She wouldn't have left her job and her home without warning, she simply wouldn't.'

'Do you know if she had any close relationships?'

'You mean a man? A love relationship?' The suggestion seemed to take Carol Ashton aback. 'I think I told you she isn't the sort of person who talks about her private life. Do you know, I couldn't even tell you if she owned a cat? But she's never mentioned anyone.'

'No one she might have bought expensive presents for?'

'I doubt it. What kind of presents do you mean?'

'We found a pair of gold cufflinks in the house, gift-wrapped and with a note indicating some sort of affectionate relationship.'

'Goodness.'

'You can't think of anyone?'

'I can't and I have to say, I'm very surprised. There just isn't anything like that about Angela.' She was thoughtful for a moment. Freya waited.

'If I had to choose a single word to describe her, I'm afraid it would be "chilly". I don't mean to imply that I don't like her because I do, and I respect her too. I respect anyone who works as conscientiously and loyally.'

'I understand what you mean, don't worry.' Freya got

up. 'There really is every possibility that she will simply return home . . . the more private she is, perhaps the less likely she would be to confide in anyone if there was some problem in her life.'

'Maybe.'

Carol Ashton looked sceptical. Freya didn't blame her, even she didn't believe in the bland reassurances she heard herself babbling.

'Will you go on trying to remember anything she may have mentioned, probably in passing, about someone she knew, someone she was close to?'

'Yes, I'll try. But I won't come up with anything.'

As they went out into the corridor a wail came from somewhere above. It was all Freya could do not to run for the front door.

'Sergeant, there was something I wanted to ask you. The other day I turned on Radio BEV and there was an appeal for any information about a missing dog . . . someone's prize pedigree . . . I wondered if there would be any point in asking them to put out something about Angela?'

'We do use local radio from time to time to appeal for information and we're always flooded with calls, not all of them relevant. But there's often something helpful. Let me check.'

'Surely it's worth a try? Someone might have seen her . . . seen something.'

They walked across the polished hall. Above, everything had gone quiet. Freya wondered fleetingly how the wailing voice had been silenced.

She returned to the car through drizzle. Lights were on in almost every house though it was barely three o'clock.

Christmas was in a few days – a poignant time of year to go missing.

For the rest of the afternoon she was at Bevham attending a seminar on Internet crime, with special reference to paedophiles. Regional HQ were setting up a special unit and keen to attract recruits. Freya Graffham was not in the least tempted to put her name forward for what she saw as a grubby, upsetting and unpleasant area of police work which involved spending too much time at a computer. But it would be useful to get the broad picture of something relatively new and it always paid to show keenness by signing up for a seminar. She had thought when she had left the Met and come to live and work in Lafferton, that ambition was something she would be glad to leave behind, together with the stress of a London that was becoming increasingly dangerous and depressing and a short, seriously unhappy marriage. Now she could feel the change beginning to heal and refresh her already. She had fallen in love with Lafferton when she had come for the interview, enjoyed the beauty of the cathedral town and its surrounding countryside. It had far more to offer than she had anticipated and she was still happy sorting out her new house.

Above all, she felt relaxed and was enjoying her job again. Enthusiasm and idealism filled her, as well as a confidence which she thought she had lost for good during her last miserable year in London.

Twenty minutes later, she was sitting in a room of about thirty other police officers listening to a profile of the typically sick, warped and secretive abuser-by-proxy of children, and discovering the latest techniques being deployed in operations to flush him out. Once or twice the details of paedophile websites repelled her so much that she closed her mind to them and went back to thinking about Angela Randall, making a mental note to call up Radio BEV the following morning.

The seminar was followed by questions. Freya had nothing to ask and most of those who did went into Internet technicalities. But the final question caught her attention, not because of what was asked, but because of the questioner, DCI Simon Serrailler, who had interviewed her, but since her arrival at Lafferton had been on leave. She was reminded at once of how young he seemed for his rank and also how unusual he was in having almost Nordic blond hair but with dark eyes.

At the end of the seminar he made his way across.

'I'm glad you could make it. Not very pretty, is it?'

'Grim. There were a couple of times when I had to switch off, I'm afraid.'

'So we won't be losing you to the new unit?'

'Er . . . no.'

'Good. Perhaps you'll come and see me tomorrow, let me know how you're settling in?'

'I will, sir, thank you. I'm enjoying it very much.'

DCI Serrailler smiled but then turned away, as someone tapped his arm.

The streets of Bevham were bright and crowded with late-night shoppers, the Salvation Army band was playing carols, and people stood with song sheets under the huge tree in City Square. 'While Shepherds Watched' came faintly through Freya's car window.

Christmas. Families reunited; home and hearth . . . the previous Christmas had been the last she and Don had spent together, almost in silence, hostility and misery like a stormy sea between them. In the afternoon, she had walked the streets of Putney and been glad to find an Indian corner shop that was open and to take refuge among its crammed, spice-smelling shelves for a while. This year, having gently rejected pleas for joining the family Christmas at her sister's Cumbrian farm, she was looking forward to shutting her new front door and being by herself with some simple food, a good bottle of wine, some new CDs and novels and the television. Her brief marriage seemed, in retrospect, to have been spent either in shouting or in acrimonious temporary truce.

At the three slow sets of traffic lights down the high street, looking at the Aladdin's cave of coloured lights and gilding and silvering, she thought again of Angela Randall. Where was she now, at this minute, at this bright, busy, happy season? Freya thought of the immaculate, impersonal, chilly little house, and its queer silence, its mundane furnishings, its sterile air; 4 Barn Close had the smell of a house into which love and friendship and laughter had never come. And the costly present in its gilded wrapping? The gift tag, *To You, with all possible love from your devoted, Me*.

Whatever the DI might say, Freya Graffham knew she could not leave this one. She wanted to get her teeth into something of her own and make her mark, that much she recognised. But that was the least of it.

She drove out of the city through the dark lanes, towards Lafferton and home, her mind full of the missing woman and a deep unease.

Ten

When the blue-and-cream bus drew up at the stop in the market square Debbie Parker had a moment of absolute panic, which turned her stomach to water and made the sweat break out in a band round her neck.

There were three buses a day from Lafferton to Starly and Starly Tor. This, at nine forty-five, was the first and she would have over an hour to kill before her appointment. She had planned it all carefully. She would find out exactly where Dava's Spiritual Sanctuary was, and then get coffee somewhere. If there was time after that, there were small shops to browse in. Starly was not much more than a village which had grown around the Tor itself, but a lot of therapists and healers had set up there, as she had discovered from the *Tor Community Newsletter* she had picked up in the health shop. For days she had been reading it, and following leads it had given her to other pamphlets and books, and Sandy had left her computer switched on, so she could access more on the Internet. Some of it sounded cranky but a few things fascinated her so that she sat up late into the night reading deeply into them, and afterwards lay awake questioning, trying to apply their principles to herself. She had so much to discover from Dava, so much guidance to receive, so many questions to ask, and whenever she glanced at the blue card, she felt reassurance and a profound certainty that this was the lead she must follow, this was what was meant to speak to her. Nevertheless, faced with the doors of the bus swinging open and the metal steps to climb, Debbie felt terrified enough to want to duck and run, back through the streets to the safety of home and her dark room, her own bed.

'Come on, love, you're holding up the queue.'

The driver-conductor was waiting, tapping a coin on the ticket box. She glanced round. Half a dozen people were pressing in behind her.

'Starly and Starly Tor via Dimper, Harnham, Bransby, Lockerton Wood, Little Lockerton, Fretfield, Shrimfield and Up Starly. Plenty of choice, only make up your mind.'

Someone pushed against her back and to save herself, Debbie had to put her foot on the bus step.

'Thank goodness for that. Where to?'

She swallowed and her throat had a hard dry lump of coke stuck in it, she could neither speak nor breathe.

'Starly.'

'Single or are you planning on coming home?'

'Return. Please.' The lump dissolved but her fingers shook, holding the white roll of ticket.

She had forgotten how beautiful the countryside round here was, even in January, how the hills sloped and unfolded one after another, with small clumps of woodland between, and streams running along the bottom of the hills, ribbons of silky grey drystone walls, sheep scattered as if they had been thrown down on the fields at random, like confetti. There was a lemony winter sun, low above the fields, and the light was wonderful, soft and clear, picking out a barn roof, a crown of oaks, a wooden gate, or slanting suddenly across an open meadow. Once, she saw a hunt streaming across, each horse jumping a long scribble of hedge, red coats and black hats and manes and tails pouring over and on.

Just looking at everything lifted her mood and calmed her. She ought to come out like this more, travel about anywhere, looking, looking, peaceful and cocooned in the warm bus. Her dark loathing of herself and her own unattractive face and overweight body seemed to have been left behind in Lafferton. Now, she was someone else, or no one else, content, unworried, happy even, in a pleasant trance of enjoyment.

She did not mind the slowness of the bus or the round-about route, the stopping and starting, all of it pleased her and kept her safely away from herself. In her pocket, the blue card was safe, a talisman, a promise and not, for the moment, anything to fear. What lay ahead, did, what was going to happen, would, and it was all meant to be.

The sun was warm on Debbie's face through the bus window. A heron, long legs dangling, flew down into a field beside a stream, and stood, erect, elegant, uncannily still. A hare raced suddenly up a slope and out of sight. She fell into a half-doze.

'Starly . . . Starly . . . all change please.' She started and for a second couldn't remember why she was sitting with cramped legs and stiff neck on an emptying bus.

'Late night, was it?'

She stood on the pavement watching the bus turn round and pull up at the stop on the other side of the street. The engine died and the driver climbed out.

Everything went quiet. The rest of the passengers had vanished and a Tuesday afternoon in January was not a day when a place like Starly bustled with people.

The little town was set on two steep slopes that formed a T, with the main shopping street on the long side. The houses were small, and all of a piece, plain stone with tiled roofs and a few white- and pink-painted eighteenth-century cottages similar to those in the old part of Lafferton. She looked round. Starly Primary School was opposite to her, next to a small car park which was almost empty. Baptist chapel. Bank. Post office. Starly Books and Stationery.

She wandered slowly past them. A small all-purpose grocer next to a butcher. These were the normal shops. At the junction of the T, the road went even more steeply downhill and at once she saw that everything that made Starly the centre of New Age interests was clustered here. Every building had either a shop or some sort of centre . . . Feng shui. Crystals. Vegetarian, vegan and whole-foods. Herbalist. The New Age Book Centre. The Starly Community Meeting House . . . Indian saris and North American Indian tribal beads, candles, incense burners, wind chimes, tubular bells, nuts, alternative lotions and remedies, beauty products not tested on animals, eco-logically safe washing powders, recycling depot. In between were doors with signs to the consulting rooms of healers, herbalists and psychics.

The street was quiet, the shops mainly empty. She wandered into a couple. They smelled of incense and dust and her feet sounded loud on the wooden floors.

Behind a counter a girl sat knitting. A woman talked to another about a homeopathic animal clinic. Debbie had expected to find the place exciting but it just seemed sad and run-down. Notices were tatty and stock looked tired, everything had a dispirited air.

She found a small wholefood café with tables and chairs in bright pine, and a noticeboard of cards for therapists and posters about meetings. They served only decaffeinated coffee and organic tea, so she had the coffee and a piece of hard flapjack. The coffee tasted odd and the girl who served her had a cold.

Debbie sat under the noticeboard. The blue of Dava's card shone out from the clutter of others. Debbie stared at it. The colour worked its magic at once, lifting her mood and the dull atmosphere of the café, exciting her all over again. She had no idea why a colour and the printing on a piece of card should seem like a voice talking directly and intimately to some place deep within her.

'Could you tell me where that is, please?' She pointed to the card.

'What's it say?'

'The Sanctuary, Pilgrim Street.'

'Oh yeah, the little side alley that runs behind here, turn up by the candle shop.'

'Thanks. It's difficult in a place you don't know.'

'Yeah, right.'

'I think I'll have another cup of coffee. My appointment isn't till twelve.'

She wanted to tell the girl all about it, talk about herself, tell her things she had never told anyone. The girl pulled the coffee jar towards her and spooned out the brown powder with a sigh. The urn glugged as the water heated up.

Debbie probed at her side tooth to extract a lump of the flapjack, and said nothing after all.

She was far too early. She walked up one side of the lane to the top, but did not find anything advertising itself as Dava's Spiritual Sanctuary.

Her calf muscles ached as she crossed and began to go carefully down the opposite side. Halfway down, she suddenly caught sight of the blue – her blue, as she thought of it now, a patch of it that seemed to glow in the dim lane. It was set into the wall of a cottage which otherwise had nothing else to distinguish it from the rest. *Dava*. There was the same dusting of gold stars. But it was not yet twenty minutes to twelve; she was afraid of looking too eager.

She was tired by the time she had walked twice round the grid of sloping streets. There were very few people about, the shops were empty. A faint smell of patchouli or musky incense drifted out of one of the doors. It was cold.

If it had not been for the blue card in her pocket, Debbie Parker would have cried, and then fled back to the bus stop and then the haven of her bedroom in Lafferton. But she did have the card.

At five to twelve, she rang the bell under the blue sign.

There was no sound and no one came. A sudden cold wind came skimming down the lane. She tried to push open the door but it was closed and locked. What were they fooling about for?

A church clock somewhere struck twelve and as the last note faded, the door opened. A woman in a long skirt and with a scarf tied round her head let Debbie in.

'Dava likes his appointments to begin exactly on time.'

They went into a hall into which coloured light came dimly through a stained-glass panel.

'Dava would like quiet now.'

She opened a door and held it open for Debbie to go inside.

There was a round table and two chairs, and the walls were hung with some sort of softly draped fabric.

'Please come in, Debbie.'

He was sitting at the table, wearing a collarless velvet coat, like a clergyman's cassock. He had long brown hair and his fingers were decorated with rings. There was a chain with a plain silver Celtic cross round his neck.

Debbie's heart thudded.

'Don't be nervous. Please – come and sit down.'

Candles were burning, giving off a sweet smell; an elaborately framed mirror reflected their flickering amber flames.

He waited in silence for Debbie to unbutton her jacket, and put her rucksack down. She fidgeted, nervous and uncertain. But then, she looked up and into his eyes. They were steady on her face, large eyes with thick lashes and they were blue, a blue as deep and magnetic and beautiful as the blue of the card. They lacked only the gold dust. Debbie felt herself drawn down into them and gave a great, shuddering sigh of relaxation; it felt like a giving up of part of herself. She was no longer anxious, no longer afraid. She was here and that was enough.

'Good,' Dava said. His voice was rather ordinary. 'Welcome to the Sanctuary, Debbie. Whatever troubles and problems and fears you have brought to me today, we will look at them carefully and I will begin to heal you and give you some new perspectives on your life. Whatever pain – mental, physical or spiritual – is lowering your energy, depleting you and dragging you down, whatever negative forces are draining you and trying to hold you back, we will deal with. Not all at once, not all today. But gradually you will begin to feel renewed and revitalised. That I promise. You will feel balanced and in harmony with yourself and the world, you will be freer, you will be in tune with your own inner being. That I promise. Some things can be sorted out very easily, others go deeper. Everything I say and do, every treatment I suggest, all the energies I will devote to helping you, are positive and good. You will come to no harm. Let me tell you how the hour will progress, Debbie.'

Listening to Dava was like listening to running water or swishing waves or breezes riffling softly through leaves, his voice was soothing and comforting. As he spoke, he looked at her steadily and the power of his eyes was so great that she was forced to look away, down at the table, covered in its deep red velvet cloth. It was like not being able to stare into the sun.

'First, I will take you through a short simple meditation to relax you and free any tensions. We will have silence together as I tune into your energies and sense the strength or weaknesses of your chakra. Then, I will read you. Once I am tuned into you, I can discover what your problems and anxieties – even illnesses – are. But you can also tell me what in particular you have come to consult me about. Are you happy with all of this, Debbie? Have you any questions or worries, before we begin? Please feel free to ask anything at all.'

He sat with his hands folded in front of him on the table. She had never known anyone sit so still. He seemed scarcely to be breathing. She remembered the heron, standing still as a carving beside the stream.

'No.' Her mouth was dry and her voice sounded unfamiliar. 'No, thank you. I'm – I'm very happy with everything.'

'Good. Good, Debbie. Then close your eyes and let me begin by focusing your mind on light and peace.'

She was lying down and she was warm; her body felt light. She was floating somewhere above the ground surrounded by a soft violet-blue haze and she was careless of everything that troubled her now or had ever done so. She was listening to soft sounds that were like music but were not, they were natural sounds, birdsong and running streams, waves hushing over sand and wind in trees . . . The music of the spheres, she thought, the music of the spheres.

She had been talking about her childhood, when her mother had been alive. Her mother's voice had been clear to her, her mother's face had been before her. She had talked about her mother walking with her through leaves in a golden wood, her mother laughing with her as they threw snowballs, her mother singing her to sleep. She had talked about her mother lying in bed pale and hideously thin, with the bones showing white through an almost transparent skin and her eyes dull.

'I was afraid of her,' she heard herself say, 'she was not my mother.'

She talked about the death and the funeral, the empty bedroom and the quietness of their house and how she had gone out and sat in the garden or walked round the streets, rather than listen to her father's weeping. She talked about her new stepmother and how she had hated her in those early weeks.

Now, she found herself floating upwards, like a deep-sea diver coming gently to the surface of the water.

'Good, Debbie . . . Rest there. Rest quietly.'

Tears were streaming down her face. She was lying on a couch and the ceiling above her was blue and dusted with tiny gold stars. She had no recollection of how she had got there.

Dava sat on a stool beside her.

'When you're ready, sit up. Take your time.'

'Have I been asleep? Was I dreaming?'

'We call it a trance sleep . . . a waking sleep. It is deeply healing. You were safe. Quite safe.'

His voice was soft and lilted a little, so that she felt she might lie down again, be rocked by it back into the wonderful other world.

'Sit up, Debbie.'

Dava got up with a swish of his long coat, and went back to his seat at the round table. 'When you feel ready, come over here again. Don't stand too suddenly, you might feel faint.'

Her head was so light it might have floated off her shoulders. She swung her legs carefully over the side of the couch and waited for a moment.

'Now, you will go home and you will sleep better than you have slept for months. But there are one or two things we should discuss . . . one or two problems to clear up.'

When she walked across the room, her legs felt full of water, so she was glad to sit down.

'You will be well. You will be very well. You have a bright shining path ahead of you, but there are obstacles in the way. You know what they are, Debbie. Tell me about them. You know what it is about yourself that you want to change.'

'I'm fat. I hate my spots. I hate the blackness that comes down.'

She had never imagined being able to speak so openly; she heard herself listing the things that she was ashamed of, as if they were items on a shopping list.

'After this consultation, I will be sending you written instructions and some prescriptions. A diet sheet – but that is so simple. Eat only vegetables and fruit. Drink only water or herbal teas. Eat nothing which is not organic. Eat only wholefoods. Eat as much of these things as you wish. Eat no animal products. No dairy, no bread, no sugars. Drink no alcohol or caffeine, no coffee or tea or chocolate. Take the vitamins I will send. I will also make up a herbal ointment for your skin. I will send this to you in a few days. The black moods will lift slowly, slowly. At first they may become worse as may the headaches. Just rest. And walk as much as you possibly can in the fresh air. Walk and dance and run in the fields, in the woods . . . wherever you feel moved to. Walk anywhere and let your soul sing, Debbie. Listen to me and listen to your inner voice.

'The process of healing and harmony has begun. I am pleased with you. I see love and light surrounding you and a joyful future, once we have cleared the darkness and the obstacles from your path.'

There was a long silence. Dava had closed his eyes.

One of the incense sticks burning in a jar on the table flaked into a pile of soft grey ash.

Dava opened his eyes and got up in one, brisk movement.

'I will send you another appointment for a time which is auspicious.'

She looked directly into his eyes but they had an opaque,

veiled look now, as if he had shut down the electricity of contact between them. His face was expressionless.

'Thank you . . . yes. Thanks.' She stumbled out of the door, feeling herself flush with embarrassment. The woman in the long skirt was standing there, so that in the dimness of the hall Debbie almost knocked her over. She said nothing. The front door swung silently open as she pressed a switch on the wall and Debbie found herself in the lane alone. It was drizzling.

Confused, and light-headed, she half ran down the steep slope and round the corner to the wholefood café, where two tables were now occupied by women with shopping bags and young children, chatting together. It was ordinary. Normal. She wanted to sob with relief.

It was only when she was halfway through her mug of sweet coffee and thick slice of carrot cake that Debbie remembered she was forbidden to have either. But she needed them. She felt as if she were thawing after her body had been frozen and the blood was flowing again through her veins. She stayed in the warmth and cheerfulness of the café until it was time to walk up the hill to catch her bus home.

She woke a little after eight o'clock the following morning, and lay trying to make sense of where she was and how she felt. The first thing she realised was that she had indeed slept deeply, peacefully and without dreaming. She waited, lying in her cocoon as calm as a baby. Fifteen minutes later, she was still lying, wide awake and blissful in the realisation that the black fog had not crept over her to blot out the rest of the day. She felt slightly detached, slightly odd, but not depressed. Not anything.

She got up tentatively, as if she might feel a sudden shooting pain or that movement might trigger the sudden descent of the blackness. But she showered and dressed and it did not happen.

Sandy was in the kitchen, putting clothes into the washing machine.

'You look different,' she said at once.

Debbie put the kettle on and reached for mugs and milk. She did not yet know how much she wanted to talk about Dava, partly because she had not yet sorted out what had happened and the things he had said, partly from some deep sense that the consultation was meant to be private. She ought to have asked his permission to talk about it. She realised she needed more guidance from him about a great many things.

'You all right?'

'A bit blotto. I slept too long. Come on, tell me about your holiday.'

For ten minutes or so, Sandy did. The kitchen was pleasant with the winter sun coming through the window. Debbie kept testing herself to see how she felt, as if she were touching a tooth the dentist had drilled to see if it were still sore.

'OK, that's enough about me,' Sandy said.

They sat in silence at the wobbly Formica-topped kitchen table and even the pattern, like a grey rash all over its surface, looked beautiful to Debbie, just as the peeling wall and the front of the washing machine and the chipped mug hanging on the peg looked beautiful. Dava. It was all because of Dava.

'Well, something's happened,' Debbie said.

The first few sentences came slowly as Debbie tried to find the right words to describe everything and to convey the power and the impact and the beauty of Dava, but then the words poured out in a stream like water over rocks, rushing together, what he had told her about her childhood, her future, her character, what he would do for her inner self, her hopelessness, her whole being. Sandy listened intently without interrupting once, occasionally looking carefully at Debbie, but mainly staring down into her mug.

The sun moved up the wall behind them.

Debbie's words dried up and stopped flowing and the kitchen was quiet. She was damp with sweat round her neck, between her breasts, down her back; the effort of concentrating and of trying to convey everything, as well as reliving the emotions, had drained her and left her limp.

'What happens next?'

'My life turns around.'

'Right . . .'

'Starting now.'

'Are you going again?'

'He'll send me an appointment . . . that's what happens. You can't make one, he sends it for exactly the right day and time . . . when it's auspicious.'

'Right.' Sandy's voice conveyed nothing, neither approval and enthusiasm nor suspicion.

'He's sending me some tablets . . . herbal things for the headaches and some skin ointment.'

'Is it expensive?'

'I don't think it can be, not very.'

'Why?'

'Because he isn't someone who would take a lot of money off you, you can tell, he isn't into getting rich . . . and he knows I'm on benefits anyway.'

'Right.'

'He said to see if the headaches got better with the tablets and walking a lot in the fresh air and the new diet, but if they don't, he could send me to someone else, he said sometimes things like that aren't easy . . . they need other sorts of treatment.'

'Where would he send you?'

'He didn't say. Someone he knows, I expect.'

'Oh, I expect so, yes.'

Debbie looked at her sharply.

'Listen, it's all OK, Sand. It's fantastic. I mean, I feel really, really better just since yesterday.'

'Great.' Sandy got up and took the mugs to the sink. She rinsed and drained them, emptied the teapot and sluiced it out. Then she glanced round. 'What are you going to do today then?'

'Go and buy the right things to eat. Clear out the rubbish from the cupboard and the fridge.'

'OK, but don't chuck mine out as well.'

'Then I'll go out and walk . . . like he said. Walk and walk in the fresh air.'

'Right.' Sandy went to the door. Hesitated. 'Listen, Debs, don't take this the wrong way – only you say you can't remember everything that happened . . . you sort of came to and you were lying on the couch . . . do you think he might have given you something, or –'

'What are you talking about?'

'Don't jump down my throat. I just mean you have to be careful. You were on your own in this room with him and –'

'Oh, for Christ's sake, Sandy. It was just like he sort of hypnotised me.' She thought of Dava's eyes and his soft voice.

'You do look better.'

'I feel like I'm reborn, you know? He's rebirthing me; that's what he said he was going to do, only it hasn't finished, but when it is I'll be new . . . a new Deborah. He said when it was complete, I would change my name – I would feel a real, deep urge to change it . . . I won't be Debbie then, I'll be Deborah. Deborah Parker.'

She straightened her back and felt herself to be a foot taller and floating above the ground as she went out of the kitchen.

The sun slid off the wall, leaving the room in shadow.

Eleven

Jim had to do something, had to be out, and besides, the house was too quiet. When the postman came through the gate, there was silence, and when the milkman whistled and the dustcart turned into the street. Silence. He had often cursed Skippy's high-pitched bark that made him start up in his chair, but he hated the silence more.

He had combed the Hill and beaten about with a stick in as much of the scrub and undergrowth as he could. Every day, Jim Williams spent most of the morning there, starting out very early, as he had done on the day the terrier had vanished, and often returning, to search and call and whistle until it grew dark.

Christmas he had spent alone and it had meant nothing. Now, it was the New Year and no one else was out on the Hill. He was waiting for the woman with the Dobermanns, who had been absent for a week. It was damp and mild and there was no sign of Skippy.

He had heard a report on the radio about a missing prize pedigree dog, and after that, he had gone through the *Lafferton Echo* the previous week, and the *Bevham Post* every night, for reports of dog-stealing gangs. Phyl had told him about them.

'They take cats, too, they go for vivisection when they don't go to the canning factory and wind up as pet food. You have to look out.'

But he had not, he had let Skippy off the lead as she never did, and the terrier had gone. He had probed down every rabbit hole he could find and stood listening for some faint bark or whimper of a dog stuck underground.

Silence, except for the wind rustling the dry undergrowth and blowing into his face down the Hill.

He should give up, he knew that in his heart. He wasn't going to find the dog. He was frustrated and angry and baffled but he should give up all the same.

But not yet, not just yet. What was a week? The terrier had chased off after something and missed a turn, found himself among unfamiliar streets where nothing smelled right, and wandered off, perhaps been into a house, or maybe he'd curled up in a garage or a shed and then been locked in.

Just a week.

He thought he might put an advertisement in the free paper.

Then he heard the yelping bark of the two Dobermanns and saw the woman striding with them towards him up the slope. Jim Williams felt like rushing to her with open arms, so sure was he that she would have seen or heard something. She had been out walking the day Skippy had disappeared, she had seen Jim, even looked back over her shoulder as he had whistled and called.

He stood, trying to get his breath now, desperate to speak to her.

She was not a pleasant-looking woman. She was large and aggressive and wore a huge, heavy sheepskin coat and a hat with ear flaps, and there was something haughty about her expression. She listened with impatience as the Dobermanns pulled at their leads.

'I know you're always up here, you were here that day, I've been waiting to catch you again. Did you see anything, did you hear anything? You know what he looks like.'

'Yes, ratty little thing, they all are, can't stand tiddly dogs. But no, I'm afraid I didn't and I haven't and really do you wonder? Let one of those off the lead and they just disappear. Run over, trodden on, down a hole. Let that be a lesson for when you get another. Have a decent-sized dog.'

She strode off briskly behind the yelping Dobermanns and when she had gone a few yards, looked back over her shoulder, in the same way she had looked back as he had shouted for Skippy.

'Sorry.'

Jim Williams felt himself begin to shake. He should have been angry, perhaps even taken her up for being so rude, but all he felt was crushed and tearful. She was right, he was to blame, it was his own fault.

'Oh Jim, honestly,' he heard Phyl say. He watched the back of the Dobermann woman going out of sight towards the trees. He wanted to rush after her and beg her that if she saw Phyl not to tell her, not to give him away.

He took out his handkerchief, wiped his eyes and blew his nose. What was he thinking about? What made him want to do that? Phyl was dead, and in any case the Dobermann woman would not have known her.

He was still shaking as he went slowly down the sloping path towards the road.

But later, having calmed himself with a good breakfast, he went out again, first to the office of the free newspaper, where he placed an advertisement, then to the telephone kiosk, where he called Radio BEV, who logged his message about Skippy's disappearance. After that, he went to Lafferton Police Station.

Twelve

Jake Spurrier took a long time to put on his outdoor shoes and zip up his jacket, partly because everything took ages these days because he felt tired, partly because he was hating the idea of a visit to Mr Sharpe.

'Jake, it doesn't hurt.'

'It did hurt. When I went for my sore throats and he stuck the needles into my neck it mega hurt.'

'You didn't have another sore throat afterwards though, did you?'

'I've got one now.'

'Hm.'

But as he turned away, Jenny Spurrier looked anxiously at her ten-year-old son. He had never been especially robust, unlike his brother Joe who was fourteen and had barely had a single day off school for illness in his life. Jake had been the one with a wheezy chest and constant ear infections, the one who caught mumps and chickenpox and was ill for a month with them, the one who went down with the first head cold in September and did not finish having them until the end of April.

Lately, he had been complaining of tiredness, and he was paler than normal. His sore throats had returned, and he had even had a couple of sties on his eyes, which children simply didn't get nowadays.

Jenny Spurrier was against antibiotics in any form, though occasionally she had given in when nothing else would get to the bottom of Jake's earaches, and if she took him to see Dr Deerbon, she knew she would have the usual battle about it. Not that this practice was as bad as the one she had transferred them all from, five years before. There, antibiotics were handed out like sweets as a cure-all for every sniffle and headache; you had been able to get them by making a phone call to the receptionist without the trouble of making an appointment to see the doctors. Things were better at Dr Deerbon's surgery, no question about that. It had been Dr Deerbon who had suggested Jenny try acupuncture for her persistent stomach pains, once every investigation had proved negative.

'I don't send people to see alternative practitioners casually,' Dr Deerbon had told her, 'but I have a great respect for Aidan Sharpe. He is fully qualified, he won't fill you with a lot of gobbledegook, and a certain range of problems respond very well to acupuncture. It's very effective for chronic pain too. A patient of mine with bones crumbling from osteoporosis and arthritis has had great relief from regular treatments with Mr Sharpe. No miracle cure, you understand . . . there is no cure for crumbling bones, but the relief of pain and stiffness has been obvious. I'm afraid you can't go on the NHS, but if you have any private medical insurance they'll usually cover it if I write the referral.'

Jenny had been to see Aidan Sharpe just twice and

her stomach pains had gone. She was able to eat normally, though the acupuncturist had recommended that she avoid highly spiced food and white wine. That had been two years ago and the treatment had also cured Jake Spurrier's sore throats and generally given him more energy and stamina. He had played football for the school team for a whole season and only missed one game because of having a cold, an unprecedented run of good health. In the last month or so though, he had become run-down again, his appetite was poor, and he had been put on the bench by the football coach.

'You know how much better you were when you had Mr Sharpe's treatment before, Jake, and you want to get back on to the team, don't you?'

Jake had grumbled, but his mother knew how to get to him . . . he was a passionate football player, and had scored enough goals the previous year to take the team as far as the county junior championship semi-finals before they were beaten. For Christmas, he had even got, via someone his dad knew at work who knew someone in Manchester, a shirt with 'Beckham 7' on it, signed by his hero.

'OK, OK.' Jake stood up from finishing his shoelaces, and began to fall towards Jenny.

'Jake, what's the matter? It's all right . . . sit down here. Bend forward and put your head on your knees.'

'Everything went all wobbly . . . the floor wasn't there.'

'You felt faint. It happens sometimes when you stand up quickly. Just sit there for a minute, I'll get you a drink of water. We won't go until you feel all right, don't worry.'

Ten minutes later, she put a protesting Jake into the front seat of the car.

'I can put the belt on myself, I'm OK, Mum, don't fuss . . .'

'Sorry.'

But he was too pale, Jenny thought, far too pale. The quicker he was sorted out the better.

When she was six, she had had three teeth taken out. In advance, her friends at school had filled her full of horror stories about the pain she would suffer, the blood and the gruesome dental instruments she would see, so that by the time she had arrived at the dental surgery she had been hysterical. She had never forgotten the gentleness and kindness of the dentist, Mr Peat. He had been tall, with a thick shock of hair and a high shiny forehead, and he had spent a long time talking to her, explaining that she would feel nothing at all except some soreness later, which would go as soon as she took 'the magic tablets', that she certainly would see no blood or instruments, and that she would go to sleep holding the surgery teddy bear and wake up only a few minutes later after a beautiful dream and with the bear still looking after her. Everything had happened as he had said and she had never been afraid of the dentist again.

Aidan Sharpe had the same quiet, calm, gentle manner as Mr Peat, although he was not so tall, and his hair and small goatee beard were both neatly cut. Now, as they walked into the bright reception area of his surgery, she felt herself relax for the first time in days. Jake was going to be looked after. Jake was going to be all right.

There was a water cooler, there were comfortable chairs and a sofa, a low table with the day's papers and a neat stack of recent glossy magazines. The table and the desk of Mrs Cooper, the receptionist, had bowls of sweet-smelling hyacinths and a tiny glass of snowdrops.

There was something welcoming about the place, an indefinable air of cheerfulness and calm, which was not at all what Jenny had expected on her first visit.

'Nothing weird,' she had said to Dr Deerbon afterwards.

'I know. That's one of the reasons I'm happy to send my patients there. Not so much as a collecting tin for Friends of the Earth!'

It was true. Aidan Sharpe's professional qualification and membership certificates were framed on the wall beside the reception desk, together with a photograph of him with the Queen. Otherwise, there were several unexciting watercolours, bland seascapes and pretty woodland scenes.

'Mum, have I got to have it done?'

But Jenny had no time to answer.

'Good morning, Mrs Spurrier . . . Jake.' Aidan Sharpe was crossing the room from his surgery, his white coat crisp, his brown brogues shining.

Behind his mother, Jake made a face, caught only by the receptionist, who winked at him.

The surgery was more businesslike than the outer room, with a desk and chair, the treatment couch and the tray with needles and steriliser. But the sun was on this side, and filling the room with watery lemon light.

'Now, Jake, how long is it since I last saw you?' Aidan Sharpe looked down at his notes. 'Nearly eighteen months. And the sore throat's cleared up?'

'It only took the two treatments,' Jenny said. 'He's been so well.'

'But they're back now, and you said there was something else worrying you about Jake, Mrs Spurrier?'

The boy sat staring down at the carpet, kicking his legs.

'Don't worry, Jake, I know how maddening it is when people talk about you not to you and I want you to tell me how you feel in just a moment. But mothers do have a way of knowing things about you, I'm afraid.'

He wrote carefully as Jenny Spurrier took him through Jake's tiredness, his recent sties and sore throat, and that morning's near-faint.

'OK, Jake, would you swap places with Mum please . . . I want to have a look at you in a good light. Great. Let's have a look at the throat first.'

He took a sterile spatula from its packet and pressed the back of Jake's tongue down, then examined his eyes, followed by a slow scrutiny of each ear.

'When you say you've felt tired a lot, can you describe that a bit more? Have you been staying up late reading or playing computer games? Not getting enough sleep? Don't worry if you have, it's not a punishable offence.'

'I can't stay awake long enough.'

'You feel tired during the day?'

'Yes.'

'Games? You're something of a footballer, I know.'

'I can't run fast, I get too tired.'

'Do you get breathless – wheezy, when you run?'

'No.'

'Do you get aching legs after games?'

'He often complains that his legs ache even when he hasn't been playing,' Jenny said.

'Right, Jake, take off your outer clothes and T-shirt and just keep on your pants. Then lie on the couch. I'd like to have a look at the rest of you.'

Jake lay, watching the sun make bright discs on the white ceiling as it reflected against the metal rim of the lamp. His legs ached now and if Mr Sharpe had stopped talking, he thought he could go to sleep here for hours and hours.

'Has someone been having a go at you, Jake?'

'No.'

The acupuncturist was touching Jake's calf and then his upper leg gently.

'Rough game?'

'No, they just came.'

'I see. Any more bruises like that?'

'I had one on my arm but I think it's gone.' He looked, but saw that another bruise had formed, larger than the first.

'Right. Have you had any nosebleeds recently?'

'No.'

'You did, don't you remember,' his mother said, 'a week or two ago, you called me in the middle of the night. I thought he must have been thrashing around and banged his face on the bedpost. I had to soak half a dozen hankies in iced water and hold them to his nose before it stopped.'

'Any more since then, Jake? At school?'

'No.'

There had been, but Jake had had enough of being interrogated and decided to practise the James Bond technique of lying under torture.

'OK, Jake, you can get dressed now and then would you just wait outside for a few moments while I go through the boring bits with your mum. Mrs Cooper has some orange squash if you're thirsty.'

'Aren't you going to stick the needles in me?'

'Not today.'

'Yessss.'

Jake grabbed his trousers and T-shirt and pulled them

on anyhow, took his other things under his arm and vanished before the acupuncturist could change his mind.

'So there's nothing much wrong after all, if you aren't going to treat him? Well, that's a relief. But I just wish you could have done something to buck him up a bit.'

'Mrs Spurrier, I think it's Dr Deerbon who will be doing the bucking up. I'd like you to make an appointment with her for Jake as soon as possible.'

'Why?'

Aidan Sharpe was looking at her steadily and with an expression she had never seen on him.

'I don't want to make any diagnosis. I'm not a doctor, you know.'

'As good as. Better than some I've known.'

'Thank you.' A smile of pride and pleasure lit up his face. 'All the same. Jake ought to see the GP and I need to have a report on him from her before I can consider giving him any treatment. There may be nothing at all wrong, but some of his symptoms need to be investigated. I'll drop Dr Deerbon a note. Don't worry, please. I am just very careful. There are far too many complementary practitioners without medical knowledge who are too ready to jump in and treat things they don't know enough about. I'm not one of them.'

He stood up.

'When I've heard from Dr Deerbon and if she's happy, we'll make another appointment for Jake and then see if I can help. There'll be no charge for this consultation.'

'Oh, I must pay you, I know you haven't given him any acupuncture but we've taken up your professional time.'

'No. It's a point of principle, Mrs Spurrier. I don't charge when I don't treat. Now, let's go and release young Jake from the acupuncturist's prison.'

Aidan Sharpe saw Jenny Spurrier and her son cheerfully off the premises, but when he returned to the reception room, his face was grave.

'Julie, I've got ten minutes before – who is it next?'

'Mr Cromer.'

'I want to sort this out beforehand. Would you try and get me Dr Deerbon – Dr Cat? If she isn't available, leave a message asking her to call me as a matter of urgency.'

But Cat came through straight away.

'Aidan? Good morning. How are you?'

'Fine and I'm sorry to interrupt.'

'No, surgery's just this minute finished. What can I do for you?'

'Jake Spurrier . . . aged ten. Felstead Road.'

'I know. Mother is Jenny. Nice family.'

'Yes. I'm afraid I'm rather concerned. She brought the boy into me this morning . . . sore throats, tiredness. I saw him about eighteen months ago for the sore throats . . . gave him a couple of treatments and they cleared up. You and I agreed they were viral anyway.'

'I remember.'

'Well, this isn't viral. I haven't treated Jake and I've suggested his mother bring him to you as soon as possible. He reports excessive fatigue, nosebleeds, aching limbs, occasional faintness, some sties, and has a nasty strep throat at the moment. He also has some bruising on his legs and one forearm. Alarm bells rang pretty quickly, as I'm sure you'll understand.'

'Pallor?'

'Yes.'

'All the signs then. Thanks very much, Aidan, I'm glad you picked up on it. I'll get them to put him in as an emergency appointment.'

'Let me know, will you? Of course, I might be over-reacting.'

'You don't, in my experience. Anyway, a blood test will tell us what we want to know pretty smartly.'

Aidan Sharpe put down the phone and swung his chair round to look out of the window on to the garden. Two squirrels were leaping from tree to tree at the far end, then running fast down the long trunks and racing across the grass, before climbing after one another in the chase again.

If Jake Spurrier did indeed have one of the aggressive forms of childhood leukaemia, as both he and Cat Deerbon expected, it would be a long time before he would be racing about, climbing and playing with such ease and abandon – if he ever did.

Thirteen

The sensation of well-being and tranquillity, as if she were cocooned in the deep blue healing aura Dava had created for Debbie Parker, did not fade or weaken during the next few days. She slept wonderfully well each night and woke calmly, happy to face the day. She cleared out every tin, packet and jar of food from the cupboard and her section of the fridge, and spent almost a week's benefit money on wholefoods and organic fruit, vegetables and cereals.

She went out every day and walked, around parts of Lafferton she had never been near before, in the park, along the towpath and on the Hill.

Sandy watched her, and said nothing. She was still concerned and she thought the diet and the exercise would be a nine-day wonder, but it was a relief at least not to see her flatmate grey and crushed under her misery, not to have to coax her out of bed in the mornings nor worry about her while she was at work.

Almost a week after Debbie had been on the bus to Starly, a package arrived.

The tablets looked and smelled like a mixture of seaweed and compost and the plastic pot of ointment was of a repellent texture. They were packed with a list of complicated instructions and a bill for £75.

She had not asked how much it would all cost and now, defiantly, she told herself that she did not care; Dava was making her better. He was gifted, he had understood her and touched something deep within her subconscious that no one else had ever reached. She had only to remember the sound of his voice and the vivid, mesmerising quality in his eyes, only to think of the blue, to feel a thrill of excitement and response, as if Dava had called to her and met with an immediate and willing reply. It did not matter if the bill had been five times £75. It had to be worth it. You could not put a price on what he had already done for her.

Later that morning, she wrote to her father, asking if he could send her £100. *'It's for some medical treatment for my skin. Unfortunately, as with so much these days, the NHS won't pay but it will make such a difference to everything for me if only I can have my skin clear.'*

The tablets were to be swallowed with pure mineral water, after a meal of raw vegetarian food, twice a day. Nothing else apart from liberal quantities of the water was to be eaten for two hours afterwards. The bottle was to be kept away from chemicals of all kinds, in a dark cupboard.

The ointment was to be applied thinly before going to bed, on skin washed in pure mineral water and scent-free soap. It smelled of tar and of something else Debbie remembered from childhood but could not place.

She undressed, washed her face meticulously, and

patted it dry, as directed, on a clean kitchen towel made of bleach-free paper. The ointment made her skin tingle slightly.

Something about the ritual, like that of preparing the organic vegetables and fruit and drinking the mineral water, made her feel in contact with Dava, and the calm feeling, as if she were drifting out to sea, lulled her into one of the new, dream-free sleeps.

Something was wrong. She was dreaming again, but the dream was part of a struggle to come awake. She could not make out whether she was in pain or could not breathe and in the half-waking dream someone had glued her eyelids together and even when she prised them apart, there was darkness and a burning sensation. Then, through it, there was a sudden, painful flash and Sandy's voice, somewhere near to her.

'Debs . . . wake up, you were screaming, you were having a nightmare. Oh my God, what's happened to your face?'

Debbie sat up. She could see a little now, through the slits that were her eyes. Her face felt strange, as if her head had somehow swollen. Her skin was burning.

'It's that bloody ointment. You're allergic to it, it's made your whole face swell up.'

Debbie's breathing hurt too, she felt as if she were pushing against a door when she breathed out, only someone was on the other side pushing it back.

'I'm going to ring the doctors. They'll come, it'll be OK.'

She heard Sandy leave the room but still there was only a slit of light. If she lay down it was harder still to breathe. She could hear her chest creaking.

'The doctor's coming and she said to turn on all the taps and get the bathroom steamy, and take you in there. Oh Debbie, what were you thinking of? Jeez, just promise me you won't go to any more cranks.'

The steam was good. Debbie felt her chest loosening slightly, but her eyes remained almost closed and her skin felt as if she had scalded herself. She tried to think of Dava and surround herself with calm and the blue colour, tried to centre down into herself as he had told her, but panic kept rising in her, scattering her thoughts. Dava seemed unreal and distant. She thought she was going to be sick.

Half an hour later, she was sitting on the couch, breathing easily through a nebuliser and calm, as the injection of antihistamine Dr Deerbon had given her took effect. Her eyelids were still swollen but she could see the doctor in a blurred outline, against the light of the lamp.

'What should I do?' Sandy said anxiously to Cat Deerbon, as she showed her into the bathroom to wash her hands. 'I'd better sit up with her, hadn't I?'

'I don't think you'll need to do that. She'll be sleepy quite soon, and her breathing is almost back to normal. Keep the nebuliser by her though, and if she gets worse again call an ambulance. But I don't think she's going to. It might be an idea for you to sleep in her room – could you do that? I've left four antihistamine tablets . . . give her one when she wakes in the morning and another at lunchtime. She'll be pretty wiped out tomorrow.'

'It's OK, it's Saturday so I'll be here.'

'Could you show me these herbal potions she got hold of?'

Sandy fetched the bottle and the ointment. 'I'm going

to pour the pills down the lav and chuck the cream away. Makes you wonder what's in them to do that to her.'

'People do get allergic reactions to all sorts of orthodox medicines, even the usual stuff you get at the chemist, just as others are allergic to things the rest of us can eat. It's a very individual thing. But I think I'll take these for now, I want to try and find out what's in them.'

'Do you think they're poisonous?'

'That's unlikely. I'd rather none of my other patients got hold of them though.' Cat picked up her bag. 'I'll ring in the morning to find out how Debbie is but I shouldn't need to come and see her. Call me if you're worried though, I'm on duty all weekend, and would you tell her I'd like to see her in the surgery on Monday?'

Cat went to check on Debbie again before she left. She was asleep, lying curled on her side, her breathing easy. Her eyelids were less swollen, and the puffiness of her face had gone down. The antihistamine was working its usual magic. It was easy to see why the girl had wanted to do something drastic to clear her skin; the acne was spread over her face and neck, ugly and slightly infected. But why had she gone to see some potentially dangerous crank among the hippies of Starly, a consultation which had doubtless cost her a whack of money, when she could have had a prescription from Cat for a course of the antibiotic which could cure her acne and, because she was unemployed, would not even have had to pay for it?

As she drove out of Lafferton through the empty night streets, Cat made a mental note to talk to one or two medical colleagues about the person calling himself Dava.

Fourteen

Freya Graffham was not a churchgoer, but on one of her first free evenings in Lafferton she went to the cathedral because there was a performance of Handel's *Messiah*. She had sung alto in it herself more times than she could remember, from her schooldays on, as she had sung in many other things, and performed on stage in light opera too, until Don had objected and, in another desperate attempt to please and placate him, she had resigned from her Ealing choir and the amateur operatic society. Don did not sing, did not like music, refused to enter a church and resented anything which took Freya out of the house without him. She had stopped playing tennis and badminton, both of which she was good at; the only exercise she was allowed to take was swimming, because Don was a swimmer. He, on the other hand, had gone skiing twice a year without her. She had been to Switzerland with him once and broken her ankle. After that, Don had simply gone skiing with a group of his friends. There had never been any suggestion that he might give it up.

As she sat in the Cathedral Church of St Michael revelling in Handel's mighty choruses, she wondered briefly again not just how she could have married Don Ballinger, but how she could ever have spent so much as half a dozen social evenings with him. Within their marriage, she had felt as if she were disappearing, her own tastes and pleasures crushed under his disapproval, her personality barely allowed to express itself beyond the confines of her job.

She still could not get used to the fact that she was free. Sitting in this glorious building listening to music she knew so well, she realised again that she did not have to feel guilty, did not have to make excuses or tell lies when she returned home but was answerable only to herself.

'Every valley
Shall be exalted.'

She wanted to join in. She knew every note, every forte and pianissimo, every alto line, every biblical word.

The cathedral was packed and though so far she recognised no one, Freya felt at home, and so much a part of all of it, that she might have lived here for a decade. London, her marriage, the Met, were vanishing bit by bit like the grin on the face of the Cheshire Cat.

In the programme she found details of the St Michael's Singers who had backed the professional soloists, and the address of the auditions secretary. When she got home, she lit a fire – one of her musts in house-hunting had been a real fireplace. She had lived with efficient, clinical and soulless underfloor central heating for too long. This fireplace was small, but drew well, so that it took her only a few minutes to get the sticks and small dry logs alight. She put the *Messiah* on the CD player, poured a glass of Sancerre and, before going back to the book she was in the middle of, wrote asking for details of the next St Michael's Singers audition.

'You are happy,' she said aloud to herself. 'You are happy!'

The audition was in the church hall the week after Christmas. Four others were there, and she and two of them, a man and an older woman, were accepted.

Freya knew that she was out of practice and her voice was slightly rough, in the aftermath of a cold. The audition was not an easy one – the standard of the St Michael's Singers was high – but from the moment she took her note from the piano, she felt as if she were soaring to the ceiling as joyfully as a bird. She had missed singing far more than she had realised.

Before they left that evening, the choirmaster filled them in on the coming season, which ran through until the end of June. They would be singing Britten's *War Requiem* here in the cathedral in May, and before that taking part in a huge performance of the Bach B Minor Mass with assembled choirs from all over the county at Bevham on Easter Saturday. Freya's heart lifted. The Bach she knew well and the Britten she had longed to have the chance to sing.

'Meanwhile, in a couple of weeks' time there's a social evening for the choir. We can always do with new people to give a hand – you know how it is, everything falls on the same old few, so if you can offer your services . . .'

Freya had volunteered, work permitting, and taken down the number of the member arranging the evening's catering. She was not a serious cook, but she had always enjoyed the chance to make puddings.

She drove back singing along to the CD player as it belted out the B Minor Mass. She loved her new house; from the start Lafferton CID had presented her with just the sort of challenges she liked getting her teeth into; she had her music back; and now her social life looked like getting established.

She tried the number the choirmaster, Alan Fenton, had given her, but there was no reply and no answering machine picked up on her call. She would ring again. Meanwhile, as she delved into a couple of the boxes she still had not finished unpacking, for some of her cookery books, Freya grinned suddenly.

'Don Ballinger, eat your heart out.'

Just before ten o'clock she tried the number again.

'Yes?' An irritable older man.

'Hello, my name is Freya Graffham, I've been given this number by the choirmaster at the St Michael's –'

'You want my wife.'

Another husband who sounded as if the less he had to do with his wife's activities the better.

'Meriel speaking.'

Freya began to explain why she was phoning but was cut short, this time by a cry of delight.

'You don't mean you're offering to help? You saint!'

'I've only auditioned for the choir tonight but we still got the third degree about everything falling on the same shoulders as usual so there is a desperate need for volunteers.'

'Good old Alan.'

'I could make some puddings for you. I love doing them. How many will be coming?'

'Anywhere between twenty and 150, my dear – they're all hopeless at replying and partners are invited. If it is 150, God help us as we're having the party here. My husband will explode.'

'I'll do half a dozen or so different things then. Shall I bring them on the day?'

'Please, though if it would be easier for you to freeze anything and drop them up here beforehand . . . ?'

'No, the day itself will be fine.'

'I hope you'll be coming to the party? It's so good to have new faces – and voices of course. Do you live in Lafferton – I don't recognise your name.'

'I only moved here a month or so ago. But I'm so pleased I've managed to get into the choir. I came to the *Messiah* and it reminded me how much I'd missed singing. I belonged to a choral society in London.'

'Wonderful. Here's the address.'

Freya took it down.

'It's about five miles outside Lafferton, a mile off the Bevham to Flimby road and you turn sharp left after the pub. Any time. I'll be in the thick of quiches and salads all day. I really look forward to meeting you . . . Mrs Graffham . . . ?

'Actually, I've reverted to my maiden name, I was divorced last summer. I'm Graffham professionally anyhow.'

'Fine. Miss Graffham . . . or maybe Ms . . .'

'Freya?'

'Wonderful. Goodbye.' She rang off briskly.

The warmth of her voice and her welcome made Freya feel good in the way you felt when the headmistress had noticed you in the corridor or the choirmaster praised your top note. Or, she thought, the DI said, 'Well done,' when you succeeded in tracking down Angela Randall.

She went back to the cookery book she had left lying open on the sofa at Chocolate Mousse Cake with Cappuccino Cream.

Freya spent most of her off-duty time during the next week experimenting in the kitchen until she was confident of having successfully mastered at least half a dozen new pudding recipes. At the first rehearsal for the *War Requiem*, her sight-reading skills were tested to their limit and at the end of the evening her voice had almost given out, but the whole experience had been exhilarating and, afterwards, she joined some of the choir members for a drink in the Cross Keys pub. New names and telephone numbers began to fill her book, she discovered someone belonging to the badminton club who offered to take her the following week and accepted an invitation to supper with a woman called Sharon Medcalf, whose car would not start and to whom Freya gave a lift. Coming to Lafferton looked like being one of the best things she had ever done. She had not felt so confident in herself for several years; but it was the extraordinary sense of being given a second chance, of starting her life all over again, which so surprised her. It must, she thought, be like this if you have had a narrow escape from death, perhaps in an accident or through illness. A new chance. She was beginning to realise how straitjacketed she had been in her short marriage, how Don had managed to crush her sense of initiative and inner strength. She had always been used to relying on herself and making her own judgements and decisions, and though she had never been impulsive in the careless sense, she had long relied on her hunches and instincts, had made up her mind quickly and acted upon it. If things then went wrong, she had been willing to take responsibility. That had helped to make her a good police officer, and was why she had been promoted in the CID.

But her unhappy personal life had quickly begun to affect her work. She had made bad judgements, wavered over things she would once have been decisive about and, when this had been commented upon, she had slipped into a trough of self-blame and uncertainty.

Now, she was climbing back rapidly. She was in touch with the woman she had always been deep down and she was determined to build on it in her new life. She was making friends, picking up the threads of old enthusiasms, getting her house exactly as she liked it without having to defer to anyone else, earning all her own money again. She had rediscovered her career ambition. The CID was what she loved, and further promotion was what she was determined to achieve within the next two or three years.

No one, she told herself, is ever going to drag me down and demoralise me again.

She spent her next afternoon off buying new clothes in Bevham. Even her wardrobe, right down to some expensive and totally impractical shoes, was going to reflect the new Freya Graffham. She came home with a cream linen trouser suit, two jumpers, and a couple of new jackets for work, one suede, one denim, as well as three scarves because she had not been able to choose between them, and a scarlet Margaret Howell cardigan in knitted cotton. Don had not liked her to wear what he had called flashy clothes. If she had stood out in a crowd, if she had been admired and complimented, he had been afraid she might move away from him, back into her old independence, so he had encouraged her to wear unremarkable clothes in grey and beige and muted patterns. She had loved him. She had tried to do what he wanted in order to please him. She had almost succeeded in totally obliterating herself and barely got out in time.

In Bevham, as Freya came out of a boutique, she had glanced up and seen the name *Duckham* over the window of the smart jeweller next door. The box containing the gold and lapis lazuli cufflinks had had *Duckham* printed on the inside of the lid.

Uniform had done the usual checks and reported nothing. Now, as Freya went back to the car park with her carrier bags she made a mental note to recheck the report before visiting the shop herself. Someone in a small, expensive jeweller's could surely be prompted to remember something about the purchase of such a pair of cufflinks.

The following Saturday, she spent the morning putting the finishing touches to a dozen pies, gateaux and puddings before packing them into bakers' trays borrowed from the station canteen.

Finding the house was easy. There were stone pillars and a drive that wound between beech trees, under which spread a mass of snowdrops and aconites. The house was probably Edwardian, red brick with tall chimneys. Here, under spreading trees on the wide lawn, more snowdrops, more aconites, and the first few ice-blue crocuses.

'You're Freya? Welcome, welcome. This is so good of you.'

She was tall and thin, with a shrewd, intelligent face. She wore jeans and a T-shirt, her hair was grey and pinned up on top of her head and she might be any-where between fifty-five and seventy-five.

She held out her hand. 'Meriel Serrailler.'

'Goodness, surely you must be.'

'Who?' And as her hostess turned, Freya saw the resemblance immediately. It was the nose.

'Serrailler. My DCI is called Simon Serrailler.'

'My son. Heavens above, you're a policewoman!'

'DS Freya Graffham, Lafferton CID.'

'Well, I promise no jokes about the singing police-woman.'

They began carrying the trays into the house. The floors were polished parquet, the curving staircase that went up to a wooden gallery on the floor above was carved, there were a number of framed drawings on the walls. The kitchen was a mix of old wooden tables and cupboards, scrubbed work surfaces, plants, and a bat-tered sofa on which slept two huge ginger cats. They made three journeys to bring in every tray, after which Meriel Serrailler took off the cloths and gazed admir-ingly at the chocolate torte, grapefruit and mint mousse, sticky ginger fudge slab with fudge icing, rhubarb and honey crumble, upside-down meringue and hazelnut and coffee pavlova, and soft-berry charlotte.

'My dear, what a feast! Why on earth are you a police-woman, why aren't you running your own pudding empire?'

Half an hour later, they were sitting at the table with mugs of Earl Grey and pieces of shortbread and Freya knew a great deal more about Lafferton, the cathedral, the St Michael's Singers, Bevham General Hospital, and the various medical Serraillers. She felt as if she had known this woman half her life. Meriel Serrailler had been a beauty but like most very thin women age had made her lined and bony.

And, Freya thought, it didn't matter a jot. Beauty may have gone, but intelligence, charm, and a lively and acute interest in people shone out.

'Now it's your turn. I want to know where you've come from and why and who you've met in Lafferton and whether you're going to stay and what you've joined.'

Curling her fingers round her fresh mug of tea, Freya was about to launch into an account of herself, recognising that Meriel Serrailler was a woman who attracted confidences and being perfectly prepared to succumb, when a car drew up outside, and someone came straight into the house.

'Now that could be anyone . . . Cat and the children, though I rather hope not with all these puddings about, and I really don't feel up to Sam and Hannah just now . . . It can't be Robert, he's gone to see Martha . . .'

But the door opened on Freya's DCI.

'Good lord.'

Freya started to get up. 'Good afternoon, sir.'

'Oh, don't start all that for heaven's sake, you're not on duty now. Hello darling, I hope you haven't come to stay, you know it's the St Michael's supper tonight and do look at all this, isn't it wonderful? I've just told Freya she's wasted as a detective.'

'She's nothing of the kind.'

Simon Serrailler sat down next to his mother and reached for the teapot. Then he glanced at Freya, smiled, and started dunking shortbread in his tea.

Afterwards, Freya thought that it was not one thing

that she remembered, it was everything, because everything came together – the winter light through the leaded windows, the warmth of the kitchen, the faint snore of one of the ginger cats asleep on the old sofa, the smell of hot tea and the sight of a pot of deep purple crocuses on the window ledge; she saw Meriel Serrailler, straight-backed and in profile, her hair spilling out of the pins at the back of her head and felt delight in this immediate new friendship, while at the same time, in her mind was the whole picture of the house, the red brick, the tall chimneys, the polished wood floors, the carved banister leading to the gallery. Everything came together, in a moment of extraordinary assurance and clarity.

For a few seconds she dared not look up. The cat went on quietly snoring. Somewhere outside a dog barked. She looked up.

He was not looking at her but at his mother. She saw the similarity of their bone structure and the complete dissimilarity of their colouring. She looked at Simon Serrailler's fingers, those on his right hand curled round the handle of the mug, those on his left spread out flat on the pine table.

He was saying, 'I promise I'll go next week.'

'It is called a *coup de foudre*,' she thought. 'It is falling in love terrifyingly and completely in an instant. It is this.'

She drank the last of her tea and stood up. She had to get out quickly, be alone in her car. She had to think. In so far as she could sort out her feelings at that moment, she recognised that she felt angry, angry and then afraid; I do not want this, she said impatiently to herself, I am not ready and it is not right. I do not want any of this.

Meriel Serrailler came with her to the door.

'You are so, so kind! I can't tell you what a difference you've made. Now, we'll see you later.'

Damn, Freya thought, damn, damn, damn.

He called goodbye to her from the kitchen, but she was going, out of the door and almost running to the car, her fingers getting into a tangle with the key and the lock.

Damn.

She heard the gravel flying up under her wheels and the screech of her skidding tyres.

For a few miles, she drove fast, before coming to a village with a small bridge. She stopped and got out. It was cold. The bridge curved over the river, and Freya stood at the foot looking down into the water, talking herself into a calmer state.

She was shocked by what had happened to her. When she had seen the DCI at the seminar in Bevham, she had thought him pleasant, young for his rank, and with unusual looks. Today, a few minutes after he had sat down at the kitchen table and smiled at her when his mother made some remark, she had looked at him and fallen in love, as she might have fallen asleep, or into laughter at a joke. She had heard of such things, read of them, and dismissed them.

Simon Serrailler's face looked up at her from the cold water. The shape of his hands and the strands of his extremely fair hair, the movement of his head as he turned it towards her and then looked down were bitten into her memory and occluded every other mental picture, every other thought.

Freya shivered.

To You, with all possible love from your devoted, Me.

In that split second, she knew what Angela Randall's note meant; she thought she could see inside the woman's mind, she understood her. Angela Randall, a middle-aged woman living a sterile, solitary life, had fallen in love; the love was probably unrequited, possibly unsuitable, and Angela Randall was in thrall to it. Women in such situations recklessly buy the object of their love expensive presents, regardless of whether they can afford it, even careless as to whether they will be welcomed.

Freya felt a vivid moment of empathy with the woman, and a certainty that she was right.

The Tape

You once told me that you came to the hospital and waited for the chance of seeing me, as you said, 'looking like a doctor'. You waited almost three hours but mine was not one of the white-coated figures who went past, and in the end you gave up and went home in disappointment. You had no idea that the students were in a different building and in any case, during the first year rarely if ever wore white coats, it was all lectures and note-taking and we wore sports jackets. But you wanted to see me because you knew that when you did you would believe that I was actually there, a real medical student. You could be proud of me then and the white coat would be a symbol of that pride. When I did begin to wear it every day, you could never have had any idea how proud I was of it too.

During those first few months it was like being a small boy again, waking up to the realisation that this was the morning of my birthday, and having to pinch myself to believe it could be true. I did not really believe for many weeks that I had achieved the thing I had longed for and worked towards since the day I had had my lip stitched at the hospital after the dog I so hated had bitten me.

The medical lectures were interesting enough but in many ways attending them felt like being back at school and I wanted the real medical training to begin. I wanted to wear my white coat. I wanted to watch operations among the gowned and masked surgeons and anaesthetists. And most of all I wanted to dissect the human body.

The first time we went into the dissecting lab and I saw the corpses on the slabs, one to be assigned to each group of us, I felt faint, but not from shock or distaste, like the others who went white and excused themselves from the room; my faintness was with excitement, so that my hands were trembling and I had to hold them behind my back. This room, with these bodies, these instruments, this smell of formaldehyde and antiseptic overlaying the smell of decomposition, was where I had wanted to be for so long, this was the focus of my dreams and the end of so many years of work. I have never got over the thrill of it, the feeling of a dreadful excitement; the sense of power. A body in a dissecting room seems so far removed from life it might never have had anything to do with life at all. The flesh is not life-coloured, it is the colour of putty. When you cut something living it bleeds, fresh, ruby-coloured blood flows from the veins, but sinking the scalpel into a corpse on the dissecting table yields nothing so vivid. After a very short time, cutting through flesh and sinew and muscle, opening stomach and heart and lungs, removing liver and kidneys, uncoiling yard upon yard of intestine becomes routine. It also becomes a sterile activity, so that the corpse might be made of plastic or rubber. It is an aid to learning, and for a trainee surgeon there is no substitute for handling real human tissue.

But these are cadavers which may have been dead for a long time. Who were they? Where did they come from? What lives did they lead? These are not questions one asks. What did they die of? What state were their organs in and what does this tell us about disease and the ageing process? Those are the questions we were trained to ask and to which we would discover the answers by patiently de-layering the corpse under our fingers. How are muscles arranged, where is the liver in relation to the spleen, where are the main arteries whose names we may have learned by heart from a textbook but which we have not actually seen until now?

After a couple of weeks, it all seemed pedestrian and I was no longer excited. Many of the others became so used to the dead bodies that they played jokes on them. They horrified me. They were treating them with disrespect which has always seemed to me wrong. The dead body deserves respect, no matter what we may have felt about the living person who once inhabited it. I was shocked when I came into the dissecting lab one morning to find one of my fellow students skipping with a rope of intestine.

I have never lost my love of the dissecting room. You know that now. But it was not enough.

I struggled through much of the learning. The chemical formulae, the physiology, the lists of diseases with their causes and symptoms were embedded deep in huge textbooks and had to be extracted and then committed to memory and I found it hard. But I would never have given up. You had sacrificed everything for me to be here and you know I have never forgotten that, don't you?

Even more, I was aroused by anticipation of what was to come.

The dissecting room was the beginning. What spurred me on after that was the prospect of going into the operating theatre and watching real surgical work on bodies which were alive, whose hearts throbbed and lungs expanded and which had blood pumping through their silken veins.

Surprisingly enough, I had hardly given any thought to the mortuary and how I would react to that. I was not even sure if we would be taken to it and when and what we might do there.

I wish you could understand what I felt when I first walked through the swinging plastic doors leading to that brightly lit, white-tiled room. I had asked a question about post-mortem examinations and, for an answer, I was sent to observe one.

Perhaps everyone who studies medicine has a defining moment which shows them the pattern of their future; those who become obstetricians hear an infant's first cry, eye surgeons thrill at the ability to give back sight, the psychiatrists talk to a patient labelled insane and believe they can reach into that person and touch sanity and nurture it back to life.

My defining moment came in the mortuary.

Fifteen

'I don't need to go to the surgery, I'm fine, aren't I?'

'You'll go – if I have to take the morning off work and drag you there myself.' Sandy Marsh ripped back the bedclothes letting the cold morning air on to Debbie's body. 'Dr Deerbon was very good coming all the way here and you were in a right state . . . anything might have happened, you might have died.'

'I wasn't going to die.'

'Come on, up and out. You can't break an appointment and you can't keep the doctor waiting. The kettle water has just boiled and I've put two slices in the toaster. Honestly, you need a minder not a flatmate.'

Sandy went to the door. She looked smart, Debbie thought, she was slim enough to wear a dustbin liner and be chic. This morning she had a black reefer jacket over a close-fitting black-and-white print skirt, high boots and a pink pashmina setting the whole outfit off. It was not a question of money, either, because Sandy never had much after the bills were paid; she bought carefully and cheaply and had an enviable knack of knowing how to put an outfit together. But it won't be long, Debbie said to herself on her way to the bathroom, it won't be long before I am slim and my skin has cleared and then I can do it too.

She looked in the mirror. The swelling had gone down but there was still a faint redness and the skin under her eyes looked papery.

'Bye, Debs. I'll ring you to find out what she said, mind.'

'OK, OK.'

But Debbie knew she was lucky. Bossy and critical Sandy might be, but she was a good friend and she owed her. She would keep the appointment with Dr Deerbon if for no other reason.

The surgery was a couple of miles away on the other side of the town, and normally she would have caught a bus, but this morning Debbie walked. The route was not interesting, but every step she took made her feel positive; she was walking in the fresh air, breathing it deeply into her lungs and she was conscious of the expanse of sky above her and the earth deep below her, to both of which she, Debbie Parker, was attached by invisible but powerful natural forces. She remembered everything Dava had said to her about expanding her mind and spirit to feel in tune with the whole earth, the heavens, the universe beyond.

'Nothing is alien to you, nothing is hostile. Everything is part of you and you in turn are part of everything. You are held securely and you can feel it to be so if you will only open your heart and mind. Walk, walk and breathe and look and listen and you will notice that every time you do you feel freer and more in harmony with all things.'

It was true, she did feel in tune with the world, the turning earth beneath her, the layer upon layer of . . . she did not know of what, but she had a picture in her mind of roots reaching down. She looked up. Above her was simply light grey cloud but she found it easy to picture the heavenly blue behind it, and beyond the blue she imagined shimmering gold, into which she could gaze.

The walk was invigorating, though she had to stop several times because she was out of breath. Still, that would improve as she walked more and got fitter. Dava had told her to classify her moods and attach symbols to them, to weigh them and give them colours and shapes. This morning, her mood was light, it weighed almost nothing; it was silvery white, and had soft cloudy edges.

One visit to Dava had transformed everything in Debbie Parker's world. She knew that she did not really need to visit Dr Deerbon this morning. Dava would shape her future and guide her through all the changes that would take place on her way to a new self, a new life. She would be slim, with a clear skin, she would be light-hearted and optimistic, equable and joyful; she would study something or get a new job. She would make more friends and her whole being would expand.

She reached Manor House Surgery damp with sweat and with a blister forming on her left heel, but otherwise happy enough to feel she might break into song. Even while waiting she felt happy. The room was full of young women with coughing toddlers and old men complaining about the delay and the magazines were dog-eared, but to Debbie everything was beautiful and part of the one harmonious whole. It seemed astonishing to her that everyone else here did not know about Dava and his powers, the great healing and help he could give them, his beauty and spirituality. She might even bring some of the blue cards and leave them on the table beside the magazines, though after a few moments she thought better of it, acknowledging that even if the patients were grateful, the doctors might not be impressed.

'Debbie Parker please.'

Dr Deerbon looked pale and had a cold. It seemed to have put her in a bad mood.

'For goodness sake, what were you thinking of, Debbie? Had you any idea what you were taking or what the stuff you put on your face had got in it?'

Debbie felt crushed.

'Let me have a look at your skin. Come over to the light.'

'I don't see that I was doing any harm.'

'Really? After what happened?'

'Well, I didn't know it would, did I? You said yourself people can have reactions to all sorts of ordinary things.'

'Yes, I did. I'm sorry. Blame a bad night but I shouldn't take it out on you. Now, let's sort out this acne. Why didn't you come here first, Debbie? This is so easy to cure now. I'm giving you an antibiotic which you'll take for six weeks. Make sure you finish the course. The acne will gradually improve and it won't come back.'

'And is that it? No creams and stuff?'

'No. You don't need to put anything on your skin and don't buy any lotions that claim miracles, the antibiotics will do the job. No – you haven't had asthma before, have you?' She looked down at Debbie's notes.

'No. I don't think so anyway.'

'Probably a one-off reaction then, but I'm going to prescribe you an inhaler. Have it with you all the time, in your bag, by your bed. You may well never have another attack for the rest of your life, but even one has to be taken as a warning. Don't be without this inhaler. After you've seen me, wait behind and the nurse will give you five minutes. She'll take you through how to use it properly – it's not difficult but there's a knack to it.'

'Right. Thanks.' Debbie stood up.

'No, Debbie, don't go. I want to talk to you about this person you went to see at Starly.'

'Oh.'

'I'm not like some GPs, who disapprove of every kind of complementary treatment. I send people for acupuncture and to the osteopath and I keep an open mind about several other therapies. But there are a lot of cranks about and the whole thing is completely unregulated, you know. It just isn't the case that if they don't do you much good they can't do you any harm. They can. I'm very concerned about protecting my patients. You've been depressed and that can make you very vulnerable. So, who did you see?'

Debbie was uncertain how much to say. She trusted Dava, he was wonderful, he spoke to her as no one else ever had, but she felt foolish in the face of Dr Deerbon's questioning.

'He's . . . he was really good, Doctor. It was just talk really.'

'Talk isn't always harmless. Besides, he prescribed the pills and the ointment. I took them away the other night, did your flatmate tell you? I'm having them analysed. What did he do?'

'It was just talking, like I said.'

141

'What, like this?'

'Sort of . . .'

Debbie was not going to tell her about the couch and the strange sense of having been out of herself and of real time, the floating feeling and the sense of having been touched by something extraordinary.

'Would you be willing to give me a name?'

'What are you going to do? I'm not making a complaint, am I?'

'Of course not. And there is nothing I can do, even if I wanted to. But as I said, I do have a duty of care over my own patients.'

'He's called Dava.'

'Dava what?'

Debbie shrugged.

'Did he give you any medical advice?'

'No. He talked a lot about spiritual things. My psyche. He said I should . . . be in tune with the universe. I should take walks and things in the fresh air. He said that would help my skin.'

'It certainly won't hurt it.'

'Food. He gave me a diet.'

'Ah.'

'I have to eat everything organic and wholefoods . . . wholegrains and fruit and vegetables, no meat, no dairy stuff.'

'Plenty of soya?'

'How did you know?'

Dr Deerbon smiled. 'Most of them seem to be keen on soya.'

'Is it bad then?'

'No. But some people are allergic to it.'

'So can I do it? The diet?'

'Yes. Make sure you have enough protein . . . some fish or eggs. The fruit and vegetables and wholegrain are good, and give yourself a bit of a treat from time to time. It's important not to be too rigid. You're vulnerable there too, Debbie, as you've been depressed. So have a cappuccino or a glass of wine or a bar of decent chocolate sometimes. Don't be hard on yourself.'

'OK. Thanks then. Is that it?'

'That's it, end of lecture.'

Debbie turned with her hand on the doorknob. 'He made me feel wonderful. Do you see? He made me see everything differently. I've never met anyone like that before.'

For a few moments after Debbie had gone to see the practice nurse, Cat Deerbon sat doodling on her notepad, turning over what the girl had said. Dava. The name was phoney and meant nothing, and it was an affectation not to admit to a surname. The advice she had been given seemed either quite positive, though nothing she could not have gleaned from a lot of magazines, or at least harmless, but one or two of the remarks Debbie had made hinted at something else, some mumbo-jumbo of a familiar kind about inner harmony and tuning into the universe. It was easy to dismiss it all, and she doubted if the tablets contained anything more than a useless mixture of mild herbs bulked up with soya, or that the ointment was dangerous; it had been Debbie Parker's bad luck that she was allergic to something in one or other of them.

Yet, Cat worried. A girl like that, overweight, with bad skin, unattractive and badly presented, without a job or much of a social life was indeed vulnerable and the fact that she had been seriously depressed sent out more alarm signals. An untrained therapist giving psychological counselling to someone like Debbie Parker, especially if it involved delving into the past, or 'regression' and 'rebirthing', could do untold harm.

She wrote *Dava* on her pad. She had no power to put someone like that out of business, and in any case, if he closed down in Starly, he could open again anywhere else he chose.

'Dava.' Cat spoke the name aloud, derisively, before ringing the bell for the next patient.

Debbie Parker did not walk the two miles home. It had started to drizzle and her blister was painful. Instead, she waited half an hour for a bus at the end of Addison Road. She felt confused. Dr Deerbon did not seem to have disapproved of some of the things she was doing as a result of her hour with Dava; the diet, the exercise – she had nodded quite approvingly at those. But there had been something about her expression and tone of voice that had made Debbie feel both uneasy and guilty. It had been like an interview with the head teacher. You felt smaller and more foolish afterwards than you had on the way in. But she was a grown woman now, so why should she be made to feel like a silly kid?

The bus was warm and steamy, and sitting in it, wiping her arm across the window to see out, Debbie remembered the last bus she had been on, to Starly. Thinking of that ride, and the time spent waiting in the café, the memory of Dava's house in the steep, narrow little lane, and of the consulting room, as well as of the amazing man himself, made Debbie both excited and defiant. He had done her more good than anyone, hadn't he? Her misery had lifted, she felt positive and happy for the first time in months. How could that be bad? She was grateful to him and she would show it. It had not been Dava's fault that she had reacted badly to the medicine, that could happen any time, to anyone. Dr Deerbon had said as much.

She got off the bus in the centre of Lafferton and bought herself a bar of organic chocolate to munch on the way home. That ought to please both of them, she thought, as she stripped off the wrapper.

There was a letter for her on the doormat. When she slit open the envelope, she saw the wonderful blue of the card immediately. It seemed to glow in the darkness of the hall and the glow made a circle of warmth around her.

Dava
Please attend for your next appointment
promptly at two fifteen on Tuesday, 30 January.
This time has been carefully and personally selected as
being the most auspicious for your therapy.

Debbie made a cup of tea and sat at the kitchen table with the card propped in front of her, gazing into the depths of the magical blue. The effect it had on her was almost as powerful as being in the room with Dava himself. She felt invigorated and changed and that her future held endless possibilities, beyond anything she could have dreamed of before she had taken that one, brave step.

The kitchen seemed to glow all day with the emanation of spiritual light from the card. But later, she realised that she wanted to do everything Dava had told her over and over again, so that when she went for the next appointment he would congratulate her and be proud of her; so, after putting a strong elastoplast round her heel to protect the blister, and then two pairs of socks inside her trainers, she went out to walk. It was half past four, and the schoolchildren were coming home, bouncing about on the pavements with their brightly coloured bags, emptying out of cars with arms full of violins and games kit, books and lunch boxes. Debbie felt a halo of goodwill and friendliness towards them surrounding her with such brilliance that she was surprised they did not stare at it.

The afternoon was dank and it was still drizzling lightly, but the snowdrops were up under the trees in the long gardens of expensive houses on the way to the Hill. She felt drawn to this ancient green heart of Lafferton; she knew that the Wern Stones were supposed to have special powers, rather like the Starly Tor. It was said that the Stones saw everything and that if they were ever split open, all the secrets of Lafferton over generations would be found engraved within. If people went on the Hill after dark to meet illicitly, the Wern Stones saw them, however safe they felt, and if a lie was told in the Stones' hearing, it would be found out, though many years might pass. Debbie thought she would ask Dava about the Hill.

It was almost dark now. A couple walked a dog along the path ahead of her but they soon turned off, back on to the road. Debbie walked briskly, lengthening her stride and swinging her arms, breathing deeply. She wished there was a moon and that she could have looked up into the heavens and seen the stars, but it was simply darkening and murky. Her trainers screeched slightly on the wet path and after a while, irritated by the sound, she moved off it on to the grassy track that climbed up between the undergrowth towards the Wern Stones and then up to the clump of ancient trees at the top. After a short time the track became quite steep and Debbie was out of breath. She stopped and leaned on a tree, bending forwards to ease the stitch in her side. Below, she saw a few dim orange lights from the town. Above, everything was blotted out. The night smelled good, of damp grass. She tried to think of the spinning earth beneath and the arc of the heavens over her head and of herself as in harmony with them and, for a moment, it seemed that she was able to conjure up a sense of being joined to the universe, a part of the spirit of everything created.

She was brought up by a slight sound, perhaps a step, perhaps a rustle of wind in the undergrowth. She turned her head to try and make it out. There was no wind, the air was quite still. It came again, a few yards below her, but whether to the right or left she could not tell.

Debbie was struck by a bolt of fear that made her numb, and as if her breath had stopped. Her heart pounded in her ears like waves rushing. She could not see and she dared not move. She was paralysed by fear and by the realisation of her own vulnerability. How stupid was she, to come up here alone after dark and without having told anyone where she was? She was acutely, terrifyingly aware of the slightest sound or move-ment but now there were none. The dark and the silence were absolute, pressing in on her, heavy and suffocating. She was disorientated, not daring to move because she did not know which way would lead her back down to the road. She gripped the cold damp trunk of the tree for support and for comfort. The tree was a living thing, part of the universe and linked to her; if she stayed in touch with it, she would be strong and safe.

Somewhere not far away in the darkness something made a slight sound, then again, but this sound was different, not a rustle or a whisper, but a faint, thin scratching.

The drizzle began again, chill on her face and hands. Then, below on the path, she saw the lights of a vehicle and then heard the engine. If she went now, quickly, if she could manage to keep her footing on the grass and get safely to the path, she might get to the car, which would have a driver, another human being, and possibly passengers too, then everything would be normal again and whatever was here scratching about in the darkness would be behind her.

Taking a deep breath and leaving hold of the tree, Debbie began to stumble down the grassy track but it was raining heavily now and the paths were slippery, so that as she came on to the lower slopes, half running, she slithered wildly and fell, crashing down with her arm out to try and save herself. She lay, crying with fear and frustration but not, she realised after a few moments, with pain. She was bumped and her palm was sore where she had skidded forwards, but when she sat up, she knew she had neither broken nor sprained anything, and could struggle to her feet. As she did so, a light glared into her face. She was nearer to the road than she had realised and the light was from the headlights of a van which had drawn up in front of her.

Her chest was hurting with the effort of breathing hard and the strain and tension of running in a panic through the dark, and when she heard a man's voice, for a moment she could not reply. But the fact that another human being was near to her and that she was safely down from the Hill made her limp with relief.

'Hello? Are you hurt?'

At first the voice came from inside the van, but then she heard the door being opened.

'Can you turn the light off, I can't see, it's . . .'

'Sorry.'

A second later, the light had dipped so that it shone on to the path, but Debbie's eyes were still blinded. She heard a footstep, and then the man was beside her. He was holding a torch. She could make out a tweed jacket, but she still couldn't see his features.

'What happened?'

'I was . . . I was walking up there and . . . it was darker than I thought. And I heard something.'

'What sort of thing?'

'I don't know, but it was scary, something scratching or rustling . . .'

'Probably rabbits or a badger. Or a stray dog.'

'Yes.' She held her side as the stitch returned briefly. 'Only I couldn't see. I just ran, but the paths are ever so slippery, I skidded.'

'Have you hurt yourself?'

'I don't think so. I've scratched my hand where I put it out to save myself but it's nothing. I banged my knee, I think.'

'You were lucky.'

'Yes. It didn't feel it up there.'

'Perhaps not the best idea then, to go on the Hill by yourself after dark.'

'Don't you think it's safe?'

'It's probably perfectly safe but you're a young woman

on her own and you can't be too careful. So maybe take a friend next time. Or better still, go in daylight. Early morning would be better than late at night.'

'Thanks. Thanks very much.'

'Have you far to go?'

'About a mile but it's through the streets, I'll be OK.'

'No, let me give you a lift. You're soaked and you've had a shock. It won't take two minutes.'

Debbie hesitated. He seemed nice, there wasn't anything funny about him. She should go, it made sense to get home quickly. But he picked up on her hesitation.

'No, of course not. That was a stupid thing to suggest. You don't know me. You shouldn't accept lifts from people you don't know, especially at night. But I do want to make sure you get home safely. I tell you what . . . you walk, I'll follow you to the main road with my lights on, so you'll be quite safe, and then you'll be among people and cars and I won't worry. And I'd better make sure you really haven't hurt yourself and are OK to walk. Is there anyone at home when you do get there?'

'Sandy Marsh, she's my flatmate.'

'Good. Off you go then . . . I'll make sure you get to the main road before I leave you.'

Debbie waited until he got back into the van, and turned it round, then headed through the gateway. There was no one about. She was glad of the man driving slowly behind her, the dipped headlights of the van picking her out clearly, so that she walked safely in a patch of light until she turned into the busier street at the end, close to a row of shops and the petrol station. She turned. The headlights of the van flashed, and as it drew away from her and off down the road, the man waved. Debbie Parker waved back, gratefully. Someone had looked after her when she wouldn't have expected it. She remembered something else Dava had said. 'You will always be looked after. You are watched and protected. Remember.'

It was true. She had heard stories of people finding help in deserted places and at dangerous moments, only to discover later that the helper had been an angel in human form.

Her heart leaped with the sudden awareness that it might just have happened to her. Why not? She had been in danger, or thought she had been, and out of the darkness had come a rescuer who had vanished, after making sure that she was safe. It all fitted, it bore so much resemblance to the stories of angelic appearances that she had read.

She couldn't wait to tell Dava.

She turned the last corner from where she could see that the lights were on in the flat. She would have a drink and a hot bath, and later, slouch on the sofa in her dressing gown watching *The Bill*.

But as she opened the door and called out 'Hi', she thought she probably wouldn't say anything to Sandy about her rescuer or that she was convinced it had not been an ordinary human being. Sandy's cheerful common sense would be like a stick poked into a delicate spider's web and Debbie wanted to cherish her angelic encounter, not have it spoiled by her flatmate's scorn. She would probably not even mention the fact that she had been by herself up on the Hill in the dark. The noises must have been made by small animals scuttling about, but now that she was safely back, she knew she had been stupid. Nowhere was safe these days, not even stuffy old Lafferton, and besides, she owed it to her rescuer not to put herself at risk again. She would certainly walk on the Hill. It had ley lines running through it, and those would help her to feel in tune and harmony with the universe. Only from now on she would go when it was light, especially early in the morning. Dawn was a propitious time, Debbie knew. That was one reason people went to dance on Starly Tor at dawn on midsummer morning.

Sinking into the soft peachy foam of her bath, she made a mental note to ask Dava about that too.

Sixteen

The luminous hands on the bedside clock showed four fifteen. Freya lay on her side, staring at them, watching the second hand click round. She was cold.

Damn. Damn. Damn. Hell. Sod it. Bugger. Shit. Damn . . .

'Oh, for God's sake.' This time she spoke aloud, as she pushed the duvet off her legs. It slid to the floor.

She needed a drink and a hot-water bottle and then to read several chapters of the book she had been immersed in before her mind had been taken over by what she thought of angrily as 'this thing'.

While she waited for the kettle to boil, she pulled up the Roman blind and looked out. The kitchen looked over her garden – grass, a lilac tree, some roses. Even a shed. There were houses on the other side of her wall and in the upstairs window of just one a light was on. Freya wondered if there was another insomniac, with a mind too preoccupied and full of whirling thoughts to sleep, or perhaps just a parent seeing to a wakeful child. She opened the window slightly and the unique smell of night, of damp flower beds and green bushes, with faint traces of smoke and car fumes, came to her nostrils, reminiscent of all the nights in her early years as a uniformed policewoman on patrol at night. She had loved it, there had always been an edge to things, and the camaraderie of the relief on night duty was different too, jokier, more supportive; you found yourself telling your colleague on night patrol things you might not even tell your life partner or could not have told your parents, and hearing their confessions in return, in the intimacy of a patrol car, or walking down a silent, dark street. She did not regret the move to CID and the promotion that followed any more than she regretted her move to Lafferton, but the smell of the night air touched a chord all the same.

She turned back to fill her hot-water bottle, and then the tea mug. She had slept on and off for no more than an hour, and otherwise, tossed about in bed until her pillows and cover were a scramble, alternately cursing, longing, or merely trying to sort out her emotions and understand what had happened.

Simon Serrailler had not come to the choir party. Freya had spent a long time choosing her clothes and doing her hair and face, and on the way there her hands had been damp on the steering wheel and her mouth dry. Like some bloody teenager, she thought furiously, turning into the drive of Hallam House. There had been plenty of cars lined up already, and the lights were shining in welcome out of all the lower-floor windows. No curtains were drawn and Freya could see figures in the rooms, but not his. She heard a sudden burst of laughter and a spurt of shyness flared through her, so that she all but got back into her car and left. She had never found social gatherings easy, but her marriage to

Don had eroded most of her poise and confidence – and in any case, they had rarely gone out except to places where they would meet work colleagues or others they already knew. Another car turned into the drive and slid alongside hers. Freya waited, wondering what car Simon Serrailler drove, desperate for this to be him, to go into the house with him. The headlights went off and a couple got out, one of whom was the woman to whom Freya had given a lift after the choir practice. She called her name. 'Sharon!' Going in with someone she knew even slightly made the evening begin smoothly after all.

Her puddings were praised and demolished, and she promised recipes to several people. She had enjoyed herself, picked up her new friendship with Meriel Serrailler at once and taken a dislike to her husband, a man with a sarcastic tongue and an expression which mixed superiority with disapproval.

The evening was a good one, but she had spoiled it for herself because she had done nothing but glance towards the door hoping that he would come in and then dreading her own reaction, and when she realised that it was after ten and he would not be coming at all, felt a disappointment so acute that she could take no pleasure in anything and so she left.

Back in bed, warm and comfortable, she plumped up her pillows and lay against them in the circle of light from the lamp, and tried again to make sense of what had happened and how and what it meant. She had been felled, instantly and completely, by the look and sound and aura and personality of a man; she had been put under a spell, had had a love potion dropped in her eyes – she called up every literary allusion she knew to what was a common enough event but one which she herself had never experienced before. She was confused and bewildered by it, taken aback that she could be vulnerable to what felt like a powerful blow rather than an emotion, and all the time in her mind's eye, whatever she was doing, whatever she thought, whether she was talking to someone else, or alone, driving her car or lying in bed trying to sleep or turning the pages of a book, all the time, she saw Simon Serrailler, as he had been sitting at the table in the kitchen of his mother's house, a mug of tea in front of him and his hand poised over it, holding the shortbread. The image never left her, as though it was on a screen at the back of her eyes. It was with her now.

She picked up her book, the book she had found so engrossing until today, the story so gripping she had rushed through washing up or taking a shower in order to get back to it. Now, she reread the same three paragraphs she had read earlier, and they made as little sense, left as little impression. Her clock showed twenty to five. The only thing she knew that might keep her mind occupied, and stop it from turning back to Simon Serrailler, was work and the only case that presented both a puzzle and a challenge in her present load was the missing woman, Angela Randall. Otherwise, there was an ongoing and, to Freya's mind, deadly dull embezzlement case, a spate of car thefts, and the ever-present drugs-related stuff. She took the pad she kept on her bedside table by the telephone, and started to make notes. She had built up a picture of Angela Randall from the search of her house, and from what her employer at the nursing home had told her. She also felt an odd bond of sympathy with her. After ten minutes, during which she had made a succinct summary of everything about the case so far, Freya felt suddenly exhausted. She was not going into the station early, because she had to do some checks at the new business park on the edge of the town relating to the embezzlement case which she could not wait to hand on to the fraud squad. After that, though, and without the DI's knowledge, she would spend some more time, preferably with the help of the keen young DC Nathan Coates, on Angela Randall.

She turned out her lamp and fell heavily to sleep.

Nathan Coates had been going steadily through the computer database of convicted drug offenders since just after eight thirty. It was now eleven and he had pepped himself with his third plastic cup of coffee ready for another round when Freya stopped at his desk.

She liked Nathan, almost because rather than in spite of his face which was a caricature of a villain's mugshot, looking as if it had been flattened by a door, the nose squashed, the cheekbones dented, the mouth large. He had ginger hair that stuck up like the bristles on a yard broom and enough odd livid lumps and bumps on his skin to remind her of Shakespeare's Bardolph; his teeth were crooked and there was a gap between the front two. He also had a grin which lit up his eyes and, together with his cheerful willingness to shoulder the most dreary of jobs which others were trying to dodge, helped endear him not only to the rest of CID but to the entire station.

'Morning, Nathan.'

He looked up and grinned.

'I've come to take you away from all that.'

'Oh, it's not so bad, Sarge, at least I get to be in the warm with caffeine on tap. Besides, I hate these druggies, honest to God, I hate them.'

Freya knew that Nathan came from a Bevham council

estate which had been governed by drug dealers for much of his growing up. He had watched school friends succumb and become addicts, several had died, others were now caught up in a shitty life of petty crime, or worse. Nathan was the fourth child of a single woman who made a habit of bearing one for every live-in boyfriend before kicking them out in favour of the next man. On paper, such a boy, from such a background, a pupil at a comprehensive school politely known as 'failing', should have gone the way of all his mates, and by now be unemployed or possibly in prison and causing regular trouble to the police force. Nathan Coates had been brighter than the rest of his family put together, streetwise and forward-thinking. He had taken a hard look around him and seen that unless he took a different road his future was grim. From the age of six, when he had been messing about the estate with his gang, he had watched the police patrol cars that were regular visitors there, and after a while, and out of sight of the others, sidled up and got talking to the officers. When he was ten he had gone to the station and asked about recruitment and meanwhile had devoured every television programme about crime and policing, which had caused few raised eyebrows at home where the set was permanently switched on and someone was always sprawled glass-eyed in front of it.

Now, Nathan Coates had been in the force for six years, in CID for eighteen months, at Lafferton from the start. He knew he could not have dealt with patrolling his own patch, arresting his own former neighbours and school-mates, and besides, he wanted to get out as the second step to a new life. He worked hard and cheerfully, he played hockey for the regional team and, to everyone's amazement, lived with an exceptionally pretty girlfriend who was a midwife at Bevham General.

'You're a star,' said Freya, 'but I need you for something else, just for an hour or so.'

'OK, Sarge.' Nathan shut down the database and followed Freya to her desk, where she filled him in on Angela Randall.

'Sounds weird.'

'You think?'

'Not the sort who'd just take off. That's kids in trouble at home, men who can't stand their nagging missus another day or ones who've had their fingers in the till and get wind that someone's sussed them. She don't fit.'

'I'm glad you agree. I'm concerned about this one, but as far as the DI is concerned, it's just another missing person.'

'File 'em, forget 'em, I get the picture, Sarge. If anyone asks, I'm like, "Who's Angela Randall?"'

'Got it.'

'What do you want me to do?'

'Go back over the missing persons file for the last year, eighteen months, see if any other case has a look of this one . . . you know the sort of thing. I can't be specific but if it's there it'll ring bells. Read up the notes on Randall first. Pull out anything and leave it on my desk.'

'Are you off again?'

'Officially, I'm back at the business park among the embezzlers.'

'And?'

'I'm nipping into Bevham to visit a very expensive jeweller's.'

'Sugar Daddy lent you his credit card for the day then?'

Freya took her jacket off the back of her chair. 'Certainly.'

If there had not been the embezzlement case and Angela Randall to take her out, she would have had to cook up something. It was better for her not to be in the station much today. She wanted to see Simon Serrailler, wanted to bump into him in the corridor, find an excuse to go to his office, attend any briefing he might be giving . . . anything. She wanted to look at him, in uniform, at work, when he was 'Sir', wanted to prove that her feelings had been temporary and ridiculous, some sort of delayed emotion related to the end of her marriage. She had looked at Simon Serrailler and been momentarily attracted to him, as anyone might, and had built on the flush of physical feeling to assume she had fallen in love.

E. J. Duckham & Son had an entry bell and a CCTV which scrutinised potential shoppers before they were allowed in. Before pressing it, Freya looked in the double-fronted windows, at diamond necklaces, earrings and brooches without any visible price, sapphire, emerald, ruby and diamond rings, Rolex and Patek Phillipe watches. She wondered who, in Bevham, could possibly be customers for any of these, as well as the more bread-and-butter silver bowls and the tiny pearl bracelets for newborn infants. Bevham had its expensive side, to the south around Cranbrook Drive and the Heights, where detached houses with long drives and huge gardens went on sale at three-quarters of a million pounds and rising, and some of the villages had the odd wealthy inhabitant, whether retired merchant bank chairman or reclusive pop star, but they were not likely to buy their baubles in Bevham. Casting a second lingering look at a delicate silver filigree and star-diamond choker, she pressed the bell for entry, and as the door swung soundlessly back, flipped open her warrant card.

The place had the sort of velvet hush special to jewellers and designer dress salons; the woman behind the counter was as impeccably groomed and coiffed as a royal lady-in-waiting, and the man who came to greet Freya had the smooth charm she associated with Jermyn Street, from where his pinstriped suit and lavender tie must surely have come.

'I do hope you've come bearing good news, Sergeant.'

'Good news?' Freya knew there had been a series of raids on jewellers' shops the previous year, and presumed E. J. Duckham had been one of them. 'If it's about the thefts . . .'

'Oh no, no, I doubt if you'll ever catch those raiders, they'll have come from Birmingham or Manchester and disappeared up the motorway very fast. No, I meant about Miss Randall. One of your officers was in here a week or so ago asking about her. I gather she had gone away unexpectedly?'

'We're pursuing several lines of inquiry as to exactly what has happened, Mr Duckham.'

'You mean she is still missing from home?'

'Do you know her well?'

'Not at all, but she has been a very good customer of ours over the past – what – eighteen months, something like that, and we pride ourselves here on personal service.'

'The uniformed officer will have questioned you about the cufflinks Miss Randall purchased in early December.'

'Indeed. Extremely nice ones. Lapis lazuli. Beautifully made.'

'Could you tell me how much they were?'

He looked disapproving.

'I understand that is not the sort of information you would normally give out but this might be important.'

'How, precisely?'

When there was no good answer to a legitimate question, you hid behind official jargon.

'It would be relevant to one of several leads we're pursuing.'

Nathan would have described the man's expression as po-faced but after another hesitation, he sighed, and went into a glass-panelled office at the back of the shop, where Freya could see him tapping a keyboard. Their pride in being old-fashioned clearly did not extend to a scorn of computers. Behind the glass counter on the opposite side of the shop the woman with impeccably coiffed hair was polishing a crystal rose bowl, which caught the light prettily. She glanced up, did not meet Freya's smile, and carried on polishing. Dirt beneath your feet then, Freya thought.

'The cufflinks were £275.'

'A present for someone Miss Randall knew well, clearly.'

'I really couldn't say.'

'But you do say that she was a regular customer . . . how regular? How often had she been in during the past year?'

'Half a dozen times. Yes, at least that, wouldn't you say, Mrs Campion?'

Coiffed Hair murmured.

'Did she just browse?'

Not that this was the sort of shop you came into on a wet Wednesday afternoon to kill time.

'Not exactly . . . obviously she always looked carefully through what she was shown before making her selection.'

'And she always bought something?'

'Yes, I think she did . . . There was one occasion when we hadn't exactly what she was looking for . . . a particular watch, but we managed to obtain one eventually.'

'What kind of watch?'

'Showing the phases of the moon. It was an Omega in fact, from the 1950s.'

'Expensive then.'

'It depends what you call expensive. We have watches costing £25,000.'

'But this one?'

'Less than two thousand.'

'Did you get the impression money was not a problem to her?'

'I'm afraid I didn't consider it. It's none of my affair.'

Freya got up. 'Would you have a photograph of the watch?'

'No. But we bought it at auction from Goldstein and Crow in Birmingham. You might try them.'

'Do you have the date of the sale?'

'I'll look it out and let you have it.'

'I'd also like to have a complete list of every item Angela Randall bought from you during the time you say she was a regular customer, Mr Duckham, with exact descriptions, cost and date purchased. Would that be possible?'

He looked po-faced again and glanced across at the woman, who had now put the rose bowl back in the case and taken out a set of photograph frames and a silver cloth. Housework by any other name.

'I suppose I can do this if you really think it is going to be of use.'

'It is.'

'But I would stress that we regard our customers' purchases as confidential.'

'How long will it take you?'

'So long as we don't have a rush of customers . . . an hour perhaps?'

'Make it forty minutes.'

Freya walked out, leaving the two of them to talk about her behind her back.

An hour later, she was in her parked car with a take-away cappuccino reading Mr Duckham's list. Poor Angela Randall – all this and for whom exactly? Someone with whom she seemed to be sufficiently infatuated to spend a large chunk of her modest salary buying costly presents for.

She finished her drink, wiped the froth from her lip and headed back to Lafferton and the Four Ways Nursing Home.

Carol Ashton was with the undertaker, the girl said, there had been a death in the night and she would not be free for another ten minutes. Freya waited in the office, refusing the offer of more coffee, and went through the list again.

1 gold tiepin. 14 April 2000. £145
1 gentleman's Omega watch. 5 June 2000. £1,350
1 silver business-card holder. 16 August 2000. £240
1 gentleman's signet ring, gold with single diamond.
    4 October 2000. £1,225

1 silver letter opener. 27 October 2000. £150
1 pair of gold and lapis lazuli cufflinks. 4 December
2000. £275

Nothing for herself, nothing for another woman, everything for a man at a total cost of over three thousand pounds in a single year.

When Carol Ashton came in, apologising for the delay, Freya said at once, 'We've no news I'm afraid, but we are following up a couple of leads.'

'Has someone seen Angela then?'

'No.'

'Then what do you mean by leads?'

'Lines of inquiry.'

'So you do think something has happened to her – you are taking this seriously.'

'I've taken it seriously from the beginning, Mrs Ashton.'

'Just tell me what you think has happened?'

'I don't know that anything has but obviously, as time goes on and Miss Randall hasn't come back, we need to go into one or two things.' She handed over the list. 'I'd like you to look at this please.'

Carol Ashton ran her eyes down it quickly and looked at Freya in bewilderment.

'These were items purchased by Miss Randall from Duckham's the jeweller in Bevham during the past year.'

'What?'

'May I ask you how much she earned with you, Mrs Ashton?'

'Just a moment – I can tell you exactly.' She went to her desk, and tapped into her computer.

'Yes, here we are. Angela was on £13,500 a year.'

'Not a fortune.'

'Wages in the care industry are low. I pay the standard rate. There are perks, of course, meals on duty, uniforms . . . and I give a bonus at Christmas.'

'I'm not criticising you.'

'I couldn't keep open, no care home could, if we had to pay some of the salaries people can get even in the NHS for example. That isn't always well known. Everyone assumes the private sector must be able to pay big wages.'

'Do you know of any other income Angela Randall might have had?'

'She didn't have another job, I'm sure of that . . . she wouldn't have had the energy. It's demanding, working on nights in a home like this.'

'Private income?'

'I have no idea. I wouldn't have thought so, but I don't actually know anything. I told you before, I think, that she was a very private person and I really knew nothing about her life outside here.'

'Have you any idea who she might have bought all these expensive things for?'

'I'm afraid I haven't a clue.'

'Are you surprised by this?'

Carol Ashton considered for a moment, tapping her finger on the side of her desk.

'I have to say, yes, I am, very. I mean, these are not things someone would buy all in one year for, say, a brother or some other relative, even supposing there were one. She might have bought one of the lesser items for – oh, I don't know, a special birthday, a godson . . . that kind of thing. But the others . . . yes, I am very surprised about those. It looks as if they were bought for . . . well . . .'

'A lover?'

Carol Ashton shook her head. 'I can't believe that. Angela was – is . . . how can I put this . . . quite a prim sort of person. It wouldn't surprise me if she had never had any serious relationship. She was always clean and neat and well groomed but she didn't put herself out to look fashionable. Sensible clothes, you know, well looked after but not much that was smart. At least, not that I ever saw.'

'Spinsterish?'

'It sounds awful, doesn't it? Patronising somehow. But yes.'

Freya got up and took the list back. 'If you think of anything at all that rings a bell, especially in connection with this, would you telephone me please?'

'What sort of thing?'

'Just something you may suddenly remember that she had mentioned . . . some remark she might have dropped.'

'Angela wasn't . . . isn't the kind of person who drops remarks. She's very guarded.'

'All the same.'

'I will, of course . . . but I doubt if you'll hear from me. I'm only astonished by what you've shown me. It just shows, though, doesn't it . . . how little you know about people you see every day?'

At the station, Freya found Nathan Coates back at his computer working on the drug database.

'Have you been through missing persons?'

'Yes, Sarge, back for two years.'

'Anything?'

'I've left a few on your desk. Nothing much though. A teenager but it was eighteen months ago and she was last sighted near the railway station. The other's a bloke.'

'Oh well. Thanks anyway.'

'No prob. Made a change.'

His grin cheered her up as usual.

The two missing persons he had pulled out of the list seemed at first sight to have nothing in common with Angela Randall, as Nathan had supposed, and certainly the teenage girl, Jennie O'Dowd, looked like the typical runaway from unhappy home circumstances.

Freya glanced at the details of the missing man and almost dismissed it, until she noticed a line Nathan Coates had highlighted in red pen.

Last sighting, 6.30 a.m. Tuesday 7 March 2000, riding mountain bike on the Hill, reported by Alan John Turner, 57, of Flat 6, Mead House, Brewer Street, Lafferton, when walking dog.

Was it worth sending Nathan out to check Mr Alan John Turner's story? Probably not, and in any case the DI would hit the roof if he found out she had taken him off the drug check to pursue what he regarded as a low-priority missing person inquiry. She could hear the word 'resources' ringing in her ears. But Brewer Street was only two minutes from her own house so there was nothing to stop her taking a short detour on her way home. She slipped Nathan's notes into her bag and was about to turn wearily back to the embezzlement case when WPC Heidi Walsh put her head round the CID room door.

'Briefing from Inspector Ford in half an hour on Operation Sapper. Oh, and Freya, the DCI would like to see you.'

Freya felt something like an electric shock zap through her.

'DCI Serrailler? When?'

'Now I suppose.'

'What about?'

Heidi shrugged. The door banged behind her.

'Freya . . . come in.'

He was not sitting but standing by the window and in the moment of seeing him, she knew absolutely that there had been no aberration, no trick played by her sub-conscious, no fleeting attraction which had owed every-thing to her own mood and nothing to reality.

I do not want this, she thought, and panic surged through her, so that she almost turned and fled not just the room but the building; she realised that she had no control over her feelings and that the only escape would indeed be to leave, to hand in her resignation on some pretext and never return. This will not go away and it has overturned and even spoiled everything. It will inter-fere with my work, my leisure, my sleep, my content-ment, my every waking moment, my happiness in having left London and come here. I am in thrall to this and *I do not want it.*

'Sit down, please. I'm sorry I haven't had a chance to catch up with you before but I came back from holiday to the embezzlement case, the usual wretched drug prob-lems which seem to grow bigger by the day . . . well, you know. But I just wanted to find out how you feel now you've been with us a few weeks.'

She looked at him and quickly away, fixing her eyes on anything else, the back of the computer on his desk, the coil of the telephone wire. She thought she would not be able to utter, her tongue was swollen in her mouth.

'I'm fine, thank you, sir. I like it very much.'

'You're getting on OK with everyone?'

'I seem to be.'

'Even Billy Cameron?'

He smiled at her and the smile was more than she could bear. She looked down at the shoe on her right foot. It was slightly scuffed at the toe. She should polish it.

'Perhaps that's unfair. Billy is the old school . . . bluff and gruff, but he's been a good detective.'

'I'm fine with him.' Don't keep saying 'fine'. Think of another word. You sound stupid.

'He'll be on your side, Freya, he's the most loyal man I've ever worked with. Worth remembering.'

'Fine.'

'What are you on at the moment?'

She wanted to tell him everything about Angela Randall, that she was only interested in that, had no time for the embezzlement stuff, was bored with anything and everything to do with drugs, of which she had had a basinful at the Met. She wanted him to approve, to tell her to spend all her time on the missing woman, she wanted a case of her own to get her teeth into and when it worked out, she wanted to go to him and tell him and have him praise her.

You are pathetic. You've regressed, you're fourteen.

'Are you working with Nathan Coates at all?'

'Yes, sir, on a couple of things . . . I think he's terrific, a real asset. He's meticulous, he never stops working, he's bright, he's ambitious.'

'And he spreads a carpet of happiness, yes, I know. I agree. Nathan Coates gives the lie to everything you would assume about a boy coming from where he does, the sort of life he's had – and managed to escape from. There's one thing worth remembering, though. He's loyal to that background. He'd find it hard to be put in a position where he had to betray it. He'd do it, of course he would, he's a copper. But it is why he's here and not in Bevham. I wouldn't want him compromised.'

'I hear what you're saying, sir.'

'Thanks. OK, I'm glad you're happy. Any problems, I'm here.'

She wanted to say something else, anything, to ask a question, voice an opinion. *Stay this moment.* She wanted to get up and run, to be outside in the air, to go over everything, every word he had spoken, every detail of how he looked.

Sod it. Sod. Sod. Sod. I do not want this.

'Thank you, sir.'

Her legs would not hold her. She would not be able to stand and walk to the door.

'Freya . . .'

She turned.

'Thank you for giving my mother all that help last week. She takes on too much and my father isn't very keen on the choir and all these social events she foists on him, so she does the lot on her own. She was really grateful for your support.'

'I'm grateful to have found the choir. I've made some good new friends.'

'And not from work. Always a bonus. I hadn't realised you were a singer.'

'I've been in choirs since I was at school . . . well, most of the time. I had a break from it for the last year or two in London, but St Michael's Singers are so good I'm lucky to have got in.'

'My mother's delighted to have found you. But watch out, she's ruthless. You'll have to learn to say no.'

'You don't sing?'

'No,' Simon Serrailler said. Not: no, I can't sing, no, I don't like singing, no, I play football instead, no, I haven't the time. Just 'No'.

He looked straight at her, coolly and steadily. Unnerved, Freya mumbled something, and left. She walked swiftly to the CID room, and without catching the eye of anyone there, took her jacket and bag and walked out again.

It took her barely fifteen minutes to reach the bridge over the river beside which she had stopped on the day it had begun.

Today, the sun was out though there had been a sharp frost that morning and the air was still cold. Freya locked the car and walked beyond the bridge to where she could get down the sloping grassy bank to stand on the narrow path beside the water.

She could not sort out her thoughts, which swirled round in a circle like the eddy around some stones a few yards away, and when she looked down she saw, inevitably, the reflection of Simon Serrailler, clear and unbroken by the flow of the water.

She put in a long dull afternoon at the business park and on the computer, forcing herself to grind at the embezzlement case, speaking to no one. She was the last to leave the CID room.

For the first time since coming to Lafferton, she was reluctant to get back to her house and be alone, and thought she might telephone one of the choir members on the off chance that they could have supper, or at least a drink. But before doing so, she turned into Brewer Street and the car park in front of Mead House. She had been too deep in embezzlement to read the full case file on the missing mountain biker and had not remembered to bring the notes home, but the name and address of the man who had reported seeing him last was in her mind.

A small Oriental woman answered the doorbell of Flat 6 and told Freya with smiles and great charm, that Mr Turner had left there a few months ago for retirement on the Costa del Sol.

Seventeen

The room was semi-dark. The cream linen curtains filtered through just enough of the winter sunlight to give a lift to the dimness but not a brightness which might have been distracting. It was quiet but into the quietness the sound of waves unfolding silkily up a sandy beach came in pulses which created their own gentle rhythm.

It was half past three. The house was quiet.

Karin McCafferty lay on the small chaise longue in her bedroom, her feet up on the raised end, her head and shoulders flat, arms forming the shape of an embrace around her upper body. In her mind's eye, she pictured a field of brilliant, luscious green spring grass dotted with small black ugly weeds that formed clumps and smirched the freshness and brightness of the meadow. She focused closely first on the grass itself, seeing its strong colour, sensing its healthy roots, full of strength and vitality and potential for growth buried in the earth, looking at the individual blades with their thin, pale veins that brought the fresh sap up through the plant.

She breathed deeply and consciously from her diaphragm, as a singer would, counting ten breaths, pausing, expanding her lungs and the muscles round her waist, then exhaling gently and slowly, feeling her body relax.

After a few moments, she pictured a gate on the far side of the spring meadow. She walked towards it across the springy turf, and unlatched it. Above her head the sky was clear, pale blue. The sun shone.

Sheep came pouring through the open gate, ewes with their lambs jumping and leaping and bouncing off the grass. The flock spread out across the whole field and as Karin watched she directed each individual sheep towards one of the dark, ugly weeds, and the sheep followed her directions exactly, though they were completely silent, she had no whistle, nor did she make any gesture. Then, at a second telepathic signal, each sheep began to eat its allotted weed, slowly and systematically uprooting it and consuming it, destroying it completely, roots, twisted, blackened, foul-looking leaves, warty stem, the entire plant. When it had finished, the hole out of which the weed had grown had disappeared, was healed over with newly sprung, fresh young grass, succulent and vibrant.

Karin watched the picture with absolute concentration, astonished at the vividness of the detail. The meadow represented her body, the grass the healthy tissue, the weeds her cancer, which the sturdy, all-powerful and obedient sheep had just consumed. The places where the weed-cancer had grown from were healthy; the tissue, flesh and skin, every cell, renewed and replenished. She lay, looking intently at the bright green, weed-free meadow as the flock of sheep trotted away, through the gate and out of sight behind a nearby hill. She was whole and healed, the cancer cells obliterated.

She was brought back to herself by the ringing doorbell and went down to find Cat Deerbon on the step.

'Say if this is a bad moment . . . I've got an afternoon off, Sam and Hannah are out to tea and Chris is picking them up.'

'It's great! Come in.'

'You have the look of someone who was asleep.'

'Do I?' Karin glanced in the mirror on the way through to the kitchen that was part of the big conservatory extension. Her eyes looked slightly bleary. 'I wasn't sleeping, I'd just finished doing an hour of visualisation.'

'So I see.' Cat was reading the book left open on the table.

'Tea?'

'Love some.'

Cat went over to the bookshelves and began to pick out title after title on alternative cancer therapies . . . *Eating Your Way Out of Cancer. The Kid Glove War: Fighting Cancer the Gentle Way. Say No to Cancer. See Yourself Well. New Life after Cancer. Cancer Therapies: the Complementary Approach. Self-Help, Self-Healing.*

'You must have spent a fortune.'

'One way of putting it. China or Indian?'

'Whatever you're having.'

'I'm having peppermint. I don't take caffeine.'

'Right.'

'I can hear what you're thinking.'

'You reckon?'

'What's caffeine got to do with cancer, how is peppermint tea going to beat a malignant tumour . . . ?'

'Wrong. I was thinking we could all do with a bit less caffeine injected into our day. I'll have peppermint as well, please . . . I like it.'

'So stop being so paranoid, Karin.'

'Something like that.'

'Anyway, this is your afternoon off, let's talk about gardening or the latest films or what's the Lafferton gossip, you didn't come to discuss my treatment.'

'It's exactly what I did come to discuss. You promised to keep me up to speed with what you're doing and you haven't. So I'm here.'

Karin smiled. 'I'm glad you're not going to give me an easy ride, Cat. I need to be able to defend myself every step of the way. I've ditched a few things before I've even started, I can tell you.'

'Such as?'

'Well, what I've been doing most of is reading, as you see. I'm sorting out what makes sense from the voodoo and the bunkum . . . God, there's a lot of that. I'm appalled, you know? How can people peddle some of the stuff they do, how can they take money for it from desperately ill people, who'll try anything? I went up to Starly . . . yes, you might well groan. That place is a shrine to quackery.'

'I know.'

'OK, here's where it's at. I'm on an organic, whole-food diet, lots of fresh raw vegetables and fruits, whole-grains. I've cut out caffeine and dairy produce and sugar, I have soya milk. I blend my own juices. I take vitamin supplements.'

'Hm.'

'I thought that's what you'd say. I do meditation and a visualisation programme. I walk two miles a day and I drink eight pints of mineral water.'

'And your bladder is working overtime.'

'Have some more tea.'

Cat looked long and closely at her friend. She was looking well. Her skin was beautiful, hair glossy, her eyes shone with health; she had a radiance Cat had not seen in her before and she told her as much.

'I feel fantastic, Cat. I simply can't believe there's anything wrong with me.'

'But you know that there is.'

'Yes.'

'I'm sorry to sound brutal.'

'It's your job to remind me. Thanks.'

'Have you been to see any alternative therapists?'

'A spiritual healer. I found her through someone at the cathedral. She gives me a marvellous sense of peace, and . . . I think I'd call it trust. I seem to be handing myself over to something else, trusting in something else . . . not the healer. I suppose people would call it God.'

'I would.'

'I've seen a homeopath.'

Cat snorted. 'That is voodoo. It's useless, Karin. It simply doesn't work and if it seems to, there are two reasons. One, the problem would have got better by itself anyway; two, it's placebo. A very powerful force, placebo. Doctors couldn't manage without it.'

'We'll have to differ then. She isn't trying to cure the cancer, she's treating me as a whole person. And please don't look like that and don't say "Right" in that tone of voice you have when you do.'

'I'll try not. Anything else?'

'I've sent for information from the Gerson Clinic and I'm spending two days at the Bristol Cancer Help Centre. Otherwise I'm reading. Thinking. Changing my life around. Still working on your mother's garden. I've cut out the others, I need to concentrate on getting well, but I love going up to Hallam House. Your ma is a tonic.'

Cat made a face.

'There is one thing you maybe ought to know about. There is a new therapist just starting out in Starly who calls himself a psychic surgeon.'

'A what?'

'I looked it up on the Internet. It's pretty spooky. There are a lot of them in places like the Philippines apparently – and all charlatans. A psychic surgeon claims to be possessed by someone who was a doctor in another century.'

'It can't mean surgery as in "surgery"?'

'I'm not sure . . . it's all magic circle stuff so far as I can make out, but it deceives a lot of vulnerable people. Two women in the café in Starly were talking about someone who'd had a throat tumour removed by this guy.'

'What?'

'They said he's better, it's a miracle, the doctors had given him up for dead – you know the sort of stuff.'

'Oh my God. What exactly is supposed to happen?'

'It's got to be sleight of hand . . . but as far as I can make out, there are instruments and there's blood.'

'This has got to be stopped.'

'How? Is it illegal?'

'I'm bloody well going to find out.' Cat looked straight at her friend. 'You're not thinking of going?'

'I rather thought I might actually. I'm quite interested in sorting the sheep from the goats.'

'Listen, you know my take on all this. It's certainly true that a good diet, exercise, a positive attitude are beneficial. Beneficial but incidental, Karin. The rest is crap, not all of it harmless.'

'I don't buy this psychic surgery stuff, you know. Give me some credit.'

Cat looked round Karin's kitchen, at the glass dome set in the roof, the plants and seedlings laid out on the wide ledges in the sun, neatly labelled, growing vigorously. The floor was laid with old French farmhouse tiles, the table a long block of polished elm, and the room was fitted with a new stereo system. Money, she thought, money and taste – Karin has it all and everything to live for, a husband who adores her, the right career at last, looks, friends, intelligence. As a doctor I know she's making the wrong decision and it's my duty to persuade her to change her mind. But as a friend . . .

'I'm torn,' she said now. 'I want to find out all about this psychic surgeon but I don't want you to put yourself at risk.'

'Come on, Cat, I'm tough, I can look after myself. Now – has your mother told you about the new hothouse she's planning?'

Cat knew better than to try and turn the conversation back to Karin's health. Besides, she quite wanted to know about her mother's latest garden extravagance, mainly so that she would be prepared when her father flew into a rage about it. For years, Meriel Serrailler had used work and family to cushion her in an unhappy marriage to an embittered and permanently angry man. Now that family took little of her time and she had retired as an NHS consultant, she had plunged herself into redesigning the large Hallam House garden which until recently had been not much more than a family playground. She still sat on some hospital and medical advisory boards, but they were not enough to occupy her considerable energies and keep her life apart from Richard's.

Finding Karin to work with her on the garden had been good fortune. They needed each other.

Eighteen

She wanted to look her best for Harry. He had always paid her compliments, always noticed when she'd bought a new frock or had her hair done and now she wanted to show him she still cared what he thought and still wanted him to admire her. It was one of the things she had promised him, and herself, straight after he had passed away. Some people let themselves go, didn't bother with make-up or having their hair done, made do with old clothes, anything that was easy to put on in the mornings so you didn't have to think, and she had sworn she would never let herself get like that. She had chosen her clothes every day as carefully as ever, picked out a necklace or a brooch, been careful to add a nice scarf over her outdoor coat and polish her shoes. She only ever wore a bit of lipstick and a dab from a compact, but she kept her skin nice with a cream every night.

But today was different. This was special.

She went through her wardrobe two nights running, discarding a few old things while she was at it, and putting others out for the dry-cleaner or to mend. She decided on the camel two-piece she'd bought for one of their anniversaries but hardly worn since, with her brown court shoes and a caramel silk scarf with a diamond pattern. Not a hat. No one wore hats nowadays, except for weddings and funerals and those fleece jobs to keep out the cold wind.

She had sat evening after evening on her own, trying to decide whether or not she should make an appointment to visit the medium, going over it all, making up her mind, changing it again, asking Harry and not being clear whether he had answered or not. She had not spoken to anyone else about it, not even to Pauline. It was too private, just between her and Harry. One evening, a couple of days after she had been to see Dr Deerbon, she had been lying on the couch in the late afternoon, a magazine on her lap, the gas fire making its gentle sounds and she had missed Harry, missed his face, his voice, his jokes, his funny habits, his shoes upside down on the hearth rail, the wheezy noise of his breathing, more than she had missed him since the day he died, painfully more. She had cried then, desperate, desolate tears, and in the middle of them had said aloud, 'Harry, what shall I do? What am I going to do?'

'Come and talk to me.'

It was Harry's voice, clear and strong in her inner ear. 'Come and talk to me.'

She had held her breath and waited, listened, urging him to go on, to say more, to explain.

'Should I go to the medium, Harry? Is that what you want me to do? Why can't you just talk to me now, I'm here, it's lovely and peaceful, why can't we be together now?'

The gas fire flickered its blue flame.

'Harry?'

But that was all. 'Come and talk to me.' She hadn't invented it, it wasn't wishful thinking, was it? He had come into her mind and told her.

'Come and talk to me.'

The next morning, she had gathered all her courage and telephoned the number for Sheila Innis, and when she heard a recorded message on an answerphone, the disappointment had been so much she had simply put her own receiver quickly down. It had taken another couple of hours, a walk to the newsagent to pay her paper bill and the post office to get her pension, and a pot of tea, before she had rung again. She had not properly taken in what was said.

'Hello. This is Sheila Innis. I am so sorry I am not able to answer your call personally but I am sure you understand that when I am working, I can't be disturbed. If you wish to book an appointment please call back between five and seven o'clock. Otherwise, please leave a message after the beep. Thank you.'

Her voice was reassuring, clear, pleasant, with a certain warmth but no false intimacy. Iris Chater listened to the message the whole way through, rang off and made a note to call that evening.

She thought she was much calmer now that she had come to a decision, and had heard the medium's voice. There was nothing spooky about her, nothing at all unusual. But at ten past five, her hand was shaking and she was so uncertain that she would be able to say anything that she fetched a glass of water and put it by the receiver.

What am I doing? This is wrong, I don't know what

I'm letting myself in for, I ought to let Harry rest in peace, leave well alone.

'Sheila Innis, can I help you?'

Miraculously, Iris Chater found she could answer.

'I'd . . . I'd like to make an appointment please. I did ring earlier and heard your message.'

'Of course. Would you give me your name?'

'Chater. Mrs Iris Chater.'

She gave her address and telephone number and her date of birth. Nothing else was required.

'I see people individually every afternoon between two and five thirty, Mrs Chater, and there are group sessions in the evenings.'

'Oh, no, I don't want to be with anyone else. It's . . . I want to see you by myself.'

'I understand. I've just had a cancellation for three o'clock on the 6th of February. Would that suit you?'

'Not until then?'

'I'm afraid not. I am always quite booked up. If you can't make that day I'm afraid we're looking at the second week in March now.'

'Oh yes, I can come then. I didn't mean –'

'I know. Once people decide they would like to see me, of course they want to come as soon as possible. I wish I could see everyone the day they ring, but I simply can't.'

'No, no, I do see. It'll be quite suitable. February 6th. I can come then.'

'Do you have the address?'

'Yes. I know the road.'

'Three o'clock then.'

'Thank you very much.'

'And Mrs Chater? You sound anxious. Please don't

worry. I think you'll feel quite at ease when we've met and you're sitting comfortably in my sitting room. Everyone's uncertain at first, of course they are, but I promise you will feel very relaxed and happy about it. I'll look forward to seeing you.' Iris Chater sat by the telephone, weak with relief. She had done the right thing, and she would not be nervous now. Sheila Innis had reassured her.

'I'm coming to talk to you, Harry,' she said, 'just like you wanted.'

February 6 was like a spring day, balmy and with a blue sky and watery sun. The snowdrops were almost over, in the sheltered spot under the lilac tree at the end of the garden, and now the crocuses had come up, egg yellow and Maundy purple, in rings beneath the trees. Harry had never been a real gardener, any more than she was, but they had both loved spring flowers and watched for them, so that she felt they were together as she walked to Priam Crescent. She set off early. She had had the back door locked all morning, so that when Pauline Moss came to it just after lunch, she wasn't able, as usual, to walk straight in. Harry had never liked that and when he had been alive and in the house, Pauline had always knocked. Lately, that had gone by the board. Iris thought she would drop a hint that she would prefer knocking to be reinstated.

She felt slightly guilty at keeping to herself the fact that she had made an appointment with the medium, because it had been Pauline who had suggested it first and found her the name. Maybe she would talk about it later. It all depended.

At a quarter to two, she had heard Pauline go out, as

usual on a Tuesday; her daughter-in-law came for her and drove her to shop in Bevham and then back to her own house for tea. It was the best day there could have been for her appointment.

She wasn't apprehensive or worried now, not in the slightest. All that was done with. She had liked the sound of the woman's voice and she knew, in her heart, that Harry wanted her to go. Hadn't he asked her, as clearly as he could manage? 'Come and talk to me.' What else could he have meant? She was happy, walking to Priam Crescent.

The house was a small detached one, white-painted pebble-dash with bay windows on either side of the front door. A hedge helped to conceal it from the road, and a long path led down to a glassed-in porch. The front garden had a magnolia tree beneath which were white and gold crocuses. Iris Chater felt her heart lift.

'Innis' was the only word on the label beside the front-door bell. This could be my neighbour, Iris Chater thought, this nice, neat, ordinary house – and after all, Sheila Innis is someone's neighbour. The idea was oddly reassuring. She did not hesitate at all before ringing the bell. Why should she, when she was doing what Harry had asked?

If she had had any shreds of uncertainty or apprehension left, the sight of Sheila Innis would have dispelled them.

'Mrs Chater? Do come inside. I must ask you first, do you object to cats because if so, I'll go ahead and move Otto to another room?'

'Oh, don't do that, I like cats.'

'He won't bother you. He's very old now and just

187

sleeps but there's a patch of sunshine in my working room at this time in the afternoon which he finds very attractive.'

She was perhaps fifty, no more, plump but not fat, with hair that had been fair and was fading and greying a little, short and well cut, swept up and back from her face. She wore a tweed skirt and a yellow blouse, a gold pendant, flat shoes. She also smiled, openly and warmly, a smile Iris Chater felt reached into her, to put her at her ease, to welcome her . . . and something more. It was the smile of someone she felt knew her. Whenever she had seen photographs of mediums, they had had elaborately styled, raven-black hair and strong black eyebrows, dark eyes, gold earrings, too much make-up. Sheila Innis could not have been less like them.

The cat, Otto, was lying full-length on the pale green carpet near French windows that looked over the garden, and had elongated himself so as to take advantage of every centimetre of sunshine. The beds in the garden near to the house and on either side of a long lawn were full of roses, now pruned down and bare, but here were snowdrops and crocuses again, as well as thick clumps of hellebores and a winter-flowering cherry giving the winter garden life and colour.

It was a pleasant room. A three-piece suite was upholstered in a damask fabric and a green slightly darker than the carpet, a polished table held a vase of yellow tulips, a handsome bureau had framed photographs – a bridal couple, several children, a young woman with long straight hair, an elderly man.

'Please, do sit down. If you lean firmly against the back of the chair you'll find a footrest shoots forward.'

Sheila Innis took the opposite chair, her back to the

French windows and the light. There was a grandmother clock set against the wall beside her. It was a lovely room, Iris Chater thought, a peaceful room. It had what felt like an air of contentment about it. She could have lived happily in this room, she thought, and not missed her own. There was nothing to make her nervous, nothing odd or worrying, there were no strange objects or pictures. She took a deep breath and leaned back. The footrest did indeed spring forward. She felt more relaxed than she had done for weeks. If nothing else at all happened, it would have been worth coming for this alone.

'Mrs Chater, have you ever visited a medium or any kind of spiritualist before?'

'Oh no. No, never.'

'I don't want you to tell me anything else about yourself. I wanted to know that because obviously, past experiences do affect people and every medium is different, we all work in our own way. So I'll just tell you briefly about what to expect. Are you comfortable there?'

'I might drop off to sleep. It's lovely.'

'Good. Now, first of all, we will both continue to sit here like this. I shan't draw the curtains or light any candles or anything of that sort. I don't work with a spirit guide either, as some mediums and clairvoyants do. I wouldn't find that helpful. I don't use tarot cards or crystals. I don't hypnotise you or put you into a trance, and nor do I go into a trance at individual sessions. But I will close my eyes to allow me to concentrate better. I'd ask you to answer any questions but only *those* questions . . . it's better if I'm not prompted. The other important thing is that nothing may happen. There may be no one from the other side who comes forward, no one wanting to make contact with you through me. That is quite possible, though it isn't usual, and if it's disappointing, I can understand, but there really is nothing I can do. I don't make things up. I won't do that. If someone – or several people – speak to me, trying to make contact and if they have messages for you, I hear them, and I can usually see them . . . it's just like a picture coming into my mind. If you close your eyes now and try and imagine, say, a tall, dark, handsome young man with white teeth and sparkling eyes . . . well, a picture will come into your mind. That is what happens to me . . . the difference is, of course, that I have no idea who I will see. Or hear. Sometimes, several people come to me together, a bit like children, jostling for attention, and then I can't hear them, I have to make out who is speaking most clearly and it isn't always easy. Am I making sense?'

Iris Chater looked across and saw the woman smile again, that warm, attractive, lovely smile. She felt wrapped in the smile and made safe by it. It was a smile she trusted.

'Yes,' she said, 'I think so.'

'Do you have anything else to ask?'

'No thank you.'

'Fine. Just relax then, Mrs Chater.'

The grandmother clock had a gentle tick. The cat stirred in sleep and its paws twitched. Through the window, Iris could see the patch of deep purple crocuses.

For several minutes, Sheila Innis sat, her hands folded in her lap, her eyes closed, silent and still. Iris waited, pleasantly at ease in the chair with the footrest. Perhaps this would be all and Harry would not come. She wondered how much she would mind.

'Nina,' Sheila Innis said. 'I have someone here called Nina . . . she's asking if you remember the blue . . . just a minute . . . she's holding something up . . . oh, it's a comb. The blue comb. You and she had a joke about a blue comb?'

It meant nothing at all. Iris tried to picture a blue comb but there was nothing.

'I'm sure it's Nina . . . no, is it Nita? Yes, I'm sorry, it's Nita.'

'Nita Ramsden? Goodness, I'd forgotten her, it's donkey's years ago.' Why would Nita Ramsden want to talk to her?

'She's laughing now. She's about . . . eighteen or nineteen with short curly hair and she's wearing an apron . . .'

'An overall . . . it's an overall. Dear God, it must be Nita. We worked together . . . it's more than fifty years ago. What does she say?'

'She's not speaking, she's just laughing. She looks so happy. She's pretty, isn't she?'

'Nita was ever so pretty.'

'She's got several young men there with her . . . one nice-looking young man is standing behind her. He says . . . I can't get his name, but he says you were all friends in a gang together. He says, what a surprise, Iris. He's quite a cheeky young man.'

'Donald?'

'Is that it? He's wagging his finger. He says he isn't going to tell me.'

'He was Nita's fiancé.'

For several moments, then, Sheila Innis was silent. Her eyes were tightly closed and she seemed to be listening intently. Nita Ramsden and Donald. How strange, when you thought of all the people since who might have come through. Why them? But thinking about it, how could she be sure it was them? She'd answered the questions, the medium had given hints and she herself had picked them up. It could all be rubbish. It wasn't what she wanted. But then Sheila Innis began to talk again rapidly.

'She's come much closer now. She has really unusual eyes . . . a greeny grey. Lovely eyes. She's saying she's sorry you had to wait for her and she couldn't tell you what had happened. You waited for such a long time in the cold. Now she's showing me a bicycle . . . I'm getting a picture of her on a bicycle riding over a bridge . . . is that a bridge?'

Iris Chater felt her neck prickle. Her hands were very cold. The room seemed cold, so that she pulled her silk scarf back up round her.

'She says it was all over in a minute but there was a second when she knew what was happening and everything seemed to go still. She knew she couldn't do anything and then it was over. She saw you waiting for her. She says . . . just a minute . . . no, is it . . . she says you had brought the biscuits. Is it that? Biscuits?'

'Yes,' Iris barely whispered. 'We took it in turns. It was my day for the biscuits . . . we used to pinch a handful out of the biscuit barrels at home.'

'She's showing me the bicycle again . . . the wheel's completely buckled, and the handlebars are forced round.'

'She was killed on her bicycle. We used to meet on the corner and that day I waited twenty minutes for her but she didn't come so I went on to work . . . and she'd been killed, she'd swerved under a tram. Oh, Nita . . . Poor little Nita. Is it really you?'

'She's saying you had good times. Didn't we have

good times, Iris, you and me and Donald and Norman. Didn't we have good times?'

'Yes,' Iris whispered, her mouth dry, 'yes, Nita, we had good times.'

'Now I've got someone else. Ella . . . Ella, no, sorry, it's Ellie. Yes. She's wearing a special brooch, a ship, yes . . . on a dark dress.'

'That's my grandmother.'

'She's frowning. She says everything was hard. She's sorry she didn't have more time for you when you were young but she had a hard time with your grandfather. Was he ill? I'm sensing he was ill for a long time.'

'He had mental problems . . . a lot of it was kept from me.'

'She says she wanted to leave you her box of treasures but she didn't have time to make a will. She passed over very suddenly. She says you'd always liked to look through it but she didn't think. She keeps telling me she's very sorry. There's a dog here . . . a dog. A small brown dog, yes. Do you know it? It's barking at you as if it's greeting you.'

'No. I don't know any brown dog.'

'Well, it's a friendly little dog and it definitely says hello, it's jumping up and down trying to attract your attention. It's a little terrier . . . a Yorkshire terrier?'

'No,' Iris said sadly. She ought to know the dog, surely, if it had come to greet her.

Sheila Innis was silent again now, her hands still resting together in her lap. The sun had moved round and the cat had moved with it.

'Is . . . is there someone who says he's Harry?'

The medium did not reply. Perhaps she ought not to have spoken. She waited, wondering about Nita, from fifty years ago, pretty little Nita killed on her bicycle. It was Nita's Donald who'd given Iris her first cigarette. They'd all started up then. They'd been friends, pals, but not really close and it had all been long before Harry. Why should Nita have come through when Harry hadn't?

'Come and talk to me,' he'd said and Iris had come but now he wasn't here, didn't seem to want to talk. She wanted to know if he was all right, just that, and for him to say something, anything, that would be proof to her, willed him to come through and say something only the two of them knew. That would be proof. Like only she and Nita knew about the biscuits.

The grandmother clock ticked on.

After a few more minutes, the medium opened her eyes, and then quickly made a gesture with her hands, running them down her body from the top of her head as if she was brushing something away.

She smiled across at Iris. 'I'm sorry,' she said, 'there's no one else this afternoon. I sense I've disappointed you. You wanted someone to come through and they haven't. Was it your husband? Did he pass over quite recently?'

'Harry. My Harry died just before Christmas.'

'That's very soon, Mrs Chater. It might be too soon. Sometimes it does take a little longer . . . but not always. No, not always. I can't make them come, you see, and I won't pretend. I could make up all sorts of things to give comfort but that would be cheating and I won't cheat people.'

'I see.'

'Would you like to come again? I'm always glad to go on trying. I don't give up easily but I just can't order people to come through if they don't want to, or are finding it difficult. That's often true when people first pass over . . . they find it difficult. They have to get help. I'm sure Harry is doing that. Perhaps leave it a month? It's entirely up to you.' She stood. 'Please don't be too downhearted. I sense Harry is very close to you and looking after you and that he's happy.'

It was the first time Iris Chater had felt suspicious. Easy words, she thought.

At the door, Sheila Innis put her hand on her arm. 'I wonder . . . I think you might be the sort of person to benefit from one of my evening groups . . . sometimes, there's an atmosphere which encourages those in the spirit world who haven't spoken . . . haven't been able to come through. We do get some remarkable results. There are just half a dozen clients. You might find what you want then.'

She wanted to escape. There was something intense about the way Sheila Innis was looking at her, something about her eyes.

'I'd . . . I'd have to think about it. I'm not sure.'

'Of course. Just telephone me. But you will. I have a definite feeling. You would find what you're searching for.'

'Thank you. Yes.' When she reached the top of the path, Iris glanced back and saw that the medium was still looking at her intently, watching her leave.

She couldn't face going home to be by herself yet, but there was a bus stop on the main road and she only had to wait a couple of minutes until one came which took her into town. She needed the town, people and cars and shops and bustle, she needed to be among things that were ordinary and cheerful and real. She bought some bread and then a bunch of early daffodils from a stall.

In the morning, she would take them up to the cemetery. After that, she went into Tilly's and had a pot of tea and a toasted teacake and spun out the time, looking at other people and listening to their conversations, until she felt normal again, normal and safe.

Pauline was at the window, waving a teacup, but she was not ready to talk to Pauline, who would know at once that she had been up to something. She was not just a nosy neighbour, she was concerned, but Iris was not ready to talk about the visit to Sheila Innis, and she didn't like to lie, so instead, she hurried inside while pretending to search deeply in her handbag. The house was very still. It was a pleasure now that the nights were lengthening just a little, so that she did not need to put the lights on until after five. She changed out of her suit and went back down to the kitchen. On the window ledge her pots of pink cyclamen glowed gently in the evening light. That had been one of Harry's few pleasures when he was so ill, seeing the potted plants she always kept up. Now, she looked at them and said his name. But there was silence and emptiness. He wasn't here, just as he had not been at the house in Priam Crescent.

'Where are you, Harry? Why didn't you come to talk to me? If I could talk to Nita Ramsden . . .'

She might have dismissed it all as baloney now that Harry had not spoken to her, if it had not been for Nita Ramsden. The stuff about her grandmother, even about the brooch like a ship, could have been a lucky strike; anyone of her age was going to have dead grandparents – parents as well, come to that. You could hardly go wrong. But Nita Ramsden, Nita and Donald, the biscuits, the fact that she had been waiting for Nita all that time on the corner on the way to work, and Nita hadn't come. The bicycle accident . . . You couldn't put it down to mind-reading because Nita Ramsden hadn't been anywhere near Iris's mind for half a century, and how could the medium ever have known a thing about her girlhood?

But she hadn't got what she went for, which was to hear from Harry. Come again, Sheila Innis had said, give it a bit longer, then make another appointment. She knew she would have to, that she would never rest until she'd made contact with Harry, but as to the evening meeting, in a group, that was different, mention of that had made her feel very uneasy. Who would the other people be, and why had the medium said things were different, and that there was often better success? What happened there that had not happened this afternoon?

The kitchen darkened gradually and the sky through the window was a deep brilliant violet blue. There would be a frost, a frost and the full moon.

After a while, she heard the signature tune to the six o'clock news coming through the wall from Pauline Moss's television. She felt a twinge of guilt. She ought to go and see Pauline, she would never want to hurt her. It was only that tonight, she couldn't have faced questions, eager, probing little questions which she could not have helped but answer. Harry had not come through to talk to her. She was more upset about it than she would ever have wanted to say to a neighbour, however well intentioned.

Nineteen

'All right, Nathan, tell me what your thinking is.'

DC Nathan Coates had a notepad open in front of him. He and Freya, sitting in the circle of light thrown by the lamp on her desk, were the only people in the CID room. It was after eight o'clock. She had filled him in on Angela Randall, and told him that the DI wouldn't countenance any more official time being spent on what he regarded as just another missing person case.

'I can't get you any overtime on this, Nathan, and I can't even justify your spending ordinary time on it.'

'That's OK, Sarge, if you think there's something, I'm up for it.'

'Thanks, but keep shtum, right?'

They had been going over a list for the past hour, since they had had the room to themselves. Apart from Angela Randall, and the missing mountain biker, a nineteen-year-old called Tim Galloway, Nathan had pulled out three more names which looked as if they might have connections, however tenuous, with the others.

James Bond ('Christ, poor bloke, imagine at school!'

Nathan had said). Aged forty-eight. Clerk. Bachelor, living alone. Had gone missing early one morning, near the river. No trace, no body found. History of mental illness, had previously wandered from a psychiatric ward and been found on Eylam Moor three days later. Went missing again two weeks afterwards.

Carrie del Santo. Aged nineteen. Known prostitute. Last seen running through the Cathedral Close in the early hours of Good Friday, 1997. On bail for soliciting and two cases of purse snatching. Not reported missing for several weeks.

Phyllis Spink, seventy-eight, missing since 1999. Lived alone in St Michael's Almshouses. History of confusion/dementia.

'OK, good, let's take them one by one. What struck you about each of them in relation to Angela Randall?'

'Right, Mr 007 . . . The last sighting was in the early morning, and the river towpath is in the same general area of town as the Hill.'

'Bit thin.'

'Yeah, I know. And the history of depression plus having gone awol before means he probably went somewhere miles away and topped himself, just never been found. Not every body gets found.'

'Not every body but most bodies, and if you commit suicide you have no control of what happens to your body after you're dead.'

'Whereas if you're murdered someone else does.'

'Yes. Keep him in for now but I don't think he fits.'

'OK . . .' Nathan took a swig of the fizzy lemonade he drank by the litre bottle, wiped his mouth with the back of his hand and belched discreetly, before giving Freya his disarming grin.

'The tom . . . gawd, another name to go to bed with, like. Got to be foreign. Got form, so had good reason to scarper. She's probably hopped it overseas, but I pulled her out because of the early-morning sighting.'

'Yes, and female. Keep her in. Check her nationality and maybe a place name but don't spend too much time on it. Then our confused old lady.'

'Mrs Spink. Female again.'

'But a history of confusion. Probably wandered off in her nightie.'

'No body though.'

'OK, keep her in for now as well. Then it's back to the mountain biker.'

'Tim Galloway. I pulled him out because he was last seen in the very early morning, and on the Hill, and he was a sportsman, though biking not running.'

'But male.'

'Yeah. I'm sorry, Sarge, but the rest just didn't throw anything at all up. Load of teenagers fallen out with the new stepfathers, or bullied at school, poor kids, or more of the depressed. Couple of blokes obviously walked out on their wives, one or two under suspicion of petty crime, fraud, cheating on their employers. Nothing to connect their disappearance with that of your Miss Randall. And besides, that's going back five years. Still, I'm surprised how many people Lafferton manages to lose. It ain't that bad. I'm sorry I haven't done any better for you.'

His young, squashed-up face looked downcast, his voice was subdued.

'You've done fine, Nathan. This stuff is always guesswork.'

'I wanted to find the perfect match for you, Sarge.'

He was like a little boy anxious to please the teacher and get a good mark.

She laughed. 'Never works out like that. But these are useful. I'm going to go through them at home, and see which look worth going into in a bit more detail . . . Come on . . . I'll buy you a drink.'

The DC's face lit up. His transparentness and the honesty of the way he never tried to conceal his reactions were part of what endeared Nathan Coates to everyone. When he was praised he glowed, when something worked out well, he walked about with a permanent grin, and when it did not, he had a face like a crumpled clown.

The Cross Keys was a few yards from the station, on the opposite side of the street. As they went through the swing doors, DCI Simon Serrailler's black police Rover pulled up into its parking space. Freya felt her stomach clench. Damn. Damn, he would see her with young DC Coates and think there was something between them, that they were an item, that . . .

Oh, for Christ's sake, woman.

Serrailler took the steps two at a time, giving them a brief nod of recognition. Freya looked back and caught a glimpse of his blond head going out of sight fast up the inside staircase.

Seconds later, two other senior officers' cars, one with a police driver, swung into the forecourt.

'Something's up,' Freya said.

'Operation Merlin.'

'Sorry?'

'Big drug round-up . . . uniform and drug squad.'

'How come you get to know everything I don't, Nathan?'

He tapped the side of his nose and grinned.

Not, she thought as they pushed into the busy pub, that she wanted to know anything about a drug op. There had been enough of them in the Met to last her a lifetime.

'What'll you have?'

'No, Sarge, this is mine.'

'Not a chance. Besides, this is your overtime pay, Nathan, so make the most of it.'

'OK, thanks, I'll have a lemonade.'

'Oh please.'

'With a whisky chaser.'

'If I spin it out and eat a bag of crisps, I'm allowed one small white wine.'

Nathan whipped round as two men left a table in the corner, and moved fast to commandeer it while Freya got the drinks.

'I suppose if it's been successful we'll hear about the drugs op in the morning.'

Nathan shook his head. 'It ain't finished yet, it's only just started.'

'Bloody hell, have you got a hot line into the DCI's office?'

'Keep my ears open, that's all.' He took a gulp of lemonade, swallowed it, and then downed his whisky in one gulp.

'How do you like Serrailler?' he asked, so unexpectedly that Freya was caught before she could prevent herself from flushing up. She bent down quickly, and ferreted for a few seconds in her bag, but when she sat upright again Nathan Coates was looking at her over his glass.

She said, 'Sorry. The DCI? Seems fine. Hardly talked to him. Now, Cameron . . . God, there were still a lot of

Billy Camerons left in the Met . . . tough as they come, all overweight, all smoked like chimneys, but if they were on your side and you needed someone to back you up, you couldn't do better. Cameron's out of the same mould.'

Nathan shrugged.

'What?'

'I think he's just coasting till he gets his pension. He's dead straight though.'

'Which is always saying a lot.'

'Serrailler's different.'

'You're not suggesting he isn't straight . . . ?'

'Christ, no. I mean he's different. Not your average copper.'

Freya stood up. 'A chaser and more of that fizzy gut rot? Crisps, sausage roll, pork scratchings . . . go on, gourmandise.'

'Nah, Em will have dinner on, it's her turn. She's had a couple of days off so she's in cooking mode. Liver and onions. I'll have to move. Thanks anyway.' He drained his glass. 'But don't let me stop you.'

'Somehow, I don't fancy drinking on my own in the Cross Keys. People might start to wonder.'

'Course they might, good looker like you, Sarge.' Nathan swung the pub door open and held it for her with his grin and a bow.

Across at the station, Freya went to her car, Nathan to the cycle racks. He and Emma lived in a flat only a few streets away.

'Thanks for the drink, Sarge. See you tomorrow.'

'Goodnight, Nathan.'

Freya glanced at the cars drawn up in the front spaces. Simon Serrailler's Rover was still there and the lights

203

were on in his office on the second floor. She wanted to wait, to hang about in the dark station yard, hoping he would emerge again on his way home, thinking she might go in through the doors as he was coming out, might exchange a word, that he might . . .

Damn. Damn, Damn, Bugger, Bugger, Sod it, Damn. Damn.

Nathan glided by on his cycle, looking at her. Then he stopped, and put one foot to the ground. Freya turned.

'OK?'

He said nothing until she went back a few steps closer to him. She thought he wanted to mention the missing persons case, and knew she would rather he didn't shout it out, even though they were the only ones on the station forecourt. He had his cycle helmet on, a gleaming electric-blue shell under which his lumpy face and ginger hair looked even odder. His expression was concerned.

'Serrailler,' he said.

She took a half-step back, further into the shadow.

'It's a hiding to nothing, Sarge. Know what I mean?'

Then he pushed off and sped away.

Twenty

Debbie Parker lay in bed propped up on three pillows, with a small sheaf of cards in front of her. Dava had given them to her the previous afternoon. The session with him had been even more affecting than the first; she had lain on his couch and been taken on a spiritual journey again, and this time, he had led her through what he called the Five Portals, gateways to her spiritual self and its unique world. She had described what she had seen – beautiful pictures of gardens with magical flowers, crystal caves shot with rainbow colours and filled with feathery angels and other beings of light. She had felt wonderful, floating on a cloud of peace and harmony, Dava's voice speaking softly in her ear through what seemed like a softly rushing waterfall and his hand touching her brow and stroking her hair, but far away, far away.

He had said that she was much better, that her energies were becoming gradually more balanced and the negative forces were slowly but surely dissolving.

'We do not fight, Debbie, there are no battle terms

used. I do not speak of overcoming and of obliterating, I speak of dissolving and disempowering. The negative forces that were causing you so much distress are weakening and dissolving. Eventually, they will retreat altogether and cease to exist.'

He had told her that she was specially protected; that wherever she went she could rely completely on the angel she had met to protect her.

'That was a rare and very special encounter, Debbie. You were privileged. To be rescued and helped in that way by one of the many angels who take on human form in order to assist us, is something to be deeply, humbly grateful for.'

'Oh, I am,' Debbie had said fervently, 'I truly am.'

'You know now that you are protected and in the next day or two you will find a sign of it. Somewhere, you will find a white feather and when you do, you must pick it up and keep it close to you. It will be symbolic of your protector. Now, breathe deeply and slowly. I want you to focus your mind on your own individual colour, which is blue. Blue but with a vibrant golden edge. Look into the heart and centre of your blue, Debbie. I am going to give you some words and phrases. You will not forget them, but I will also give you some cards to prompt you. Read them over and over. Each card is a talisman.'

The cards were different-coloured, and printed with Dava's phrases. He had signed each one.

BLUE
Peaceful. Musical. Spiritually healing. Artistic. Sensitive. Sincere.

BLUE

Brings peace, tranquillity, faith in oneself.

BLUE

Inspires calm, faith, trust.

BLUE

Is your note of harmony with the universe.

The other cards were printed with diagrams of the chakras, and drawings of her own healing flowers and herbs, her own special dates for the coming year highlighted on a calendar. She had read them until she was beginning to know them by heart. Now, she looked at the card which told her about her auspicious times of day. The first of these was seven thirty-five in the evening, a strange time, with which Debbie found it hard to identify, in spite of the complex phases of the sun and moon and the links to astrological charts. The second, though, she related to immediately. Her name had been filled in by hand at various points, so that as she studied the card she felt a personal link with Dava through his elaborate, flowing black script.

DAWN

The hour between the first lightening of the morning sky and sunrise is your most auspicious time. It is now, DEBORAH . . . that you come most alive and are most in tune with the universe. At this hour, DEBORAH . . . you are at your most vibrant and hopeful. Your energies are finely tuned, your aura, which is a particularly unusual and beautiful one, DEBORAH, is vividly coloured and singing with life. This is the hour when you should give thanks to the maker of the universe, the hour which is most propitious for you to take new decisions, your most creative hour. Rise early and celebrate your dawn hours and sleep when your energies begin to fade, after sunset.

There was also a card with suggested lines she should read in her chosen 'sacred place' at dawn, together with a prayer she should recite.

She read until she was too tired to read more and then she put out her light and lay on her back, marvelling at the fact that she felt so totally different since seeing Dava, happier, more confident, optimistic about her future. Her skin was beginning to clear too, and the blackness she had felt every morning for so many months was more like a thin veil through which she could see clearly than a dense cloud.

If she continued to move forwards like this, she knew she would be well enough to start looking for a new job, part-time at first, which in turn would lead her to new circles of friendship. She had taken down the names of several groups that met in Starly to focus on ecology, astrology and healing, and New Age therapy, and before long, she knew she would feel well enough to sign up for one or two of them. But she planned to take Dava's advice. If most of her benefit money was being spent on her appointments with *him* and on the tapes and books which she had bought from him as well, it was money spent to good purpose, an investment for her future health and happiness.

She let herself relax, felt her breaths come more slowly and deeply, and then began to focus on the circle of vibrant blue she conjured up in her mind, with its shimmering golden rim and its heart of deepest violet.

The healing power of it flowed into her mind and her veins.

She fell asleep.

Earlier, Sandy had accidentally knocked Debbie's handbag off the kitchen table and, in hastening to apologise and pick up the spilled contents, had found the card for her second appointment with Dava.

'Oh, Debs.'

'Thanks, I can manage,' Debbie said stiffly, almost pushing her flatmate out of the way, afraid that she would find the other cards and scoff.

'Look, it's none of my business –'

'Right.'

'OK, but . . . and there is a but and you know it.'

'I haven't taken anything, I haven't got any more ointment if that's what you're worried about.'

'But you'll have to pay another bill, won't you?'

Debbie pushed the last couple of things back into her bag and zipped it up with a sharp rasp. Her defiant expression said everything words did not. Sandy sat down at the table and looked at her.

'I worry about you, Debs, I'm concerned about you, I care about you for goodness sake.'

'No need. I'm good thanks.'

'Well, you weren't.'

Debbie hesitated. Sandy's voice was full of true anxiety. She did worry, she was a friend. Debbie sat down opposite her.

'Can't you see how much better I am?'

'That's Dr Deerbon's tablets, isn't it? Come on.'

'I don't mean my skin. I expect you're right on that, but I mean me. I've only been to see him twice and he's changed everything, Sandy, he's changed the way I think and feel and the way I am about myself. I'm not unhappy any more, I want to get up in the mornings, I'm going to look for a part-time job soon. I am just learning so much. You haven't got anything to worry about, honestly.'

Sandy sighed. She was still frowning. 'It's costing so much though. I just wonder if you can't get some sort of counselling on the health service.'

'It's not counselling.'

'Well, what is it then?'

Words swirled round Debbie's head, Dava's words, the words on the cards, words that were new to her and meant something impossible to convey to plain-speaking, clear-thinking, straightforward Sandy. Harmony . . . aura . . . vibration . . . energy . . . peace . . . protection . . . angel . . .

She could not say any one of them out loud, for fear of sounding stupid, of being mocked, being misunder-stood. The words had become sacred, like words from the Bible or prayers in church, they were not words to be passed casually between them across the chipped Formica kitchen table of the flat.

'I promise I'm fine. I know what I'm doing. If it hadn't felt right and if it hadn't made me so much better I wouldn't have gone again. But thanks anyway. I mean it. Thanks.'

She had gone round the table and given Sandy a hug, and hoped that everything was right between them and that Sandy wouldn't go on at her again. Because there really wasn't any need. She knew what she was doing. Things were fine. Really fine.

*

Her alarm buzzed on low vibration at six the next morning. She was anxious not to wake Sandy. Through the kitchen window she saw only darkness but it was not raining and when she opened the back door, she felt mild air blowing in gently. She had a glass of orange juice to avoid putting on the kettle that whistled so shrilly when it boiled, ate a soya yogurt and put two Penguin biscuits in the pocket of her fleece jacket. She clicked off the light softly, and even more softly closed the back door. Out in the street, she paused and looked back. The flat was still in darkness. She thought fondly for a moment of Sandy, neatly asleep in her pretty primrose-and-white bedroom, with the fluffy bedside mat and the two Dutch dolls in their primrose-and-white gingham caps and aprons, sitting on the small shelf with their wooden legs dangling down. She saw Sandy's make-up exactly lined up on the dressing table which had a yellow-and-white frill around its base, her magazines stacked in date order between yellow wooden bookends on the shelf, Sandy's frame of photographs on the wall, each in an individual oval frame within the whole – Sandy and her sister as babies, as toddlers, as angels in a play, as Brownies, on ponies, in bikinis on a sunlit beach, Sandy's parents, Sandy's various cats and dogs. Every Saturday morning, Sandy cleaned, dusted, swept and polished her room and rearranged everything precisely as before on the furniture, on the shelves. One day, she would make a fantastic married home, for which she would personally sew every curtain and flounce, paint every wall, stencil every border, following ideas cut out of her magazines. Suddenly, Debbie felt a flutter of panic. It would happen, of course it would, sooner or later Sandy would leave for that new home, having met an

Andrew or a Mark, a Steve or a Kev or a Phil, and when she did, Debbie would be by herself. She had no idea how she might cope.

The streets were empty, just as before. Away on the main road, there was the noise of light traffic, the occasional lorry, the first bus, but she saw no one else walking along the pavements or even riding a bike to an early shift somewhere. Two of Dava's special cards were in her fleece pocket and she carried a small torch, the size and shape of a credit card, but which had an intense beam that shone a surprising distance ahead of her. She had seen it in a gift shop in Starly when she had been buying a scented candle which Dava had said would purify her room and help to concentrate and focus her thoughts.

She scarcely needed the torch through the avenues and crescents towards the path, but once she was on the track at the foot of the Hill she switched it on, determined not to be caught out and frightened half to death by a rabbit or a stray dog like the last time.

But nothing about this morning was like the last time. The air smelled soft and fresh, the feel of the ground beneath her feet steadied her, and she climbed easily up the track. As her torch beam picked out the Wern Stones, she went happily towards them and when she reached one, put out her hand and touched its cold damp surface, then ran it down to where there was a slight unevenness and roughness. The ancient stones had been there aeons of time, nobody knew how long or why they were there, but Debbie imagined them being in place maybe even at the beginning of the world. She felt its heaviness pressed into the earth and how the strength of ages was coming to her through it. How could she have been afraid that other time when she had been in the charmed circle of the Wern Stones? She turned and looked up at the sky. There was a thin line of light at the horizon. She felt suddenly excited. Imagine how it must be at Starly Tor or Stonehenge at dawn on the midsummer solstice. Well, she would discover in June when she would be there with all the others, dancing and celebrating the birth of the light. From somewhere below, she heard a faint whistle. The dog walkers came here early too, but it was still too dark to make out any figures.

She climbed on, past the bushes and undergrowth where she had been so terrified before, but this time, pointing her torch beam right into them and seeing nothing but innocent twisted roots and branches, briers and brambles and scrub and rabbit holes. On and up. She was getting out of breath now. Dava had told her that she must learn to feel when her body was right, her weight in tune with her height, her emotions, her spirit, learn to sense everything about herself for herself. Since going on the organic wholefood diet she had already lost a few pounds, though she had not been able to give up the chocolate bars or biscuits yet, and felt for one now in her pocket, stripped down the metallic wrap and bit deep into it. Dr Deerbon had said she had no idea and nor did anybody else really whether chocolate made a bad skin worse, though she had suggested Debbie try and cut down the amount she ate gradually. OK, so she had cut it down. Well, a bit.

Now the light was strengthening steadily. She had almost reached the top of the Hill, where the great circle of ancient oaks stood, a landmark for the whole of Lafferton. The bare branches stirred slightly, making a dry noise and the breeze moved Debbie's hair. There was a stone bench, just a slab placed across two other slabs and she sat, turned towards the east and the lightening sky, now tinted faintly rose red in a thin line where it joined the dark earth. She was acutely, thrillingly conscious that this was her own special time, when she was most keenly in tune with the forces, the universe, the natural world, the harmony of the spheres . . . things she did not fully understand but which she was sure she could now sense. She would always find this time her strength and her solace, she would recharge her energies and plan for the future, place herself in the guiding hand of the light. She could hear Dava's voice as he had spoken on and on so softly in her ear as she had lain on the couch, like a stream flowing and never pausing, never changing its rhythm.

The light filled out in the sky, creeping over the darkness and dissolving it, and then the rim of the sun and the rose-red flush came gradually up over the edge of the world. Debbie held her breath. From somewhere just ahead of her in the trees a bird began to sing, though she had no idea what bird it was. Later, in the spring, she knew there would be a chorus of birds and that people came up here just to hear them. She wasn't sure if she would like that. She wanted this place, in her time, to herself.

Somewhere on the lower slopes, far down, she heard a whistle. She could make out the cathedral clearly now, the stone tower touched by the rising sun. It was amazing. The world was being recreated before her eyes, as if it had been dead and was coming back to life, or like a picture that was being painted by some invisible hand as she looked on.

She took out the cards and read them, then read the invocations aloud, though quietly, feeling slightly foolish.

'My time,' she said joyfully, 'this is my time.'

Sandy would be getting up now, pottering into the bathroom in her crisp lemon-coloured dressing gown, turning on the dodgy hot-water heater for her shower. The ordinary day was beginning. For ordinary people, Debbie thought suddenly, because she had a sudden, strange sense of not being ordinary, not being like others, all those people in their little houses and flats and cars and bungalows below her in Lafferton, but being different, chosen, picked out for special knowledge, given special, privileged insights. She was not the same old overweight unhappy Debbie Parker with a bad skin, she was Dava's chosen one, a hand had been laid on her and she was transformed.

She wanted to sing.

She was also hungry and needed to go to the loo. The dawn was up, her special time was over. She slipped the torch in her pocket and headed joyfully back down the track.

At the bottom, as she turned on to the path, she recognised the white van, parked at a funny angle across it. Her heart lurched. She was sure, sure, this was the van that had been driven by the man who had come to her rescue, the one who had driven away and vanished, not human but angelic. She stopped.

Someone seemed to be half slumped on the front seat, almost hanging out of the open van door. There was no movement at all.

Either the man was leaning in to fiddle with something down near the foot pedals, as he might if the van had broken down, or he was hurt or had been taken ill.

She went nearer and pushed herself between the open van door and the bushes, thinking quickly, wondering if she should run for help or shout, whether she knew how to give first aid. That she ought to help him she had no doubt, just as he had helped her. He had come to her rescue, and seen her safe and now she had come to his.

The branches of the hedge fell back and she was beside his legs as he lay across the front seat of the van, but then he moved, pulling himself quickly backwards with a single strong movement. So it was the van then, not him. She felt very relieved, realising that she had been dreading what she might have found, blood, or him dead of a heart attack.

He stood upright and looked straight at her, smiling. It was him.

'Hello, Debbie,' he said.

She didn't stand a chance, caught by surprise and off balance as he knew she would be. One minute she was standing there, full of concern, about to speak, the next he had her in a swift and powerful armlock. He bent her neck backwards, tipping her off her feet in the same well-rehearsed, confident movement. Debbie felt a moment of astonishment, a second of excruciating pain, and then the sky was a black vortex filled with burning stars and her body was rising and falling again, rising and falling. The pain was everything she was and the darkness something to fall into. One thing she did not feel, had not had a chance to feel before everything happened, was fear.

Three minutes later, her body was cooling in the refrigerated container section of the van, as it was driven away at a careful, steady speed, off the path, and out on to the main road.

The Whipple Drive Business Park on the outskirts of Lafferton had been built just over a year previously and contained well-designed and spaced-out units of various kinds, including fully equipped offices in two-storey blocks, together with some smaller storage units and lock-up garages. The whole was pleasantly landscaped, with sloping lawns and newly established rowan trees.

The white van drove down the still-empty service road, and turned right at the far end, to where the block of cabin units gave out on to the perimeter fence and beyond, to the waste ground leading to the main railway line. The last unit was the largest, and had its entrance at the side. There was a small office in the front and a large area behind, to which the van backed up. The doors were opened, then those of the unit, revealing steel runners on to which the refrigerated box containing Debbie Parker's body was rolled straight to the back. Then the doors were closed and double-locked again, and the van driven into the garage.

From there an inner door led through to the unit.

In the office, with its door marked FLETCHER EUROPEAN AGENCIES, he switched on the fluorescent overhead lights, and then the percolator.

While the coffee was brewing, he slipped off his jacket and shoes, opened a metal locker, and took out a set of green overalls and a pair of rubber overshoes. The cream slatted blind was permanently pulled down, hiding any view of the office and its occupants from the path outside, though there were rarely any passers-by.

He sat calmly at the desk drinking the hot, arabica roast. It was seven ten. He had an hour in which he could do some preliminary work and before he would have to leave the unit for the rest of the day – work which he could not wait to do. That was partly why he went through the ritual of making the fresh coffee, to spin out this first excitement, as well as to calm himself after the dangerous few moments on the path at the bottom of the Hill. Here he felt safe, here he was on his own territory, in charge. There, anything might go wrong, within split seconds; nothing much ever had, though the young mountain biker had been difficult, strong and agile. That one had made him sweat.

The fat girl had been easy, trusting and friendly, caught completely off guard. He had planned it well this time, left nothing to chance, and it had worked like a dream. He was proud of himself. He was never going to be foolhardy enough to think it had become easy and that he could not make a mistake. Pride would come before the fatal fall. He was not going to allow that to happen.

Because he had not finished, not by any means.

He unlocked a side drawer of the metal desk and took out a folder. Inside was a typewritten list. He read down it now, for pleasure.

> Young man, 18–30
> Mature man, 40–70
> Elderly man, 70 plus
> Young woman, 18–30
> Middle-aged woman, 40–60
> Elderly woman, 65 plus

He had never added the word 'Dog'. Dog had not been part of the plan, Dog had been on the spur of the moment, because seeing Dog had brought the raging jealousy foaming up inside him at the recollection of that dog, her dog, the hated dog. It had looked exactly the same, breed, colour, size, everything. Dog might have been a clone of that dog. He had taken Dog before he had thought what he was doing.

Dog had been disposed of.

Two entries on the typed list had ticks in red pen beside them and now he took the same pen out of the drawer and let the point hover beside Young woman, 18–30. He remembered the feel of her fat neck as he had locked his arm round it and pulled her back. She had made little sound, only a deep, choking gurgle.

He placed the pen point on the paper and formed the red tick mark, lingering over the short downward and the longer upward stroke.

Three ticks. Six entries.

He wondered if six would do. But there was no hurry, and besides, the search for the right one might take months. He was unlikely to be so lucky and quick again, and it was the selection and the planning that were so vital if he was not to make any mistake.

The small clock on the desk read seven twenty. He placed the paper back in the file and locked the drawer, then went across the room and through the inner door to the store. He switched on the overhead lights here and at once the place was lit in exactly the way all the pathology rooms he had known were lit. There was a steel sink in one corner and a channel in the rubber floor leading into a central drain. Against the wall, what looked like the doors of large filing cabinets gleamed greenish grey. Propped up beside them was the metal table. He wheeled it to the centre under the main light and over the drain, then opened it out. A metal trolley with rubber wheels was set up in the same way, with a sliding drawer attached to one side by hooks and bolts. The drawer swung out at an angle to reveal the instruments arranged so that the whole was like a display that gave satisfaction to the eye by its order and symmetry.

He stood back, checking.

When he was satisfied, he crossed to where the rectangular box stood on its metal runners, and swung it round until it was level with the table.

Debbie Parker's body was already cool to the touch. Sharp surgical scissors slit her fleece jacket, trousers, jumper and underclothes, all of which were dropped into a black bin bag, to be disposed of later. Her wristwatch, house keys and a small credit-card-sized torch went into a separate box. There were three cards in one of her pockets. He studied the writing for a second or two and finding the New Age claptrap of no interest, dropped them into the bin on top of the clothes.

Then he stood beside the metal table, looking down at the girl's flabby naked body, with its pitted facial skin and acned shoulders. He felt nothing. That was correct. At post-mortems the pathologist felt nothing, no emotion, no sorrow or sympathy, only curiosity and intellectual and professional interest. The first pleasures, those that accompanied the hunt, the swift capture and the kill, were over. The rest was to come, and it was different, more clinical and unheated, and much slower. The other was furtive, hurried and frightening. His blood pressure rose, he sweated, his heart pounded. He was taking an appalling risk. Now, he was sure that there was no risk at all, because everything had been planned so carefully, for so long, and practice helped.

He walked round the table slowly, looking at the body, and as he went, he began to dictate, as the pathologist did, noting everything about the body on the table under his scrutiny, quietly and professionally, in the tone of voice he had heard and admired so many times and imitated by himself over and over again. He was proud of his own expertise now, confident that he could take on any of them, the best in the world, and was proving the bastards wrong about him. They had had the power to fail him, to judge him unworthy to join their ranks and now he was getting his own back.

When he was ready, he took up the scalpel. He had too little time now but he wasn't able to wait and tonight he could come back and spend as long as he liked, here at the heart of everything, expertly taking Young woman, 18–30, apart. From the moment he had taken her round the neck from behind, Debbie Parker had ceased to exist as a human being with a personality and a name as well as a life. That was why he could operate on her dispassionately. They all could. It was how they did the job. She was a sample, a specimen of her sex and age, no more.

He bent forward and made the first precise incision.

Twenty-One

Cat Deerbon had succeeded in her aim of keeping one room in their farmhouse out of bounds to children and dogs. As a result it had become known mockingly as the Smart Sitting Room and it was in there, on two matching sofas and deep armchairs upholstered in cream leather, that they had now gathered. Supper had been eaten, and they had brought glasses of wine in with them. A cafetière and a pot of tea were on the low table. It was rare for Cat to be able to hold a meeting at home, but it was half-term and Meriel Serrailler had taken Sam and Hannah overnight to London for assorted treats including the Eye, the Planetarium and the Hard Rock Café. Cat had been able to cook a decent meal, make the house and herself presentable and put together some notes which were now typed out on a sheet of paper in front of her.

The others, sitting back comfortably with their wine and coffee, were Chris, the osteopath Nick Haydn, Aidan Sharpe the acupuncturist, and Gerald Tait, senior partner at a GP practice on the other side of Lafferton and someone both the Deerbons greatly liked and respected, as a man and as a doctor. He represented the older generation but his outlook was up to date and his sympathies were broad.

Over supper, the talk had been partly medical but of a general nature. Now, they were to focus.

Cat set down her glass. 'It was my idea to have this informal meeting of minds but of course it is informal and I'm not sitting here as any sort of chairperson. We're all on an equal footing and everyone must say exactly what they think.

'OK. Chris and I have become increasingly concerned over the last few months about some of the – I don't know what terms you prefer – alternative therapists, complementary practitioners, working in our area. I should use the words "quack" and "charlatan" about many of them and I daresay you would too. You know that quite a large community of people has mushroomed in and around Starly Tor, because of its history and dubious reputation as an ancient site of – well, take your pick – witchcraft, Druid worship, healing, ley lines . . . a lot of New Age travellers appear there with the spring, and all the usual shops and cafés and so on have moved into Starly as a result. None of that matters, they're usually harmless. There's a bit of dope smoking – though oddly enough, my policeman brother says there are fewer serious drug problems up there than in Lafferton and certainly fewer than in Bevham. No. Drugs are not the point. What have come to our attention and become a matter of real concern are the quack practitioners. At best they take a lot of money from gullible people who can ill afford it, and even that wouldn't really be anything to do with us. But a number of these so-called therapists are not harmless. The point is, as you know, neither Chris nor I – nor most of the other GPs in Lafferton – are against properly trained and qualified alternative therapists working in proven disciplines. That's why we asked you, Aidan and Nick . . . I've sent patients to Nick who sorts out the bad backs, I've sent them to Aidan, because I know there are some conditions that respond well to acupuncture. But you two know what you're doing and you follow the first principle of all orthodox doctors: 'Do no harm.'

Aidan Sharpe cleared his throat. 'Thank you, Cat – sorry to interrupt you but I am grateful for that and I'm sure Nick is. We are properly trained and qualified, as you rightly say, but I'm afraid we still come in for a good deal of hostile criticism for what we do.'

He had a strangely precise and formal way of speaking. It probably went with the exactness and precision of his skills, Cat thought. She had talked to Aidan Sharpe about traditional Chinese acupuncture and noted how it seemed to combine an elaborately laid-down scientific system of mapping the body and what could go wrong with it, with the need for an intuitive, almost artistic flair for diagnosis. She did not pretend to understand or accept the theory behind the whole thing – it contradicted much of what she had been taught – but she respected that it had a long and honourable history – and that it often worked.

Nick Haydn sprawled at one end of a sofa, a big, broad rugby player with huge hands, a therapist who could manipulate people's bodies with energy and strength when necessary, his way of working in contrast to that of Sharpe – for whom, Cat noted, he seemed to have a certain antipathy. Well, they were at opposite ends of the spectrum as people as well as therapists. Nick wore a clean but creased sweatshirt emblazoned with 'Guinness is good for You' over baggy corduroys; Aidan Sharpe wore a well-cut suit and a bow tie in a paisley pattern. Nick's hair was curly and needed cutting, Aidan's was neatly combed; Nick was clean and scrubbed but needed a shave, Aidan wore a goatee beard. Cat liked and respected them both. It was good that they complemented one another.

'What has brought all this up now? Starly's been the haunt of hippies and New Agers for years,' Nick said. 'They don't take any business away from me – my appointment book is always full.'

Aidan Sharpe nodded across at him in agreement.

'Two things really. Firstly, I had an emergency call recently to a young girl who had consulted a practitioner up there about her acne. She got some herbal capsules from this guy and also a vile-smelling ointment. She had a serious allergic reaction to one or both and her flatmate had to call me out. She was fine but I had the stuff analysed by a mate at BG. The tablets were rubbish – dried parsley mainly – but the ointment contained several things that I wouldn't allow near anyone's skin.'

'Who in God's name gave her the stuff?' Gerald Tait looked angry. 'This is the reason the new EU regulation on over-the-counter medicines has been drafted – dangerous substances peddled by profiteering crooks.'

'But that EU directive is throwing out the baby with the bathwater,' Aidan put in, 'because if it comes into force people won't be able to buy some very useful supplements.'

'I'd rather that than see harm done.'

'The trouble is, people like this practitioner in Starly will never conform to the regs.'

'Who is the man anyway? Do we know?'

'He rejoices in the name of Dava.'

'Dava what?' Nick asked.

'Oh, he has nothing so orthodox as a surname. Just Dava.'

Nick snorted in derision.

'There's worse.' Cat looked down at her notes. 'A psychic surgeon has started practising up there.'

Gerald Tait looked round at the others. 'This is a new one to me. What in heaven's name is a "psychic surgeon"?'

'May I interpose here?' Aidan put up his hand to straighten the bow tie which was not in the least crooked. I know what it is about bow ties, Cat thought, it's not just that they're prissy, it's that they remind me of all the smoothie gynaecologists I've met.

'I do happen to know a bit about psychic surgery. Though I confess I'd no idea we were graced with a local practitioner and I must agree, it's an appalling thought. It is overwhelmingly a foreign practice and of course it's a form of trickery done usually quite cleverly, but anyone who can bust a magician or knows a bit about conjuring can tell you how it works. They prey upon the poor and the gullible and they treat those without hope. But of course there has to be a success rate of sorts, otherwise they'd quickly run out of clients, so they have accomplices.'

'Like all the best magicians,' Chris said. 'The girl who helps with the sawing in half, the plant in the audience who volunteers himself to be blindfolded before picking a card.'

'Exactly. The accomplices pose as patients with anything from an apparent broken leg to an intestinal tumour. They come along with case notes, letters from bogus consultants and so on, and, of course, they are cured and proclaim that a miracle has been performed on them, so lo and behold, the queues form.'

'Dear God, are there no limits to what people will do to con others out of their money?' Gerald said. 'Haven't we taught the British public anything in several centuries of successful orthodox medicine?'

'You'd be surprised,' said Aidan, 'if you knew how many people come to me who should have gone straight to their GP – which is where I send them, I hasten to add. But if I were unscrupulous I could do a lot of damage and make a fortune into the bargain. People want to believe. They want to believe that an acupuncturist can cure congenital blindness and Down's syndrome and a club foot and even reverse the ageing process. Don't imagine I treat even half those who come to me. Perhaps the same goes for Nick.'

'Less so,' Nick Haydn said. 'Osteopaths are seen as practically orthodox – we're thought of in the same breath as physiotherapists. But I've had plenty of people come to me with broken ankles and even once a broken neck because they thought I'd sort them out better than A & E would.'

'I'd like to hear more about this psychic surgery,' Gerald Tait interrupted.

Cat listened as Aidan Sharpe gave them a lecture on the practice. The 'surgeon', even though he was practising sleight of hand, actually touched and manipulated the bodies of his clients, scoring their flesh with his thumbnail or a round-ended stick which he had palmed, to mark and bruise but not cut, and then he pretended to remove tissue of various kinds from inside the body.

'And you're telling us, this is what is going on ten miles from here, Cat? Dear God. Something has to be done.'

'That's why I wanted us to meet. The point is, Gerald, we need to show somehow that we, as orthodox medics, approve of genuine alternative practitioners like Aidan and Nick, then maybe people would guess the others don't have our imprimatur?'

'Can't the police do anything? Can't you ask your brother?'

'I've actually been trying to do just that for the last week, but Lafferton police are up to their necks in a drug operation and I haven't managed to speak to him, but I do plan to talk to him about it.'

'Good.'

'Meanwhile, I think it's very good that we're meeting like this and I do want to thank you – 'Aidan said in his precise way, 'for your hospitality of course, but also for your gesture of faith in Nick and myself . . . it is very much appreciated.'

'Seconded,' Nick said, making a face at Cat while Aidan had turned away.

Aidan offered his coffee cup for a refill. 'This is a wake-up call to everyone, if I may so express it.'

'Look.' Nick uncrossed his long legs. 'We're all agreed that there are some cranks about and one or two may possibly even be dangerous but I just wonder if we have any authority at all to try and hound them out of town. We have to be very careful here. I think the legal aspect has to be crystal clear before we attempt to do anything.'

'I agree,' Chris Deerbon said firmly, 'and I'm more anti the whole complementary scene than anyone here. We can't play God, however much we'd like to.'

They argued round in circles for some minutes. Cat was frustrated. Her idea had been to establish a consensus straight away and then draw up a battle plan and it was not working out. But then Aidan took charge.

'We're getting nowhere,' he said. 'I think we need to look hard at what we want to achieve, focus on what seems the most urgent and leave the rest aside. Firstly, Cat, I take it that one of your ideas was to form some sort of group or alliance between ourselves and perhaps other interested GPs and qualified complementary therapists, so that you, the doctors, know which of us you would be happy to have your patients consult, if they ask you, and who you would not.'

'That's more or less right, yes.'

'But secondly, your concern is to weed out those who may be actively dangerous. There's plenty of baloney but then people will always lay themselves open to that and I really feel it's up to them – astrology is baloney, crystal healing is baloney.'

'Candles in children's ears.'

'Iridology.'

'Reflexology.'

'No, that's respectable,' Nick Haydn put in.

Cat raised her hand. 'Carry on please, Aidan'

'Thank you. What really worries us, I think I'm right in saying, is the therapist who hands out medicines and the therapist who may do some actual physical harm – your psychic surgeon.'

'I would also want to add that those who may do the most harm are the ones who, through inadequate knowledge, miss something really serious in a patient. They are doing harm by default.'

'Should we perhaps divide things between us? Cat,

you were going to ask your brother about the policing aspect.'

'Fine. And we can all start keeping notes of any alternative therapists we come across.'

'Maybe a nice colour-coding system? Red for danger, blue for OK, green for thoroughly recommended,' Nick suggested. 'Bags I be green.'

'It's the reds that are important,' Aidan Sharpe said.

The Tape

Of course I didn't tell you. How could I have told you? This is the first time you have heard anything about it. I managed to conceal it from you for all those years and I'm very proud of that because if you had ever found out I would have had to disappear to the other side of the world, because although it was not my fault, you would have blamed me as you always blamed me for everything.

I had worked incredibly hard, staying up night after night learning the things that were so difficult for me, the grind of chemical formulae, pharmacology, tropical diseases – everything I found uninteresting but had to know. They were a means to an end and it was only the thought of the end that got me through. I didn't go out, never socialised, and after a time, no one bothered to invite me even for a quick pint in the bar at the end of the day. They had soon learned that they would be rebuffed. I was a misfit and a swot, they couldn't get the measure of me and they couldn't be bothered to go on trying. I would have liked a few friends, people to talk to in depth, but I hated the noisy camaraderie of the medical school bar, the crude humour, the smutty talk and especially the practical jokes. So when I was not studying or attending post-mortems, I went running. I became extremely fit and I loved that feeling of power and speed as I pounded off through the streets and out into the country, crossing the moors or making my way down to the miles of flat beach. Running. I wish I had kept it up. I am still fairly fit and do my half-hour of exercises morning and evening, but after I broke my leg I could never run as far and as fast so I stopped. I like to do everything well or not at all.

I worked. It often seemed as if I did nothing else – working and running, working and running – but I was focused on the end purpose.

If only I had not been impatient and tried to hurry that end forward. If only I had not made my single mistake and been found out.

I was truly shocked to discover quite recently that medical students in many schools no longer dissect corpses, just as school pupils studying biology at Advanced level no longer dissect dogfish and frogs and so on, as we did. Computer programs, virtual reality, charts and diagrams and plastic models are all replacing the dissection and the first time many medical students now put a scalpel into flesh is in the operating theatre.

We learned our trade properly. But the bodies we dissected in those first years bore little relation to real human beings or even to the freshly dead. They were wizened and ancient, preserved and unreal, and although they served their purpose and I found them interesting enough, I wanted more, and when I entered the pathology room for the first time, I knew that I had found it. I became a joke with the teams there but the senior staff admired my ambition and seriousness, I know that, and were privately marking me out as one of their own, a future colleague. They didn't get so many that they could afford to treat me with indifference. Medical students who long to become forensic pathologists are few, even in these days of graphic television drama.

The place became a second home. Towards the end I was observing a post-mortem just about every day, sometimes several.

After a time, of course, watching did not satisfy me, it was not enough. I wanted to start doing the job myself and the knowledge that I would have to wait several more years until I qualified and got through my other specialties was deeply frustrating. I lived with that for about a year. Then, one night I looked up from 'Congenital Diseases of the Eye' and knew what I was going to do. It was so obvious I could not understand why I had not thought of it before, but the moment I did, I jumped from having the idea to starting to plan how I would carry it out in a couple of minutes. I set aside the textbook, forgot the eye and began to think, and the excitement that welled up inside me was like none I had experienced before.

Twenty-Two

Sandy walked from the shower into her bedroom wrapped in a towelling dressing gown at the moment the pips sounded for the eleven o'clock news on her bedside radio. As she heard them, she felt a flicker of anxiety. Debbie had not said that she would be out or left a note and that was unusual, but she had been going to the occasional meeting of one of the groups she had joined at Starly – weirdo groups, Sandy privately thought, but she had said nothing because she was so glad her friend was cheering up and getting together the beginnings of some sort of social life. The meetings did not usually go on late though – until tonight, Debbie had been back by ten, drinking her mug of the vile-smelling herbal tea and telling Sandy all about New Age beliefs, chakras, auras and goodness knows what else. Sandy always listened and asked interested questions and she had to admit that Debbie was looking better, far better – her skin was clearing up, though that was almost certainly because of Dr Deerbon's antibiotics, her eyes were clear and her hair, which she had had well cut in a becoming shorter style, was no longer lank and greasy, and she had definitely lost weight. You couldn't knock something that was so clearly doing her good.

Sandy got out her manicure set and bag of nail varnishes, and took them into the sitting room, where she watched an old episode of *Friends* while removing the Peony Pink from her fingernails and replacing it with Sugar Icing. *Friends* was particularly funny and she revelled in it. Debbie would have done too, she thought, when it was over. It was five past twelve now. Sandy began to wander about the flat, putting on the kettle and making a cup of tea which she left to go cold, switching on the radio and turning it off again. Once, she even went out into the street. It was empty and quiet and few lights were still on – everyone around here had to go off to work early in the morning. Sandy waited for a moment. It was a lovely night, mild and dry. Debbie would come at any minute, walking briskly down the road or maybe even arriving in a minicab as the last bus would have gone by now. A black cat streaked across the road and vanished into the hedge. A car turned in at the top of the avenue, but it was not a cab and simply sped by and away.

At ten to one, Sandy went to the telephone. She had got dressed again, feeling uneasily that she might have to go out, that Debbie could have had an accident and would need her at the hospital. She lifted the receiver but then put it down again, hearing what she thought was an engine. She looked through the front-room curtains and saw a car turning into a driveway on the opposite side of the road and dousing its lights.

Half past one. She went into Debbie's room and looked around for the book in which she kept addresses

235

and phone numbers. There might be a note of a meeting. Then she saw Debbie's handbag hanging over the back of a chair. Sandy stared at it. Wherever she had gone, she would have taken her big brown bag. She hesitated then unzipped it and looked inside. Wallet, lipstick, comb, tissues, notebook, a paperback about meditation, some paperclips . . . all the usual rubble. Her house keys had gone, and her inhaler, which Dr Deerbon had prescribed after the asthma attack and told Debbie she must always carry on her.

Sandy was puzzled. There was no way Debbie would have gone out to a meeting or an evening with one of her new friends at Starly without her bag. She went back to the telephone. It was twenty minutes to two.

The patrol car was at the door within five minutes, bringing a cheerful older policeman and a young policewoman who seemed irritated by Sandy's story. They declined her offer of tea and sat in the kitchen asking the usual questions.

'I'll go and look at her room if you'll show me please,' the young WPC said. She had given her name as Louise Tiller.

Sandy took her into Debbie's bedroom. 'You won't find anything, I'm afraid,' she said.

'If you could leave me to be the judge of that.'

'But her handbag is here and she would never have left that if she'd been going out for the evening.'

'Well, she might have taken another. People do have more than one.'

'No,' Sandy said, 'she doesn't actually.'

'How long have you two been together?'

'What, flatmates? – about a year.'

'Flatmates is all it is then?'

Sandy flushed. She had taken a great dislike to WPC Tiller.

'Yes, it is.'

'OK. This the bag?'

'Yes.'

The policewoman picked it up, crossed over to the bed and tipped the contents out so that they spilled in a pile in front of her. She then began to rummage through them, picked up the notebook and flipped the pages over.

'I imagine you've telephoned all these people to check if she's with them?'

'Well . . . no . . . she wouldn't have gone out for the evening without her bag.'

WPC Tiller sighed and walked out of the room abruptly, leaving the contents of the bag strewn on Debbie's bed. Sandy followed her.

'Nothing there, Dave.'

He stood up. 'Look, Miss Marsh, I think you'll find your friend went out, it got late and she's stayed overnight with someone.'

'She'd never do that. Not without telling me. Not without ringing. And she wouldn't have left her handbag behind.'

'She did that, did she?'

PC Dave Grimes frowned. His own wife seemed to be joined at the hip to whichever bag was currently in favour – she carried her life in it.

'She's shacked up with a man she met at the pub then,' the policewoman said in a bored voice.

'No.'

'What makes you so sure?'

'Debbie isn't like that.'

'Like what?'

'Debbie doesn't go to pubs and . . . look, I know her, I live with her, she's been my friend since we were at primary school. This is just not like her. She – she was pretty depressed until recently, but now she's been feeling better and –'

'It's all right, I know what you're trying to tell us.' The policeman spoke gently to her. 'This is out of character. Some people go out until all hours and all over the place and no one would dream of reporting them as missing unless they didn't come home for weeks. Other people would never dream of doing it – they ring in, they leave messages or they just don't go off at all.'

'If there's a psychiatric history it puts a different complexion on things though, doesn't it?'

Sandy stared at WPC Tiller. She could hardly speak for anger and distress. 'What do you mean?'

'A history of depression.'

'All right, Louise. There isn't really anything we can do tonight, Miss Marsh, and I'm sure your friend will come home in the morning. If you haven't heard from her by then, let us know and we'll take it further.'

WPC Tiller had already stalked out of the door. The constable reached for his helmet. 'It won't be easy, but try and get some sleep. You did exactly the right thing by calling us.'

Sandy was grateful to him and dismissed the WPC as an uppity cow. All the same, what she had implied was worrying. Debbie had been better, much better. But depression was a funny thing, Sandy knew, and it might have come over Debbie again suddenly and without warning, so that she might . . .

'Stop it,' she said, 'stop that now.'

She made herself a drink, filled a hot-water bottle and

went to bed with the Maeve Binchy paperback she had bought earlier that day. Perhaps she might read herself to sleep.

It was half past three before she dropped off, six when she woke again. She got quickly out of bed and went straight to Debbie's room. It was empty and exactly as they had left it the previous night. The rest of the flat was empty too. Sandy sat at the kitchen table looking at the rectangle of pearly-grey sky above the next door roof. She felt wretched, tired and with aching muscles from sleeping so tensely. But there was something else, which she did not at first recognise, almost like a pain in her chest. Then she realised that it was fear. She was afraid for Debbie. Whatever casual assurances WPC Louise Tiller had made about her having stayed overnight with friends, Sandy knew that she had not done so, never would have done it in a thousand years. But what had she done? Where had she gone? Why had she not come home?

She went into the sitting room and checked that the phone was working, and then found her mobile and checked that. Then she rang Bevham General A & E. No casualties answering to her description of Debbie. Her next call was to work, to say she wouldn't be in. After that, she showered, dressed, burned her mouth drinking a mug of tea which was too hot, and went to Lafferton Police Station.

DC Nathan Coates picked up on the routine report about a missing girl. When Freya came, a copy was on her desk.

'What do you think, Sarge?' he said.

She scanned the details. 'Hospitals?'

'Nothing.'

'Hm.' Freya went to get herself the first coffee of the day. The phrase 'psychiatric history' had jumped out, making it likely this was a depressed girl who had taken herself off because of a particularly low mood and who would turn up, hopefully alive but possibly dead if she had been suicidal. She stood on the landing, sipping from the plastic cup. That was the most likely scenario, and yet . . . there was something about this one, something not right; Freya had never trusted colleagues who talked about having hunches about cases, but once in a while she had to admit that she herself got just such a gut feeling. She had one now. This was one missing-person report which she did not intend to see filed away to gather dust.

Nathan came through the swing doors behind her. 'Sarge, the flatmate is downstairs. Come in just now to report still no sign.'

If it had not been the sort of business about which there was nothing remotely amusing, Freya would have smiled at the look of eagerness on his face. He had latched on to the case of Angela Randall and here was something new and possibly relevant to it. Nathan sensed action and after too much time trawling through records at the computer, action was what he needed. Freya threw her empty cup in the bin and headed for the stairs. On the whole, she was with him.

By the time she had finished talking to Sandy she was more than satisfied that the links were positive. The missing girl's flatmate had been white-faced and almost incoherent with anxiety and it had taken all Freya's skill to soothe her and extract the detail. The first thing she asked about was Debbie Parker's mental state and the girl had leaped to her defence angrily.

'Look, she was depressed for a bit. She lost her job and she . . . she had really low self-esteem . . . she's a bit overweight and . . . Look, I don't want to be disloyal, I'm not criticising her, you do understand that, she's my best friend and I feel responsible for her.'

'That's exactly why you need to tell me everything, Sandy. And of course you're not being disloyal. You want her found fast and we will put everything into it, but you mustn't hold anything back out of misplaced feelings of loyalty.'

'Yes, I see. OK, well, she's more than a bit, she's quite a lot overweight. That got worse after she lost her job and got depressed and she's had bad acne. But she was just coming out of all that, you see, she went to see a therapist up at Starly and he gave her a really good diet – not a slimming diet, not dangerous, just really sensible eating.'

'Have you the name and address of the therapist?'

'Well . . . just a name. He calls himself Dava.'

'Dava?'

'Debbie's never mentioned a surname. I said she was to be careful but I think it was harmless . . . well, apart from the stuff he gave her to take.'

Freya looked up sharply. 'Stuff?'

Sandy told her about Debbie's allergic reaction.

'Is it in the flat still?'

'No, Dr Deerbon took it away. She said she wanted to find out from someone at the hospital what was in it.'

Freya made a note. 'Do you think Debbie could have gone to see this man last night?'

'I doubt it. We don't have secrets even though we lead different sorts of lives. Besides, she'd never go anywhere far without taking her bag.'

The bag. Freya had flagged that mentally as soon as she had read the first report. No female went out for an evening, or even for an hour, without taking her bag, and according to Sandy, it was the only one Debbie Parker owned and everything had been in it.

'Only she took her house keys,' the girl said now.

'You might do that if you slipped out to the corner shop for a pint of milk.'

'We don't have a corner shop and she didn't take her purse.'

'Now, you're quite sure . . . think hard, Sandy . . . quite sure, that she hadn't had any bad news, or had a sudden really low patch? Depression's a treacherous thing, it can strike again even when people feel they've turned a corner.'

'I know she was better, I know it. She was feeling good about herself for the first time in ages, she was losing weight, looking pretty, she talked about looking for another job in a while. She was taking exercise. That's why I didn't worry when I first got in. She sometimes went out for long walks . . . she said she wasn't up to jogging or running yet but when she got fitter she would.'

Oh God, Freya thought. 'If she went out for a long walk she wouldn't have taken her handbag, would she?'

'No, it would just get in the way. It's a big bag.'

'But she would take her house keys.'

'Yes. So that's what I thought. At first. Just for an hour, but then it got dark and time went on and I knew she wouldn't have been walking until after midnight.'

'Did she walk anywhere in particular, take a regular route, do you know, or did she just go where the fancy took her? That's what I think I'd do.'

'In the daytime she might walk all the way into town, perhaps go to a shop or have a coffee there. But mostly she went on to the Hill.'

Freya's heart sank at the same time as she felt a surge

of excitement. That made three, three for definite. The mountain biker, Angela Randall and now Debbie Parker. Three people who had gone walking or running or riding alone on the Hill. Three people who had disappeared without trace, leaving no message, no hint or clue. Three people who, so far as anyone could tell, had no reason to go missing deliberately, and of whom there had been no report or sighting anywhere.

'What will happen now? What will you do? You are going to look for her, aren't you? Only the policewoman who came last night seemed so dismissive, and I really don't think you should just be –'

'Dismissive in what way exactly?'

'She didn't seem to take it very seriously. I got quite upset actually, because she seemed to think it was obvious that if Debbie had been depressed she must have . . . must have, you know . . .'

'It is not obvious at all. I believe you, Sandy. You know your friend, you should be able to tell. I don't think it at all likely that Debbie felt depressed enough to want to harm herself. But I had to ask you the question, you do understand that?'

'Yes, and anyway, how you asked it was different.'

'OK. I think you might go home now, in case Debbie comes back.'

'I ought to ring her dad and stepmum, oughtn't I?'

'Hold on a bit – maybe till lunchtime. Then if she hasn't come back, yes, but try not to panic them. I'd like to put out a message on Radio BEV, asking if anyone has seen Debbie. Could you go through her things and see if you can work out what she was wearing when she went out? I'll come and see you later and we'll go through with you what I want them to broadcast so you can make sure it's right. Now, here's a card with the station number, and my extension. If I'm out and you need to leave a message or just talk to someone, speak to DC Nathan Coates who'll be working with me on this.'

She watched the girl walk slowly away across the station forecourt, her head bent, slight, pretty, desperately worried. As well she might be, Freya thought, heading up the stairs to the DI's office.

He wasn't there. Freya went back to the CID room to where Nathan was patiently entering data on to the computer. When he heard her brief report on the missing girl his face lit up.

'We go for it, right?'

'Yes, except that Cameron isn't in his office.'

'Cameron's off,' someone shouted from another desk. 'Got a hospital appointment.'

Freya knew that the DI had been waiting to see a consultant about what he called his 'dodgy stomach' for several weeks. She tapped her pen on the side of her desk for a few seconds. So he was off, maybe for the day, certainly for the rest of the morning, which meant she had no alternative, didn't it? This one couldn't wait.

'Is that drugs op still on?' she asked Nathan. He shook his head. 'They wrapped it up yesterday, for the time being.'

'Successful?'

'I heard they landed a few small fry. The big fish got wind. What's next then, Sarge?'

'That,' Freya said, making for the swing doors, 'is just what I'm off to find out.'

Interestingly, because it was work, and she was keyed up about it, Freya did not feel the trembling sense of anticipation at merely seeing and talking to Simon Serrailler that she had been unable to control the last time she had knocked on his door. Angela Randall and Debbie Parker were at the front of her mind and she wanted to get the wheels turning. She was pleased DI Cameron was off, mainly because she thought that being able to bypass him might mean that happened faster.

'Come in.'

As she heard his voice her heart jumped.

'Freya . . . I hope you've got good news. I could do with it.'

'Not exactly, sir, sorry.'

He shoved the fair hair back from where it flopped over his forehead. He looked tired.

'Heigh-ho. What have you got? Sit down, sit down.'

She outlined the facts about Debbie Parker, and then quickly related her case to that of Angela Randall, with the relevant links to the mountain biker neatly placed at the end. It was the sort of summary she knew she was good at, succinct but comprehensive, highlighting the most important points for him to pick up, ignoring incidental detail about which he could be briefed later if necessary. He gave her his full attention, listening without interruption. When she had finished he was silent for thirty seconds or so, then he gave a funny little jerk of his head which she was to recognise as a sign that he had digested information and made a decision.

'You're right. Your instinct was sound. The three together – and certainly the two missing women – look like more than coincidence. We've got to find this girl, Debbie Parker . . . What do you propose?'

'Local radio appeal for information. Piece in the evening paper, tonight if possible, with her photograph, as prominent as they'll do it. Posters, but on hold for say forty-eight hours. And a full search of the Hill. Interview the therapist at Starly Tor.'

'Good. What about the father and stepmother?'

'I told the flatmate to hold off a bit longer in case Debbie turned up.'

He looked at his watch. 'No, they need to be told now. Get them down here. I want every blade of grass on the Hill looked under. I want the reports on Angela Randall and the biker on my desk and I'd like you to go up to Starly and take this hippie practitioner apart.'

She got up. 'I'll get on with it.'

'Who do you want with you?'

'Nathan Coates. He's already doing some checking for me and he's raring to go.'

Serrailler laughed. 'Perfect. And good work, Freya.'

She made for the door. There was nothing like it – suspecting that an incident was important, having your suspicions taken seriously, making out a good case and being given the go-ahead. This was what she loved best about the job; cases like this were what had made life at the Met bearable through the dull patches, the frustrating jobs and the sordid ones, and certainly what had enabled her to close her mind to her disastrous marriage during working hours. It had been a case at which she had worked away quietly by herself for weeks because she hadn't been happy when it was officially downgraded, and about which she had been proved triumphantly right, that had clinched promotion. She thought about DI Cameron and his hospital appointment. She would never wish serious illness upon anyone but, on the other hand, Nathan had hinted more than once that Cameron was only marking time until he could retire . . . which would mean a vacancy for DI.

She crossed the CID room almost at a run, signalling thumbs up to Nathan on her way.

'We're on. The DCI is going for it. Uniform will be combing the Hill, and there's a local radio appeal going out. I need to have the flatmate in here again – can you get a car to pick her up, Nathan? – then ring Radio BEV newsdesk and alert them. I'm going to write the appeal for info and we're passing that to the *Echo* for this evening as well. Oh, and can you ask Sandy Marsh to bring in a photo of Debbie if she can find one, the more recent the better?'

Nathan jumped for his phone. 'What's for me after that, Sarge?'

'You and I are having a drive out to Starly. We can have a dandelion sandwich at the wholefood café.'

Twenty-Three

'Radio BEV serving Bevham, Lafferton and the county. This is Robbie Muncaster with your local news and weather on Friday lunchtime. Police at Lafferton are appealing for any information about a missing girl. Twenty-two-year-old Debbie Parker of Pyment Drive, Lafferton, has been missing from her home for about twenty-four hours and police say they are growing increasingly concerned. Detective Sergeant Freya Graffham from Lafferton CID.'

'This is a disappearance quite out of character. Debbie Parker has never gone away from home without warning before and we're particularly concerned because she left her handbag with all her belongings in her flat, so she clearly can't have meant to go far or stay out long. We're very anxious for members of the public to report any sighting of Debbie or to give us any information they think might be relevant, however insignificant it may seem. If you think you have seen her, please get in touch with us urgently.'

'The missing girl is described as about five feet four,

plump and with mid-length straight brown hair. She may have been wearing trainers and a fleece jacket and police are particularly interested to hear from anyone who may have seen a young woman answering to her description on or in the area of the Hill. If you have any information at all, please telephone Lafferton CID on 01990 776776.

'A Bevham man has received four thousand pounds in compensation from the firm for which he worked for seventeen years, Wakes Electronics, after . . .'

Sandy Marsh turned off the radio and the kitchen went silent. None of it could be happening. Any minute, Debbie would walk in the front door and the nightmare would be over. Any minute, she would ring and ask what all the fuss was about. Any minute.

Sandy felt guilty, as if by going to the police she had turned Debbie's absence into something sinister and frightening. One minute, she just hadn't come home, the next, the police were on the radio talking about her and it had all got out of control. I should have kept quiet, she thought, then she would have just come back. I should have waited here and . . . Of course she shouldn't. She put the kettle on for yet another mug of tea, because she had to do something, anything to stop it all going round in her head.

Half an hour ago she had rung Debbie's father and stepmother in Stafford but had told them not to come straight down, that Debbie would be in touch, would as likely as not walk in, either to the flat here or maybe even to their house as a surprise. As if, Sandy had thought.

She hadn't told them about the police appeal.

The Detective Sergeant had rung two or three times to check things, and then to read out what was going to be said. She was very nice, very understanding.

'Oh God, Debbie, where are you? Come home, please, just walk in. Please God, let her just walk in.'

She dropped a tea bag into her mug and filled it. Debbie was her friend and her flatmate and she cared about her but what must it be like if it was your child who had gone missing, or your husband? She couldn't go to work, because she knew she would be good for nothing there. She'd told them exactly what was going on, not given them some lie about feeling ill. They'd been really good, told her not to think of coming in until Debbie was back, and asked if she wanted anyone to come over to the flat to keep her company. Last week, it had occurred to her that as Debbie was so much better, she might see if there was a job for her at Macaulay Prentice, maybe part time. Her old job at the building society would be good experience for working with credit control.

Where is she? Sandy drummed her fist suddenly on the kitchen table. *Where is she?*

The phone rang, making her leap up. It wasn't Debbie but her father, wanting to know if there was any news. Sandy tried to sound reassuring, not to alarm him, not to dramatise things. Not yet. But if Debbie hadn't returned or rung by the time the *Echo* ran its piece, DS Graffham had said the family ought to be asked if they wanted to come down to Lafferton.

Sandy had found a snapshot of Debbie taken at an ice rink they'd gone to last winter, for a Saturday-afternoon laugh; they'd blow that up and have it on the front page of the paper. It was real. It was happening and she wouldn't wake up out of any dream. Debbie had been missing for – how long was it? As she tried to work it out Sandy realised for the first time that when she had got up and left for work the previous morning, she hadn't actually seen her friend. In the old days, she had made a point of going in, drawing her curtains, taking her tea and trying to get her to start the day, but since she had been so much more cheerful, and Sandy was not worried about her spending the whole day miserably in bed trying to blot out life, she hadn't done that. Mostly now, Debbie was up at the same time as her, but occasionally she had a lie-in, and Sandy left her to it. She knew it was only for an extra half-hour. She didn't worry now.

Had Debbie been in bed asleep when she had left for work yesterday? She had assumed so but now it dawned on her that she did not actually know, could not have sworn to it. She had definitely been in the previous night, though; they had watched *Coronation Street* together and then the video of *Ocean's Eleven*.

She probably had been in bed asleep the next morning but once or twice, since she had first seen the Dava man, she had gone out for one of her new long walks early in the morning.

Sandy went into the sitting room and from there into her bedroom and then came back to the kitchen again, unable to calm down, not knowing what to do, whether to ring the police station, whether she had done wrong not to think of all this earlier. It wasn't that she had been holding anything back, it had just never occurred to her. And after all, she didn't know and she couldn't be sure either way. Debbie might have been in. Debbie might not have been in. Debbie probably had been in. Debbie –

The phone rang again.

'Sandy, Freya Graffham. I thought you'd like to know we've already had a lot of calls in response to the Radio BEV appeal, several of them are quite helpful, and we're following them up.'

'Has someone seen her then? Do they know where she is?'

'Nothing specific yet. There are some obvious hoaxers but that's quite usual and we can weed them out at once. How are you?'

Sandy swallowed. 'OK. Listen . . .'

'Have you remembered something?'

'Yes,' Sandy said, 'No . . . it's . . .'

'Hold on . . . don't try and tell me over the phone, Sandy, you sound upset. I'll come round.'

An hour later, having heard what Sandy Marsh had to say, Freya drove up to the Hill to find a full search underway. Police were spread out in a line moving slowly up the steep paths combing the ground, others were beating the scrub and undergrowth. The whole area had been sealed off. As she got out of her car, she saw Simon Serrailler talking to the uniformed inspector in charge of the search, and went across. The hunt for Debbie Parker was at the forefront of her mind now and all her energies and attention were focused on it, but a part of her reacted to the sight of him with a spurt of pleasure; she suppressed it, putting her feelings into a locked area of herself, to be ignored as far as possible while the investigation was going on.

'Freya?' He turned to her at once. 'Anything?'

'Not sure.' She nodded to the inspector who detached himself and went back to the police van which was the meeting point of the search team.

'I've just been to see Sandy Marsh, Debbie's flatmate. She's very distressed. It suddenly occurred to her that she didn't actually see Debbie yesterday morning. She was certainly there the previous night. They spent the evening in the flat watching television and Sandy went into her room later to borrow some tissues at about half eleven. Debbie was in bed and already fast asleep. So Sandy slipped in and out without waking her. But Sandy wonders if she might have got up before she did the next morning and gone for one of her long walks.'

Serrailler frowned. 'Any response from the radio appeal?'

'Lots of calls, the usual time-wasters, nothing concrete. Sir, I think we ought to put out another appeal and mention Angela Randall's disappearance as well. Time has gone by on that one but I'm sure the two are linked. Someone's memory might be jogged by this into remembering the other woman.'

'It might, but I'd rather we held off until Debbie's parents are here and we've had a chance to fill them in. I don't want them hearing a radio mention of another missing woman before they know the full picture from us and I don't want the press having any excuse to start howling "SERIAL KILLER" in foot-high headlines.'

'Right.'

'What are you doing now?'

'I'm going back to the station to pick up Nathan Coates and then to Starly to track down this therapist.'

'Dava.' The DCI made a face. 'I'd like to hear my mother on the subject.' They smiled at each other, recognising a mutual understanding of Meriel Serrailler.

'Your mother has asked me to help her with a spring fair, by the way.'

'Well, watch out. She has jaws of steel.'

'I'm not even sure what it's for . . . a day centre?'

'Yes. She's patron. It's a day centre for the elderly with

dementia and related problems. Once she's landed you for that it'll be St Michael's Hospice.'

'Of which she is patron?'

'President.'

It was pleasant, standing in the winter sunshine, talking to him, both of them relaxed, jokey, for a moment setting aside the reason for being here. He had a way of meeting her eyes and smiling, not flirtatiously but simply as if he liked her and wanted to talk to her about other things in their lives than work. Stay the moment, Freya thought, stay the moment.

'I owe a lot to your mother. She's made me welcome and introduced me to people, friends. It isn't easy starting again in a new place.'

'I can imagine. You'll find Lafferton a bit of a gossip shop though. We're really a hick market town with a cathedral. Still, it must be easier to make new friends here than in London.'

'Do you know, I don't think I ever want to see London again.'

'You will, you will.'

'There's no one I miss.'

He met her glance again. He was direct, she thought, he did not evade.

'Starly, DS Graffham,' he said now.

'Yes, sir.'

She carried his smile with her for the rest of the day.

Twenty-Four

'Colin . . .'

He had never before heard Annie shout and this wasn't a shout you ignored. The place could have been on fire.

'Colin . . .' She came in without knocking.

'Have you heard the news on Radio BEV?'

'Well, of course I haven't, I've had clients all morning.'

'It's one of them has gone missing. Headline news.'

Colin Davison, aka Dava, had hung his robe up and was shrugging on his denim jacket. He had had clients wall-to-wall since nine o'clock, with only time for a mug of coffee – real Blend 37, not the dandelion muck – and he was hungry. But what his secretary had just said was alarming.

'Who are we talking about, Annie? Calm down.'

'She came earlier in the week and once before, I've looked her up. Debbie. Debbie Parker.'

'You know I forget them ten seconds after they've left the room.'

'Plump girl with spots.'

He remembered perfectly well. She had been one of the instantly trusting ones, drinking everything in and determined to turn her life around. The second time she had been, the change had already been noticeable. It took so little, he had thought, nothing they couldn't have done for themselves, yet they came to him, and came back for more, needing permission, needing to be led by the hand, without any confidence in themselves. He felt sorry for them really.

'So what's happened to her?' He checked his pockets. 'Have you got a fiver?'

'In my desk drawer, but listen . . . it was headlines, I said. The police are appealing for anyone who's seen her. She hasn't been home.'

'Yeah, right, lots of people don't go home, home stinks, they've had it up to here with home, you can't blame them.'

He walked out of his room through to the cubbyhole Annie had as an office and got the tin out of the desk. Seventy-five pounds.

'The last two paid cash,' Annie said coming up behind him, 'but don't take it all, Colin, there's an electricity bill to pay.'

He took thirty.

'Do you think you ought to ring them? Say she was up here?'

'What for? I shouldn't think I was the last person to set eyes on her.'

'They asked for any information.'

'Nothing we can give them.'

He looked down at the appointment book. Just one and not until three o'clock and tomorrow, again, just one in the morning. Not good.

'Time to do a spot more advertising,' he said to Annie. 'I'll give it some thought over my sarnie.'

Colin Davison looked ordinary, walking down the hill towards the Green Man Wholefood Café, an insignificant man anywhere between forty and fifty with nothing of the charismatic Dava about him. Something happened when he dimmed the lights and put on his robe, something came over him to give him power and presence whenever a client walked in. He felt it and he knew it worked. Colin was no cynic. In his own way he believed in what he did, though by no means in everything he said. Look at this girl, Debbie . . . See how she'd benefited from it. He did what other people could not – doctors, psychiatrists, even beauticians.

If he tarted it up a bit, that was harmless enough and it all helped – the blue card, the appointment at the time 'most propitious for you', the music he played, the lines he gave them to learn. They needed him.

The café was quite full, and as he went in Stephen Garlick saw him and indicated a spare seat next to him in the window. Colin got a plate of cheese-and-tomato quiche and salad and a cinnamon muffin and took them over. He liked Stephen, who kept the shop that did next-to-no business selling candles and incense burners, wind chimes and dream catchers, eco-friendly washing powder and face creams not tested on animals, and books about everything from feng shui to vegan cookery. He was a bit of a dreamer, and a 100 per cent believer, recycler and animal rights activist, honest and incorruptible. Sometimes, when he was with Steve, Colin felt slightly ashamed.

'Hi.'

'Health and happiness,' Steve said. 'I was hoping to catch you.'

'Problem?'

'Yes, but not mine. Or, well, not only mine. Have you heard about the person who's taken 12 Hen Lane?'

Colin shook his head, his mouth full of the warm and very good quiche. They could cook here, especially the pastry. You just had to avoid some of the weirder stuff.

'His name is Anthony Orford.'

Colin looked blank.

'No one is sure exactly where he's come from, possibly the north of England though somebody else said Brighton. He moves around every few years, maybe when things get a bit hot for him.'

'God, you're not on the grapevine, you *are* the grapevine. Who is this guy?'

'An alternative therapist.'

Colin put down his fork. 'That's worrying. There are enough of us up here already and too few clients to go round. What's his line?'

'He calls himself a psychic surgeon.'

'Oh my God. I've heard of him. He opens up, he's chock-a-block for months, word gets round about him really fast and they come from all over the country to see him.'

'What's he do exactly?'

'Claims to be taken over by the spirit of some doctor who lived like a hundred years ago and performs operations . . . only they're not. But people seem to think they are.'

'Come again?'

'I'm not sure how he does it but his reputation goes before him. He's cured people of big things . . . tumours, ulcers, MS . . . Once people discover where he is, the queues will form and the rest of us will be empty.'

'It won't do me any harm . . . or this place.' Stephen looked round. 'And I shouldn't think you need to worry, it's different from what you do.'

'Yes, but people choose between us, not many of them go the rounds.' Debbie Parker came to his mind. She'd been to other therapists, she'd told him so, though all of them in Lafferton.

'Did you hear the lunchtime news on local radio? Annie came charging in to tell me. Apparently, there was a police appeal for a girl who's gone missing.'

'Why, do you know her?'

'She came to see me. Fat girl with a bad skin. Nice. Innocent sort of kid. I wouldn't want her to have come to any harm.'

Stephen drained his mug and got up. 'I've got to get my bike's new brake pads put on before I open up.' Stephen was strongly anti-car, though he just about tolerated the fact that Dava needed his old van to travel the seventeen miles from home up to Starly every day.

'Do you know when this chap is opening up?'

'The psychic surgeon? No idea. They're doing work there now though, the decorators are in. Can't be long.'

Colin groaned. He had read enough about Anthony Orford to know he was a serious threat to his own business. He was unsure exactly how he gained his reputation, or whether there was anything to it, though he suspected not and he didn't think he liked the sound of it. Talking to people, getting them to relax and meditate and focus on things outside themselves, even prescribing vitamins and herbal treatments, all the things he himself did, were fine but he had never pretended to be a healer, never claimed to cure any illnesses, though he was sure a lot of people who came to see him were relieved of some stress-related symptoms. Headaches and tiredness and irritable bowel syndrome caused by tension might disappear, though he would never make promises. Cancer and heart disease and multiple sclerosis – that was a whole different ball game and pretending to perform operations on people was way out of line. It shocked him. People like that gave decent therapists like him, trying to make a living and give unhappy people a bit of help, a seriously bad name.

He finished his lunch, walked down to the newsagent to pick up the *Guardian* and then took his usual three-quarters of a mile detour round the town at a fast pace, which was all the exercise he could fit in during the day. As he turned into the top of the lane leading to his consulting room, he saw a black Rover 45 draw up outside. A woman and a man got out and after searching round for a few seconds, as everyone did, found the bell. Colin stayed where he was and watched as Annie opened the door, and let them inside.

He had no clients until three so what was this? He went down the hill and looked at the car. It was anonymous, and there was nothing at all on any of the seats or the parcel ledge, nothing in the door pockets except a folded road map. What kind of people had a completely clean and empty car? He put his key in his door.

'Colin? There you are.' Annie's face was dramatic. 'The police are here.'

Of course. He went into the cubbyhole that served as a cloakroom, washed his hands, rinsed his mouth and retied his ponytail. He had better be like this, ordinary in a jacket, than wearing his robe with his hair flowing. Annie had put them in his room, where the man was examining the wallcharts of the chakras and astrological signs and the woman was sitting with one leg over the other – good legs, he noted – writing something.

'Sorry, I was out on my lunch break. I'm Colin Davison.'

He had always believed in being charming to the police, even if it was only when they stopped you because the exhaust was hanging off the van. It was surprising how often it paid off.

'Detective Sergeant Freya Graffham, and this is DC Nathan Coates.'

Colin shook hands with them both and sat down at his desk. No point, he thought, in pretending he didn't know what this was about.

'I take it you must be here because of Debbie Parker?'

If the policewoman was surprised by his directness she did not acknowledge it by a flicker.

'That's right. How did you hear about her?'

'I didn't, actually, it was Annie, my assistant – she heard the news bulletin on Radio BEV and came in to tell me straight away. It's awful.'

'Debbie was a patient of yours?'

'I call them clients, Sergeant. I'm not a doctor. Yes, she came to see me twice. The second time was only this week. Nice girl.'

'Can you tell me why she saw you? Was she ill?'

'Well, as I said, I'm not a doctor. If someone's actually physically ill and they haven't consulted their GP, I send them straight there. If they have already been and they just need some spiritual uplift and aid with the deepest part of their psyche to help in their healing, that's fine and we work on that.'

'And did Debbie say she'd been to her doctor?'

'Yes.' It seemed better to lie. They weren't going to

know. 'Her real problem was her lack of self-esteem. She needed a lot of work on that. I was beginning to get her to look deeply into herself and discover her true nature, her true path. She had no knowledge of the guidance she could find and she was very responsive.'

Gobbledegook, she was thinking. It might as well have been written across her forehead.

'How'd she seem when she last came here?' The young man, who had one of the ugliest faces he'd ever seen. He and the Debbie girl would have suited one another.

'Well, I told you, we were working together on some of her deep-seated –'

'Yeah, yeah, but did she seem just dead unhappy? You know what I'm saying – as if she might try and run away?'

'If you mean do I think she was suicidal, then no. Nothing like.'

'Do you take any details of your client's personal lives, Mr Davison?'

He quite liked the woman. She was straight, not asking one thing and getting at another. He gave her one of the smiles that never failed.

'Not really. I discover a great deal as I get to know them . . . by intuition, by meditation with them, by what they choose to tell me of themselves. I have names and addresses obviously, and any family relationships which may be inharmonious are often uncovered. I can always sense them. But bare details of parents, siblings, all that, I don't put down.'

'Did Debbie say anything at all in the course of her sessions which you think might give us any lead as to where she might have gone?'

He sat looking at his desk for a long time. The room

was silent. Neither of the detectives moved or interrupted.

In the end, he said, 'I'd need to meditate about it. Debbie had a lot of things that needed straightening out, stuff from her childhood that still affected her . . . I'm not a psychiatrist, you understand, but people recall things that have happened and that are clouding their present well-being, and meditation and other therapies help to clear them away. Debbie wasn't happy about herself but she was getting in tune, getting more positive, beginning to see her way. That's a very exciting time when it happens. She was moving forward.'

'So not as likely to run away as she had been?'

'Her way of running was down into herself, into the darkness.'

'Did she mention any friends – anyone she was thinking of going to see?'

'No.'

'What kind of treatment did you give her?' The man again.

Colin sighed. 'I suggested she change her diet. Wholefoods, fruit and vegetables and wholegrains, plenty of organic mineral water to drink. No dairy fats, sugars or caffeine.'

'Penance then.' The detective constable was grinning at him. It improved his face 100 per cent.

'It benefits most people.'

'I bet. Anything else?'

'Exercise. Debbie didn't take any, or not to speak of. Again, it's advice most people need and it's always beneficial. A lot of what I do is to suggest very obvious lifestyle changes and at the same time we work on spiritual energies and inner harmonies.'

'What kind of exercise?' the sergeant asked.

'She was too unfit to start running or even jogging, and to swim, which is the best of all, she'd have to travel to Bevham. I suggested she start by walking, going a bit further each day, good brisk walks. She needed to be in the fresh air as much as possible, preferably in natural surroundings.'

'Do you know where she went to walk?'

'She mentioned the towpath by the river but I wasn't keen on that. Running water is very therapeutic but towpaths are just the sort of places where flashers and that kind of damaged person lurk. Not a good idea for a young woman on her own.'

'Do you know Lafferton?'

'Yes, but I don't live there.'

'Is there any other place she might have liked to walk?'

'Well, obviously, the Hill. The Wern Stones up there have ancient origins, it's a place of very positive energies. As well as fresh and a good healthy climb.'

'So you suggested she go on the Hill?'

'I can't remember if I actually suggested it – I mean, that might have come from her. She lives near it, doesn't she, and it's the most well-known bit of Lafferton apart from the cathedral, so it would be obvious, wouldn't it?'

'Did she tell you she had actually been walking there? Perhaps when she came back to see you the second time?'

'I don't remember. I've a lot of clients, you know, my appointment book is full weeks on. I think she definitely said she'd been walking . . . and I noticed – you can tell when someone's started to move with the rhythm of the natural world.'

'So she never mentioned going on the Hill to you?'

He didn't like this. He'd been open and straight and given up the time and he didn't like them digging and digging, going on about one thing. What did they think?

'I said –'

'You said you have a lot of clients, yeah, right.'

The woman seemed suddenly warmer and more sympathetic as she leaned slightly forward, holding his glance. 'What you've told us so far is really helpful, Mr Davison. But this is very important. Even the smallest thing someone remembers may help us. We have a major police search covering the Hill at the moment.'

The atmosphere in the room had changed. Suddenly, they were talking life or death. He could picture the line of uniformed men beating with sticks to and fro, to and fro, creeping slowly forwards.

'I do understand,' he said quietly, meeting the woman's eyes. 'I know that the Hill was mentioned as a place she might go as against the towpath but I honestly can't remember if I suggested it or she did. Is that where she was last seen?'

'We're gathering information all the time, Mr Davison.' The sergeant stood up. Her expression was closed as she came out with the bland official language, her moment of apparent intimacy with him finished.

She handed him her card. 'I'd like you to think hard about both your meetings with Debbie Parker. If possible, check any notes you may have made. And if anything, the smallest thing, occurs to you, please phone us as a matter of urgency. It doesn't matter if it turns out to be nothing – let us be the judge of that.'

'Of course. I'll meditate about it tonight after my appointments are over.'

'We'd really appreciate that.' The young man's tone was ironic but when Colin looked at him, his face was blank.

Twenty-Five

'Better, much better. Now we'll take it just once more from the top.'

The choir groaned faintly. They had worked harder tonight than they felt they had ever worked before and it was nine thirty, time for thirsts to be quenched.

'When you're ready, ladies and gentlemen.'

'Sadist,' someone said, just audibly.

The choirmaster, David Lester, smiled.

'Thank you. Now, *Dona nobis pacem . . . Paaaa . . . cem* and please remember, the word means peace . . . Baritones, do not boom . . . concentrate and . . . three four.'

'*Dona nobis pacem . . .*'

In spite of tiredness and dry throats, the music still flowed out of them, inspiring them to better singing than ever. Freya had never felt so absorbed in music nor so moved by what she was singing, difficult though she found it. She listened as the altos rested for several bars, imagining how Britten's mighty oratorio would sound when they had a full orchestra with them in the cathedral rather than just the assistant choirmaster, good as he was, on the piano.

The sound died away softly. No one coughed or stirred for several seconds. David Lester frowned slightly. They waited for him to say he wanted it again, and again . . .

'I do wonder why I have to wait until pub time for you to give of your best. That's all. Thank you, choir.'

They broke up with a clatter of chairs and music stands.

'See you in the Keys?' Joan Younger, who sang next to her in the altos, touched Freya's arm.

'Not sure. I'm whacked tonight.'

'I heard about that missing girl.'

'Yes. Big op.'

'All the more reason why you need to relax.'

'Probably.'

Freya packed her score away in the old black music case she had had since she was at school, and extricated herself from the throng. She had told the truth when she said she was tired, and she had a headache. Days like this were stressful for everyone no matter how case-hardened. She had come to the St Michael's Singers rehearsal in spite of feeling more like a hot bath and early bed, because she knew she needed not only the distraction of the music, but the balm it poured into her and the uplift the act of singing provided. It hadn't failed. She felt more at peace within herself but she didn't feel like an hour of drinking and shouting across the crowded, smoky pub. She had arrived after seven thirty and had to stumble her way through her row when everyone else was already in place. David Lester had stopped and called attention irritably to the nuisance latecomers caused. Now, she walked out alone into the cool, starry night, joyful at being in the fresh air again. Her car was on the other side of the cathedral as there had been no place left when she had arrived, and as she turned the corner, away from the main west door, everything went wonderfully quiet. The houses around her were dark, but there were street lamps, old-fashioned ones like lamps from story books, from which pools of topaz light fell on to the cobbles.

On such a night it was a joy to be walking slowly through these ancient spaces, but as she did so, Freya's mind was filled again with the two missing women. They had been walking or running somewhere alone – but then what had happened and where were they now, safe or in danger, alive or dead? She shivered, not because she was afraid, especially not here in a sacred and protected place, but because inevitably her professional mind returned again to scenes of violence and its aftermath. This was the first case since she had come to Lafferton which had engaged her as fully as many of those she had dealt with in the Met. In spite of herself, she had begun to identify with the two women. She felt under a personal obligation to them. She must do for them what they could not do for themselves.

The search of the Hill had been called off when it grew dark. Nothing had been found. It would be resumed at daybreak and continue either until there was something or the whole area had been combed without result.

She walked the last few yards to her car. She wanted to clear her mind of the case and she could not, would not, now, until it was resolved one way or another. That was the nature of the job and her own nature too. A DI at the Met had once told her it was her weakness.

'To climb right up the ranks you've got to learn detachment, Freya, and you don't seem able to do that. You can't leave things at the end of the day. You take them home. You take them to supper, you take them to bed with you. You'll burn out.'

In a sense, that was exactly what she had done – burned out of the Met. But Lafferton had given her a new life and a new sense of commitment. She knew she let some cases get to her, take her over, insinuate themselves into her dreams, but she was what she was and forcing herself into a different mould would be a betrayal. It would also, she was sure, make her a less effective officer.

Thinking deeply, she took a step off the path as a car swung round the corner, picking her up in its headlights. Freya turned as the driver braked and hooted.

'Freya?'

She was blinded by the glare. The window of the silver BMW slid down as the headlamps dipped.

'Who is this?'

But as she took a couple of steps nearer she saw him with a shock of pleasure.

'Sir?'

'What are you doing walking in the close alone?'

'Coming from a choir practice in the cathedral. I was so late I couldn't get a space so I had to park my car down here.'

'Was my mother singing?'

'Not half. She's gone to the Cross Keys with the others but I didn't feel like it tonight.'

'Hang on.'

He swung his car into a space beside one of the darkened houses, switched off the engine and got out.

'Are you here to look for Meriel?'

He laughed. 'No, to come home. I live here.'

'Good heavens. I didn't think anyone did, I thought this end of the close was just offices.'

'Pretty much. There are offices and there's me. The clergy are all at the top end near the cathedral.'

'Well, well.'

'Come up and see. Come and have a drink at the end of a bad day.'

How easy momentous words often sounded, she thought, how casually spoken a sentence which she would carry with her like a precious object perhaps for the rest of her life. 'Come up and see. Come and have a drink.' She followed him into the dark, silent building and up the stairs, looking at his back, his head, the white-blond hair, his long legs, the shoes he wore, the colour of his socks, remembering, remembering. When you were young you pinched yourself to see if this was really happening, if you were you and awake and alive. Now, she could scarcely breathe but the sense of unreality was the same, the disbelief, the heightened awareness. The joy.

Serrailler. She stared at his name on the plate beside the door. *Serrailler*. The letters were not ordinary letters. The name was illuminated. *Serrailler*.

He walked in ahead of her. Lights went on. Freya stood in the doorway of a room that took the rest of her breath away.

He glanced at her and smiled, the smile he had which lit up his face, the whole room, the space between them. 'Drink? Coffee?'

'It had better be coffee,' she said. Her voice sounded odd but he seemed not to notice.

'Do you mind if I have a whisky?'

'Of course I don't.'

'Sit down.'

He went through a door on the left. More lights, brighter lights on pale walls. The kitchen.

Freya went to the window. The shutters were open and she looked down into the still, lamplit Cathedral Close. In spite of the emotion of being here, in this amazing room at Simon Serrailler's invitation, in spite of her shaking hands, it was the missing women who filled her thoughts again. She feared for them, and the frustration of knowing nothing, having discovered nothing, was unbearable. Every hour that passed meant time during which something might have been done, something vital uncovered. She had gone over and over the case notes, trying to see something she might have missed. She turned and looked again at the room. It was perfect. It had everything she might have chosen, but designed and arranged better than she could have done it – furniture, rugs, pictures, books, the lighting exactly right, the spaces between exactly right. She walked across to look at a set of four framed drawings in a group above the chocolate-brown leather sofa. They were of Venice – the domes of Santa Maria Salute and San Giorgio Maggiore, plus two churches she did not know, the line vibrant and clear, the detail minute and yet beautifully economical. The initials SO were just visible in each lower right-hand corner.

'Here we are.' He came out of the kitchen with a tray and set down cafetière, milk and sugar and small pottery mug on the low table.

'Who did these? I love them.'

'I did.'

'I didn't realise.'

'Intent to deceive . . . O is my middle initial.'

'Simon, they're beautiful. What are you doing in the police force?'

'Ah, but would I enjoy art so much if I did it twenty-four/seven? Drawing keeps me sane.' He went to a white-painted cube on the wall, opened the front and took out a whisky bottle and glass.

'Do you paint as well?'

'No. It's line I love – I work in pencil, pen and charcoal, never colour.'

'How long have you done it?'

'Always. I went to art school but I left because no one was interested in drawing or the teaching of drawing. It was a bad time. Everyone wanted conceptual stuff. Installation art. I wasn't interested.'

'But then –' Freya sat down on the sofa – 'the police force?'

'I went to university to read law so that I could come in on fast track as a graduate. It was always either drawing or policing.'

'But your parents are doctors.'

'My entire family going back three generations have been medics. I'm the black sheep.'

'I'd have thought you were a refreshing change.'

'My mother has come round to seeing it a bit like that now.'

'Your father?'

'No.'

He said it in a way that defied her to ask more. She did not, but pressed the plunger on her cafetière and watched it sink slowly down, crushing the layer of coffee grains to the bottom.

Simon took the deep easy chair opposite to her, crossed his long legs easily, and leaned back, whisky in hand. She could scarcely breathe. It was not possible to look at him.

'I didn't get back to the Hill before the search was called off but I presume nothing was found?'

'Nothing at all.' She poured her coffee to keep her head down, her hand shaking.

She wanted him to talk, to get to know the sound of his voice so well that when she had left here she would be able to hear it exactly, carry it with her.

'But we're off duty. How long have you been a choral singer?'

An hour and a half later, Freya had talked about herself and her past life more intimately than she had ever talked to anyone. Simon was a listener, prompting only occasionally and then with nothing more than a word or two, looking at her all the time as she spoke. She found herself talking about her family, her training, the Met, her marriage and its breakdown, and wanting to go on and on, wanting him to know her and everything about her. After a while, she was able to glance at him, to look at his face in the light from the angled lamp behind his chair, in profile, as he drank his whisky, as he faced her again.

She was absolutely in love with him, she knew that now, but tonight had changed things. She no longer wanted to reject this, to swear it away, no longer said Damn, Damn, Damn at the thought and the sight of him and the acute awareness of her reaction. She had never known a man who had given her such full and concentrated attention, who had listened to her and looked at her in this way, as if she were important, what she said mattered and there was nothing else and no one else of interest to him in the world.

The cathedral bells chimed midnight, making her

aware of how long she had talked, how much of herself she had yielded up. She fell silent. His room, this flat, in this corner of the quiet close was the most beautiful, tranquil place she had ever been in, with an atmosphere like no other. Just to sit here, in the silence opposite him, made her tremble.

'Goodness,' she said now.

'Thank you.'

'What for?'

He smiled. 'Telling me so much. People are not often so generous with themselves.'

It was a unique, extraordinary way of putting it. But he is unique, she thought, there can be no one else like him in the world.

'I have to go.'

He neither tried to stop her nor leaped up, eager to see her out. He simply sat on, relaxed and still in the light of the lamp.

'Thank you for this,' Freya said. 'I went to choir so that my mind would stop spinning the case round and round, and singing and then coming here really have given me what I needed.'

'Rest and refreshment. It's important to get as far away as possible from this sort of case . . . if not physically, then spiritually, mentally. It can drain you otherwise.'

Then he did get up and stroll across to the door with her. 'I'll come down,' he said.

'No, I'm fine.'

'It is late, it is dark, there is no one about at this time and you are on your own.'

She laughed. 'Simon, I'm a police officer.'

He put the flat door on the latch and looked at her, his handsome face stern. 'And two women are missing.'

She looked at him for a long minute. 'Yes,' she said quietly.

'I wish I was not thinking about them the way I am,' Simon said, touching a hand to her back to guide her as she began to descend the stairs. The touch burned into her.

At her car, he held the driver's door for her. She hesitated a fraction of a second. He did not move.

'Thank you again.'

'My pleasure. Goodnight, Freya.'

He lifted a hand and stood watching until she had driven down the close to the arch at the far end and away.

Twenty-Six

Mr Victor Freeborn disappeared from the Four Ways Nursing Home some time after four o'clock in the afternoon. No one had seen or heard him come downstairs and go out of the front door, which Mrs Murdo the secretary found unlatched when she slipped out to the postbox at five to five.

It was not until twenty past six that the police patrol car brought Mr Freeborn back, having found him sitting on a bench beside the river wearing nothing but pyjamas and slippers.

It had happened before, but because of Angela Randall's disappearance, Carol Ashton was in a greater state of anxiety than usual and it took the whole house a long time to settle down, by which time a carpenter had fitted a new, and more complicated, lock and they had had a staff conference about how else to tackle what the housekeeper Pam Thornhill called 'the Houdini problem'.

So it was after eight o'clock when Carol got home and picked up the *Echo* to read over a much needed gin.

The disappearance of Debbie Parker was the main front-page story. Her photograph, a fat girl giggling on an ice rink, was blown up to a dramatic size. Carol read the report quickly, looking for some mention of Angela Randall. There was none. Yet the two cases seemed to have plenty of similarities.

But if the links were so obvious, why was there no reference to Angela? What were the police doing? Had her case simply been filed away and forgotten? Carol recalled the young, pretty, efficient-seeming Detective Sergeant Graffham, who had certainly not given the impression that she would put her notes of their conversations in a drawer. She felt upset. Someone else was missing, Angela still was, and Carol thought she owed it to her colleague to remind the police of her name; she also felt angry, that she had reported something important and been sidelined.

She finished her gin and tonic, poured herself half an inch more, capped the bottle and went to the telephone.

'I'm sorry, DS Graffham isn't in,' the voice answered. 'Can anyone else help you?'

Carol hesitated. She didn't want to have to tell the whole story from scratch to someone who knew nothing about it.

'Can you tell me when she will be available?'

'You could try tomorrow morning.'

'Can I leave a message?'

She gave her name and number and asked for the sergeant to call her urgently.

But she won't, she thought, going into the kitchen to start preparing herself something to eat. In her experience, people, however charming and well intentioned, seldom did ring you back. She started to beat two eggs for an omelette, but by the time she had got some salad things from the fridge, she was too restless to leave things until the next morning. She left the kitchen and went back to the phone.

'Bevham and District Newspapers, good evening, how may I help you?'

A few minutes later, she was speaking to someone called Rachel Carr. Forty minutes later the same Rachel Carr was ringing her doorbell.

'Mrs Ashton, tell me about this lady who you say is missing – Angela Randall. I gather she works for you?'

She did not scribble notes in a spiral-bound book, she had put a small recording machine on the coffee table between them. Carol watched the little chocolate-coloured spools go round as she talked, about herself and the Four Ways, about Angela, about her disappearance, about speaking to the police twice, and finally, about the shock of reading that another single woman had gone missing.

'So of course I looked at the report expecting there to be something about Angela . . . well, it was obvious. Only there just wasn't.'

'Have you contacted the police this evening?'

'Yes, but the person I saw wasn't there. They just suggested I ring tomorrow morning.'

'Not really good enough, is it?'

'I just don't understand why they didn't mention Angela.'

'So you feel the police are being rather lax?'

'Not exactly . . . I mean, we don't know what's going on, do we? I want to find out, that's all. I'm puzzled. I owe it to Angela. She hasn't got anyone else to fight for her.'

The machine clicked and beeped and Rachel Carr reached down to change the tape over. She was a tall, sharp-faced young woman with oval designer spectacles and an expensive-looking pale suede jacket.

'I know this is a difficult question to answer, but – what do you think has happened to Angela Randall? You seem quite sure she is not the sort of person to go off alone without telling you or making contact.'

'She's the last person to do anything like that. The last person.'

'Then?'

Carol looked at her own hands. The tapes hissed round and round. She was suddenly reluctant to say what she thought out loud, superstitiously fearing that to speak her worst fears might somehow make them come about.

'In your heart, you think something has happened to her, don't you?'

Carol Ashton swallowed. 'Yes,' she said. Her voice came out as a whisper. She cleared her throat. 'I've no real reason for saying that, except . . . as time has gone on, I can't see what innocent explanation there can be.'

'I agree with you. And when you read about this other missing girl – Debbie Parker – what was your reaction?'

'As I told you, I wondered why there was no mention of Angela . . . another Lafferton woman who has gone missing in what seem like similar circumstances.'

'Then what did you think?'

'That there must be a connection between the two.'

She looked at the reporter, whose expression was both grave and expectant.

Then Rachel said, 'I don't want to distress you, Mrs Ashton, but after all, you're not actually a relative of Miss

Randall's so perhaps this isn't too insensitive. Do you think it likely that by now she may be dead?'

'It's what I'm afraid of.'

'Do you think this other young woman might be dead too?'

'Dear God, I hope not. It isn't long, is it, she might have been found by now . . . it's only a couple of days, not like Angela.'

The reporter said nothing, just looked at her and waited.

'It's too awful to think about . . . two of them.'

Silence.

'If there were a connection, it seems . . .'

Rachel Carr raised her eyebrows slightly but still let Carol speak.

'It's too awful to contemplate.'

'Do you blame the police for the delay in finding anything out about Miss Randall?'

Did she? She wondered if she had already said too much, implied things she was not really sure about. All the same . . .

'I'm angry,' she said, 'and I'm upset. It's too long. And now this new case . . . I'm quite frightened. I think anyone might be, don't you?'

'You think other Lafferton women have good reason to be frightened at the moment then?'

Did she? If it came to the worst . . .

After a moment, Carol Ashton nodded.

Rachel Carr broke the speed limit on her way back to the newspaper office – but then, she always did. That was what her red Mazda MX5 was for. She was also extremely excited. This story had legs, she thought, and she had been waiting for something like it for weeks; she could lead with it, give it some attitude, ask awkward questions of the police, stir up what she regarded as the semi-comatose Lafferton public. She imagined her byline across the front page day after day as she spearheaded a major press campaign.

Don Pilkington, the *Echo*'s editor, had gone by the time she got back but the news editor, Graham Gant, was still at his desk. Rachel pulled up a chair and began to talk, not pausing for him to interrupt until she had filled him in on everything and outlined her plans.

Looking steamrollered, he reached for a copy of one of the national papers. 'The police are a step ahead of us. The Commissioner of the Met has just admitted they all got it wrong when they took bobbies off the beat and lost public confidence in them at the same time. People need to feel safe and bobbies patrolling make them do that. They're recruiting hard and they plan to put foot patrols back.'

'Yeah, right, like our government plan to put more doctors in hospitals and more teachers in schools . . . and how many have we seen? Have you been up to Bevham General lately? Lafferton isn't the Met, things take a long time to filter down, and in any case, the point is not what might be going to happen in the future but what is – or isn't – happening here and now. I want us to go big on this one, Graham. Two women are missing so why have the police only told us about one? Both were known to go out alone on the Hill, neither was the sort to vanish without notice, there are no traces of them and neither has been in touch . . . what are the police trying to cover up – their own incompetence? Why isn't the Hill policed properly – it's just the sort of place where weirdos hang out, like the towpath where that flasher keeps jumping out on runners. Why haven't the police caught him? Why –'

Graham Gant held up his hand wearily. 'Whoa, one thing at a time, Rachel. OK, you can get on to Lafferton and ask about this other missing woman. I think that's important. Anything else, and certainly anything in the nature of an anti-police campaign, you have to run past the editor.'

'I'll ring him at home.'

'You won't get him, he's at a big Masonic dinner in Bevham.'

Rachel snorted.

'Let's get the details about this other woman, do everything you can on that, we'll headline it tomorrow if there's still no news on either of them – the police want us to keep this other missing girl in the public eye anyway. But wait till you can talk to Don before you start whipping up public anxiety.'

Rachel stormed across the room to her own desk in frustration. It was always the same, the big boys in league with one another, covering up for one another, scratching each other's backs. Half the police were Freemasons, that was well known, as well as half the lawyers, bankers and big businessmen in both Lafferton and Bevham, big boys playing little boys' games. But that didn't matter. When it came to deceiving the public and conspiracies of silence, it bloody well did.

Rachel sat at her desk staring into space for a moment, picturing the campaign she fully intended to get permission to run, one way or another – and she was good at wheedling Don – and then taking her fantasy one step further to the point where her work on the *Echo* was noticed in Fleet Street and a call came in for her to go and see the editor of the *Daily Mail* . . . Rachel Carr did not intend to remain in the backwaters of Lafferton for long.

She picked up the phone and put in a call to the police station, but by now it was nearly ten, no one was in CID, and the duty sergeant could only give her the party line on the missing girl, said there was no recent news and would not comment on any other missing persons.

'I suggest you ring back in the morning.'

'And speak to?'

'DS Graffham.'

'What time does he wander in?'

'She. DS Freya Graffham. Any time after nine. If she isn't available, you could ask to speak to DC Coates. Sorry I can't be of more help to you tonight, madam.'

Rachel slammed the receiver down. She didn't relish having to wait until the morning to get permission from the editor, then speak to some poxy woman detective, who would probably give her the stone-wall treatment or make her hang about until there was another press briefing.

An hour later, she had written what she thought was a pretty cutting-edge piece. The story, and her angle on it, were too high-profile to be confined to the *Lafferton Echo* and, after all, she had tried to speak to the editor, had she not? It was hardly her fault if he was out at a Masonic dinner. She called up her address book and clicked on an entry. ed@bevpost.com ccnewsed@bevpost.com

I am attaching a piece on the news which broke today on the missing Lafferton woman. I have key info which has not been released. Story has implications of interest for the wider readership of the *Bevham Post*. I have been unable to contact my own editor but feel the news story is too urgent to leave overnight.

> Good wishes,
> Rachel Carr
> rcarr@laffertonecho.com

She hesitated for a split second before clicking 'Send' and watching the message and its attachment fly off her screen.

Within five minutes, she was heading the Mazda for Hare End and the barn conversion she shared with her lover, county rugby captain Jon Blixen.

Twenty-Seven

DCI Simon Serrailler was not given to shouting. He preferred to make his anger known by speaking softly and icily.

'Freya, come in here please. Bring Nathan with you.'

The knock came in twenty seconds.

'Come in.' He pointed to the newspaper on his desk. 'I take it you will have seen this morning's *Post*?'

'Yes, sir.'

'Gawd knows where it came from, guv, only not out of here, I can tell you.'

'Freya?'

'Categorically not, sir.'

'So how does this reporter – Rachel Carr – know about the other missing woman, how has she found out her name, her address, where she works? Someone must have talked to her.'

'No one in the station. To start with, not many people here even know about Angela Randall, she was just another name in the missing persons file. Nathan and I have been the only ones looking into the case in detail and neither of us briefed this reporter.' There was a sliver of ice in Freya's own voice.

'OK, I take your word for it. But these are exactly the sort of headlines I wanted to avoid . . . look at some of these provocative questions – "Can Lafferton women now feel safe in their own town?" . . . "Have the Lafferton police failed to keep those enjoying the town's prime open space, the Hill, safe from a serial killer?" Serial killer, for God's sake, there isn't even a body. Right, we'd better anticipate them. I want a press briefing called for twelve noon. I want local radio, regional television, the news agencies, the lot – and get on to it now before they get on to us. I've put the search team out on to the Hill again but they'll have finished by this afternoon. Any joy at Starly?'

'What? With Dava the Diva! Gawd, what a plonker.'

'I doubt if he knows anything about Debbie Parker's disappearance,' Freya said. 'She had two appointments with him and he gave us all the New Age psychobabble, but I didn't get the impression he had anything to hide.'

'All the same, we'll keep him in the frame for the time being. Apart from anything else, Debbie seems to have made some new friends up at Starly and her flatmate might not have been told everything about them. It's a better lead than any other as to where she might have gone.'

'With the raggle-taggle gypsies, O. I used to fancy being a gypsy when I was a kid –'

'Thank you, Nathan, save the childhood reminiscences and get on the phone. I want this press briefing to be and to look orderly, organised and hyper-professional. We're in charge, we're in control and we have to get that message across. Public confidence is going to take a knock from this rubbish. Oh, and if national press get wind and call up, put them on to me. Say nothing.'

'Sir.'

Freya looked at Serrailler as she turned away, to see if he would catch her eye with some flicker of intimacy. He did not. She hesitated for a second, letting Nathan go first out of the door.

The telephone rang.

'Serrailler. Good morning, sir. I have read it, yes.'

Freya fled.

More press came into the conference room for the noon briefing than had attended for a long time. They sensed that a major story might be about to break and they smelled blood. DCI Serrailler walked smartly into the room as the clock struck and took the rostrum with Freya, Nathan and Inspector Black, who was in charge of searching the Hill.

'Good morning, ladies and gentleman. Thank you all for coming. As you know, an appeal was made to the public yesterday for any information about a local woman, Debbie Parker, who was last seen on the evening of the 31st and who may have left her home early the next morning. She has not been seen or heard from since, she left no message, she has not been in touch with her family or friends and so far as we know she has no reason to go missing of her own accord. She did not take any belongings with her apart from her house keys. Her handbag and all other personal possessions and outdoor clothes were left in her flat.

'We are becoming increasingly concerned for Debbie Parker's safety and as well as the broadcast public appeal for information, have had search teams out on the Hill and its surrounding area, where it is thought she may have been out walking.

'As I am sure you are aware, people go missing for many reasons; they may have a history of depression or other mental health problems, they may have domestic, family or monetary problems. They usually return of their own accord. We always take a missing person report very seriously, but in some cases we have more reason for concern and this is true of the young woman, Debbie Parker.

'Another Lafferton woman, Angela Randall of 4 Barn Close, was reported missing by her employer at the Four Ways Nursing Home on 18 December last year, but although we took full reports and made an investigation at the time, we had no reason to see Miss Randall's disappearance as suspicious. However, in the light of the disappearance of Debbie Parker, we are looking at that of Angela Randall again as there are certain links between the two.

'We have had calls from the public as a result of our broadcast appeal and we are following up a number of leads but so far we have no definite information which may lead us to her. We will be making a similar appeal to the public about the disappearance of Angela Randall. We'll naturally keep you all closely informed of developments. Meanwhile, I would be grateful if the press would refrain from wild and lurid speculation, which is not only unhelpful, but distressing for the families and friends of the missing women and causes general public alarm.'

Rachel Carr stood up. 'Chief Inspector, surely it must occur to you that the moment you put out an appeal for information about a missing young woman it gives rise to what you term "general public alarm"?'

'Of course people will be concerned but we put out the request for information in as undramatic a manner as possible, precisely so as not to cause alarm, while at the same time alerting people to the case.'

'Why did you conceal the disappearance of Angela Randall?'

'No one has concealed anything, Miss . . .'

'Sorry, Rachel Carr, Bevham Newspapers . . .'

'Yes, I rather thought that's who you might be.'

There was a ripple of amusement. Rachel Carr's spikiness and naked ambition did not make her popular with her colleagues.

'Well, Miss Carr . . . that is exactly the kind of phraseology to which I was referring. Angela Randall's disappearance was reported to us and we made initial investigations. But we do not and cannot put out a general appeal or public statement about every person who goes missing, even within a place the size of Lafferton.'

'But you're taking her case seriously now?'

'As I said, we take every case of a missing person seriously. Are there any more questions, as Miss Carr seems to have decided the debate is open to the floor.'

'Jason Fox, County News Agency. Chief Inspector, are you worried for the safety of one or both of the missing women?'

'As neither has been in touch, and as time goes on without any news, then yes, there is cause for concern. But I would stress that we have no evidence at all that any harm has come to either woman.'

The questions came fast now.

'Is this a murder inquiry?'

'Has the search of the Hill yielded any trace of either woman?'

'Why has no search been made of other parts of the town?'

'Are people advised to stay away from the Hill?'

'Are women on their own to be concerned for their safety in Lafferton?'

And, from Rachel Carr again, 'Why is Lafferton inadequately policed? Why are there no patrols in the area of the Hill on a regular basis?' And yet again, 'If you are, as you say, concerned for the safety of these two women and if, as you say, you feel there is a link between their disappearances, are you looking for anyone in connection with these missing women? Do you think it likely they have been abducted or murdered? Is there a serial killer preying upon the women of Lafferton?'

Jim Williams had heard yesterday's Radio BEV appeal for information about the missing girl and afterwards he had sat down in the comfortable Parker Knoll reclining chair to think. Now, this morning, he had gone out, as usual, the half-mile to Akre Street to buy the *Post* and his packet of Mintoes. It was a beautiful day, too beautiful – too warm, the daffodils too far out, the birds singing too joyously. That could only mean a return to sleet, east winds and hard frosts at night. He had taken off the white fleece with which he lovingly draped the camellias in their pots outside on the terrace but he would look at the thermometer just before the ten o'clock news and go out to wrap them again if it looked like dropping too low.

He thought about camellias all the way back home. The *Post* was folded under his arm. He did not indulge himself in opening it in the street, partly because it spoiled the pleasure of reading it over his tea and because

291

he had a vague sense that just as it was common to eat in the street, so it might be common to read the paper there too.

He had not forgotten the news bulletin about the missing girl. He was still turning it over in his mind as he made his bacon and eggs and mushrooms, sliced and buttered the bread, put the teapot ready and the kettle on to boil. He opened the kitchen window and the unmistakable smell of spring drifted in. Once the first person in the street cut their grass it would be even sweeter.

Ten minutes later, he was sitting at the table, his full plate in front of him, his tea poured, and the *Post* propped up against the pot. The missing girl was headline news. But as he read on, he was most taken by the mention of another woman, Angela Randall, who had disappeared before Christmas. Both women had been known to go running or walking on the Hill and as Jim studied the photograph of Debbie Parker, he felt fairly sure he had indeed seen her up there, though it was not easy to tell from the rather blurred picture of a girl wobbling about on ice skates. Still, she looked familiar and if he closed his eyes he thought he could see her out walking. But the police would want to know more than that; dozens of people might ring in to say they 'thought' they 'might' have seen the girl on the Hill, though they couldn't be sure exactly when.

But as far as the other woman was concerned, Jim felt more confident. There was no picture of Angela Randall but there was a good description of her. The main thing that jogged his memory though was the fact that she had last been seen running off towards the Hill, wearing a light grey tracksuit, very early on that December morning when it had been so foggy. Jim had been out that day with Skippy, and early too because he hadn't been able to sleep and he remembered the fog because when he had left the house it hadn't seemed too bad, not much more than a mist, but by the time he had got on to the Hill, it had been quite dense and damp too, a fog that clung about your face and hair and chilled you.

He cleaned his plate round with half a slice of bread, and went to the fridge to check what he would have for his tea later. There was a pork chop he could have with potatoes and greens, and the individual apple pie he had bought yesterday from Cross's bakery which he could have with a tin of Devon Custard. It was his favourite sweet, though in the summer he generally ate the apple pie with ice cream.

He reread the article in the *Post* carefully. No, he probably hadn't enough on Debbie Parker to bother the police with, but the more he thought about it, the more he thought he should go to them and tell them that he had seen the other woman running through the fog.

Having decided, he folded the paper, cleared the table and washed up the pots, before settling down in the living room to watch the football previews. Beside him on the small stool, the *Radio Times* lay open on that day's page, with the programmes he planned to watch highlighted in red. He went through it from cover to cover on the day it arrived, scheduling his viewing week. This afternoon he had almost three hours of enjoyable television sport ahead of him and then it would be time for him to take his short walk to the end of the road, round the corner and back the other way, before making his tea and settling in for his evening viewing. Therefore, he would go to Lafferton Police Station now, this morning. He would make sure that he told his story not to whoever was on the front desk but to someone properly on the case. He knew about messages that were never passed on, notes that were slipped into files and never looked at again.

He switched off the television and put on his coat and cap. He'd tell the police all he could remember. For some reason, he felt he owed that not only to the missing woman, but to Phyllis – and after her, to Skippy.

As Freya walked across the CID room after the briefing, the phone on her desk started to ring.

'DS Graffham.'

The desk sergeant was calling up to report an elderly man who had been in.

'Said he had something he wanted to say about the missing woman, Angela Randall, but he wouldn't tell me what, he wants to talk to someone directly involved.'

'What sort of elderly man, Roy?'

'Seventies, raincoat and cap. I don't think it's a wind-up, he seemed genuine.'

'Where is he now?'

'Gone home. He waited a bit. I've got all the details here.'

'Give them to me, will you?'

She scribbled down the name and address. As she put the phone down, it rang again.

'Freya, would you come in for a minute, please?'

This time, she went down the corridor to Simon Serrailler's room without Nathan in tow.

'Thanks,' he said as she opened the door,

'That young woman from the *Echo* is out for blood.'

Simon made a dismissive gesture. 'She's just a local terrier. Now, Debbie Parker. The only real lead we have on her is Starly. That was something new in her life, she was caught up in it, and I have a feeling that if there are going to be any clues as to why she went off and where she is now, we'll find them up there. You saw the one therapist, but I want a lot more. I want Starly saturating with uniform, every shop, consulting room, café . . . tepee. House-to-house near enough. Get that picture of Debbie on Have You Seen leaflets and spray them round the place. We want anyone who recognises her or knows her. We've drawn a blank on the Hill.'

'Sir. But what about Angela Randall?'

'What about her?'

'Well, so far as we know she had nothing to do with Starly.'

'No.'

'So . . . we don't have any leads for her at all.'

'No. The only lead is the very tenuous one of the Hill and we've nothing there. Until anything new comes up about her, we concentrate on Debbie Parker.'

'Right.'

Personally, she might be more in love with Simon Serrailler every time she set eyes on him, but professionally, she was in disagreement with his dismissal of the Angela Randall case. The picture of her sterile, lonely little house came to Freya's mind, the soundless rooms, the dreadful, bleak, silence that hung over the place, and then the picture of the golden parcel, the expensive cufflinks with their note. It was the note that gave her deepest and most private feelings away, the note that reached out to Freya and struck such a chord with her. She knew, walking back to her CID room, why she was not prepared to let Angela Randall's case slip out of sight. The note attached to the gift was somehow one of desperation, a revelatory note, in spite of the absence of names, a note that revealed an obsessive passion. Angela Randall loved a man to whom she regularly gave expensive presents, presents for which she must have dug deep into her savings made from a modest salary. Freya understood her, and what motivated her, only too well.

So far, she had told no one about what she had discovered from the Bevham jeweller.

'Nathan?'

'Sarge.'

'The DCI wants a house-to-house up at Starly, posters, leaflets with Debbie Parker on, a total blitz. He thinks anything we may find is going to be found up there.'

'Gives me the creeps that place. I bet she's up there. She's joined some bonkers coven.'

'Well, if she has, by the time uniform have saturated the place she'll be found.'

'Is there anything for me, Sarge?'

'At Starly?'

'Anywhere. Only Matt Ruston wants me to help him on the drug data. There's a helluva lot to be gone through.'

'You trying to tell me something?'

'Don't be daft, Sarge, I love you to bits, die for you I would, only if it's back to Starly . . .'

'It isn't, it's off to see a little man who will only talk to important people in CID, and when we've done that, there's something I want to run past you.'

Nathan flashed out his monkey grin. 'Gimme five,' he said, raising his hand.

Twenty-Eight

'Is this a good moment or are you feeding children, doing children's homework, giving hay to horses . . .'

'Hi, Karin. Children fed and homeworked and horses hayed, now catching up on GP paperwork so all interruptions welcome. How are things?'

'I'm reporting in as requested.'

'Good. What have you been up to?'

'Reflexology.'

'Don't, I couldn't bear anyone tickling my feet.'

'They don't, they press, and quite firmly. It's utter bliss. I nearly went to sleep. They burn lovely scented candles. Sweet girl too. I didn't tell her anything and after a bit she asked if I had any problems in my breasts.'

'Good guess. Women of your age often have.'

'Cynic. I felt terrific afterwards.'

'I'm all for that.'

'I'm keeping a diary.'

'About what you are doing or are you putting down your feelings as well?'

'Everything. There'd be no point otherwise. I have to be honest with myself, Cat.'

'So what's next?'

'I've another appointment with my spiritual healer on Wednesday morning. That really is the best thing so far. I come out feeling I could climb Mount Everest but I also feel very calm and positive.'

'Can I make a suggestion here?'

'That's what you're for, you're my doctor.'

'I think you should go for another scan.'

'Why?'

'I want to see what is actually happening . . . as against what you feel.'

'I want to think about this.'

Cat sighed. She was restraining herself as much as she dared, being as open-minded as far as she thought professional, but every day she had misgivings. Karin looked well and felt well. Cat needed to know what had happened to the cancer.

'Are you being fair?'

'To who?'

'Well, actually, to me. I'm giving you a lot of rope here, Karin.'

'I just need a bit longer.'

'What are you afraid of?'

'What?'

'Sorry, Karin – I can't believe I said that.'

'You think I'm afraid of facing what you would call "facts".'

'I don't know what the facts are until we find out.'

'Just not yet.'

Cat hesitated then decided not to push her for the time being.

'OK, so where next? Feng shui?'

'The psychic surgeon.'

'No, Karin, absolutely not.'

'Listen, this one isn't about me. I don't believe in it, I think it's trickery and I think it probably ought to be stopped, but at the moment all we have is rumour. Someone has to go and find out and then bring back a proper account. I'm doing everyone a favour here.'

'Then I'm coming with you. I want to know what's going on as well. I hear what you're saying and maybe you can be a guinea pig. But you're vulnerable.'

'It's Thursday morning at ten fifteen. You'll be in surgery.'

'Yes, and Chris will be at BG lecturing. Damn. OK, but if anything worries you, come straight out. We're not talking scented candles here.'

'I know.'

'By the way, has my mother rung you?'

'About her dinner party? Yes she has and we're going.'

'Excellent.'

'Do you know who else will be there?'

'Us, Nick Haydn, Aidan Sharpe and a rather attractive detective sergeant who works with Si. Possibly David Lester, not sure. Bit of a liquorice allsorts, but you know my mother. I think she might be matchmaking.'

'Or fundraising or trying to get up a working party for the hospice bazaar.'

'Or just winding up Dad. He'll hate it, of course.'

'She never seems to notice.'

'Oh, she notices. Her way of dealing is to bat on regardless.'

'I'll have been operated on psychically by then, of course.'

'God, what a conversation stopper. And, Karin . . .'

'I know, I know.'

'The scan. This is your doctor speaking.'

'Goodbye, Cat.'

Karin was in Starly by nine thirty the following Thursday morning. It was a day to make anyone feel better, she thought, driving through the lanes whose hedgerows were sprinkled white with blackthorn. She had been determined about taking charge of her own health, determined and positive. She believed in what she was doing. Nevertheless, in the dark watches of the night she had misgivings, when she imagined the jaws of the crab eating their way through her. Then she wondered what she had been thinking of, rejecting Cat's advice and proven medical treatment, and fear that her delay meant that she would now be beyond help gripped her. But in the day, when she read the books so full of miracles and success stories, so bubbling with optimism and confidence, and listened to her tapes and was transported by them into realms of beauty and calm and vibrant health, everything changed; her night terrors receded into their hollow caves and she felt fit and sure of herself again.

She felt like that now as she pulled into the car park behind the market square at Starly. It was quiet, the sun caught the trunks of the trees with lemon-coloured light, and a mother with a laughing, dancing toddler and a new baby in a sling went past; she and Karin exchanged a remark about the springlike weather and the child blew a stream of bubbles from a wand and plastic tub of liquid. The bubbles drifted up, gleaming with iridescent rainbows.

Karin walked down the hill, looking in shop windows

at dream catchers and jars of organic honey and small crystals. One of them, a pink quartz like a chunk of solid-ified rose petals, caught her eye; she felt a magnetic power emanating from it towards her. She bought it for five pounds, and when she put the package into her bag, she felt a lifting of her spirit.

She bought a newspaper and took it into the pine-tabled wholefood café, to read over a glass of home-made lemonade. 'If life seems like a lemon, make lemonade.' She had read that, along with a great many other opti-mistic little mottoes, in one of her American books, the one that also told her she should wrap herself in white light, weave her own cloth of gold and reach out every morning as she woke to touch her own rainbow. She liked the lemonade advice though.

She looked out of the café window and felt good. She told herself so. She felt happy and positive and well. She was sure of it. She was also full of foreboding about the appointment ahead. Reflexologists and aroma-therapists were one thing, a psychic surgeon quite another. She curled her right hand round the mobile phone in her pocket for reassurance.

At ten past ten she walked through the door of a house at the bottom of the hill whose glass panel had 'Surgery' written on it in black; the word 'Dental' had been roughly erased. As a dental phobic, Karin was not reassured.

'Good morning. Have you an appointment?'

The middle-aged woman in the camel-coloured jumper could have been the receptionist for a Harley Street consultant. Karin gave her name.

'Yes, thank you, Mrs McCafferty. Would you take a seat? Dr Groatman will be with you shortly.'

'I'm sorry?'

The woman smiled. 'Dr Groatman. That is the name of the consultant who treats patients through Anthony.'

'I see. And I take it this doctor —'

'Lived in the 1830s in London.'

'— Right.'

The woman smiled before turning back to her computer.

'Do many people come here?'

'Oh yes, the doctor is fully booked for some weeks ahead. People travel long distances for a consultation.'

Karin picked up a copy of *World Healing*, but as she looked at the cover, the inner door opened and an elderly woman came out looking confused and rather pale.

'Mrs Cornwell? Please come and sit down for a moment and reorientate yourself. I'll get you some water.' The receptionist went to a cooler at the far end of the room. 'It's important that you drink this, Mrs Cornwell. How are you feeling?'

The woman took out a handkerchief and wiped her face. 'A bit faint.'

'That's quite usual. Just drink the water slowly and don't get up. Have you any discomfort?'

The woman looked up in surprise. 'Well, no. I haven't. None at all. Isn't that odd?'

The receptionist smiled. 'It's usual.'

Then the door opened again and a man came through and went straight across to the desk without looking at either woman. He was slight, with sandy hair and an unmemorable face. He entered something on to the computer, typing with two fingers, then looked briefly at a folder on the desk, before walking back across the room and closing the inner door behind him. There was silence. Mrs Cornwell sipped her water and wiped her face and continued to look bemused, the receptionist returned to her work. Karin opened the magazine again.

A buzzer sounded.

'Would you go through please, Mrs McCafferty?'

Karin's legs felt weak and her throat dry. It was exactly like the dentist. She didn't want to go. She wanted to turn round and get out, now, while she could.

The receptionist was smiling. Karin looked at the other patient. What happens? What is it like? What does he do? What are you here for? How do you really feel? The questions tumbled round her head.

'Straight through the door. Dr Groatman is waiting.'

Oh God, I must be mad.

She wished Cat had come with her. She went slowly across the room.

The man was very bent and walked with a pronounced limp. He wore a caliper and one shoulder was slightly higher than the other. His hair was the same sandy colour as the man who had walked through the reception room, but tousled and sticking up from his head. He wore a white coat and stood by an examination couch. The room was lit dimly, with slatted blinds shielding the window. There was a sink with a tap. A bare vinyl floor. Nothing else.

'On the couch, please. What is the name you use?' His voice was gruff with a slight accent she could not place.

'Karin.'

'Lie down, please.'

Karin lay. He stood above her and passed his hands rapidly over her body without touching it.

'You have cancer. I feel your cancer in the breast and the glands and spread to the stomach. Please unbutton your shirt but do not remove and do not remove the clothing or the underclothing.'

Now the accent was definitely foreign, perhaps German or Dutch. While she unbuttoned her shirt he looked away.

'I should remove this growth here in the neck gland. This is the core tumour. We get rid of this, others will shrink and disappear. They feed off the parent tumour.'

Everything in her wanted to shut out the sight of him. He needed a shave, though his skin and hands seemed clean. He reached under the couch and swung out a tray of instruments. She heard the sound of a bucket being moved. Karin forced herself to watch, to observe everything as closely as she could, remembering his face, his hands, his body. He took an instrument from the tray and seemed to fold his hand over it.

Then he reached towards her neck.

'You need not be afraid, nothing to fear. Look at your heart rate, far too quick, ridiculous. Calm down. I am making you well. The tumour will go, you will be well, what is there to be afraid of?'

Then the hand moved swiftly and she felt him take a fold of the flesh in her neck, low down, then a curious sensation, as if something were being drawn across her skin, and the hand twisting and moving within her neck. She watched his face. He had his eyes half closed, but she knew he was aware that she was looking at him. The twisting movement sharpened, she felt a stinging pain, and a wrench.

'Ah. There. Good.'

His hand moved swiftly away from her and down. Something dropped into the bucket at his feet. When his hand came up the fingers were bloody. Now his hands were hovering just above her again, and he was mumbling what sounded like an incantatory prayer.

'You are in God's hands, Karin. Safe now. You will be fully well. You need to rest and you should eat well, do not starve, do not deny your body. Give it what it asks for when it asks. Drink water, plenty of water. Rest. Goodbye.'

He stood motionless. Karin lay, slightly light-headed, slightly bemused, but after a few seconds, she swung her legs off the couch and got up unsteadily. Dr Groatman neither helped her nor spoke and his facial expression did not flicker. She thought he was the man in the sports jacket who had come through the reception room, that he had twisted his body, padded his back and shoulder, mussed his hair – thought, but could not be sure.

As she put her hand on the door leading back into the reception office, he said softly, 'Mistrust and suspicion are dangerous companions. Keep an open mind and a generous heart, Karin, or you will negate my healing work.' His voice was unpleasant and whatever accent there had been was quite gone.

Karin almost fell into the outer room.

Two people were waiting.

'Please sit down and drink a glass of water, Mrs McCafferty.'

'No, I have to go, sorry . . .'

'You really must. You need to centre yourself. Please.'

Trembling, she sat and sipped the paper tumbler of water; the woman was right, she needed it, she was thirsty and unsteady. The buzzer sounded for the next patient.

'Do I pay you now?'

'Yes please. Take your time; wait until you feel quite calm again.'

'I'm fine. Thanks.' Karin stood. She did not faint. The room remained still. She crossed to the desk and the smiling woman handed her a small card. *Mrs K. McCafferty. For treatment: £100. Please make cheques payable to SUDBURY & CO.*

She came out into the fresh air, doing sums furiously. She had been in the consulting room perhaps ten minutes, no more. But say one patient every half-hour, allowing for the waiting, from nine till five – sixteen patients a day, with an hour for lunch, fourteen patients, fourteen at £100 = £1,400.

Back in the wholefood café, she sat at a window table in the sun, and over tea and a carrot cake which was rich and delicious, she wrote pages in the loose-leaf notebook she had brought while the visit was fresh in her mind – smells, sights, sounds, what he had said, what she had felt.

Back in the car, she rang Cat.

'Dr Deerbon is out on an emergency call. Can I take a message?'

Karin left her name, and asked Cat to ring her that evening at home.

She drove back slowly to Lafferton, delighting even more in the sunshine, feeling released and relieved and trying to put the morning's experience out of her mind. She had planned to spend the afternoon in the garden clearing space for the seed potatoes. She went into the house, took the mail from behind the door, and went into the kitchen to put the kettle on before changing into her old jeans, jacket and boots. The sun was shining through the huge vase of daffodils on the table, making them blaze. Karin took the mug of tea over to the sofa with her letters. Five minutes later she was asleep. She neither stirred nor dreamed and when she woke, over two hours later, lay still, feeling an extraordinary sense of peace and refreshment. The sun had moved across the room and was making oblong blocks of brightness on the white wall. Karin stared at them. They seemed to radiate energy and to be beautiful beyond explanation or words.

She remembered the morning – Starly, the strange consulting room, the man with the bent back and lame leg, his odd accent, his brusque remarks. She had been nervous and suspicious, relieved to get away. Yet now, lying looking at the white wall, she felt full of strength and well-being, as if something within her had indeed changed and her spirit been renewed. She wondered what she could say to Cat Deerbon now.

Twenty-Nine

He wanted to know what was going on. There had been reports on the radio and in the local paper, which had been picked up, although only in small paragraphs, by some of the national press. The place was buzzing with talk. Worry. Speculation.

It would be too dangerous to go in the van.

He had spent the previous evening with Debbie Parker. He had written his post-mortem report and filed it and then she had to be restored, the organs replaced, wounds sewn up. He liked to think he always did an immaculate job, and that he was respectful, always respectful. They had taught him that. There was often crude humour in the mortuary and at the post-mortem table, especially when the police were present; it was their way of dealing with what they witnessed and keeping the horror at bay, but he had never approved of it, and certainly had never joined in, and now that he was alone, he worked in silence, or occasionally, to music. For Debbie he had played Vivaldi.

When he had finished, he sheeted her and slid her

body into the cold store beneath the others. Each drawer had a label but the names were what he chose for them, not their own, and he gave each one careful thought.

Achilles.

Medusa

He had written *Circe* neatly in black ink and slipped the card into the slot on the drawer containing Debbie Parker. Then he had unzipped his green lab suit, stepped out of it and put it into the washing machine before dressing in his own clothes and locking the unit, each section separately with its own double padlock, and going out by the side door, which rolled down and bolted to the concrete floor.

He left the van in the car park of a public house and walked in the pleasant early spring evening towards the Hill.

It was still cordoned off with police tape and warning signs were placed at every entrance point. No one was about. The police and their vehicles and equipment had all left.

He walked round the perimeter path, looking up at the deserted slopes, the undergrowth, the Wern Stones, to the crown of oaks at the top. There was no indication of how long the police would keep it closed, but even when the Hill was reopened it would take a long time for people to return as normal there. They would be anxious now, rumour would feed on rumour, no one would feel safe, everyone would be watched and the police would patrol visibly and regularly.

He walked away, taking a different route back to the parked van. You could never be too careful, never drop your guard.

He went into the public house bar, which was empty,

bought red wine and a hot pasty, and borrowed the evening paper from the counter. It was a large, anonymous room, a public house for passing travellers. He was served without interest and would not be remembered. Two groups of men came in and did not spare him a glance.

The *Lafferton Echo* had another article about Medusa and Circe. The pasty was delicious. The evening sun fell in ruby red through the glass lozenges of the window behind him, on to the newspaper. He felt content.

Thirty

Sharon Medcalf had not been at choir practice that week, having sent a message that she had a bad cold, which had thrown Freya's plan. Now, Sharon's phone number was in front of her but she was still hesitating. She needed to talk to someone about Simon Serrailler, to get answers to some of the questions that preoccupied her whenever her mind was not focused on work, and on both occasions when they had talked privately, Sharon had revealed herself as an enthusiastic gossip.

So why am I dithering? Freya asked herself now.

She walked away from the phone, poured a glass of wine and sat down to think. She wanted to talk about him, to hear his name and speak it herself, find out more about his life. Who else was there to ask? The people she had got to know best since coming to Lafferton were work colleagues. Apart from acquaintances, mainly other choir members, the only person she could call a friend was Meriel Serrailler, who was naturally ruled out. Which left the dauntingly well-dressed Sharon Medcalf, who was divorced and owned two designer boutiques in Bevham. But Sharon was a member of the choir and when the conductor had asked her to sing a few bars of a solo aria in the *Messiah* to illustrate a point he wanted to make, Freya had looked at her with new respect. Her soprano voice was glorious, rich and clear with impressive top notes. The rest of the choir had listened with absolute attention. There was more to Sharon Medcalf than expensive clothes. Freya had ceased to curse when her mind turned to Simon. Deep inside her a small, furious, independent voice muttered scornfully from time to time. It also murmured warnings. She ignored them.

She switched on the television, hopped from a garden makeover programme to one about house-buying to a European football match and switched off again. She had caught up with the day's papers and had no new book to read. She drank the last of her wine and pulled the phone nearer.

'Is that Sharon?'

'It is.'

'It's Freya Graffham . . . I just rang to find out how you are. The message to choir was that you'd lost your voice.'

'Bless you, yes, it's been a stinker but I'm feeling much better today. How was choir?'

'Good. It's really shaping now, but the sopranos are definitely thinner without you. The other reason I rang was that I have a day off on Wednesday and I wondered if you'd like to have lunch? If you're well enough.'

'It'll be malingering by then. I'd love to. Where?'

If they were going to talk about Simon, they had better not be anywhere in Lafferton.

'Somewhere out of town . . . what about the Fox and

312

Goose at Flimby? The food's excellent but it only gets really crowded in the evenings.'

'I haven't been out there for yonks. If it's a day like today it'll set me up nicely. Thanks, Freya.'

'Shall we meet there at half twelve?'

Freya wanted to sing. Sharon had talked about the Serraillers when she had given her the lift home. She might not know Simon well but she would surely be able to answer the one question that had been gnawing at her since Freya had been to his flat. She could neither ignore it nor dismiss it. She needed to know.

She went to run a bath and while she was soaking in it worried not about Simon but about work. The only piece of halfway positive information about either of the missing women had come from Jim Williams who was, so far as they knew, the last person to see Angela Randall, running through the fog. But fog was what shrouded her after that and there were no leads at all on Debbie Parker. The search of the Hill had yielded nothing. A couple of people in Starly recognised her photograph and one had known her name but no one had seen her up lately. House-to-house inquiries, posters everywhere, another radio appeal, more in the papers – and nothing.

She wondered vaguely about Jim Williams's dog Skippy. That had been last seen on the Hill and it, too, had vanished apparently into thin air – or thick fog. But dogs did run away, chasing after a smell, or burrowing too far down a rabbit hole, and a missing dog was not a missing person. People stole dogs. Jim Williams had seen no one but he had reported hearing a vehicle. Did dog snatchers drag their victims into cars and roar off down the road? She remembered Cruella de Vil.

*

Spring had retreated and winter was delivering a late blast as she drove out to Flimby two days later. The wind drove sleet and little pinheads of hail at the windscreen and as she parked at the Fox and Goose a biting north-easterly was driving straight across the fields towards her.

The pub was quiet and the log fire and amber-coloured lamps on the tables welcoming. On the far side of the hatch she could see that the snug had its small complement of the old countrymen who still lived in and around all the villages. The low burr of their voices was like the humming of bees.

Freya bought a vodka and tonic and bagged a small table near the fire. There were women who could lunch out in country pubs like this every day if they fancied, but surely they would not get such pleasure from it as she did on a precious day off? In London she had never enjoyed such leisurely days. Her free time had been a rush of catching up on domestic chores and trying to prove to herself, by preparing elaborate dinners, that she loved making Don happy.

Not any more, she thought, curling her toes up inside her boots, nor ever again.

As if a light had been switched on she saw Simon's flat in her mind's eye, the long, tranquil room with its pictures, books, and pieces of modern and antique furniture in harmony together. She wanted to be there now, for all that she was enjoying the very different room she was actually in, with the gingham curtains and horse brasses. She wanted to be absorbed into Simon's room so that she belonged there, fitted as perfectly as a vase or a stool or one of his drawings on the wall.

'God, what a day!'

Sharon Medcalf was beside the table taking off her

long suede coat. Freya had spent an hour choosing her own clothes and making herself ready, determined not to let herself down in the face of Sharon's designer presentation, and when she had looked at herself in the mirror before leaving home she had been rather pleased. She had some decent clothes and she had mixed them with what seemed to be a bit of panache; she spent her working life in clothes that were neither oversmart nor overcasual, and did not call too much attention to themselves; she had enjoyed the chance to make more of a splash. Confronted by Sharon now, she wondered why she had bothered. Sharon wore Armani with a startling scarf and dumped a Louis Vuitton bag on the floor beside her.

Freya could not resist reaching out to finger the pure silk of the vivid blue, white and fuchsia patterned silk.

'That is amazing . . . I've never seen anything like it.'

'You won't . . . it's vintage Ungaro.'

Freya sighed.

'Oh, poof, it's the job, I'd just as soon wear jeans from Top Shop.'

'Hm. Anyway, how are you?'

'Much better. Freya, thank you for asking me here. I value your wanting to be friendly.' She said things like that and somehow they didn't sound false.

Sharon Medcalf was probably late forties, very tall, very slim, with very long, well-cut blonde hair which must cost a fortune to be so discreetly coloured. Her make-up could have been done professionally that morning.

'I haven't been to this place for years and I am starving.'

'The menu's on a blackboard behind the bar.'

'I know and I can't see it.' She hauled up the Louis Vuitton and took out her spectacle case.

'Dior? Chanel?'

Sharon put the YSL glasses on and made a face. 'OK, food.'

They ordered and Freya replaced her empty vodka glass with mineral water and settled back. She had no idea how she might bring Simon Serrailler's name into the conversation but, in fact, it was relatively easy. When their crab cakes had arrived, Sharon said, 'You know the choir AGM is next month and Peter Longley and Kay aren't standing again?'

'No, I haven't really found my way round that side of things yet.'

'Meriel was mentioning your name. She wants you on board.'

'Really? I've only just joined.'

'Yes, she rang me. She's an amazing woman, Meriel, knows everyone and she is just so clever at roping them into things.'

'She's roped me into making six chocolate truffle tortes for a hospice do and to help with the spring fair. She must have been pretty high-powered when she was a consultant.'

'People still speak of her in hushed tones though I gather students quaked when they were on her ward round. She's the kind of person who should never retire. Now she has to divert all that energy into her charities.'

Their main courses arrived, the monkfish in thick meaty chunks surrounded by its lightly curried sauce, with big bowls of fresh vegetables. Freya went to the bar to get more mineral water. She wondered if Angela Randall had ever come to a pub like this with the man for whom she had bought the expensive presents; she hoped so and that she had had some return for her extravagance. How had she met him? Where was he now? She was sure the gifts tied in with the woman's disappearance but was still without a single lead. Debbie Parker, she thought, putting the deep blue bottles of water on the table between them, would almost certainly not have been to the Fox and Goose, with or without her new friends from Starly. Freya felt guilty that she did not find Debbie very interesting.

She sat down, poured herself a glass of water and then said, 'It's a real medical establishment, the Serrailler family.'

'Going back three generations. Do you know the others?' Freya bent her head to her plate. 'No. Though I work with Simon, of course.'

'Yes, he's the odd one out. His parents weren't best pleased when he decided to become a policeman, of all things. God, I can't believe I just said that.'

'Don't worry, we know we're a pretty low form of pond life.'

'But, to them, a Serrailler who is not a doctor is not a true Serrailler. You'd think two out of three triplets as doctors would do, wouldn't you?'

'Do you know him well?'

'Richard?'

'I meant Simon, but yes, Richard too.'

Sharon looked at her quickly, put her knife and fork together and leaned back.

'Hardly,' she said. 'He and Meriel don't come as a couple, if you see what I mean. She does her own thing.'

'I didn't take to him when we met.'

'Nobody does. I think she's had a tough time. He's a very bitter man.'

'What, about a son becoming a copper?'

'That and Martha. Do you know about Martha?'

'No. Do you want pudding?'

'How do you think I get into my clothes. Coffee though.'

They ordered espressos.

'Martha is the youngest Serrailler, about ten years younger than the triplets. She was born severely brain-damaged. She's in a home on the other side of Bevham. From what I've heard, it killed Richard. Martha represents failure to him. He had to have the perfect family, moulded to his design. It didn't work.'

'Poor Meriel.'

'Yes, she's the one who suffers. That's why she's always in this whirl of activity, most of which takes her away from him.'

'Presumably he's retired too?'

'Yes. He was a consultant neurologist. No one knows what he does with himself now. It certainly isn't giving help and support to his wife.'

The coffees came, with a plate of four chocolate truffles. Sharon pushed them away. 'How do you find Simon to work with?' she asked.

Freya was caught off guard. Sharon was looking at her carefully.

'He's a very good DCI. Runs a good team.'

'And?'

'Sorry?'

'Don't say you haven't fallen in love with him. Every other female who has ever come up against Simon Serrailler has.'

Freya swallowed a mouthful of scalding coffee. Pain shot down her throat. Sharon leaned forward. Eager for confidences and confessions, Freya thought. Be careful, be careful. But she was desperate to talk about him and careless of everything except to know more.

'OK,' Sharon said, 'I get it. Now listen –'

'I need to know just one thing, Sharon. Is he gay? It sort of seems obvious that he would be – must be, of course he must.'

'Good God, no,'

Freya felt sweat running down her back. Her head was swimming.

'It's a bit of a mystery what he is. Everyone's tried to crack it, no one ever does. You're a detective, you've got as good a chance as any. I don't know Simon well, it's Meriel I know, but I've met a lot of people who've been bruised by him. He's a charming man, handsome, cultivated, warm, good company. He's fast-tracked up the career ladder, which is also an attractive trait. But he has broken more hearts than I've had hot dinners, Freya. He charms women, he's friendly, he makes them feel they're the only one in the world, he gives them his full attention, listens . . . he's a very good listener. Now whether it is that he simply doesn't have a clue, I don't know. He certainly isn't a sadistic woman-hater, I'd put money on that. But he backs off when they start getting keen, and when he backs off he cuts off, big time. They don't know what's hit them. And there's something else – no one knows where or what, but he definitely has another life away from Lafferton and the two lives never, ever meet – they probably don't even meet in his own brain, if you see what I mean. I'm going to order another coffee – you?'

Freya nodded. She could not have spoken a word. Sharon got up and went over to the bar. The buzz of happy conversation and laughter boomed and buzzed round the room, the smell of coffee and whiffs of cigar smoke floated in the air. It was an atmosphere she could hide in, while she struggled to sort out her emotions.

Sharon was sharp enough to have unmasked her at once. Be careful, she warned herself again, be careful.

When she came back, she said, 'Listen, Sharon . . .'

Sharon raised a hand. 'I know. Don't say anything to anyone.'

'There isn't anything to say.'

'Whatever. You work with him, you don't want it getting round. I'm not an idiot.'

'There is no "it" . . . really. I'm just curious.'

'Right. Curious.'

'All right, attracted as well.'

'I just wanted to warn you.'

'Warn me – or warn me off?'

'Absolutely not – a) not my type, and b) I'm sorted. But I've seen too many women made very unhappy by your DCI.'

'Thanks, I am warned. After having one man ruin some of the best years of my life, I'm not about to let it happen again. I tell you what though – if he were gay, might he not have to keep it under wraps and away from home for one reason.'

'His father?'

'From what you've said.'

'Could be.'

'OK, that's quite enough of men. If I came to one of your shops, how much discount would I get off a pair of Armani trousers?'

On the way home, Freya made a detour to the Hill. No one was about. The tapes were still across the entrances, whipped about by the wind and giving off the reminder of death and disaster common to every crime scene. If this is a crime scene . . . she thought, walking slowly up to one of the gaps that led on to the green slopes, now bare and bleak in the waning light. It was easy to conjure up ghosts here as well as images of fear and violence. On a sunny summer day, it would emanate charm and playfulness, with children running about, people strolling with their dogs, runners sweating in singlets and lycra.

What had happened here? She knew it was here, she had a gut feeling and there were too many links. The young mountain biker had last been seen here. Jim Williams had seen Angela Randall running into the fog. Debbie Parker had taken to walking here in the early morning because she had been told it was an auspicious time. Even Skippy the Yorkshire terrier had run away from Jim Williams into the undergrowth and vanished.

What was happening and why? Where was the link, not only between three people and a dog all last seen on the Hill, but in any other sense? Was there one? If so, it was obscure and she could get no handle on it.

She looked round again. What had always motivated her as a police officer was a sense of owing something to the victims of crime, those who could not, for one reason or another, speak for themselves, defend and even avenge themselves, because they were either inarticulate, intimidated, or dead.

She had the same conviction now. She had to work on behalf of the missing people, even the missing dog. None of them had disappeared of their own accord, she had no doubt.

She got back into the car and drove away, but the melancholy and loneliness of the empty Hill clung to her all the way home.

Lunch with Sharon had been enjoyable and a complete

change, regardless of the real reason behind her invitation. With some slight reservation, Freya liked her, and would try and sustain the friendship, though she would never trust her with secrets, there had been too much of an eager gleam in her eye, and a longing for gossip. Freya could keep silent about anything to do with her work. But it was not work that she had wanted to talk to Sharon Medcalf about.

For the rest of the afternoon, she involved herself in displacement activity – supermarket shopping, washing and ironing. She cleaned the bathroom and had a shower. She watched the early television news.

At half past eight, she went out. She had no plan, she simply went, parking at the side of the cathedral where she ought to have been the night of the choir practice.

It was dark. The streets were quiet. The Close was empty apart from a woman on a bicycle and three boys walking towards the choir school. Freya lingered until they had gone in, then she walked, keeping to the shadows, towards the end houses.

He might still be at the station, or out on some police business. His flat would be in darkness and she would have wasted her time. If the lights were on, meaning that he was there, she would be happy. She could stand and look up, picture him in the room, stay as long as she needed. There was no question of her ringing his bell. She was not such a fool.

As she stepped across the grass at the side of the path, she heard a car. Simon Serrailler drove past her. Freya stopped dead. If he turned, he would see her. She stepped back into the shadows.

A couple of other cars were parked outside his house. Simon drew up beside them and the headlamps were doused but in the light of the street lamp Freya saw both car doors open. He got out first, and then a woman. She was slim and slight, and wore a pale trench coat.

Freya felt suddenly, horribly sick. She wanted to run, she wanted not to see but had to see, had to stand watching, taking in every detail.

They walked towards his building, but instead of going in, stopped at one of the other parked cars. Simon had his arm round the woman's shoulders and was bending to say something. At the car, she turned to him and he held his arms out to her.

Freya turned away. She could not run, she was paralysed, if she had been caught now, she would have been as frozen as a wild creature in headlamps. She did not want to see any more, she wanted not to be here, enduring all this. She was furious with herself.

She heard the car door slam, the engine start, the wheels turn on the cobbles. She looked up quickly. Simon was standing in his doorway, his hand raised. Then, as the car drove quickly away, past Freya, he turned, pushed open the front door, and went in.

Freya waited. It had begun to rain. In a couple of minutes, the lights went on at the top of the dark building. She pictured the flat, the lamps, the pictures. Simon. Then, she walked away.

Thirty-One

He thought he knew everything about himself. He had spent so much time alone, searching his own soul, trying to trace everything he did and thought and needed back to its source, that he would have said he could never be surprised again.

He had known for so long what he must do, and why. He had known what gave him the satisfaction that was only ever temporary, the pieces of knowledge which were gradually making the whole. He had never had any real interest in the chase and the capture. They were means to an end. He had to find the people, to select them carefully, to stake them out, track them down, pursue them one final time, and then of necessity still them. He avoided the words murder and kill and death. But none of that gave him pleasure. Sadists and psychopaths, evil people, obtained gratification from the act of murder, and possibly from everything that led to it. He was not like that. The idea horrified him.

What he did was altogether different.

So he was shocked to realise that he longed to return

to the Hill, now that temporarily he could not do so. He wanted to retrace his steps, to stand where he had stood with each one of them, to recall everything. If the police had not cordoned off the place to the public, he might never have found this out. The previous night, he had looked at his list and something else had troubled him. There were three examples left. Mature man. Elderly woman. Elderly man.

The others were accounted for, had been examined, dissected, recorded and filed away. His research was unique. No one else had experimented in the way he had, comparing the way each had been killed and the minute differences between them.

It would soon be over. He would have done what he set out to do. There would be no need for more. It was when he realised it that he knew he was not an obsessive but an addict. Even the thought of being deprived of it for ever, even the phrases 'the end' and 'the last time' and 'never again' caused him to break out in a sweat which ran cold and unpleasant down his back. He had to get up and pace about the room, then go out and pace the street before he felt calmer.

How could it ever be over? He would have nothing to live for. If there was no more work to be done, there would have to be another reason for going on and he needed to go on. He needed the fix. He needed it to keep him alive and functioning, to stop him from going mad, to help him stay in control.

He dared not take the van and he could not go in his car. Too many people knew it, knew him and might wave cheerfully to him. He would have to walk and it must be in the late evening; in daylight he would be too conspicuous. People avoided the Hill now. He knew he ought to avoid it too because going there would be breaking every rule. He had been able to continue with his work precisely because he knew what those rules were and had always obeyed them. He knew that most people were caught because they broke the rules and that they broke the rules because they became arrogant and careless and because they were stupid. But he was clever; he had a trained mind; he was systematic in everything he did; he had never acted on impulse, always checked and double-checked. So why was he so desperate that he was prepared to take a risk now? He felt the need building up inside him and he understood that only this had power over him. He must ignore it, he must control it.

For hours, he thought of the Hill. For several nights he lay awake re-enacting every occasion when he had been there, 'to work' as he liked to think of it.

He had come to love the place, for its sense of ancient history, its deep roots in the past, its Wern Stones on which so much superstition had been focused for so many centuries. He loved its silences and the different sound the wind made around it depending from which quarter it blew. He loved the way its furrows and shelves and stone outcrops were arranged, and the clumps of scrub and undergrowth and the coronet of oak trees. He loved its rabbits and its rabbit holes. He had chosen it for more practical reasons, but he had come to love it for sentimental ones.

To calm himself, he drove down to the business park. It was after seven o'clock. Everyone had left, the units were locked and in darkness. He let himself in at the side door and slipped into the cool, silent building. How astonished they would all be to discover what he had achieved here; the men who had dismissed him and ruined him had almost certainly never given him another thought once he had left the medical school buildings, but they had lost someone who would have brought glory to the place. Why had that never occurred to them? If he had been allowed to continue and follow his chosen path, he would have been at the top of his profession by now but they would have taken the credit for having trained him. Now, he took every last jot of that credit for himself.

He clicked on the white-blue fluorescent lighting and stood for a moment, hearing the silence of the dead. Then he walked down to the door set in the concrete wall at the back and went into the heart of his kingdom. It was so small, the back half of a garage, but everything that mattered was here. He hesitated, his hand hovering over one drawer handle before moving to the next, but finally, it was the second on the right that he settled on. He had checked the electricity feed, the thermometers and dials, as he did every day. He was meticulous. He could not afford to be anything else.

He reached out.

Angela Randall lay facing him as the drawer came forward silently on its runners. He stared down at her white marble face. Angela Randall. Her obsession with him had been flattering at first and when the presents had begun to arrive he had been rather pleased. No one had ever conceived a passion for him before. He had never allowed it. But after a time, the letters which gave off such a pathetic smell of desperation, the gifts, the invitations, the pleas, had become irksome. In the end he had despised her. Not that she was here for that reason; emotion had never been allowed to influence his work in any way. She was here because she had been the right age, sex, size at that stage in his research and because she had been easy to track down on the Hill.

He slid the drawer fully out to look at his own handiwork. He thought he had done a better job on Angela Randall than on the others, precise, unwavering, clean. Everything had been removed, examined, dissected, weighed, recorded, before being put back. He knew her body parts as well as he knew the back of his own hand, had studied them as closely. Now she was restored, the seams pale and shining between the surgical stitches.

He wondered what she would have given him next.

Before he rechecked the electricity and the thermometers, switched off the lights and padlocked every door, he had spent some time looking at them all. He was a little dissatisfied with his work on the young man, who had been so fit, so lean and well muscled, and wondered if it ought to be repeated. But the capture had been the most difficult, the boy had struggled, he had been very strong. Not like poor fat Debbie.

Three drawers remained empty. One of them had not yet been allocated. The others were for the elderly, for Proteus and Anna. But if things continued as they were on the Hill it would be some time before he would be able to welcome them. He walked around the inner room and then the outer, pacing, frustrated, impatient. He did not lose his temper because he never had. Loss of temper, even in minor, everyday matters, was dangerous. He would not have come so far as this in his work if he had been prone even to the smallest displays of it. But he felt like a channel that had been dammed up. This was not a delay of his own making and it was not part of the plan. Yet surely it was a weakness in him not to have allowed for the unpredictable, simply because it was a force in life and it was life he had to deal with first.

He walked around the building until he had his feelings under control, then left, to return home and revise his plans.

Thirty-Two

The weak afternoon sunshine had no warmth in it though it lit the surrounding fields prettily. Karin and Cat walked round the paddock in the teeth of the east wind, which bit through their thick sweaters, fleeces and supposedly weatherproof jackets. Hannah Deerbon sat on her rotund pony Peanuts, both of them smugly unaware of the cold. She had been led round three times and as they reached the gate, Cat said, 'OK, this is the last time and I mean it. Karin and I have no hands or faces left.'

'Don't be silly.'

'All the same, this is it, Hanny. Karin, give Peanuts a shove up his backside to get him moving.'

Energetic movement was not part of the pony's game plan and he treated the couple of slaps on his rear administered by Karin with contempt. She had rung Cat to say she needed to report on her visit to Starly, but when she arrived, Cat had been getting her daughter and pony ready.

'No school?'

'Training day. Mum's been here this morning. I promised I'd be back by one thirty but of course it was five to three. Still, she knows all about that. She said she wasn't actually expecting me until four.'

They had set off into the wind, Karin borrowing a jumper and outdoor jacket, but it was difficult to talk out here.

Karin had woken from the deep sleep into which she had fallen after her visit to the psychic surgeon, feeling rested and slightly light-headed. The experience had seemed strangely distant and it had not been until later in the day that she had been able to sit down to go through it carefully, and form an opinion. As she did so she had become more and more uneasy. Cat had been in mid-surgery when she had telephoned.

'Come up for tea at home tomorrow, we'll talk then.'

'Move, lazy Peanuts, move.' Hannah lifted her legs until they were almost horizontal to her body and brought them down with a smack on the pony's sides. This time it had the desired effect. Cat and Karin found themselves running to keep up as the pony shot forwards, and Cat struggled to hang on to the lead rein. As they reached the gate, Peanuts skidded to a halt, Cat let the rein go and slipped on her backside in the mud. Hannah sat in the saddle, cheeks pink, eyes like stars, laughing, laughing.

The whole incident tipped the three of them over into a riotous mood, from which they had not fully recovered half an hour later. Hannah had gone to watch children's television with her tea on a plate, leaving Cat and Karin in the kitchen.

'This is what I miss,' Karin said. 'All this stuff with ponies and *Blue Peter* and school satchels and packed lunches. And don't tell me I don't know how lucky I am.'

Cat poured out their mugs of tea. 'No, and I'm not going to tell you motherhood is hell because the hell is only purgatory and there are good stretches of heaven. If I have sympathy for one group of patients more than another, it's the women who can't conceive.' She looked across at Karin. 'And for those who might have done but left it too late.'

'It would have been tough on any children I might have had with things as they are.'

'That's true. OK, spill the beans.'

Karin was quiet for a moment, assembling her thoughts. The cat jumped on to the sofa and curled up beside her.

'It's worrying. I think he ought to be stopped, I really do.'

'What happened?'

Karin told her, in as much detail as she could, quoting everything she remembered that he had said to her, describing what he had done. Cat listened without a word, sipping her tea, occasionally frowning. From the television next door came the sound of a recorder band playing 'Morning has Broken'. Outside the wind bent the beech trees at the end of the garden. When Karin had finished, Cat said nothing, only got up to refill the kettle, before going to check on Hannah.

Karin waited. She envied Cat not only her children but something indefinable about her house and her family life, a warmth and a happiness, together with a confidence in the future, which affected the spirit of every visitor. Whenever she left here, in spite of the times she had seen Cat white with exhaustion at the end of a punishing day, or with anxiety about a patient at the same time as one of the children was ill or had some problem at school,

Karin had still taken away something that healed and refreshed her from the atmosphere in this house. Since her own change of career and her satisfaction in what she was doing, she had known some of the same deep-seated contentment in her own life, which at times came close to making up for the absence of children in it. Everything had clicked into place at long last. She had vowed never to say, never even to think, 'It's not fair,' and 'Why me, why now?' about the cancer.

Cat returned and dumped Hannah's plate and mug on the draining board.

'OK, I've taken it in. I'm horrified. This man is dangerous, you're right, though I'm not sure if he is doing any physical damage and it sounds as if he was very careful not to ask you to undress or to touch you in any way or place that could lay him open to a charge of assault. You're quite sure about that? Because if he did, then we've got him. I can pick up the phone to my brother now.'

Karin shook her head. 'It was uppermost in my mind from the minute I walked into the room. He was very, very careful.'

'Of course he would be with a woman who was obviously watchful and intelligent. Would he behave so impeccably with a young girl, or even a child . . . does he see children?'

'I don't know. The people waiting were all older.'

'The wickedness is the deception, of course . . . and the fact that he gives people false hope with this pantomime. He will also convince at least some of them that they are cured and don't need proper medical treatment, which is the worst of it.'

'I found it quite frightening.'

'I bet you did. Dear God, imagine if you were old and

333

frail and you actually believed he was cutting you open and taking bits out of you – you could perfectly easily die of shock. I wonder if anyone ever has.'

'To find that out you'd need to discover where he came from, where he's worked before.'

'I'm going to do some research when I have half a moment.'

'I can help there. I'll trawl the Internet and I've a friend on the *Sunday Times* I might ring. They're good at digging up people's unsavoury pasts. They might even do an investigative report.'

'Good idea. We've a meeting of this new committee of doctors and complementary therapists. I'll report to that. The trouble is it all takes time. And I'm on call tonight. It's the one thing I'd cheerfully give up, and yet it's often when you get to know your own patients best – when the chips are down at four in the morning.'

'You're a national treasure. I hope you know that, Dr Deerbon.'

'No. I haven't succeeded with you.'

From the television room the hornpipe marked the end of *Blue Peter*.

Karin stood up. 'Thanks for the tea. I'll leave you to enjoy some quality time with your daughter.'

Cat made a face.

Outside, the wind cut across the garden, slamming the car door out of Karin's hand. She looked back at the lighted kitchen window, watching Cat lift Hannah up on to the worktop beside the sink, both of them laughing. Yes, she thought. Children. But the check she kept on herself came at once. 'Don't whinge.' Self-pity and dissatisfaction ate into the spirit, which she was determined would remain positive, optimistic and thankful.

As she reached home, her mobile rang.

'It's Cat. I'm going to check out this guy for myself. Can you text me his number?'

'What if he susses you're a doctor?'

'He won't. And anyway, so what?'

'You might have to wait a bit, he claims to be very booked up.'

'Give us both time to do some digging. I want to go there knowing every last thing I can find out about our psychic surgeon.'

It was almost midnight when Cat telephoned her brother.

'I didn't think you'd be tucked up.'

'I've only been in half an hour.'

'And I'm on call so there's never any point in going to bed early – or going to bed at all come to that. Si, have you anything doing up at Starly . . . officially?'

'Sort of. We did a house-to-house the other day, trying for info on the missing girl Debbie Parker. Drew a blank though.'

'Yes, I knew she'd seen a therapist up there. She was my patient.'

'Is . . . I like to remain optimistic.'

'Did your people encounter a chap calling himself a psychic surgeon?'

'A what?'

She repeated Karin's story.

'He's new to me. I can check whether our people saw him. They'll have been to the house, they went every-where. I haven't had a report about Debbie Parker having been to see him though. She favoured a chap in blue robes who calls himself Dava.'

'She told me about Dava. Listen, Si, this Dr Groatman,

or Anthony Orford, or whatever his real name is – he's dangerous. For all sorts of reasons, he ought to be put out of business.'

'You were certainly right to ask Karin if she felt he'd laid himself open to any charge of assault, but it doesn't sound as if he did.'

'Can't you get him for something else?'

'Such as? He isn't breaking any law. You know yourself anyone can set up as an alternative practitioner, no training, no qualifications, plate on the door and Bob's your uncle. There are no regulations. If we could prove he had actually taken an instrument and opened someone up, we could certainly arrest him. Has he?'

'It's all sleight of hand.'

'Does he claim to operate on people . . . is that what he says in his literature?'

'Oh, I think he's too clever to have any of that.'

'How does he get patients?'

'Word of mouth. People tell of his miracles.'

'How long has he been in Starly?'

'Not long. Karin is going to try and find out where he was before.'

'And why he left. I'll get some checks run tomorrow, but from what you've told me we've no reason even to question him. Someone would have to come to us with a formal complaint.'

'Shit. I'm really wound up about this one. Think of the people he's conning, think of the money he's raking in. Think of the serious illnesses people might be taking to him instead of coming to us.'

'There's one thing you might do . . . What is the next best thing to setting the police on to him? Possibly even better?'

'Not a clue.'

'The press. Get a reporter to pose as a patient and then nosy around Starly. Ten to one they'd never get an interview out of him, he'll be too fly, but if a good journalist gets to the bottom of him and there is any dirty linen, it'll be hung out all over the district.'

'Can you think of anyone who'd be interested?'

'Oh, indeed,' Cat heard the smile in her brother's voice, 'I know just the person. Got a pen?'

Rachel Carr was in the office by eight every morning. She had found out long ago that the early news reporter caught whatever worms had been turned up overnight and she was never going to let a colleague beat her to them. There was also fun to be had in the Mazda on half-empty roads. By ten past eight, the traffic coming into town and the school-run mothers took all the joy out of her precious toy. So when Cat Deerbon rang she took the call and within a few seconds of listening the adrenaline was pumping.

By mid-morning, Rachel had the go-ahead from her editor, put in a couple of calls to people who might come up with something about the psychic surgeon and made an appointment to see him herself. Having been told that he was fully booked for six weeks, she pleaded acute pain and distress, slipping in mention of a friend who had said the surgeon had worked a miracle on her and saying that he was her only hope.

'Hold on one moment please.'

The receptionist was back within twenty seconds to say she could fit Rachel in at the end of the coming Friday afternoon.

'Dr Groatman does try to keep some spaces for people who are in great pain.'

Rachel thanked her tearfully and profusely.

'There may be a small further charge to cover the extra administration.'

'I don't mind, I'll pay anything, it doesn't matter what it costs. Thank you so much.'

She put the phone down, went straight on to the Internet and keyed Dr+Charles+Groatman+psychic+surgeon into Google.

The website it gave her was out of date. Dr Charles Groatman, aka Brian Urchmont, advertised himself as practising at a clinic in Brighton. Beside his photograph were extracts from letters of thanks, praise and recommendation from grateful patients and details of surgery hours. When she rang the telephone number given, a BT message told her it was unrecognised. Rachel thought for a moment, then remembered Duggie Hotten, who had been a senior reporter when she was starting out and had gone on to the *Brighton Argus*.

She was put straight through.

'Rachel. Carr, of course I remember. What are you doing now?'

'Chief reporter at Lafferton.' She hoped no one was listening.

'Great stuff.'

'I won't be here for ever.'

'*Daily Mail* next stop then?'

'Watch this space.'

'What can I do?'

She began to tell him but he was there before her.

'God, just start me on the subject of our psychic surgeon. We've a mountain of stuff on him but he's always come out of it smelling of roses – sort of. So he's in your neck of the woods. Good luck.'

'I'm doing an investigative. Can you let me have any clippings?'

'Sure. He's a tricky one, Rache. Watch your back. He's got a nose for a journalist and he screams "Libel" like a stuck pig. He also turns up all sorts of people to defend him, grateful patients whose lives he saved, you know the stuff. We had a mountain of letters.'

'What happened?'

'We dropped it. Too much flak. Besides, he isn't doing anything illegal. He's very, very careful.'

'Great stuff, Duggie, I owe you.'

'A word in the ear at the *Daily Mail* once you're there. That'll do nicely.'

Thirty-Three

The only day Sandy Marsh had missed going to work had been the day Debbie had disappeared. Since then she had gone in early and stayed late, because she couldn't bear being in the flat and because at work she could keep her mind off Debbie for a good part of the time.

Today, she walked down the long open-plan office shortly after eight, expecting there to be no one else in for another half-hour. But Jason Webster was there, putting some daffodils into a vase at Sandy's desk. Everyone had been brilliant to her, Jason most of all, the place had changed from an office to a home full of caring relations. People took over some of her work, brought her coffees, invited her out every lunch hour and to their homes for supper most nights so that she was not left to spend an evening in the flat alone unless she wanted.

'Those are beautiful, Jase. They look like the spring.'

'Keep you smiling.'

Sandy dumped her bag and coat and gave him a hug. The daffodils shone like sovereigns in the rather sterile grey and steel office.

'Coffee?'

Sandy turned on her computer and looked at the new file left on her desk late last night by the section manager. More people in debt, more firms asking for time to pay, more excuses. Sandy was in the area of credit control where the desperate ended up, those who had had virtually every warning and not only failed to pay but failed to communicate or proffer explanation, reason or excuse. 'Last Chance Saloon' someone had printed out in scarlet and pinned over Sandy's work station ages ago.

She enjoyed her job. She was meticulous, she liked working with figures but figures which had people not far in the background, and she liked being able, just sometimes, to haul people in before they fell off the edge of her desk into the bankruptcy court.

'I put sugar in it as well.' Jason set down the tray. He had brought two cups of coffee and two ring doughnuts.

'No, Jase . . .'

'You're wasting away, Sandy. I don't like it.'

It was true that she had lost almost half a stone since Debbie had gone missing. Jason sat on the edge of her desk. 'No news then?'

Sandy shook her head. She had given up ringing the police station. Not that they weren't always very nice to her, said of course they'd be in touch at once if . . . everything being done . . . following up a lot of leads . . . In other words, not a thing.

'I've been thinking,' Jason said, 'they searched the Hill, right?'

'Crawled all over it.'

'But what were they looking for? I mean, they didn't know Debbie, you did. They might have overlooked something you'd have spotted.'

'Like what?'

'That's the problem.'

'I don't think they could have missed anything . . . there were so many of them, Jason. Though I suppose they were . . .' she swallowed, then said quickly, 'they were looking for bits of her clothing – or blood or . . . things.'

'It's OK, don't get upset.'

'It *is* upsetting. Sorry, I don't mean to snap, sorry.'

'No, you're fine, don't be daft. But I still wonder if there might be a point in you and me going up there, having a poke around.'

'It would make me feel I was doing something. There's not much else I can do except go over and over everything she said, everything she did, anything that might be a clue. But that's just made me stay awake all night. I wouldn't dare go up there by myself, but you're right. I might just get some sort of feeling. Sounds stupid.'

'No it doesn't.'

'I thought last night – I've begun to get angry with her, you know? If she's gone off on purpose and she just isn't letting anyone know, whatever the reason, whether she was depressed again or what, then I'm angry. I know that's wrong but I can't help it. Then I think, that isn't Debbie, it just isn't in her nature. She's a very considerate person, she's really thoughtful. She'd never, ever put us all through this. She'd have rung me or her dad or texted me. I've been her best friend since we were five, first day at infant school, Jase. I know Debbie. I just know something's happened to her. But no one seems to want to do any more. They don't talk about extending the inquiry or going nationwide with the appeal but they won't say why. It's really getting to me now. I'm angry all the time. If I'm not angry with her I'm angry with them.'

'And it ain't doing you any good. So what about going up there?'

'Isn't it still cordoned off?'

'No, all the tapes and stuff have gone, I drove by this morning.'

'That means they've given up then.'

'Whatever. We haven't.'

'But what could we do?'

Jason got up. 'I don't know, babe, I just think you'd feel better for it.'

'No. I couldn't be there without thinking horrible thoughts. But thanks.'

'You're welcome.'

He picked up his coffee and the remains of his doughnut and wandered off down the room to his own desk.

Sandy clicked on to the first file of the day and settled down to work. She was busy, which helped, and when three of the girls suggested a quick lunch in the bistro nearby she agreed with pleasure.

That evening, for the first since Debbie had gone, Sandy stayed home in the flat alone. She had been trying to avoid it and for a short while that had helped, but she was not a person to flinch from difficult things and having changed her mind and resolved to go to the Hill with Jason at the weekend, she was determined to face the empty flat now.

As soon as she got in, she put on the radio, found a station playing old hits and turned up Blondie singing 'The Tide is High'. Sandy took it through to the bathroom, where she poured some purple liquid called Intensity into the water which brought foam frothing over the edge and on to the mat. It smelled exotic and she wallowed in it, while the music changed to Wings with 'Mull of Kintyre'.

Come on, it's not so bad, you're doing fine.

After the bath, she spent half an hour giving herself a manicure and pedicure, fiddling about with different nail polishes, put on a face mask and then some rejuvenating cream she had bought that lunchtime, along with two new tops which were in carrier bags on the bed, to be tried on again later, after she had cooked pasta and fresh tomato and mushroom sauce with Parmesan and drunk a glass and a half of some white wine she found in the cupboard, left over from Christmas. Then there was *Coronation Street* and *The Bill*, a couple of cheques to write, and a new Penny Vincenzi novel to start. She should have done all this long ago. Running away never did anyone any good.

She went to bed not long after ten with her book and a cup of tea. She had changed the sheets, so that it felt cool and fresh.

She had read two pages of her book when, without warning and as a response to no particular thought or reminder, Sandy started to cry. She sat up and reached for the tissue box and then she cried for twenty minutes, tears of fear and anxiety pouring down her face, tears that released all the pent-up strain of the past week, tears that came with great gulping sounds. She missed Debbie, she dared not imagine what had happened to her or where she was but she was terrified that Debbie was not alive.

The thought had been pushed down inside her for

days; she had been optimistic and cheerful, determined there was a logical explanation – maybe not a simple one, or one that she would like, but an explanation all the same, and that when she had heard it, from Debbie, she would be able to sort things out.

Now, she accepted that there could be no explanation other than the worst of all. She had spoken the truth when she had told Jason that Debbie was the last person to disappear without warning. Wherever her friend had gone, if it had been to try and solve some problem she had never spoken about, she would still have been in touch, with her of all people. They had never failed to tell one another things that were important since they had been little girls in the playground. Debbie was dead. Someone had attacked her and taken her away. Someone had killed her. Someone was hiding her. She said it over and over to herself as she wept, and in the end had to go to wash her face in cold water in an effort to calm herself down.

Then she went back to bed, and lay, still crying, not wanting to put out the light, not able to read, but for hour after hour wondering, wondering and dreading.

Thirty-Four

The blue suit, the brown-and-pink print two-piece, and a plain mauve jumper and tweed skirt were laid out on the bed, but she was no nearer deciding which would be right to wear, and then, suddenly, she saw the funny side of it. There had to be a funny side.

Here I am, Iris Chater thought, dithering about what clothes would be right, as if I were going out to a smart lunch when what I'm going to is ... but she could hardly bring herself to think the word. Still, it was funny; as if it mattered what anyone wore when they went to a group evening with a medium, as if people were going to judge her by her clothes, or even notice her at all.

She put the blue suit and the two-piece back in the wardrobe and kept out the jumper and skirt.

It had taken her a long time to decide. She had left the idea alone, after she had visited Sheila Innis the first time, partly because it worried her, but mainly because she was still upset about Harry not having come to speak to her. All the rest had been too strange to sort out and the suggestion of going to a group had taken some working through as well. In the end it was curiosity that had decided her. Now she had met the woman, and not been frightened by sitting with her alone, hearing things about her own past she had all but forgotten, getting messages from people she hadn't thought of for fifty years, she had known she would go to the seance eventually and then it had just been a case of waiting until what seemed like the right moment.

She was feeling brighter in herself and the lighter mornings and evenings helped, and the fact that she could get out to do a bit in the garden. The end of the day was the worst. She missed Harry the most then and never seemed to be able to settle easily to anything. But in the day she went out more, even if it was only shopping, and once a week to the hairdresser and twice she and Pauline had gone on the bus into Bevham for the day, with lunch out. She saw plenty of Pauline but not in the same dependent way. In the end, though, Iris had told her about the visit to the medium; it had been Pauline who had first suggested it after all, and secrets always came out in the end. She wasn't ashamed. Pauline had been interested and very understanding and sympathetic about Harry's silence.

All the same, something held her back from saying that she was going to a group seance. Maybe she would talk about it eventually, maybe she wouldn't.

She would get the bus part of the way there, then walk the last bit, and if it was very late finishing, she might get a taxi home. Harry had never been happy about her being out by herself after dark, and made her take taxis once he had stopped driving the car, so she always had the numbers with her. She couldn't imagine

Mrs Innis would mind her ringing for one. She had said to be there at seven. 'There'll be six others, Mrs Chater, and you'll find everyone very friendly and the whole meeting quite informal and relaxed.'

She had gone on to ask Iris about herself, whether she was feeling more able to cope.

'The only thing is, there are days when it doesn't seem as if he's in the house at all and he was always there, at the beginning as soon as I walked in, I said, "Hello, Harry," because I knew he was there.'

'He's still with you all the time, but you have been getting out more, spending less time thinking only about him, focusing on him.'

'I still miss him, I do still think of him a lot of the time.'

'We have to move forward. Our loved ones don't want us to try and live in the past. But they're never far away.'

She'd felt better then.

When she left the house, the biting wind had dropped so that, although it was cold, it was pleasant to walk. As planned, she got off the bus a stop early, to calm her nerves.

All the stories her mother used to tell about table-turning and Ouija boards revolved round her head, all those spooky happenings behind drawn curtains. Everyone went to seances then, they were an entertainment, but when she was young, she had hated to hear about them, hated the relish in her mother's voice when she talked about whoever had 'come through' and what the medium had looked like in a trance, 'all white-faced and peculiar'. She tried to keep the pleasant room in Sheila Innis's house in mind, the comfortable chair and the vases of flowers and nice curtains, the fat cat Otto.

As she turned into the avenue, she heard footsteps behind her. An elderly man walked past and nodded 'Good evening', as he went on ahead.

A couple of minutes later, she saw him turn into the gate of the medium's house, so that they stood together on the doorstep.

'Same destination, then. I don't think we've met here before, have we?'

'No, this is my first time . . . well, I've seen Mrs Innis.'

'But not been to a seance? You'll find it very interesting, very. I'm Jim, Jim Williams.'

They were shaking hands as Sheila Innis opened the door.

This time it was a different room with a long table and chairs. The curtains were drawn and the lamps lit, so that when she walked in, Iris Chater felt quite comfortable, almost at home, and Jim Williams took the seat next to her after leaving his coat. There were five others, four women all middle-aged to elderly and a younger man. He looked unhappy, Iris thought, ill at ease and downcast; he was pale, with a bad skin, and dark circles beneath his eyes, and when he showed his hands, she saw how bitten the nails were.

Sheila Innis came in. 'How nice to see you all. Good evening, everyone.'

They all murmured except the young man, who seemed to slip down in his chair as if hoping to disappear.

The medium took her place at the top of the table. She wore a cream blouse with a row of blue beads and a pale blue jacket. Smart, Iris thought, and wondered if she should have worn the two-piece after all.

'We have to welcome just one new guest this evening.

Iris, if I may introduce you in that way. We don't like to be too formal.'

They all looked at her and smiled, and Iris felt welcome and as if she belonged with them. She wondered why she had been so nervous. Only the young man looked away. The medium hadn't introduced him as new, so he must be familiar with it all. Iris wondered about him. A tragedy, she decided, a young wife? Something he's never recovered from.

The lights dimmed, though no one had got up to touch a switch. There must be a clever arrangement under the table. One standard lamp set behind Sheila Innis remained a little brighter, though it left her face shadowed. Everyone had gone very still.

'Let us bow our heads and ask for a blessing on our circle tonight. Let us invite our spirit guides to join us and for our loved ones on the other side to come near. Let us at the same time warn any disturbed, malicious or mischievous spirits to leave us and to seek guidance and peace in other realms.'

It was like praying, but not quite the same. Iris closed her eyes and folded her hands and imagined herself in church, saw the altar and the cross. Then, she tried to picture Harry but could not. She opened her eyes again quickly. Bent heads, hands folded on the table. The lamp shining on the medium. The quietness in the room. Her heart began to beat too fast. She looked at Sheila Innis. Her face was stiff and without expression, her eyes closed, her head tipped slightly back. No one spoke. Nothing moved. Iris saw the leather binding on the cuff of Jim Williams's sports jacket, out of the corner of her eye.

'I have someone with me . . . a young woman, a very attractive young woman. She has an unusual bangle on her wrist . . . I can't see it closely . . . come nearer, dear, show me the bangle . . . thank you, now she's holding it up. It's silver . . . and in the shape of a snake . . . the head and tip of the tail come together at her wrist but don't quite meet. I've never seen anything quite like it. Does anyone . . . ?'

'It's Carol. My Carol had a bangle like that, she went on holiday to Bali and brought it back, it wasn't long before she was killed, it was her last holiday. Is she saying anything? Does she look all right?'

'Can you speak louder . . . ? Is it Carol? She's nodding now and laughing and holding up the bangle. Now she's drawing something in the air . . . still laughing . . . teasing us, I think . . . she's drawing big circles with her arm. I don't know what they're meant to be . . . she's saying you . . . yes, that you took her to the fair. She went with Kerry –'

'Kenny . . . her brother Kenny, my son. Oh, they did, we did, we all went to the fair and she went on the big wheel. It is Carol!'

Iris looked at the woman opposite. She was smiling and crying at the same time, and wiping her eyes on a tissue someone had handed her, so that her mascara smudged and smeared her cheeks.

The medium's face had not changed and now her voice had taken on a strange, expressionless tone, as if she was talking in her sleep. Iris wondered when Harry would come – if he would, among so many other people. He had been shy, he hadn't liked groups of strangers. Maybe he would rather not get in touch here.

The person to Iris's right clutched her hand suddenly, making her start. The woman was staring huge-eyed at Sheila Innis but holding on to Iris. Something Iris would never have imagined or believed was happening, something she did not understand, and could never have described or explained afterwards. She'd heard of it somewhere but dismissed it as a joke. Looking at the medium now, she saw that it was no joke.

Sheila Innis was not Sheila Innis any more. Her face was changing as they watched. Instead of a pale middle-aged woman who looked as if she were asleep, the face was ageing and caving in at the mouth, the nose seemed larger, and the cheeks more sunken, the chin more prominent. The face was that of a very old woman, scowling and unpleasant, with a malevolent stare out of intense, pinprick dark eyes. Iris gripped her neighbour's hand in return.

'Someone did away with me. I was put away. I was locked up. Someone didn't want me to see the light of day. Was it you? Was it you? I know which one of you it was and you know, don't you? You never thought I'd come back to accuse you, you thought you could get rid of me, out of sight out of mind, and take the money when I was dead. Well, you took the money and much good it did you. Your conscience can't be clear, can it? Are you going to speak to me. You know my name. You know who you are and I know who you are. Look at me, look at me, look, look . . .'

There was a slight movement. The younger man had bent his head but his face was a terrible yellow colour, waxen and sick. His hands were on the table and the fingers were locked together. He said nothing.

They went on staring at Sheila Innis who was no longer Sheila Innis, speechless and horrified.

But what came next was almost worse, and it came so suddenly that Iris thought she might faint, her heart seemed to freeze and then leap painfully in her chest; she could not breathe easily.

The old woman was fading from the medium's face and for a second it seemed as if it was returning to the familiar pleasant face of Sheila Innis. Then out of her mouth came a series of yapping barks, the noise made by some small ferocious dog defending its territory. The barks would not stop, they grew louder and more frantic until Iris wanted to put her hands to her ears, or run out of the room. The dog sounded as if it were trying to escape from somewhere, the barks became yelps, and then the yelps were painful, and mingled with whimpering and whining, then more strangulated barks.

Iris became conscious of Jim Williams at her side. He had pushed back his chair and when she looked at him, she saw that his face was flushed, his eyes wide open in horrified astonishment. He put his hand to his throat. The barking went on and on, the medium's mouth was opening and shutting and her head was shaking, making her hair flop down over her eyes.

Jim stood up. 'Skippy,' he said pleadingly. 'Skippy. Skippy. Where are you? What's happening to you? Skippy . . .'

None of them knew what to do. Jim stood with his hand to his throat, his shoulders heaving.

The lights went up abruptly. Sheila Innis was sitting with her eyes open, looking as if she had been woken out of a deep sleep. Jim Williams slumped down into his chair.

A minute later the door opened and a man with a moustache and a blue shirt and tie came in carrying a large tray of teacups and saucers, which he set on the table, smiling round as if, Iris thought, he'd happened into a meeting of the WI instead of a seance that had become sinister and frightening.

People began to move and take the cups. The man left the room and then reappeared, with a second tray, of teapot, milk, sugar and biscuits.

Sheila Innis smiled. 'Thank you, dear,' she said.

Everything seemed normal, nothing might have happened. Jim Williams's face was still flushed and distressed; when he reached for his cup his hand trembled.

'Are you feeling all right? That upset you, didn't it?'

He managed a gulp of tea, then quickly set it down again, fearful of spilling it in his agitation. 'I lost the little dog,' he said. His voice was husky. 'Skippy. She sounded just like him. That was Skippy.'

'It's terrible losing a pet. People never realise. If they haven't had one they think it can't be much, not like losing a person, but it is for a while, it really is.'

'He went. Just vanished. I blame myself, I should never have let him off the lead, Phyllis never did, never would have, I used to think she was making a fuss but she was right, you see, I shouldn't have let him off, and when I did, he vanished. And that barking was him. He's dead then. It must mean that.'

'Where did you lose him?'

'On the Hill. He just vanished into the bushes. I called and called, I've been up there almost every day, until this police business.'

'That poor girl?'

'And the other. There was another went missing, you know, an older woman, before Christmas. I saw her. I've told the police. I told them about Skippy as well but of course they weren't really interested, well, you can't blame them, if it's people and a dog, well, there's no contest, I can see that. But I feel as if I've let Phyllis down. She trusted me with Skippy, you see. I've let her down.'

'But he might come back. Don't give up hope. Dogs run off, they lose their scent of home, he might have been picked up by someone . . . Have you tried the dog rescue? Or you could put an advert in the free paper, have you thought of that?'

Jim shook his head. 'I might have done,' he said. 'Not now. Not now I've heard that.' He looked up at the medium.

She was standing behind one of the others, holding her teacup, chatting. As if it was all normal, as if nothing had happened and her face had never turned into that of an evil old woman, and there had been no yapping dog. If it hadn't been for Jim, Iris might have thought she was going mad. She'd given up hope of hearing from Harry now. He wouldn't come with all of this going on.

'My husband died,' she said to Jim. She hadn't known she was going to say it. He patted her hand. 'Just before Christmas. It was a merciful release, he'd been so ill, only . . . well, it's still hard, isn't it? Still really hard.'

'Have you heard from him? She gets a lot of people coming through . . . sometimes there's four or five. Don't give up, like you said about Skippy. He might come, you know.'

'Do you come every week?'

'Mostly. Well, it's interesting. I find it interesting. And it's company. I read a lot of books about the spirit world. I've made quite a study of it.'

But it hadn't prepared you for hearing Skippy bark, she thought. He seemed better; his tea was finished without a spill, and his face looked quite cheerful. She imagined coming every week, just out of interest and for the company. She'd rather sit at home for a month without seeing a soul.

'How are you, Mrs Chater? I do hope we hear from your loved one in the second part of the evening. I'm sure several will be waiting to come through now. I use the board this time. I get very good results.'

Iris stood up. 'I'm afraid I have to go, I have to be back for . . . my neighbour. She isn't well. I promised I wouldn't be out for long, you see.'

Sheila Innis put her hand out and placed it on Iris's arm. It felt warm. Soothing. Iris stared at her face, trying to see the old woman again, but there was no resemblance, none at all.

'Don't worry, Mrs Chater. Sometimes things are a bit strange, perhaps even worrying, when you're new . . . Of course, I don't know what happens, I'm in trance, I don't have control over any of it. It's very different from the individual sittings – well, you've gathered.'

But Iris had her handbag over her arm. The room felt hot and something in it smelled strange, sickly sweet and unpleasant in her nostrils.

'I'm sorry.'

Jim got up, pushing his chair back. 'I hope you come again. I hope you like the company.' His eyes were watery and they pleaded with her.

'And I hope you find your little dog. You try putting in that advert.'

People were talking together. No one else took any notice of her going except the young man with the bitten nails and bad skin, who looked up and stared, out of pale, vacant eyes.

The hall was empty. There was no sign or sound of Mr Innis.

Iris opened the front door, slipped outside and when she had closed it quietly, leaned on it for a second, trembling, as Jim Williams had trembled, but with a great wave of relief. The air was mild and cool and smelled of hedgerows and car exhaust. It smelled wonderful, Iris thought, as wonderful as anything she had ever smelled in her life.

As she turned into the road, she saw that the light behind the drawn curtains in the front room had suddenly dimmed.

She realised that, in leaving the house so hastily, she had not asked to phone for a taxi, but because the evening was pleasant, she didn't mind the thought of walking on into town. Taxis for hire never came down roads like this but perhaps she would be lucky and a bus might appear.

She began by walking fast, but after a few yards, she was so breathless, she was forced to stop. When she began to walk again, her legs felt watery and the breathlessness was worse. Iris sat down on the low stone wall of a house. There were lights on. If she felt no better, she would ring the bell and ask them if they would phone a taxi for her. People never minded being helpful in that way.

Yes. That was what she would do. She stood up, but then two things happened at once. She was afraid, quite suddenly, with an awful sense of foreboding and doom. It was not fear, it was mortal dread, it was the certainty that something appalling was about to happen to her. At the same time, a pain in her chest gripped her in metal pincers and crushed the breath from her. A second surge of pain. If she could get to the front door of this house, if she could make them hear. Iris struggled with the pain, struggled to stand, struggled against the wave of fear, tried to call out, but then she was safe, someone was coming. She managed to stand, even lifted her right arm a little to wave to the car, and it was all right. It was coming nearer and as it came, it was slowing down. She felt the brightness of the headlamps envelop her in warmth and light and safety. She looked up and saw the car stop beside her. The light was beautiful.

'Harry,' she said. But no more.

Thirty-Five

DS Freya Graffham had spent most of a long cold day with Nathan Coates and DC Gary Walsh, alternately hanging about an underpass of the Bevham road to the Sir Eric Anderson High School, Lafferton's comprehensive, and visiting addresses on two housing estates.

For the rest of the time, they had sat in parked cars, watching, waiting and drinking paper cups of coffee. The drugs operation was in its fourth week and it was known that suppliers were using the underpass to target high school pupils. Also, though the heart of drug dealing in the area was in Bevham, the Hartfield Estate at Lafferton contained a major artery. Several characters had been picked up in the underpass, but they were next to nothing. It was the leading operators they needed to find and someone at Bevham had decided the Hartfield might yield one or two of them. It was unlikely. Large old houses at Flimby and Woodford Poins, detached executive homes on Mill Road were where the bosses would live, with private schools for their kids, Jaguar 3 litres for themselves and Gucci handbags and charity lunches for the wife. But there was no hard evidence. Without it, the rich and well connected of Lafferton and district would not welcome a knock on the door and a warrant card flipped open in their faces.

Freya was cold and full of the pent-up irritation that a pointless day without anything to show for it always brought on. Drug ops were the worst of all, and the next day looked like being equally frustrating as she trawled through more records, attempting to link thefts of white goods from newly built houses. Someone was working a clever scam, but trying to find out who by spending six hours or so at her computer was a depressing prospect.

The kids had long gone, the cleaners were in the school buildings and the underpass was deserted. The housing estate calls had turned up plenty of foul-mouthed residents and a dead cat. No one had even answered the door at most of the addresses they had.

'OK, that's it. Operation home time.' Nathan gave a thumbs up and started the car happily. As they moved off, the one parked a few yards away flashed its lights and pulled out to follow.

'Thought for a moment you was going to offer overtime, Sarge.'

'Waste of police resources, Constable.'

'Yeah, like the rest of the day. You going out anywhere special tonight?'

'You sound like the girl who does the washes at my hairdresser's.' Freya imitated: 'Got anything special planned for the weekend, then? Going somewhere nice for your holiday, are you?'

'Well, are you?'

'No. Choir tomorrow.'

'Night in with the cat and the telly then. You should live a bit more, Sarge . . . come clubbing with me and Em one Friday.'

'Sure, gooseberry really suits me.'

'Nah, we'll fix you up first. Some really nice young doctors at Bevham General.' Nathan gave her a quick sideways glance. 'Unless you've got your own arm candy lined up.'

'That will do, DC Coates.'

'Blonds, isn't it?'

'I said don't push it, Nathan.'

'Sorry, that was a bit out of order.'

'More than a bit.'

'Only, I like you, Sarge. I don't want you pining away.'

'I am not pining away.'

'There's a poem . . . dunno who wrote it, not my thing really, only Em heard it on the radio. It's about how to cure love, know what I mean?'

Nathan screeched to a halt as the traffic lights in the town centre turned red.

'Go on.'

He turned to her, his monkey face cheerful in the light of the street lamp. You get away with murder, Freya thought, and you probably always will.

'See, this poem says there's two ways. You can spend hours by the phone, pining, waiting and hoping, counting the minutes . . .' He put the car into gear and raced satisfyingly ahead of a BMW that had been pulled up beside them in the next lane. 'Yeesssss.'

'Or?'

'Or. A better way is you get to know him better.'

Freya laughed. 'OK, very good. Now let's hear about you, Constable.'

'Me, well, you know. Very happily shacked up with my Em.'

'Exactly.'

'What?'

'Shacked up. For God's sake. And how long is it?'

'Be two years.'

'Time you did the decent thing then.'

'What decent thing would that be, Sarge?'

'How like a man can a man be? Marry the girl, Constable Coates, propose to her, go down on bended knee, spend your overtime money on a diamond. They had some lovely ones in the window of Duckham's in Bevham last time I looked.'

'Prospecting was you?'

'Seriously. Your Emma is lovely. She deserves more than "shacked up". If she'd be mad enough to say yes, of course.'

'Yeah, yeah.'

'Don't you *want* to settle down?'

'I am settled.'

Freya shook her head. 'It's different.' She had meant it. Her own mistake had not made her disapprove of marriage in general and the pretty, delightful and eminently sensible Emma was what Nathan needed.

Nathan slewed the car neatly into a space in front of the station, and they went inside.

Freya entered the emptying CID room and looked round. It had the usual seedy, end-of-the-day air, bins overflowing with screwed paper and empty plastic coffee cups, desks littered with computer printouts, chairs anyhow. Her own was not much of an example and she spent five minutes clearing, tidying and sorting it out so that she would not feel too depressed at the sight of it in the morning.

Her computer was still switched on and for a moment she hesitated over spending another hour going through the drug data, or even going back over the stuff that had come in – what little of it there was – on the missing women.

But she was tired and irritable and hungry and the hour would more than likely be wasted. Home, she said, taking her suede jacket off the back of the chair and knotting the cream pashmina round her neck; home, a piece of fillet steak with mushrooms and tomatoes, two or three glasses of red wine and half an hour going through the score of the B Minor Mass ready for tomorrow evening.

She switched off a couple of lights, said goodnight to the only other person left in the room, pattering away at his keyboard, and went out and down the corridor.

A light was on in Simon Serrailler's office and the door was slightly ajar. Freya hesitated. Don't do it, don't do it, leave it. If Nathan had noticed, how many others might have done so? Don't do it, where's your pride?

She tapped on the door.

'Come in.'

He had his jacket off, tie loosened, blond hair all over the place. The files on his desk were a foot thick.

'Freya – thank God, an excuse to stop. Come in, please, please come in.'

'Don't tell me this is all drug stuff.'

'A ton of it. Any joy today?'

She shook her head. 'There was never going to be.'

'I know what you think about all this. It's not the minnows we want and it's only minnows who are going to be hanging about the road tunnel to the Eric Anderson and nobody but minnows are going to live in flats on the Hartfield Estate. But first of all, the minnows can and do lead us to the sharks, and secondly, there have been enough public complaints, especially from parents, about drug pushing to the school children, that we have got to be seen taking it seriously. And as you know, there's not a lot of point in putting cars full of uniform out to warn the dealers off until the fuss dies down. Grin and bear it, Freya. It has become pretty serious recently and we might well get somewhere. We've half the county's forces on drug ops.' He looked at her for a second. 'But that isn't why you're here is, it?'

Freya went still. What did he mean, what was he going to say? What had he noticed?

Then the DCI stood up and pushed his chair back. 'I've had enough. I'm absolutely bushed. So are you. How many cups of takeaway coffee have you had today?'

Then it was easy. 'Enough to know I don't want another for a week.' She turned to go, remembering the steak and the glass of wine and the Bach score. There were worse things to have waiting for you at home.

'Sandwiches? Bags of crisps, KitKats . . . ?'

'I passed on the crisps.'

'Right, we both need a decent dinner. Do you know the Italian place in Brethren Lane?'

The floor lurched beneath Freya's feet.

'If we go in my car, we can leave it in the close and walk to Giovanni's, it's five minutes. You can keep yours here and get a taxi home. That way we can enjoy a bottle of wine.' Simon was at the door, tie pulled straight, jacket over his shoulder. He glanced round. 'Or – not?'

These are the times you remember until you die, these ordinary, unplanned, astonishing, joyful things, these spur-of-the-moment, unexpected things. You remember every word, every gesture, the colour of the tablecloths in the restaurant and the smell of the liquid soap in the cloakroom, so that for the rest of your life, when you smell it again, you are there and you are the person you were, on that day, at that time, thinking what you thought, feeling as you did. These are the times.

'God, sorry . . . I was miles away. Thanks – sounds good.'

'Low blood sugar. Makes you tired and faint and cross. Giovanni's fegato alla Veneziana will sort it. Come on.'

They ran down the concrete stairs and out through the doors to his car laughing. Stay the moment, Freya thought quickly, looking up at the starless, moonless night sky, please God, stay the moment.

In the car she realised that she looked as if she was at the end of a long day at work, not at the beginning of an evening out. The cream-coloured pashmina was as near as she got to being dressed up. The next thought was that he must like her if he invited her out no matter how she was looking.

The restaurant was a glowing warm oasis, one of the small, old-fashioned Italian places that made no concessions to interior design and twenty-first-century food fashion.

'I love it because it's straight out of the sixties,' Simon said, as they were greeted effusively by the proprietor and given a cosy table in an alcove near the window. 'Look, the candles really do come in Chianti bottles with straw waistcoats.'

'I hope there's a proper pudding trolley.'

'Oozing cream from every pore.' The menus arrived, the specials of the day were described lovingly by a waiter with the sort of Italian accent people used to joke about. 'The difference is that the food is fantastic. There may be prawn cocktail but it contains huge, salty fresh prawns in the most wonderful creamy home-made mayonnaise and the veal is thin as tissue paper and the liver melts in your mouth.'

'The best sort of comfort food.'

A bottle of Chianti arrived and was poured, ruby red, into huge glasses.

'Comfort drink,' Simon lifted his to her and smiled, that devastating, extraordinary smile. The restaurant was full but there was no one else at all in the room, in Lafferton, in the world. This is happiness, Freya said, this, now. Perhaps I have never known what it was until tonight.

And then they talked, as they had talked on the evening in his flat, filling in more of the spaces they had left then, discovering more about each other's lives, talked about Simon's last visit to Italy and the preparations for his next exhibition, a little about the choir – but he didn't sing, wasn't interested in music, liked silence; about cricket, which he played for Lafferton police and also in his mother's village; about his childhood again, which Freya thought he was still trying to explain to himself as much as to her; his being a triplet and also the different one of the three seemed to intrigue rather than trouble him. They moved to her childhood, the Met, and then her marriage which she had glided over quickly the last time; it was like Simon's childhood – she needed to try and understand and explain it to herself, and as she talked about it to him now, she thought she might at last have begun to do so. They went on to books – they had similar tastes in fiction – food – he cooked but was not, he said, unacquainted with Tesco's Finest range

– Meriel's charities. They did not talk about work. The restaurant food was exactly as he had said, old-fashioned and unfashionable 1960s Italian, wonderfully cooked, wonderfully fresh. They gazed at the pudding trolley for several nostalgic moments – tiramisu, sherry trifle, coffee and brandy mousse, crème brûlée, chocolate gateau, with jugs of golden cream – but in the end passed it up in favour of cappuccinos.

The restaurant emptied. They sat on, talking. Rain battered suddenly against the windows.

Simon Serrailler caught her glance and held it. 'Thanks for this,' he said and smiled again.

Freya heard Sharon Medcalf's voice in her head. God, he's broken more hearts than I've had hot dinners. And chirpy Nathan's, his face worried for her. Barking up the wrong tree there, Sarge.

She looked across the table. Oh no, absolutely the right tree.

Simon stirred his coffee. 'You like it in Lafferton, don't you?'

'Love it. I should have moved long before I did. I've been lucky to find friends so quickly too, lucky with people at work. Lucky.'

'Sorry to have blighted it all with the drugs op.'

She waved her hand. But then, for a moment, broke out of her trance of bemused delight, remembering the others, remembering what she owed them.

'Just one thing, sir – it's work though, so if you'd prefer not . . .'

'No, fine. And it's Simon in here.'

She felt herself flush. Focus, she said, focus. 'I'm unhappy that the missing persons case has been downgraded.'

Serrailler sighed. 'I know, I understand how much you've put into it, but the Super had a good look at the files and said enough. I couldn't honestly justify putting up a fight. The public appeals drew precious little and we've no evidence of foul play. Without that, we simply can't give it high priority any longer. You know that. We've thrown an awful lot at it, you know.'

'Supposing these women have been murdered?'

'But we've no reason to suppose they have.'

'Something has happened. They didn't go off voluntarily. I just know that. Nor did the mountain biker, and nor for that matter did Jim Williams's dog.'

'I think we'll leave the dog out of it.'

'There's something . . . I know there's something.' She crushed a sugar cube into fragments on the tablecloth with the back of her spoon. 'Come on, you agree with me, don't you?'

Simon shook his head. 'Probably. But whatever gut feeling you and I have won't –'

'– justify any more resources. God, I hate that word.'

'What – resources?'

'Why don't we all just say what we mean, which is money? It all boils down to money. People's lives boil down to money.'

'No. The first tiny scrap of evidence that any of these missing people has come to harm and we upgrade the whole thing and put everything we've got on to it.'

'I'd better go through the scrap heaps again then.'

The waiter was ostentatiously brushing non-existent crumbs off the table next to them.

'God, we're the last. What time is it?'

Simon laughed. 'Twenty past twelve.'

Freya reached for her bag but he was already on his

feet and Giovanni was coming over to him, handing him the bill. The whole thing was accomplished swiftly and smoothly. He's done this plenty of times. He's been here plenty of times. Who? When? How many . . . ?

Stop that. It doesn't matter. You are here, this is now.

'I'll walk you up to the taxi rank in the square.'

'No, it's not far, you're almost on your own doorstep.'

They went out into the narrow lane and at once heard the bolts being drawn across the restaurant door.

'I think we may have outstayed our welcome,' Freya said. 'Look, I'm fine on my own.'

'Not at this time of night, even in Lafferton.'

'I've been on the beat in some shady bits of London.'

'Forget you're a copper. Think of yourself as a young, attractive and therefore vulnerable female.'

This is now. This is the beginning. This is all.

They reached the empty town square. At the rank on the far side, a couple of cabs waited, both empty, but as they neared them, a driver appeared.

'In a puff of smoke,' Simon said. 'They go into holes in the ground for warmth.'

A wind came snaking down the open square towards them. Freya pulled the pashmina up more closely around her neck.

And then it was over, the engine had started, Simon opened the cab door and closed it after her so quickly she was mumbling her thanks as they were moving off. She looked back to see him raise a hand briefly, and then go off in the direction of the cathedral and his flat. She came crashing to earth, in the back of the taxi which smelled of cold leather and stale smoke. He had not made a move to kiss her on the cheek, to touch her shoulder, to do anything other than smile again, say goodnight, and put her into the cab. But her reaction lasted only until she stepped inside her house and switched on the lights. It was still comfortably warm. She sat on the sofa and went over every moment of the evening, every word he had spoken, every look he had given her, every nuance of everything, and when she went to bed, could not sleep and so went over it all again.

It was not until the following morning that she remembered the night she had gone to stand in the dark close outside his building and seen him arrive with the small woman in a trench coat and walk with his arm round her, to her car.

Giovanni's, she thought at once, they had been to Giovanni's.

She walked the whole way to work. It took forty minutes and the wind was so bitter Freya could hardly feel her face as she went in through the doors. DC Nathan Coates came fast down the room as soon as he saw her.

'Thought you were never coming, Sarge.'

'What's up?'

'Elderly woman gone missing. Neighbour reported her going out at about half past six yesterday evening, on foot . . . hasn't come home all night.'

Freya pulled off her coat and scarf and flung them on to her chair. 'Go on.'

'Neighbour has key. Went in last night. Everything normal, but there were some clothes laid out on the bed as if she'd been choosing what to wear.'

'Coat and handbag gone?'

'Yeah, she hadn't just slipped to the letter box.'

'This morning?'

'No sign. Everything the same as when the neighbour went in. No note or message.'

'Relatives?'

'No. Widow. No children.'

'Age?'

'Seventy-one.'

'I need some coffee.'

In the canteen there was the usual morning smell of frying bacon, the usual hubbub. Freya bought two coffees and they went over to a table by the window.

'Right. Similarities with our other missing women?'

Nathan stirred three packets of sugar into his cup. 'Woman out on her own. No apparent reason to disappear. No messages. No note. No traces. Though it's early – we haven't done the full checks yet.'

'Uniform will have to go to the railway station, bus terminal, hospital and so on. Differences?'

'She was nowhere near the Hill.'

'That's the most significant.'

'She'd got dressed up properly to go out.'

'So had the others in their way – the biker and Angela Randall were wearing gear for cycling and running and following a known routine, Debbie Parker was wearing clothes to go for a walk. I mean, none of them had slipped out in their nightie and curlers.'

'What do you think, Sarge?'

'I think we'll go and see this neighbour – and then I hope we can get the DCI to take it seriously, upgrade the whole inquiry again, before someone else goes missing.'

Across the room, a table of uniforms exploded with bellows of male laughter. She had always liked the camaraderie of the station, watching the different ways people unwound and let off the tensions of a difficult shift, with jokes, laughter, backslapping and loud mutual support. There were disagreements, and friction – not everyone got on well, not everyone trusted everyone else, but that was inevitable in places where people worked together closely under pressure, punctuated by long spells of boredom. Whenever there was a particularly upsetting case – a murder, child abuse, a bad accident – ranks closed, quarrels were set aside, everyone pulled together in unspoken agreement. Policing would be intolerable if that were not the case and Freya had always been grateful for it, in London, and now here.

She drained her coffee cup and tidied up Nathan's sugar bags neatly.

'Gawd, Sarge, it's worse than having a wife. Is this what it's going to be like, I ask myself?'

'Do I hear right?'

She glanced at Nathan as they swung through the doors out of the canteen. His pock-marked, lovely-ugly face was beetroot red.

'Hey!'

'No, no, listen, I haven't said anything, hold on . . . only you made me think, that's all.'

'Well, don't think too long. *Do*.'

'It was you saying that about not losing Em . . . I mean, I don't know what it'd be like not having her. If she got fed up of waiting for me and went off. Like you said.'

At her desk, Freya picked up a clean, empty plastic pot and dropped some loose change into it. 'OK. It's a start.'

'What?'

'I'm saving for your pop-up toaster.'

She picked up a Magic Marker pen and wrote in large black letters 'NATHAN'S WEDDING PRESENT'.

He grabbed it from her and wiped it off with his sleeve. 'Get out, they'll have my trousers off next time I come in, whoever sees that. Have a heart, Sarge.'

'OK, but the clock's ticking, Nathan. Now come on.'

'I love these little streets,' Freya said as they turned into Nelson Street and drove down slowly looking at the numbers. 'They can't have changed much since they were put up by the Victorians as working men's cottages. There are a lot in London like this, though most of them are yuppified now all the old ladies who used to whiten the step every morning have died off. They suit people and they always did – unpretentious, good gardens at the back, neighbourly. Just right.'

'You missed your vocation, Sarge . . . there's 39. Should've been an estate agent.'

Pauline Moss was looking out for them from the window and came to the door as the car drew up. She wore an overall, and looked distraught.

'She isn't back, there's been no call, nothing . . .' she said, leading them into her crowded living room and shifting a tabby cat off a chair. 'Here, let me just wipe it before you sit down, you'll be all over his hair.' She scrubbed vigorously at the cushions with a cloth and her hand, and inspected the result carefully. 'I left it till half past eight, only then I just had to ring you, it isn't normal. I've been up all the night worrying about her. Where's she gone, she never goes off like that, she hasn't spent a night away from home for years – not since long before Harry was ill and that's at least three years, must be.'

'I take it you know Mrs Chater well?'

'Ever so well, we've been neighbours nearly thirty years. When her Harry and my Clive was alive, we were all friends together. Then Harry was ill for so long and after he died I've kept an eye out for her. She's been brave, really brave, and tried hard to keep going like before, but it's been a struggle. We don't live in each other's pockets you know, we have our own – what is it they say now, our own space – always have respected that. But we see each other most days, we have coffee or tea, or maybe go shopping or she comes into mine to watch a programme she likes, or I go to her and we maybe have a game of cards.'

'When did you last see Mrs Chater?'

'Yesterday morning. She was pegging out and I called her for a cup of coffee. I'd just baked as well. I'd had a letter from the council and I wanted her to have a look at it. Then we talked about going on a day outing next month. A coach outing, you know? We used to go sometimes, all four of us, but after Harry was ill, of course, we couldn't, but I've been trying to get her to do one or two things again, pick up the reins – you have to, don't you? She did the same for me when Clive went.'

'Did she seem to like the idea of a day out?'

'Yes, she did, she said it was time to look forward a bit. We talked about it a lot, I had a brochure. We liked the idea of Chatsworth. You can have a lovely day out there, they've beautiful grounds, you can have your lunch. It's not too far. I was going to book, we'd just got to choose a date.'

'So there was nothing to suggest she was going away somewhere else on her own?'

'She'd never do that, never in a million years. Besides, you don't go off without telling anyone, and in the evening, do you? Of course you don't, whoever you are. And she'd only her handbag.'

'I gather Mrs Chater had no relatives?'

'No. They'd no children. It was always a sadness, that. Harry had a sister but she died, oh, five years back and I don't think Iris kept up with them, they live up in Scotland somewhere, Aberdeen, that's it. No, she was on her own when Harry went. I'm different, I've two sons live close by.'

'Has she other friends?'

'Well, yes, not close, but we both know plenty of people round here, though not so many as we used to, of course, it's all changing, isn't it? She did used to go to the cathedral but she stopped when she found it hard to get out. Harry had to be looked after all the time.'

'Did you see her go out?'

'No, I was in the bath. I heard her front door go and her footsteps pass . . . that was all. I didn't think much of it, only that she hadn't mentioned going out, but then, as I say, we don't live in each other's pockets.'

'So you've no idea where she was going?'

Pauline had an idea but she didn't want to mention it. Had Iris gone back to the medium? Iris had been so disappointed that Harry hadn't 'come through'. Had she given it another try? Well, it was up to her, private business, she'd clearly not wanted to talk about it. It didn't seem right to mention it to two strangers, without Iris's permission, even if they were police, and Pauline didn't see how it could matter. But she kept the thought in her mind all the same. Maybe later, if Iris didn't come back. Only she was going to come back, of course she was.

'How has she seemed recently? Was she still depressed after her husband's death?'

Pauline looked hard at the young man. He had a face only a mother could love. 'I don't think that's the right word, you know,' she said firmly. 'There's too much talk of people being depressed. She'd had a bereavement, her husband of forty-one years had passed on. She wasn't depressed, you aren't, you're grieving, you're sad as you can be, but it's normal, isn't it? If you weren't, what kind of person would you be? But not depressed like when you have to have tablets.'

'Sorry, love.' He may have that face, but he had a winning smile. Pauline got up. 'I'll make us a pot of tea?'

'Thought you'd never ask. Let's give you a hand.'

Freya smiled, and stayed behind in the sitting room. Nathan could charm the birds off the trees as well as pots of tea out of ladies and it invariably helped him to find out little things that had been 'forgotten'.

She looked round Pauline Moss's room. Pity the original fireplace had been ripped out and replaced with a hideous electric heater. Once there must have been a wooden sash window, now there was an aluminium, double-glazed monstrosity.

She heard laughter from the kitchen and the chink of china.

The pot of tea was accompanied by home-made scones and ginger cake, all borne through on a huge tray by a grinning Nathan. Freya rolled her eyes but he gave her a conspiratorial wink. So he had gleaned something useful when chatting to Mrs Moss. Freya let him get round to it after tea had been poured, scones buttered, and Nathan had tucked in as though making up for lack of breakfast and pre-empting lunch.

Freya had a scone, and talked generally about the changes in these homely streets and how life used to be even thirty years ago when Pauline Moss and her husband had first moved in with their two young boys, about neighbourliness and its decline, working women and the loneliness of those who were left, retired and out of the loop.

'We've been very lucky, Iris and me,' Pauline Moss said, 'we've had the same houses, same streets, same shops, and each other . . . it helps you, you know, when you're left on your own, that some things stay the same. You rely on that. I did, Iris has. I feel for them on their own without knowing who's next door, everything different, or being moved to some new place by the council. Not that it's happened here, thank God, but in Bevham they pitched so many of them out when they did all that rebuilding, it killed a lot of the old people.' She chattered on easily, occasionally reaching out to ply Nathan with another cup of tea, another scone, more cake. Freya waited.

A nut feeder hung at the window from which blue tits came to eat with little, darting movements and bright, watchful eyes, before flitting off again. The garden was well tended, with a rockery down which a small water-fall ran into a pool. A contented life, Freya thought, the old-fashioned life still lived by so many people up and down the country in ordinary places . . . home cooking, gardening, neighbourliness, shopping, a day's outing on a coach to a stately home, perhaps bingo occasionally, and otherwise, evenings with the television and books from the library. Pauline Moss and Iris Chater played cards together.

Middle England, traditional values. Don't knock it, don't ever knock it, she thought. This is what we have come from, at bottom, this is what we are, and this is absolutely what we, Nathan and I, are here to cherish and to protect.

Nathan picked a couple of crumbs off his plate and turned a beam of appreciation on to Pauline Moss.

Freya waited a few seconds more. Nothing. She glanced at Nathan. He wasn't giving anything away.

'Mrs Moss, you've been really helpful. Now, I wonder, do you have a key to Mrs Chater's house? I'd like to take a quick look.'

'I don't think you ought to go poking into her things.'

'Of course. But there may be something you didn't notice or think was important. We want to find Mrs Chater as quickly as possible.'

Pauline stood up. 'You've got to do your job. I'll let you in.'

'Thank you.'

Freya watched a blue tit dart away from the feeder, alarmed by the movements through the window. Imagine living your whole life on the verge of a nervous breakdown, never being able to enjoy a quiet meal. Memory of the dinner she had enjoyed with Simon was a safe craft on which she was gliding through the calm waters of the day.

They followed Pauline Moss into 39 Nelson Street. Another empty house, belonging to a woman who had disappeared, another set of rooms full of another person's life and private affairs. But there was a warmth and a comfort here which had been so absent from Angela Randall's sterile little house in Barn Close. Iris Chater's rooms were crammed full of furniture, ornaments, pictures, knick-knacks, clocks, tapestries, fire screens, plants in bowls, standard lamps, doorstops, knitting, jigsaw puzzles, rugs, mats, tray cloths, photographs, bowls, vases, containers for everything, covers for everything. Nothing was out of place, yet there was a pleasant muddle.

They looked round. In the hall, Freya examined coats and scarves, in the cupboard under the stairs looked at boots and shoes and a vacuum cleaner and suitcases. The bed was neatly made and covered with an embroidered satin quilt, the toilet seat with a fluffy lilac cover. On the bed were laid out some sensible clothes.

Iris Chater was a home person. She had not gone away. She had meant to come back. The whole place gave out that message. It was as clear to Freya as was her certainty that this missing woman was linked in some way to the others. She did not need to probe further in this cosy, cluttered, comfortable little home.

'Thank you, Mrs Moss. We don't need to do any more here. If you remember anything you think might be relevant, please ring. Here's the station number – ask for either of us. DS Graffham. DC Coates.'

They went out into the sunshine. Pauline Moss closed the door of 39, making sure it was locked firmly, and turned to face them, the key in her hand. But it was Nathan she spoke to. 'I don't like to ask this, only I can't help it, it's been in my mind all night.'

Nathan put a hand on her arm. 'What is it, my love?'

'That missing girl there was a search for on the Hill . . .'

'There's nothing to say your neighbour has been up there, so don't you worry.' Nathan's voice was soothing.

'Thank you,' she said. Nathan patted her arm again.

Freya pulled out into the road. 'You missed your vocation, DC Coates. You'd make a lovely vicar. Such a way with the ladies.'

'Comes in handy. There's something Pauline Moss hasn't told us yet.'

'Yet?'

'Oh, she'll come out with it. I'll pop back later.'

'Time it right, she'll have made a fresh tray of scones.'

Simon Serrailler listened as attentively as he always did to any of his team – it was one of the best things about him that he was never dismissive, never poured scorn, even if in the end he came down on the other side. He leaned back in his chair while Freya filled him in.

'No obvious links, I recognise that, but this is just one too many.'

'I agree. Mrs Chater had been bereaved and that is sometimes a reason why people go missing . . . But I'm not arguing with you. High priority then, please . . . house-to-house, hospitals and stations, radio appeals, get the press on to it.'

Thirty-Six

It was not his fault. He was methodical and cautious, he took his time and he planned everything. He had always disliked acting on impulse and right now he could not afford to do so. That was the way mistakes were made and, besides, he despised those who blundered into situations, or allowed their emotions to fire up and cause them to lose control of their thinking, those who killed because their inner selves were in turmoil and their passions had control over them. Such people murdered when they were drunk or out of their minds on drugs. Such people killed their neighbours, because they lost their tempers over an argument about noise, or their wives, in a fleeting fit of jealousy, or else they murdered prostitutes in the throes of sexual rage. He despised them all. When he read about them he wanted them caught and punished and would have offered his services to the police if that would have led to such an outcome.

So, it was not his fault then, he was clear about that. The police had cordoned off the Hill and crawled over it. The public had been first barred from it and afterwards were too afraid to go there and who could blame them?

But it had spoiled his plans. He had had things so well worked out and everything had gone so smoothly, but now there was no plan and so he had done what he had sworn he would never do and acted on impulse, without preparation.

It seemed to have been successful but he was not settled, not satisfied. He felt on edge, he needed to go over and over it all trying to spot the flaw, the tiny mistake which might prove his undoing. There did not seem to be one and yet he could not rest, could not sleep, did not feel, as he had felt each of the previous times, calm and in control. He could not enjoy himself.

To begin with, he had not planned to go out that night. But he had been writing cheques to pay bills, doing accounts, going over his records and VAT returns, and the room had been stuffy. He had been cramped. He wanted fresh air. He had simply walked down to the letter box and the air had indeed felt good, had cleared his head and soothed him. Something smelled new, something smelled of spring. It had excited him, so that when he had reached home again, he had been filled with a restless need to do something else, go somewhere else and the restlessness had felt like something effervescent in his blood.

The van, of course, was at the unit. He had locked his front door and taken the car, and begun to drive, slowly, aimlessly, about the streets. He was not going anywhere, nor looking for anything. Or anyone.

When he saw her, everything clicked into place. He knew at once.

Elderly woman.

She was leaning against a wall, as if to get her breath. Anyone might have been concerned for her, and stopped, any conscientious passer-by. As he got out of the car, she began to slump and slide sideways, down on to the pavement beside the wall. The street was empty. No one walking, no car. Every house had curtains drawn.

He bent over her. She seemed to have suffered either a stroke or a heart attack. He knew the signs. But when he raised her up, she was still alive – barely breathing, her colour bad, but alive.

He lifted her and opened the back door of the car and watched her fall heavily sideways on to the seat.

He did not know at what moment it happened. He was driving, fast, but by the time he reached the unit, she was dead. Then he had had to be quick, because of the security patrol that came round intermittently . . . though, he knew, not as often as they were paid to – most of the night, they parked up and drank from flasks of tea and watched porn channels on tiny televisions in the cab. Once, perhaps, they sailed round the empty streets of the business park without getting out. He knew. He had spent weeks sitting in the dark in the office of the unit, checking their movements, plotting them on a time sheet. But he did not know whether they had already been round tonight and, he was in his car, which they would not recognise. Supposing they came and in a guilty fit of efficiency, logged his number?

He worked very quickly, which he hated. It made him sweat and he hated sweating.

He carried her round to the side of the unit and unlocked it, swung up the door. It was a struggle to keep hold of her and switch on the light. It was not as usual. He did not do things like this.

But then everything went as it always had and she was undressed swiftly, bagged and put away, the drawer slid out and back and it was done. He checked the gauges. The clothes and the handbag went into the usual heavy-duty black bin liner. He did not take anything at all from either her bag or her pockets, did not even look into them. He had never done so. He was not a common thief. The dustmen came on Thursday, when the black bin liner would be put out for them along with several others. The more obvious and normal things were the better. He knew that. He did not draw attention to himself by taking full sacks to tips to be disposed of, he did what every other person on the business park did and put his rubbish out for the binmen on the correct day.

He left the unit and got into his car more tense and anxious than he had been for years. When he drove away, his heart pounded and his hands were slippery on the wheel. But he saw no one. The security patrol did not come. He was out on to the main road and speeding home.

But it took it out of him. He was awake for hours, sweating with fear, his hands shook when he poured a drink. The next morning, he pleaded a temperature and bronchitis and stayed in alone. He was afraid that he could no longer trust himself, no longer rely totally on his absolute self-control, his iron will, his determination. He had acted impulsively, without warning or planning. Perhaps it had been all right, and he had not been seen or heard, perhaps luck had been on his side. But he did not rely on luck, or trust to it. That way madness lay. He had only ever trusted himself and he had never been let down. Until now.

Thirty-Seven

Freya picked up the evening paper on her way home.

MIRACLE WORKER OR CLEVER CONMAN?
by Rachel Carr

'It's a miracle. That's all I can say. He's given me my life back again.'

I was listening to Mrs Glenda Waller of Orchard Park Close, Lafferton, sing the praises of the man she believes cured her from a potentially fatal medical condition when orthodox doctors could do nothing.

Mrs Waller is in her late thirties, and had been suffering from stomach pains for some time. 'I was in agony, bent double with the pains. I couldn't walk properly, couldn't eat so I was losing weight, but when I went to the GP he said it was just indigestion. It got worse, so I went back, and he sent me to hospital, but no one there could find what was wrong with me and all the time I was getting worse. Some days I could hardly get up, and it was a struggle just to do the ordinary things. It was affecting my marriage, my family, everything.' Mrs Waller is married to Rob, a long-distance haulage driver, and the couple have two teenage sons. 'They were all very good but they began to lose patience and I was getting very depressed. I was sure I'd got something very serious but then why did no doctor manage to find out what?'

When I saw Mrs Waller, over a cup of tea in her cheerfully cluttered family house, I found it hard to believe she had been so ill. She is cheerful and radiates good health. I had heard her story from someone else, who told me they knew 'a woman saved by a miracle'. Although that isn't a claim made every day, I was naturally suspicious. We've all heard the sad stories of desperately sick people who believe they have been cured whether by orthodox or alternative treatment, only to find, sadly, that it was merely a temporary remission. But I was intrigued by Glenda Waller's story, not least because the person she claims worked a miracle on her is, to say the least, a practitioner out of the ordinary.

'Go and see him for yourself,' Mrs Waller urged. 'It's easy to be sceptical. Heaven knows I was – sceptical and scared. After all, you hear some funny things. But as soon as I met Mr Orford, I had a feeling something amazing was going to happen to me. And it did.'

So with Glenda Waller's words ringing in my ears, I set off for the hilltop village of Starly Tor, six miles outside Lafferton. I had an appointment with the man whose real name is Anthony Orford, but who also claims to be Dr Groatman.

Starly is a pretty, compact village with steep streets of houses, leading down to a small square in which a few shops and cafés have sprung up to cater for the visitors who come in their hundreds every year to consult the many New Age and alternative therapists.

I was unimpressed by the crystals and incense sticks, beads, dream catchers and dubious potions on sale, and frankly cynical about some of the therapists who advertise on noticeboards in every shop window . . . Ancient Chinese Healing, Dream Healing, Past Life Regression, Flower Therapy . . . They make plain old reflexology and aromatherapy look positively orthodox.

But if they all sounded faintly batty, then what about the man I was due to see? What on earth was I going to find? If it had not been for Glenda Waller's firm recommendation, I might have headed straight back for the safety of home.

Instead, I walked up one of Starly's calf-muscle-stretching streets to ring the bell of what looked very much like a dentist's surgery – which is exactly what Mr Orford's consulting rooms used to be.

My first impression was that quite a few dentists could learn a thing or two from the bright and welcoming reception area, with its huge windows overlooking a pleasant garden, fresh flowers, water cooler, and charming greeter, Mrs

Esme Cox, who has worked for Mr Orford since he set up practice in Starly at the end of last year.

'I see people come in here looking frightened and strained, and of course often sick,' she told me, 'and I watch them leave with a new confidence, a spring in their step and a light in their eyes. I hear about the wonderful things Mr Orford has done, the cures, the miracles – yes, I really believe that is sometimes the word . . . and all I can say is, I am just grateful and humbled to be working with this remarkable man.'

You might think she would say that, wouldn't she? So I sat flipping through one of the shiny new magazines and waited for the doctor.

'No,' he said at once, as he shook my hand, 'you must not call me that. I am not a doctor.'

Anthony Orford is an ordinary, pleasant-looking middle-aged man, with an educated voice and a tweed jacket. Nothing alarming there then. He led me into his consulting room, which was in semi-darkness – the window blinds were down – and contained only a couch, a sink with a tap – and a large bucket. I looked at the bucket with alarm.

'No point in staying in here,' he said. 'I just thought you might like to see where I work. Perfectly mundane surroundings, you see.'

'Like the dentist's without the machinery.' It seemed I couldn't get dentists off my mind.

Back in the waiting room, Mrs Cox brought us tea. I wanted to take the conversation back.

'Dr Groatman . . .'

'A remarkable man, quite remarkable, diagnostician, clinician, surgeon . . .'

'But dead,' I said.

For the first time, the warm smile chilled a little.

'There is no such thing as death, Miss Carr . . . not in the sense you mean.'

I wondered what sense he thought that was.

'Dr Groatman lived and practised in Limehouse in this life during the nineteenth century. Now, he practises through me, from the other side. He guides me, teaches me, operates through me.'

'When you say "operates" . . .'

'Indeed. Psychically.'

I asked him what exactly that meant but his reply seemed a little evasive. When I pressed him, the chilly smile disappeared into the freezer altogether.

It was at this point that I began to feel uneasy. Nothing had happened to me, nothing had been said to make me shudder, yet as I sat there with this respectable-looking man, I did just that.

'People come to me in pain and in distress. They may have seen many doctors, may have been told either that there is nothing wrong with them, or that what they have wrong is incurable. Even terminal. Dr Groatman, through me, discovers what the illness is and treats it – usually operatively, sometimes not. He treats it psychically, removes a tumour perhaps, or a polyp, dissolves a gallstone, cuts through an inflammation or sterilises some deep-seated infection. The results are remarkable.'

'And you feel you have nothing to do with it?'

'I have nothing to do with it at all. As I say, I am merely a channel.'

'A well-paid one.'

The silence in the room went chilly too. Odd that. But I knew that the psychic surgeon charged high fees. Mrs Waller told me she had paid him £150. Money well spent, she assured me. I suppose, for relief from months of pain, it might well be.

'If you aren't a doctor . . .'

'I am absolutely not.' Mr Orford was making quite sure I got that down.

'Then how can you perform operations?'

'I don't.'

'But . . .'

He sighed and I began to feel like a very stupid child.

'Dr Groatman operates. Psychically.'

'You mean he cuts people open?'

'In a manner of speaking.'

'Psychically?'

'Yes.'

We were going round and round in circles.

'Where did you practise before you came to Lafferton, Mr Orford?'

'Brighton.'

'I'm amazed anyone would ever want to leave Brighton. I certainly wouldn't.' I was hoping to hear a lot more about Brighton. I wanted Mr Orford to tell me about the cures he – or rather, Dr Groatman – had performed there. After all, wouldn't all his new patients be impressed – not to say reassured – by hearing some earlier success stories? But he seemed reluctant to go into any detail at all.

We chatted for a few minutes longer, but talking to Anthony Orford is like talking to a smoke haze. The more direct my questions, the hazier his answers, though he was always courteous.

He stood up and put out his hand. I had obviously overstayed my welcome. At the door, I asked him yet again to explain to me a bit more about how Dr Groatman worked.

'If ever you are ill – and naturally, I hope very much that you will not be – and your GP seems unable to help you, make an appointment. Then you will learn for yourself.'

The smile came out again as I said goodbye. But the thermostat was still below zero.

I left Starly feeling puzzled.

So who is Anthony Orford? Who was Dr Groatman? And have either of 'them' a licence to practise in the way 'they' do? Apparently so. There are no regulations at all governing alternative therapists. Only those fully qualified are allowed to practise as doctors. But Mr Orford was at pains to stress to me that he does not claim to be one.

I found it all very alarming.

So I went back to see Glenda Waller, and asked her to explain exactly what had happened at her consultations with Orford/Groatman. I got a surprise. Because the man she now described to me as 'the doctor' was certainly not the man I had seen that afternoon. Apparently, when Anthony Orford is taken over by Dr Groatman, he changes. He shrinks, his back becomes a little bent, his face becomes lined and his hair thinner. The voice Glenda Waller described was not that of Anthony Orford.

'He wears a white coat,' she said, 'and you get into one of those gown things in a cubicle. Everything is proper, and he has a tray of instruments. Like the dentist really. First of all, he sort of runs his hands over your body but not touching it, above it, you know? Then he finds out what is wrong and where it is. Then, well, he takes one of these instruments.'

What happened next to Mrs Waller sounds frankly unbelievable. The psychic surgeon appears to make some sort of incision in the patient, and quickly removes diseased tissue, tumour, infection or whatever is said to be causing the problem. Glenda Waller claims to have felt 'something' but not pain. She also says that she saw 'something bloody, mixed with tissue and cotton wool' pulled out of her body and dropped into the bucket beneath the couch.

I asked her how she had felt. 'A bit faint,' she told me, 'a bit light-headed. But I wasn't worried or frightened and you'd think I ought to have been, wouldn't you?'

I would indeed. I felt worried and frightened just hearing about it.

'But I trusted him. I just knew he knew what he was doing and that it was all going to be all right. And it was, wasn't it?'

I had to agree with Glenda Waller. She looks radiant. Whatever was wrong with her is wrong no longer. She is out of pain and no longer depressed. It would be unfair to doubt her, churlish not to be impressed.

Nevertheless, there are some questions about psychic surgery which need to be answered. If the practitioner has nothing to hide, why was he so reluctant to answer so many of my questions fully and frankly? What exactly goes on in the consulting rooms and on the 'operating table' of this man – or should I say, these men? Only they really know – but they are not telling.

Miracle worker or conman? The jury's still out.

The article was spread across the whole of the middle pages of the *Lafferton Echo* and accompanied by photographs of Starly Tor and the outside of the psychic surgeon's consulting rooms. There was also a photograph of Rachel Carr in a neat box beside her name. Smug, Freya thought, smug and arrogant.

For now, she had other things on her mind, as she bathed, washed and blow-dried her hair carefully, chose a dress, changed her mind, chose another, and finally rejected that one too in favour of her black silk trousers, black satin jacket and shocking-pink and low-cut silk shirt.

Lately, Freya had come increasingly to trust her inner feelings and it was those which told her now that Simon Serrailler was almost certain to be at his mother's dinner party.

But when Meriel led her into the drawing room where

people were having drinks, Simon was not the first person she saw. That was the slim, slight, woman with whom Simon had driven up to his building on the night Freya had been hanging about outside it in the dark.

She felt nauseated as her stomach plummeted as though in a fast-descending lift. Simon was here, then, in some other room but about to return to this one, and to the woman who wore a plain grey cashmere jumper over a long darker grey skirt. She wondered how she could leave, now, whether she could plead sudden sickness – which would not be entirely feigned – how she could get out without even seeing him.

Meriel had hold of her arm. 'Freya, I don't think you've met Cat?'

The woman smiled. It was an open, warm, welcoming, friendly smile. Freya hated her. The woman held out her hand.

'Hello. I've heard a lot about you.'

Freya could not speak, she smiled and shook the woman's hand.

The woman laughed. 'Oh, don't worry . . . nothing bad, all good.'

'Sorry?' She managed the word. It sounded peculiar. It was in a foreign language.

'I hear a lot about you from Simon.'

She imagined she must look as vacant as a fish in a tank.

Now the woman touched her shoulder. 'You work with him, don't you?'

She had not forgotten how to nod and then, somehow, words miraculously came out of her mouth. Bubbles from the fish, she thought. 'How do you know?'

'God, this family is hopeless . . . Mother didn't even

introduce you properly. I'm Cat Deerbon. Deerbon formerly Serrailler. Simon's my brother.'

The room settled back into place.

Freya was introduced to Cat's husband, to a large osteopath with a thick neck and to a tall and very beautiful woman in an enviable long coat of printed velvet. The group, Cat Deerbon said, had been in the middle of discussing an article in that evening's paper.

'Not the psychic surgeon, by any chance?'

'Yes. Does this mean the police are interested?'

'No, no . . . or not officially anyway. I clocked it all the same.'

When they went into dinner, it was clear that the party was complete. Simon was not there. It was like being a child again, bitterly disappointed at the cancellation of some treat, a teenager, instantly cast down by a cutting word from an admired teacher . . . and just as easily uplifted again. But not tonight, she thought, taking a forkful of gleaming fish terrine into which the coral of scallops had been beautifully studded. Tonight you enjoy who is here, you do not pine for he who is not. Tonight is for making more new friends. Cat, she thought, glancing at her across the table. Yes, definitely Cat and not only because she was Simon's sister, for all she did not look like him. Cat because she was warm and engaging, intelligent and quick, the sort of person Freya responded to immediately. For the moment, though, she had to attend to those on either side of her. She had been put on the right hand of her host but at the moment, Richard Serrailler was going round the table pouring wine. Freya turned to her right.

'We haven't been properly introduced,' she said.

He was probably in his fifties, with an immaculately

cut dark grey suit and, she noted, surprisingly elegant, well-manicured hands. Surgeon, she decided, and real not psychic.

'Aidan Sharpe. How do you do? I take it you sing in the choir with Meriel?'

'I do. She took me under her wing . . .'

'Meriel has a way of scooping people up and involving them in her doings. She wraps the wonderfully rich blanket of her world around them and before they know it, they're manning a stall at the hospice bazaar.'

'Funny you should say that.'

Freya finished her terrine. Her neighbour had cut his into the finest slivers, before picking each one up carefully on his fork. Surgeon, definitely.

'Are you a doctor?' he asked.

This was the moment. Freya collected people's reactions when she told them her job. She wondered if Simon did too. Some were shocked, some alarmed, some immediately began complaining to her aggressively about the rise in crime/lack of bobbies on the beat in their area/unfairness of traffic forces . . . others were avid for inside information about almost anything to do with policing in general and CID in particular.

Now she looked Aidan Sharpe straight in the eye and said, 'No. I'm a detective sergeant.'

His eyes widened fractionally but otherwise his expression did not change in the slightest. He was a good-looking man – would have been better without the goatee, Freya decided.

'May I guess at your profession?'

He smiled. 'I always enjoy this.'

'Oh?'

'Do you remember – no, of course you don't, you're

far too young . . . there was a television programme called *What's My Line?*. People with unusual jobs were quizzed by a panel – I think they were only allowed to answer yes or no – and the panel was supposed to work its way towards discovering their job. They performed a mime at the beginning but that was the only clue.'

'OK. Do your mime.'

'Lord . . . I don't think I can.'

'You must be able to.'

'Could you? Locking a pair of handcuffs, I suppose.'

A girl in a white apron was going round the table, removing plates. Meriel brought in a huge casserole dish and set it down on the serving table.

Freya looked round at the faces of people talking and laughing in the warm candlelight. Nice, she thought, good company, good food. Happy. Yes. But Simon . . . She turned back to her neighbour. 'Come on.'

He sat silent for a moment, then put his thumb and forefinger carefully together and made a single, careful, almost delicate forward movement with them. Freya watched. It meant absolutely nothing and she said so.

'In fact, I had you down as a surgeon. But if you are, then I don't know what you were doing then.'

He smiled again.

'Are you a surgeon?'

'No.'

'Damn.'

And so it went on, a light-hearted, amusing exchange, which made her feel relaxed. After a few moments, and a pause while their plates were heaped with duck in a rich apricot gravy, Freya said, 'OK, I give up.'

'Sure?'

'I shall probably kick myself for not getting it.'

'Somehow I don't think you will.'

'Go on.'

Aidan Sharpe gave her an almost flirtatious look. 'I am an acupuncturist.'

They both laughed, Freya with astonishment, Sharpe with delight. 'No one has ever guessed. Ever.'

'I didn't think much of the mime.'

'No, I'm afraid it's almost impossible to do one.'

'Well, well. In that case, tell me what you think about this man Orford . . . the psychic surgeon – if you've heard about him.'

Aidan laid down his knife and fork. 'Oh, I've heard about him all right,' he said, 'and it makes me very angry. Forgive me if I become quite irrational at any moment.'

The conversation got no further for the moment. The vegetables came round and Freya turned to hand a dish to Richard Serrailler.

'Thank you, Sergeant.' There was no mistaking the heavy sarcasm. He turned away abruptly to pass the vegetables on, then picked up his knife and fork.

'I'm not on duty,' Freya said lightly. 'Freya is fine.'

He merely grunted.

Richard Serrailler was as handsome as his son, with the same nose and brow, the same straight forward-flopping hair, only grey. But his lean face seemed set in a permanent slight sneer and his eyes were cold.

'I work with Simon,' she said.

'I could wish you didn't of course. He may have told you.'

Deciding to play both dumb and charming, Freya looked at him with widened eyes. 'You mean you disapprove of me? But please explain why. You must have heard something derogatory.'

'Nothing to do with you.'

'Now I'm very confused. Do sort this out for me, Dr Serrailler.'

He did not offer the use of his Christian name, merely said, 'My son should have been a doctor. He would have made a decent one.'

'He makes a more than decent DCI.'

'Strange choice of job.'

'No. Exciting, challenging. Dangerous. Important.'

'You have a high opinion of yourself.'

If the man had not been Simon's father she would have asked if he enjoyed being offensive, whether or not she was a guest at his table. Instead, she ate a mouthful of duck very slowly before saying, 'How many doctors are there in your family exactly?'

'Seven living – four of us are now retired. Two generations behind us.'

'In that case, you can afford to spare one son.'

'That is for me to decide.'

'Not for him?'

But Richard Serrailler had already turned pointedly to the man on his other side, the osteopath Nick Haydn. Freya ate, letting her rage subside. She wondered what had caused Serrailler to be so bitter, so dismissive, so downright unpleasant.

'Difficult,' she heard Aidan say quietly.

She grimaced.

'Don't worry, my dear, it's not you, it's everyone. Forget it.'

'Thank you for that.'

He smiled and reached out to pour her more wine but she put her hand over her glass.

'Water?'

'I can –'

But he was on his feet, and bringing the bottle to her from the other side of the table. The acupuncturist might not be obviously and immediately attractive, even were she looking for an attractive man, but his manners and kindness were appealing after her brush with Serrailler. At the end of dinner, she made her way into the drawing room behind him, and went straight to where he had made a group with Nick Haydn and Cat Deerbon. Coffee and teapots were placed on two small tables.

'I wanted to ask you more about the psychic surgeon,' Freya said. 'Partly out of curiosity after reading tonight's article, though there is a police angle as well, I'd better say.'

'The person you should talk to is Karin,' Cat said, nodding to the beautiful woman sitting next to Meriel Serrailler on the window seat. 'She's actually been to him.'

'What?' Aidan looked horrified.

'Ask her. But it sounds very much like an extremely clever magic trick . . . the sort that makes you blink, it's so effective. I don't think this man is actually doing anything other than conning people.'

'That's more than enough, isn't it? Gullible people, vulnerable people . . . it's snake oil again.'

'I couldn't agree more.'

Cat looked at Freya. 'Has it anything to do with my missing patient?'

'Which one?' Freya asked levelly.

It was ten minutes to one before the party broke up.

'Freya, here's my home number,' Cat had come out to her car, 'do let's meet up. I don't have a lot of time, what with job and family but I get half a half day and there's always Sunday . . . maybe you could come to lunch then?'

Freya took the card with delight. It was something else, someone else, that drew her closer to Simon, a part of his family, inviting her in.

She turned out of the drive into the dark lane. Meriel had kissed her on both cheeks and given her a warm hug. Richard Serrailler had shaken hands and said nothing, nothing at all.

There was a message on her machine from Nathan.

'Evening, Sarge . . . message from the DCI. Case conference about the missing women. High priority. Nine sharp. Cheers.'

Thirty-Eight

'Good morning, everyone. I'll get straight into it. As you know, we now have three women reported as missing in Lafferton.

'May I draw your attention to the fact that until the disappearance of Angela Randall, precisely four women have gone missing from Lafferton in the last six years, and of those, one was subsequently found to have committed suicide, one was found dead of natural causes, one eventually contacted her relatives, after having gone away of her own volition, and the fourth, an elderly lady with dementia, was found wandering and admitted to hospital. So when three women disappear without trace in a few weeks, we must regard it as highly suspicious.

'Right. I want to know what we've got so far in the way of any links. Are there any links? Did these women have anything in common?'

'Well . . . the fact that they are women obviously,' Freya said. 'But they differ in age – one twenty, one fifty-three, one seventy-one.'

'The Hill links two of them.'

'Two of them live alone.'

Serrailler nodded. 'Angela Randall is single and it appears has no close relatives. Mrs Iris Chater is widowed and lives alone. She has no children.'

'Yeah, but Debbie Parker has a dad and stepmum. I know they don't live here but it breaks the pattern,' Nathan Coates said.

'The longer I look at it, the more it seems to me that they have nothing in common beyond their sex,' Freya said.

'What about that dog?'

The DCI looked blank for a second.

'Jim Williams, sir,' Freya said.

'Oh, right, the man who last saw Angela Randall. His dog ran off. I can't see how that's relevant. Dogs do run off.'

'It disappeared without trace, on the Hill. So did Angela Randall, so, probably, did Debbie Parker.'

'Possibly. OK, any other contributions? Anything at all.'

'Angela Randall,' Freya said thoughtfully. 'I found an expensive pair of cufflinks, gift-wrapped and with a cryptic message on the card, in her wardrobe. When I checked with the jeweller in Bevham – Duckham's – I found out that she had bought a number of expensive gifts – a watch, a tiepin, a silver letter opener, things for men – from the same jeweller in the course of eight months or so. Now we know from her employer at the nursing home that she apparently had no close relationships, and from her neighbours that she never had visitors. So who were the expensive presents for? The gift card said, "To You, with all possible love from your devoted, Me."'

'If there was a man in Angela Randall's life he's the only one in the case. Debbie Parker didn't have a boyfriend, Mrs Chater lost her husband just before Christmas.

'Let's get another radio appeal out, another press conference. I'm going to get uniform to do a house-to-house for the whole of central Lafferton . . . We've done the streets in which all three women live and the area around the Hill but I want this extended. We'll get the divers into the river, and we'll get every area of waste ground, every playing field, the lot. Saturation. I don't want anyone in Lafferton to be left in ignorance of the fact that these three women are missing.'

'National press, sir?'

'Yes. I'm going to talk to the Super. But national press, television and radio as of this evening. Unfortunately, all this coincides with the fact that the drugs op is moving up a gear as well. We've had some excellent information, as some of you will know, and we're going to be acting on it during the next few days. We're stretched. I'm heading up the drugs op, but I want to be kept informed about everything, absolutely everything, to do with these women. Freya, I want you in charge for the moment. Everyone else reports to you. We've got to find these women and so far we have barely a clue – no sightings, no traces, no bodies, alive or dead. That in itself has to be extremely unusual.'

'Off the record, sir, where are you putting your money?' Nathan asked.

Simon Serrailler frowned and thought for a moment. Then he said quietly, 'I'm afraid – and this is off the record, Nathan, this is a private opinion, right? We have no evidence and I don't want this getting out.'

'Sir.'

'Then I think we are looking at three women who have been abducted, very cleverly abducted, by someone or some people, who know how to cover their movements and leave no trace.'

'Murder, then.'

The room went dreadfully still.

'I'm ruling nothing out,' Serrailler said quietly.

The Tape

It was over six months before I could bring myself to
tell you that I was no longer a medical student. I kept
up the pretence very well. But then naturally came
the question of money, as you were paying towards
my fees. I wrote to you and I lied. I did not want to
see you – I never wanted to see you by then – but I
knew there had to be some explanation and so you
remember that I said I had been advised not to continue with my studies on medical grounds. I had
always had mild asthma but it had become so much
worse that it could strike at any time and a serious
attack might weaken my heart.

After that you had no idea where I was for almost
two years. I simply slipped out of your life, like someone
diving into the sea and resurfacing thousands of miles
away. I did not know what you thought, whether you
made attempts to find me, if you ever contacted the
medical school. It was not you I worried about.

I spent some years trying to work out a future for
myself and during that time, I simply took odd jobs

so that I could live, clerical jobs, mainly, and always on a temporary basis. I registered with an agency and there was always plenty of work. I was meticulous, reliable, hard-working, methodical, neat, all qualities that recommended themselves to employers. I did not make trouble, I did not waste time, I did not gossip, I hardly socialised. But throughout that time, like an underground force, my mind was working on my future, trying out ideas, planning, scheming. I could not be a doctor but I had never given up the desire to work in some area of medical treatment, and because I so loved bodies, I often toyed with the idea of simply becoming a mortuary attendant, or an assistant in some hospital path lab, probably abroad.

But I could never have played second fiddle, never have stood unable to take part, never have bowed and scraped to some 'qualified' pathologist, never have done the drudgery like a servant week after week, unnoticed, unregarded, because I knew as much as they knew, I could do their job. I would have exploded with frustration.

I went through some months planning to take up my medical training again, forging references perhaps, lying about my age, going abroad, but deception was not something that came easily to me then. The only person I had ever deceived and lied to was you. I did not want to behave like some petty criminal and if I had been discovered the humiliation would have been traumatic, more than I could have borne. I had had enough of humiliation. My hatred of those who had condemned me, poured scorn on me and made me feel small was and has remained absolute, a pure, bitter hatred, not like a poison but like an acid.

Every other medical career I considered, even to the point of reading about it in detail in some reference library, I rejected because it was inferior, second best and with a low status. I would not become a nurse, or work in the ambulance service. Perhaps I might have taken up dentistry but I rejected it because it was too like medicine, I might have been victimised again.

I want you to know everything. There is no harm in it because you cannot react in a hurtful way, you cannot sneer, as you so often did, you are unable to humiliate me. You wanted to be proud of me and you would be, now. Now, you are no threat to me and would not wish to be. I had to work everything out for myself, be responsible for myself and answerable to myself. I had waited all my childhood and youth for that.

I missed the hospital and the pathology lab desperately. I dreamed about it. I dreamed of carrying out one post-mortem after another and making astonishing discoveries, solving problems, finding out bodily secrets. When I was working at one or other temporary desk, in my mind I was walking the corridors of the hospital, putting on my green gown and cap, picking up the instruments. I lived in two worlds and yet I never neglected the work I had to do, I was able to satisfy my employers quite easily while I conducted my other life.

But after a time, I became frustrated. I had to do something, make some decision, find out the course of my life.

In the end, it happened by chance. I was asked to take on a temporary job in the head office of a company hiring out vending machines. It was some distance away from the room I had rented, in an area I did not know. I took a train and then walked for ten minutes, a dull walk but one which I could vary each day by taking a short cut, or a side route down one of several different residential avenues. They were much alike, but the houses were large and of varying styles and periods and I liked to speculate about their owners, wondering what occupations brought in a salary high enough to afford Aldine Lodge and Manor House and West End and The Poplars. One house had a brass dentist's plate. Sometimes, people were driving out as I passed, in large, comfortable, expensive cars to match the status of their houses.

I was not envious, though I would have enjoyed living somewhere less cramped and run-down than the bed-sitting room to which I was confined.

But I always knew that this was only a temporary home, like the temporary jobs, and that my real life and destiny were waiting for me to discover them. I never despaired, and I was never depressed because of this. You would have been proud of me at this time, proud of the fact that I dressed smartly and looked after my clothes and my body and that I never lost confidence in myself.

I remember the morning very clearly. One does remember the days when destiny strikes. I have never forgotten the decoration around one of the photograph frames in the room in which the head of the medical school dismissed me. If I close my eyes, I can still see the thin twisted rope of mock gilt.

So it is not surprising that I remember everything about the day I walked down Spencer Avenue, one of the two long, treelined roads which took me by a slightly circuitous route to my office. The houses were mainly gabled and mock Tudor or real Edwardian, the hedges mainly forsythia which was in full, vivid yellow bloom on this rather damp, mild spring morning. You would have liked Spencer Avenue. It was the sort of road you aspired to though you had no hope at all of achieving life in such a place. But when I was a boy and still loved you, still talked to you and told you things, we used to go for walks rather like this one and I would point out to you the houses I might buy for us when I was a famous doctor, and you would choose the colour of the curtains and the shrubs you would grow in the front garden.

I was early. I always was. I have never been able to bear unpunctuality, in myself or in others. I did not have to hurry.

It was two-thirds of the way down, on the right-hand side, the side down which I was walking. The house was an imposing one, though not especially attractive. It had black-and-white half-timbering and leaded light windows, which made it gloomy. It was large, the drive was immaculately gravelled, and there was a lilac tree in full bloom to the right of the house. But it was the plate attached to the gatepost which drew my attention. Another dentist? Or a medical consultant, a gynaecologist with an extensive private practice? A psychiatrist? An ophthalmic surgeon?

I was startled when I read what was actually there, under the name, John F. L. Shinner.

I had never considered it, did not even know a great deal of what exactly it involved – there were few of us about in those days. But I stared at the plate with a sense of revelation. I did not need to make a note of the name and address, they were already engraved in my memory.

I began to walk quickly, not because I was late but because I was excited. I saw my life opening up in front of me. I would train, and I would practise. I would have my name on a house like this, in a tree-lined road. It would be very like practising medicine and I would be answerable to myself only. For the first time, I found it hard to concentrate on the work in hand, and the moment one o'clock struck I went out to the public telephone box in front of the General Post Office, obtained the number and phoned to make an appointment. I explained that I did not need treatment but that I wanted to discuss the possibility of training to join the profession. After a moment, the receptionist put me straight through.

'I'd be happy to see you. I hope I might be of help. When exactly did you become interested?'

'I did three and a half years of medical training but I failed one set of exams and almost immediately afterwards I became quite seriously ill. I'm well now, it was some time ago, but by then I was unhappy with the way I was being trained. I became very interested in some of the alternative ways of treating the sick.' I found that I believed passionately in what I was saying, even as I heard the words that came out of my mouth.

'Have you talked to other therapists?'

'I looked into the possibility of homeopathy.'

'And?'

'I was never interested in pharmacy. Chemical treatments and homeopathy seem somewhat akin. I find it hard to explain but homeopathy seemed too cerebral to me.'

Mr John F. L. Shinner chuckled. 'Our training is very rigorous – just as much as orthodox medical training. But I would not call the discipline too cerebral. It is about whole-patient assessment, treatment and care. You are dealing with people, not just symptoms.'

'I am not interested in "just symptoms".'

'Then come and see me. If I can be of help, I will.'

I could not sleep that night. In the end, I went out for a walk at two thirty, through the narrow, run-down streets, where lilac trees and forsythia and the set-back houses of Spencer Avenue might have been a thousand miles away and yet were so certain a part of my future that they were more real to me than the streets down which I walked. I noticed nothing, only smelled the rancid frying of fat from a fish and chip booth and the smell of diesel from the arterial road nearby. I had an absolute certainty about everything, as if I had been guided towards Spencer Avenue, and the brass plate of John F. L. Shinner which marked my destiny. It was strange, this feeling of fate. I was not familiar with it but for the time being, I allowed myself to succumb to it.

I do not know why the attraction to my future career was so strong, so compulsive, for I knew very little about it or how long it would take me to study, how much it would cost, where I would have to go. But uncertainty over these matters was trivial, and with time everything would become clear. I had no doubts, none at all. But I knew that I would tell you nothing, that I would not communicate with you until I had achieved it all.

I have never regretted anything or looked back or

been in doubt for one instant. I knew that I was right and so it proved.

As for the other matters – I believe they were always there, lying below the surface of my mind. I was to be fulfilled and satisfied in a career I was good at but the old needs had not been defeated. I had been cut short before I had done what I must do, wanted to do, and there would have to be another way of accomplishing it, but it could wait. In the end, it had to wait for years, but that did not matter. I have succeeded in the end, haven't I? I have done everything.

John Shinner was most helpful. I made an appointment to go to the house after he had seen his last patient and after my own working day. I walked down the avenue with an extraordinary sense of elation.

He was a small, tubby man, and although his name was apparently English, he was clearly partly Oriental.

'Our discipline originates in China,' he said. He was showing me the room in which he practised, and which I took immediately as my model, it was so orderly, so sterile, so neat. There were no superfluous decorations, no pictures, nothing save what was directly relevant to his work. The walls were painted cream, the leather of the treatment couch and of his working chair was black. There was a wonderful calm and harmony about that room which I have always tried to emulate. My patients have told me that they are aware of it and that it adds to the efficacy of the treatment I give.

'There are few regulations governing complementary therapies,' Mr Shinner said. 'Anyone can set up in practice, without training or qualifications. Would

413

anyone set up as a dentist or an orthopaedic surgeon without training and qualifications? Of course they would not, yet nothing is done and the public can be put at risk. Ours is an ancient and proven discipline. You will study for accreditation with our national institute. You will study hard and you will never stop learning, even after you have practised for years. I learn every day. Yet we are disregarded by the medical profession, disapproved of, treated with disdain and contempt, laughed out of court. Have they observed our operations – the removal of organs, Caesarean sections – carried out on patients who are wide awake and can be seen talking, laughing, quite without pain or discomfort throughout the procedure? Our critics dismiss us as liars. But of course, most of our work is nothing like so dramatic. We help, we give hope, we sometimes heal entirely, we give pain relief, we ease chronic symptoms of incurable conditions. We affect body, mind and spirit, we touch the deepest parts of the psyche as well as the most superficial areas of the body.'

He spun round in his chair and stared at me for a long time, his eyes steady and deep.

'What makes you feel that this is where your future lies?'

'An inner conviction.'

'Do you hope to be a rich man?'

I laughed. 'I don't expect to become a millionaire.'

'You don't answer my question.'

'I am not here because I expect to make a fortune. But I have been poor and I confess I have found it a miserable experience.'

He said nothing more, but got up and went to his

desk, where he jotted down some names and addresses.

'Write for information, find out all you can. Any of these people will advise you. Mention my name. But if you succeed – be prepared for ridicule and hostility. Could you cope with that?'

'Yes,' I answered confidently. I have never had any interest in the good opinion of others.

Finally, he lent me three books to study. 'By the time you have read them carefully and thoroughly and then thought about what you have read, you will know. One way or the other.'

I thanked him and got up. I was anxious to get home and to begin reading them, to open the first doors on to my future life. But the certainty was mine already.

Thirty-Nine

'Sarge?'

'Hi, Nathan, what did she give you?'

'Chocolate cake to die for.'

'And?'

'And the old girl was going to a medium. Trying to get in touch with her Harry.'

'Why didn't the neighbour tell us that before?'

'Said she felt it was a sort of betrayal, like, didn't think Mrs Chater wanted any Tom, Dick and Harry knowing . . . well, she wanted Harry to know, if you get me, only –'

'Cut the bad jokes.'

'Sorry . . . anyway, she said, Mrs Moss, only I got to call her Pauline –'

'– I bet you did.'

'She said it was all a bit secret . . . apparently, she were the one found out the name of this spook-raiser and she give it to Mrs Chater who went once, then went all quiet about it. I think Pauline was trying to protect her really, you know, from everyone taking the mick.'

'Did you get the name?'

'On my way.'

'Good boy. By the way, the DCI's going for a recon-struction – Debbie Parker walking down her street in the early morning, and round the perimeter road of the Hill.'

'When's that?'

'Thursday morning. They're looking for a girl now.'

'What about you?'

'I'm off to the jeweller in Bevham . . . I want you to go up to Starly, interview our friend Dava again, give him a real grilling.'

'Hold on, Sarge, when do I get my lunch?'

'You don't need lunch, you've had half a chocolate cake.'

'Sarge! Have a heart.'

'OK, you can have a cup of dandelion tea in that green café.'

Nathan made a retching noise and rang off.

The jeweller was polite, cool, willing to be helpful but sure he could tell her nothing more.

'I would like you to take your time and think back very carefully to Miss Randall's visits here. Can you remember the conversations you had with her when she was choosing the items and purchasing them? I want you to try and remember if she said anything at all that might give us a clue as to who the recipient was.'

'Or recipients?'

'What I'm getting at is that people usually have some sort of conversation when buying items of this kind . . . it isn't a quick purchase, like buying a bar of soap at the chemist. If I came in here to buy something expensive and special for someone . . . say, a birthday, I would take my time choosing it and I would involve the salesperson in the purchase . . . it's part of the fun, if you like. Especially when items are costly and you don't buy them every day. I would probably say this gold chain is a christening present for a new niece, or ask if you would recommend a particular type of cufflink for a brother's fortieth birthday.'

'People do that, yes.'

'Often?'

'Quite frequently, yes.'

'But not Angela Randall? Never? Not once? Didn't that strike you as odd.'

'Miss Randall simply asked me to show her items of a certain type or within a certain price range . . . she never discussed why she was buying them.'

'Or for whom?'

'No.'

'And you didn't ask her?'

He looked prim. 'Certainly not. It is none of our business unless a customer chooses to tell us.'

'Did you ever get the feeling that these were gifts for a lover?'

'No. She wasn't that kind of person.'

'So what kind of person was she?'

He thought for a moment. 'Restrained. Private. Pleasant but . . . yes, private is the best word – not the kind of lady who made small talk.'

'Do you think she would tell, say, her hairdresser, her business?'

'No. And we, of course, are not hairdressers.'

Which makes them a pretty low form of pond life in your world picture, Freya thought as she left the shop and crossed the street towards her favourite café.

It was just emptying after the lunchtime crowds, and she found a table in the window, ordered a brie and salad ciabatta and a large cappuccino, and got out her notebook. It always helped if she could think quietly for half an hour after an interview, jotting as she went along if anything came to her. But nothing did. The visit to Duckham's had been a waste of time. She decided to go back to Angela Randall's sterile little house. But the whole investigation was going nowhere except up against an impenetrable fog. Fog. Angela Randall had last been seen running into one. It seemed appropriate. But at least she had been seen by someone. No one had seen Debbie Parker or Mrs Iris Chater.

Freya bit into her ciabatta and the salad dressing dribbled out of the bread and down her chin and hands. As she started to wipe them with the paper napkin, she glanced up and saw someone on the other side of the café window, looking in and trying to attract her attention. It was Simon Serrailler's sister.

Any interruption to such a frustrating circle of thought was welcome, but Cat Deerbon more welcome than anyone else Freya could think of, save her brother.

'Isn't it typical? Someone always catches you when you dribble salad dressing down yourself. There's no way of eating this thing politely.'

'Like éclairs.'

'Join me – have a coffee? Or one of these?'

Cat Deerbon sat down, and dumped a couple of large carrier bags on the floor.

'Child shopping – bor-ing. Vests, socks, pyjamas, knickers . . . I'd love a large espresso and – not a sandwich. What?' She looked at the menu. 'A toasted teacake. How nice to see you again. Aren't you on duty?'

'Oh yes, I've just been interviewing someone. But we're allowed to eat. You?'

'Half day. And the children look like waifs their clothes are so outgrown. I had to do something about it.'

Freya looked more closely at her. When you knew that she and Simon were brother and sister, you could see a resemblance, about the eyes, and the mouth, but their colouring was different, Simon looked older and it would never have seemed likely that they were two of triplets.

Cat bit into her teacake and the hot butter ran down her chin. They giggled.

This is Simon's sister, this is his flesh and blood. This is not only a woman whom I like, and who might become a real friend, this is someone who knows him as well or better than anyone. I want to ask her about him, I want to hear about him, everything, his tastes, how he behaved as a child, his relationship with his father, where he goes on holiday, who his friends are . . . the women Sharon says have been in love with him, the hearts he has broken.

It seemed impossible to begin. But Cat brought the conversation round to Starly. 'You know, people have lots of reasons for wanting to become doctors . . . not always good reasons, but I guess in the main they're respectable ones. I just can't fathom what lies behind someone setting up as these extremist alternatives. What is this guy, the psychic surgeon so-called? Is he mad or bad?'

'Same question as we ask about people who commit certain crimes. Paedophiles, some killers. Mad? What's mad? You can answer that better than I can.'

Cat shook her head. 'Only in the most obvious and clear-cut cases and they are pretty few, you know. Truly, certifiably, permanently "mad" – deranged, out of all touch with normal human reality. It's rare.'

'Bad then. I don't know if any of these people are simply bad. Misguided.'

'There has perhaps been some thwarted desire to do good, to heal ... and it's become channelled in the wrong direction, or warped in some way.'

'It must be a power trip as well. Especially when people are so grateful they call you a miracle worker.'

'I sometimes think all of medicine is a bit of a power trip actually. I can think of quite a few consultants who get off on power.'

'You see, what puzzles me is that this guy – and not only this one – does actually seem to have an effect. People claim to be cured.'

'Most conditions that are not life-threatening get better on their own anyway and the power of placebo should never be underestimated. I'd like to talk to someone who has claimed to be cured of cancer or multiple sclerosis or motor neurone disease by a psychic surgeon or a crystal healer. I'd like to talk to them every six months for the next ten years and see if they still make the claim. They won't, of course.'

'Do no harm . . . isn't that your first principle?'

'Yes. But I'm a qualified doctor.'

The waitress came to clear the table.

'Another coffee?'

'I ought to get back.'

'So ought I.'

'Then we'll have another coffee. And there's something I need to clear up . . . was my father very rude to you the other evening?'

Freya made a face. 'Ish.'

Cat's face coloured quickly. 'God, he makes me so furious. He does it to wreck anything Mother does, anything to stop other people having a good time, anything to put a curse on an event.'

'He seems rather bitter.'

'He is.'

'Has he had disappointments?'

'No. Well – Si not going into medicine was a blow. As if there weren't plenty of Serrailler doctors to keep him happy. He hated retiring, hated it. He was resentful, depressed, angry . . . whereas my mother just accepted the inevitable and got on with the rest of her life.'

'And how.'

'Absolutely. Dad wallowed in self-pity for a couple of years and then took to being rude. I'm sorry you copped it and I apologise.'

'I've coped with worse – don't think about it. I was more puzzled than anything else.'

Their coffees came and Cat stirred her espresso several times, before she looked up at Freya and said, 'There's Martha too, of course. Has Si mentioned her?'

'No, but . . .'

'No, I suppose he wouldn't tell people at work. He finds it difficult.'

'I have seen Simon outside work.'

'Oh?' Cat looked at her sharply.

'We had dinner.'

'Right.'

Freya wanted desperately to tell Cat about the evening in Simon's flat, about the dinner at the Italian restaurant, about her feelings. The conversation might open into a new realm of intimacy between them. Instead, Cat said, 'Martha is our younger sister . . . ten years younger than us. You know we're triplets? There's Ivo as well, in Australia.'

'Yes, Simon told me.'

'Martha is very seriously handicapped, mentally and physically. She's always been so. The only surprise is that she didn't die as a child. She lives in a special home at Chanvy Wood. It has eaten my father's life away and he barely mentions her – I don't think he and I have had more than two or three conversations about Martha in my life. If anything made him bitter and angry and resentful it was that.'

'Hard for Meriel.'

'Very. But then, a lot of things have been hard for her and she has simply shouldered them and batted on. I may not always get on easily with Ma – she drives me nuts sometimes – but I admire her more than I can express.'

'Does your father blame anyone – or anything for Martha's condition?'

'I've no idea. Oh, himself, probably, deep down in a place no one would ever be able to get to. Of course it's nonsense, it was simply a chromosomal accident. There's no history of it in either family. But it's hard to be rational about something like this when it happens to you. I know, I've dealt with patients in the same situation.'

'I wonder why Simon didn't mention it.'

'Simon has a lot of my father in him, but just in a more positive way. He's very private too . . . there are places just as deep in him. You just don't go there.'

'No one?'

Cat gave her a long look. 'No one. It's none of my business, Freya, but . . . just don't try. I love my brother dearly but I'm probably the only woman in the world apart from Mother who can do so.'

She drained her coffee and reached down to get her carrier bags together. 'I must get off home with my vests and knickers.' She started to get out her purse but Freya put out her hand. 'No, these are on the CID. You've been helping the police with their inquiries. Actually, you have – I needed to talk over this Starly business.'

'Come and see us at home, will you? If you could bear the chaos of Sunday lunch?'

'I'd love to.'

'I'll ring.' Cat bent down suddenly and touched Freya's cheek with her own. 'I'm really glad I looked in through the window.'

Freya watched her leave, bundling with her bags through the door, and felt elated, in spite of the warning about Simon, the same warning that had come from Sharon Medcalf. She liked Cat for herself. She also thought that, in spite of the dutiful speech, Cat liked her and might even see her as good for her brother. Please, she said, putting her notebook away, yes, please.

Forty

He had gone to the unit at half past five that morning
in order to look at the real Debbie so that he had her
clearly in mind, as she was now and as she had been.
When he arrived on the perimeter of the Hill, they were
already there, crowds of them, police vans, reporters, television crews, like a film set with all the hangers-on those
entailed. It was early but plenty of people had heard
about it and come to stare, women mainly, and a few
teenagers before they went on to catch the school buses.

He had been determined to stay away, knowing perfectly well what all the psychologists and the profilers said
about people like him. 'They will always return to the
scene in some way or other. They can't keep away. If there
is a search, they may offer help, if there is a public appeal,
they may come forward with spurious information, if
there is a reconstruction they will hang about to watch.'

He had no need. What had happened on the Hill was
unimportant, merely a necessary prelude. What mattered
was what he did in the unit. He was not interested in
the hunt, the capture, the kill. He understood perfectly

why bodysnatchers had been employed in those dark streets of Edinburgh centuries ago. If he could have employed people to bring the necessary bodies to him, he would have done so.

What drove him to the Hill this morning was the desire to see how the police managed things, what mistakes they made, how far they got it wrong. There could be no outcome of course. However many people came to watch, however many came forward, none of them could be of any use because none of them had been there. No one had been there. He was the only one who knew what had happened.

He hesitated. In the group of uniformed police around one of the vans, he saw the young woman he had met at the dinner party, Freya Graffham. If she saw him, he would have to speak to her, would have to have a reason for being here. He moved out of her line of sight a little and began to think. But it came to him quite quickly and easily, as things always did. He knew what he was going to say and rather looked forward to saying it. But the scene was set, the actors were waiting, the curtain was about to rise. He went to the left a little along the path, to get a clear view.

He could see at once that they had got it wrong. The girl was not fat enough and her hair was slightly too fair. But the fleece jacket was right, and the dreadful acne. Another young woman was talking to her, head close, talking, talking, gesturing with her hands. The flatmate.

Someone called for quiet. There was a moment of absolute stillness. Then the girl began walking and the cameras started to roll, the television crew walking backwards in front of her, the men with the furry microphones alongside.

The clothes were identical and she walked in almost exactly the same way. Almost. He watched. She was crossing the road now, heading for the opening that led to the Hill itself. He wanted to shout directions to her, tell her to move faster, tell her to change her expression, and to look up at the Hill, not ahead. Whoever the girl was, she was too conscious of the camera ahead of her, the walk was too hesitant.

Everyone else watched intently, some of them, including Freya Graffham following in a group some yards behind the girl. Freya had not seen him, he was quite certain of that. Better that way. His story would be of more use later.

The girl was on the Hill now and the others were staying back. The weather was not right but as he watched her, apparently alone, going towards the point at which they had met, he realised that excitement was rising in him. He knew what was going to happen, it was running in his head, reeling out like a film he had already seen and whose ending was perfectly right. For a few seconds, she veered in the wrong direction and he wanted to call out to her, but then she turned again and then everything was right, it was as though she knew, as though she was Debbie, not a stand-in, and he felt a surge of power. It was extraordinary. She was doing as he wanted. She was obeying his silent orders, as if she were one of the remote-control planes boys flew on the Hill on Sunday mornings. Every footstep was as he directed. He had to hold himself from running to meet her. She was almost there, poor, fat, badly dressed, spotty girl. How could there be two of them in the world? He had no need of two but if he had been on his own, he would have taken her all the same.

She was a few yards away. He held his breath until his chest was strained. Someone shouted. The woman. Freya Graffham.

'OK, Caroline, OK, you can stop there.'

Freya came running up and the pack of them followed. Everything was ruined, in the last few seconds, the last few strides. The film had broken down.

He watched Graffham, her hand on the girl's shoulder. He could no longer hear her. The girl had taken him to the edge and then the policewoman had pulled him back.

He wanted to kill her.

By the time Cat Deerbon drove round the perimeter road on her way to the surgery, the Hill was empty, but she had deliberately taken the detour to try and remember anything at all about Debbie Parker that might be useful. She had been a funny girl, on the one hand seriously depressed, disfigured by the acne, overweight – and yet when she had come into the surgery, she had not made Cat feel drained and tired, as so many of her patients with low moods did. They had joked, Debbie had made sharp, observant remarks, there had been a wit and a warmth there, beneath the doleful outer layer. And now, where was she? Off with some gypsy-hippie tribe, travelling in an ancient bus and never washing? On the road to the gurus of India? Neither seemed likely.

The disappearance of Mrs Chater was even more troubling. Cat thought of the hours she had sat in the hot front room with her and her dying husband. No, she was not a woman to vanish without warning either. She was made of tougher stuff, the type of woman who would soldier on for however many years she had left, and make the best of things. She was a stayer not a runner.

Cat thought the same was probably true of Debbie.

She pulled into the surgery car park and sat for a moment after turning off the engine. In the pit of her stomach, a hollow, slightly painful sensation made her uneasy. Dead, she thought. They are both dead. How do I know that? Why am I so sure? Freya Graffham had asked her if there was anything she could tell her about the two women and in one sense there was a great deal – everything she had just been thinking. But what did that amount to, in terms of a police investigation? Nothing. Vague ominous feelings. They would not be worth ringing in to describe.

But she wanted to talk to Freya again. She liked her. She had enjoyed their chance meeting and lunch. And she wished very much that Simon did not have a place in the picture. She had recognised the signs given out by Freya only too well. There had been enough of them in the past, heaven knew. Si attracted women, unsurprisingly. Si liked women, enjoyed their company, took them out, talked to them and, even more important, listened to them carefully. After which, he panicked. Besides, there was presumably still Diana.

Cat was the only member of the family, and possibly the only other person at all, who knew about Diana Mason. Simon had known her for five or six years, after they had met in Florence, where he had gone, as so often, to draw. They had struck up a conversation, discovered their hotels were in the same street. That might have been that, but for some reason, it was not. When they returned to England, Si had telephoned her.

Diana Mason lived in London and had been widowed over twenty years before and never wanted to remarry. Instead, she had wanted to find the career she had never begun, and with the money her husband had left her, she had bought her first small restaurant, in Hampstead. Now, all those years later, she owned a chain of nine, all called Mason, in London, and in smart, cleverly chosen places like Bath, Winchester, Cambridge and Brighton. Masons were relaxed brasseries with excellent food, open from ten until ten, serving the best coffees, ices and salads in an American style, welcoming to children and families and students, with exactly the right atmosphere, furnishings, staff, drinks. Diana had designed and chosen everything, every detail was decided upon by her, and she now took the sensible view that she had found a winning formula and should stick to it. She worked hard at it, constantly driving between her restaurants checking details, talking to staff, eating in each branch in turn. As a result, she had made a lot of money. Several larger restaurant chains had offered to buy her out but she had always turned them down, saying that when she was no longer having fun she would quit, but that for now, she was still enjoying herself. The relationship between Diana and Simon was unorthodox, and it suited them both. Cat had long ago decided that they were not in love with one another, and that for this very reason, it worked well. They were fond of one another, enjoyed one another's company, saw one another for a weekend several times a year, once or twice had gone on holiday again. But they were both independent people who, for different reasons, preferred not to have permanent ties. They both liked their work and their own space, their own friends, their own lives.

Added to which, Diana Mason was ten years older.

Simon almost never mentioned her, even to Cat, who had sometimes wondered how much either of them would mind if the other fell seriously in love with someone else. Probably not much.

Still, women like Freya Graffham, nice women, worried her. Si was either obtuse or chose not to notice the broken hearts that regularly lay about him. In a way, he was indifferent, even callous, and Freya, for one, deserved better. But how to warn her, how to broach the subject at all was a problem Cat would shelve for the time being. Apart from anything else, she knew from experience that if Freya was as in love with her brother as Cat suspected, she would be beyond the stage of taking kindly to any warnings whatsoever.

An hour or so later, Cat was washing her hands after attending to a child with a suppurating eardrum – why couldn't the mother have so much as given the poor kid a clean pad of paper tissues to hold against it? – when the phone rang.

'Can you take a call from Aidan Sharpe? He says he can call back later if not.'

'No, I'll take it, give me a break.'

'Tea?'

'You read my thoughts. Thanks.'

The outside line connected in with a click. 'Aidan? Good morning.'

'Cat, my dear, is this a very inopportune time? I did say I would be happy to call back.'

She smiled at his rather old-fashioned way of speaking, his extreme courtesy. Chris always said Aidan Sharpe's manners went with bow ties.

'It's fine. I could do with a break.'

'Bad morning?'

'Busy. You?'

'As ever. But I had a cancellation, and there is something I really do want to mention to you. I've been worrying about it but this morning, I don't know if you were aware, but the police were doing a reconstruction of the last known movements of that young girl who is missing.'

'Debbie Parker, yes. I drove by. I didn't see you.'

'Oh, I was like you, passing. To tell you the truth, I didn't know what was going on at first. I thought someone must be making a film until I saw the police vans. But, you see, it is precisely this that I've been worrying about and I really feel terrible. I should have thought earlier, I should have done something but I simply didn't.'

'About what?'

'Cat, the young woman came to see me. I treated her.'

'Good Lord. She didn't tell me.'

'Dear me, was she your patient?'

'Oh yes. I've seen her several times recently as a matter of fact.'

There was a silence, and then a small sound, which might have been a sigh, or an intake of breath.

'Aidan, what exactly is the matter? You say you treated her?'

'I did, just once. I asked her to make more appointments but she never did. I'm not sure she liked needles, to be frank. But her acne was really quite serious and we do sometimes succeed with it, though I rather suspected she needed a course of oxytetracycline as well.'

'I gave her one. She came to see me about it eventually . . . she ought to have come earlier, but Debbie was rather into – alternative therapies. She'd started going up to Starly to see a New Age healer.'

Aidan groaned. 'Which one? Dear me, it is the poor little girls like Debbie one so worries about.'

'A rather wafty character in a blue robe called Dava. He gave her some potentially dangerous skin cream and some herbal stuff to which she had a serious allergic reaction. I had to go out to her as an emergency.'

'This is precisely the sort of thing you've been talking about, isn't it?'

'Yes. But Aidan, I don't quite see why you're worried just now about Debbie. What has it to do with you?'

'Well, surely I ought to have reported it to the police? It is information.'

'I shouldn't think it is the least relevant to her disappearance. Would you?'

'Well, no, but they wanted to hear about anything at all . . . I had simply forgotten and I'm appalled. I seem to be losing my grip.'

Cat laughed. 'You'd better not. I've got a couple of intractable arthritic pains for you to see and you always manage to help.'

'My dear, you are very kind. I can't tell you what it means to have your confidence in this way.'

'You do. And meanwhile, don't worry about Debbie Parker.'

'I'm afraid I do. I just do. I have a very uneasy feeling.'

'So do I, between ourselves.'

'I really think I might go to the police.'

'If it will ease your mind, then yes, I think maybe you should, Aidan.'

Cat put the phone down. Aidan Sharpe was an old woman, but she liked him and respected him. It was typical of him to fret because he had temporarily forgotten that he had treated Debbie Parker. She wondered, as she pressed the buzzer for her next patient, what had led him to acupuncture. He was an unlikely practitioner. One day, she would ask him to tell her his story.

The door opened on a heavily pregnant young woman, clutching a toddler by the hand and carrying a one-year-old baby. So much for the hours I spent at the family planning clinic, Cat thought wearily.

'Hello, Tracey. Come and sit down.' She smiled at the tired-looking girl. 'Not long to go now. How are you?'

Tracey sat down, perched the baby on her lap somehow, yanked the toddler towards her with her foot, and burst into tears. Morning surgery flowed on.

The desk officer was about to ring up, when Freya Graffham came through the door into the lobby and stopped.

'Mr Sharpe? Hello. Is there anything I can help with?'

'Aidan, please.'

'I wasn't sure if this was official.'

'My dear, nice as it is to see you, I'm afraid this is official. It's about the missing girl, Debbie Parker.'

'Right, we'll go in here.'

He followed her into a small interview room.

'Do sit down. Sorry about the furnishings. Can I get you a coffee?'

'Cup of poison, you mean.'

'In the case of station coffee I have to agree with you.'

'Well, remind me to tell you one day just what frightful things coffee does to your entire system, mental and physical.'

He sat down. She was prettier than he remembered, sharp-looking, with such a shining cap of hair. He had been right, of course, to come down and not to telephone, and the timing had been right too, to arrive as she was leaving the building. He sat down, looking across at her with pleasure. She would listen too, what he had to say would not be dismissed, if only because they had met socially, and she had good manners. Adrian Sharpe smiled.

'Now, Debbie Parker. We did a reconstruction of her last known movements early this morning.'

'Really? Her last known movements? So it is known where she was last seen?'

Freya made a small face. 'Not exactly. We are pretty sure she went for a walk, and we are also fairly sure it was in the area of the Hill. That's where she had taken to walking quite a lot in recent weeks, and from what we can piece together, it was likely to have been very early in the morning. We hoped someone might just have seen her . . . memories can be jogged surprisingly long after the event if we get it right.'

'Have you had a lot of response?'

Freya shrugged. 'This and that. There are always a fair few cranks, of course . . . people who would have seen the moon turn pink if we put it about that we wanted them to contact us about it.'

She seemed so charming, so relaxed, so friendly, but she was clever, she was giving nothing away, she was throwing up the usual smokescreen. He was not deceived for a moment. The reconstruction had brought in no response from the general public that was of any use to them. But then, that was always going to be the case.

'I'm DS in charge at the moment, so if you do think you have anything that might help us, I'm the person to tell.'

He leaned back in the uncomfortable chair and sighed. 'I don't know, I simply don't know. All I know is that I've been worrying about it. It is going to sound very feeble and pathetic if I tell you that I haven't been here before simply because I forgot. No excuse. I forgot.'

'What did you forget?'

'That Debbie Parker had been to see me.'

'You mean as a patient?'

'Yes. She came just once. She had rather bad acne, poor thing . . . frightful skin, and she was depressed, partly as a result of her appearance. She was rather over-weight too. I don't know if you know that?'

Freya merely nodded.

'Acupuncture does have a proven effect on skin conditions. It's one of the areas we really can see benefits from the treatment over time.'

'What, you mean not everything responds?'

'By no means. We have our strengths . . . just as Nick Haydn – you remember you met him at Meriel's dinner as well?'

'The osteopath, yes. I didn't get much chance to talk to him.'

'His discipline has enormous success in some areas and is quite unsuited to the treatment of others. You wouldn't send anyone with acne to him.'

'When did Debbie Parker come to see you?'

'I looked it up in the database. It was October. She had an initial consultation, which is quite long, and one treatment. I suggested she come back for three more but she never did.'

'Did she contact you to explain why?'

'No. I wasn't surprised, in fact.'

'Why?'

'She seemed uneasy. Nervous.' He thought about the expression on Debbie's fat, unattractive face. 'Some people simply cannot take the needles. They don't hurt, but people are afraid of them. They can't relax. Debbie was an unhappy girl.'

'Unhappy enough, in your opinion, to take her own life?'

He paused. 'That is always very difficult to answer.'

'Just an opinion. But it could be important.'

'Then – in my professional opinion, yes. I think she was just the sort of young woman to do so.'

He looked into Freya Graffham's face, but it gave nothing back. Did she believe him? He could not have said, and the fact annoyed him.

'Did she mention having suicidal feelings?'

'Oh no. Nothing like that. So far as I remember, she said she sometimes felt "a bit down" – but then, so do many patients.'

'You didn't think there was immediate risk of her committing suicide?'

He sighed again and shook his head. 'But you can see why I now blame myself, can't you?'

'We have no reason at all to suppose Debbie has taken her own life – that she is dead at all.'

'Off the record, don't you think it the most likely explanation?' Tell me, he thought, urging her, tell me what you think, tell me what the official police verdict is going to be, tell me.

But Freya Graffham merely shook her head slightly. 'I'm grateful to you for coming in. It's never too late. It just slots another piece into the puzzle. So thank you. And don't worry about not remembering earlier.'

Efficient. Cool. Professional. But not tough, he thought, certainly not tough.

She walked out of the station and down the steps with him.

'I don't suppose you would remember if either of the other two missing women had consulted you?'

It was a typical ploy, to leave one last question and then spring it, as an afterthought, unimportant, scarcely worth mentioning, but . . . He was not remotely taken by surprise, did not stumble, did not hesitate.

'I read about one other woman. I'm afraid I can't remember the name though.'

'Angela Randall.'

He stood, thinking for a moment, then shook his head. 'I'll check of course, but I don't think so. But you mentioned that there were two others besides Debbie? Isn't this becoming rather worrying to you? How many women normally go missing in a small place like Lafferton in the course of a year, let alone a few weeks?'

'Not too many. There was an appeal about the three of them on local radio and television.'

'Then I'm afraid I missed it.'

'The third hasn't been seen for a couple of days.'

'Oh, in that case . . .'

'Yes?'

She is watching me. She is looking at me and trying to discover something. 'How long is it before you panic?' he asked, smiling.

But she did not smile back. 'We don't. We take everything more or less seriously according to individual circumstances.'

'And what were these?'

'Different from the other two.'

Yes. Different. Unplanned. A mistake.

'I doubt if I'll uncover any more patients among your missing persons but give me a name.'

'Chater. Mrs Iris Chater.'

'Age?'

'Seventy-one.'

'I'll go over my records carefully . . . for how far back, do you suggest?'

'That's up to you . . . try a couple of years initially. Do you keep full records for longer?'

He pressed the remote control and his car headlights flashed in response. He walked over to the driver's door, opened it, and only then turned back to her with a smile.

'I never destroy any records at all. I'll check and telephone you. May I have a number?'

'If I'm not here at the station, a message will always reach me.'

She stood on the bottom step and watched his car move off. As it turned out into the main road, Aidan Sharpe waved.

'Can you look up a man called Aidan Sharpe?'

'Hang on, Sarge . . . Let me grab a pen.'

'S-h-a-r-p-e . . . he's an acupuncturist. Been in Lafferton a few years and I don't know where before that. Look up the national register, double-check his qualifications . . . it's unlikely there's anything else, I'm sure he won't have form, but run it through.'

'What am I looking for?'

'I don't know. Anything. Nothing probably.'

'Thanks a bunch. How hot is this, Sarge? – only the DCI's gone mad, twenty-four hours to find every dealer and user in a fifty-mile radius, search every garage and lock-up, pull in everyone with ten minutes over on their parking time, I don't know who's on his back.'

'Bevham. It's out of control, they know it and they're trying to shift the focus. Spare me five minutes.'

'What is it about this guy Sharpe?'
'He wears a bow tie.'
'Girl's blouse then.'

Freya's phone rang.
'Sarge? Your bow tie.'
'Anything?'
'Nope. Fully qualified, got all his letters and that.'
'Where did he train?'
'London and China. He got a pigtail and all?'

The Tape

I am frightened. You always knew what to do when
I was frightened. You left the lamp on low, you talked
to me in a quiet voice, you stayed close to me. But
now I need you far more than I did then and you
don't hear, you don't reply, you have withdrawn yourself and that is cruel of you.

Forty-One

The phone drilled into Cat Deerbon's strange dream about a white pony. It was half past three. She answered automatically, before remembering that she was not on call.

'Cat? It's Karin . . . listen, I'm so sorry to wake you . . .'

Cat sat up. Chris stirred, mumbled, and slept on.

'It's OK, don't worry, but just hold on a few seconds. I'll put this phone down and pick up the other.'

She slipped out of bed and went quietly down to the kitchen. The cat was on the old sofa at the Aga end, and Cat settled next to it.

'OK, I'm here. What's wrong?'

There was a silence. Cat waited. Instinctively, she knew that Karin would respond better than if she were pumped with questions.

The dishwasher hummed faintly on the last stages of its cycle. The kitchen was wonderfully cosy.

'I'm scared. I've been awake for a long time. I couldn't not ring you.'

'I'm glad you did. Is Mike there?'

'No, he's in New York. Anyway, I can't talk to him.'

'OK.'

'I know I'm doing the right thing, I still know that. There's no way I can go down the other road.'

'This isn't just pride talking, is it? If so, forget it. Doesn't matter.'

'It isn't pride.'

'Has something happened?'

'No . . . not really.'

'I'll take that as a yes, then.'

'I've had awful backache. I don't mean gardening backache.'

'Where?'

'In the middle and a bit lower down. Not between the shoulders.'

'All the time?'

'On and off.'

'But more on.'

'Just for a few days.'

'Do you want me to come over now?'

'Christ, no, please. I'm just scared, Cat. I haven't been scared before. I've had it all under control.'

'Part of the problem?'

'I don't know. But tonight . . . everything . . . death . . . tombs . . . earth in my mouth . . . oxygen masks . . . going under . . . pain. Awful pain they can't do anything about.'

'Give me half an hour.'

'No, listen –'

'And I shall need a double espresso.'

Cat clicked off the phone.

*

In the field, the grey pony loomed out of the night and stared at her, ghostly white, over the fence. 'You broke my dream,' she told it, and let the car slide down the slope for some yards before starting the engine and turning out into the dark lane.

Karin opened the front door. She was wearing a long white waffle dressing gown, and her hair was tied up. There was never anything unkempt or dishevelled about her, Cat thought, even in the early hours of the morning. But she had lost weight, too much weight too quickly, and her face had a new look – something about the eyes, something about the prominence of the bones.

Cat kissed her on both cheeks and gave her a long hug. Her body felt slight.

'You're a saint,' Karin said.

'Nope, just a doc.'

'And a friend.'

'That first.'

'Did you really mean double espresso?'

'Maybe better tea?'

'Definitely better.' Karin filled the kettle. 'I didn't even ask if you were on call, I was in such a state.'

'It's irrelevant.'

'It got to me. I don't think it has until now.'

'It had to.'

'I didn't know what to do. I've never been so scared. I haven't looked death in the face like that until now. I didn't care for its expression.'

'Apart from the frights, how have you been?'

'OK, until I got backache. That's a bore. What do you suppose it is?'

'I'll have a look at you in a minute if you like. I don't know. You said it wasn't gardening backache but have you been working out there? You know how it is – first warm days of the year, everyone goes out to dig and we get the fallout.'

'I haven't been working in the garden.'

She set two full mugs in front of them. Cat noticed that, for once, Karin's was plain Indian tea too, not herbal.

'Anything else?'

'Not really.'

'What?'

Karin shrugged. 'Tired. That's nothing.' Her skin, always beautiful, had a transparent sheen.

'Will you go for a scan?'

'Oh, Cat, what's the point? We both know what it is, what's happening to me. Why have it underlined? I'd rather not know.'

'That isn't like you.'

'It's like this me.'

She lifted her mug, took a sip of tea, set it down again, and looked across at Cat, her eyes brimming with tears. 'What's going to happen?' she said.

'I am being absolutely truthful when I say that I don't know. I need something to go on, Karin.'

'Educated guess.'

'No.'

'OK then, I'll do it for you. Secondaries. Probably in the spine. I've been coughing as well. So, lungs too. But I'm *not* going to go to hospital, I'm *not* seeing an oncologist. When I need a doctor, I'll have you if that's OK. I'm going on with my healer. I've an appointment tomorrow. It really helps.'

'I know.'

'I'm being stricter with the diet as well.'

'What are you eating?'

'Raw, organic.'

'What?'

'Vegetables, a bit of fruit. Water. They recommend coffee enemas.'

'Absolutely, categorically not, Karin. You can do yourself a lot of harm. Listen, it isn't what you are eating that's worrying me so much as what you are not – you need good nourishment. Of course you need fresh fruit and veg, but you also need milk, eggs, bit of cheese, lots of fish, a bit of yeast to give you extra vitamin B, wholegrains – oats are best. A couple of glasses of good red wine every evening.'

'You've just crammed a dozen toxic substances into one sentence.'

Cat snorted and poured herself a second mug of tea.

'What can you do about my back? And my general mopes? Do I live with those while I get better?' Karin's eyes were huge and anxious on Cat's face.

'Depends. If you had a scan so that I knew what was wrong with your back I'd feel happier about treating it. I mean, paracetamol is all very well . . . I would like to prescribe a mild antidepressant . . . one of the newer kind, the SSRI group. But I suppose they're full of toxins. Some aromatherapy is said to have uplifting properties but I'm no expert. It's nice and cosy though.'

'I know, I go every week. It's cosy . . . not sure it's much use.'

'If we do pinpoint what's wrong in your back, I'd possibly send you to see Aidan Sharpe. He's very careful, I have a lot of faith in him . . . he wouldn't treat you at all if he didn't think it was right. It might well help the back pain.'

'OK.'

'But he would want you to get a scan too.'

'OK.' Karin sounded suddenly exhausted and defeated. She sat, staring down into her empty mug.

'I think you should start on the course of antidepressants. They'll work quickly . . . a week and you'll start feeling better. If you're still serious about tackling this your way – or my way, come to that – you need to be on top and you're not. Let's get your mood up and your fighting spirit will come back. Deal?'

Karin was silent for a moment. 'Go over it all again.'

'Right. See me later this morning. I'll get them to put you in at half eight, before the rest of surgery. I'll have a look at you, prescribe your tablets so you can start at once. And book an MRI scan at BG. For a time when I can come with you. It's a bit scary. Meanwhile, you go and get a double dose of sweet smells and then come to lunch and I'll put some decent food inside you. Don't look like that, it's our own eggs and they're organic. Let's go from there. And don't let things get like this again. Talk to me, talk to Chris, ring us whenever. Don't ever sit here brooding, especially when Mike's away. Things grow.'

'God, they did.'

'There's a trick about the nightmares too. Write down the gist of them – keep pen and paper by the bed. In the morning, take the paper and put a match to it. Watch it burn and grind up the bits to ash. You're burning up the nightmares so you won't have them again. Old-fashioned trick cyclists' tip.'

Cat wound her scarf round her neck and picked up her car keys. 'I'll see you in the morning.'

Chris was awake when she got back into bed. 'Is Karin OK?'

'No.'

'What?'

'Frightened.'

'You're a good girl.'

Cat pressed her face into his warm back. 'She had that look,' she said. Chris grunted, understanding.

A week later, she drove Karin to Bevham.

Something had happened since her visit in the early hours of the morning. Karin had lost her vibrant and powerful confidence in the road she had chosen to take and twice telephoned Cat, once to ask for the scan, the second time to agree to the blood test which would tell them more about her condition.

'Though I don't understand what anyone can see from looking at a blob of my blood.'

'They'll look for tumour markers.'

The result had been worrying and the blood test had also shown that Karin was anaemic.

'Which accounts for your tiredness lately. We can help with that.'

It was never easy, knowing how much to tell a patient and in what detail. When she had first come to the surgery Karin had preferred to get on with following her own treatment plan, taking each day as it came and not investigating too much into her physical state. So long as she felt well, she was well, had been her firm line.

Now she did not feel well.

'I want to know. I have to be able to see what I'm up against. You can't fight an enemy if you don't know how strong it is.'

'OK, I'll try and help, though these things are always relative, you know. Seeing what a scan or a blood test looks like is one thing, making any sort of prognosis is another.'

Now, as they went along the bypass towards Bevham, Karin said suddenly, 'Do you believe in ghosts?'

Cat laughed. 'No. No, I don't think I do.'

'But you do believe . . . ?'

'If you mean in God, I have to. I've seen too much to let me believe otherwise, and I couldn't do my job if I didn't.'

'Why not ghosts then?'

'Not sure . . . I suppose I think they're unnecessary. And there's so often a rational explanation of so-called ghostly sightings.'

'So you don't think we come back?'

'Not as ghosts in the usual sense. Do you?'

Karin did not reply, but after another moment said, 'What about places which have a bad atmosphere. People would usually say haunted, but anyway, places that have a definite sense of evil surrounding them.'

'Yes,' Cat said quietly, 'I do believe in those. I don't know why it is so, but it sometimes definitely is. We once went into a house in France when we were on holiday, before we had the children – a pretty house, charming really, and it was a lovely evening. We were looking for a room to stay in for the night and someone had sent us there because the hotel was full. When we walked in I had the most appalling sense of fear . . . there was evil in there, it hit me in the face the moment I walked in. Nothing happened, there was nothing to see . . . but I couldn't have stayed there. I couldn't wait to get out again.'

'Did you find out why?'

Cat shook her head.

'I've had the same experience with people. I remember a waitress in a restaurant in London . . . Just some pleasant ordinary little bistro, about twenty years ago. When she took our order it started and it got worse . . . she was a witch. I'm still convinced there was real evil about her . . . the friend I was with felt it too. But what was it really? She didn't look at all unusual but I didn't want her near me.'

'Have you been having night frights again?'

'A bit . . . nothing much. Your coming over jinxed them.'

'Good. But if you do, talk about it. Don't bottle it up.'

'I'm still afraid.'

'What about your healer?'

'I talked to her about it yesterday. Now there's the very opposite in a house. I've never been anywhere like it. When you walk into the garden, before you even get to inside, you have this incredible sense that it is a healing place. There is such an air of peace and goodness. When I go, I just drink it in. I want to stay and be wrapped in it. Nothing can get to me there. These places . . . good vibes, evil vibes . . . I want to understand it.'

'Yes.'

'Is it to do with being near death, Cat?'

'I don't know,' Cat said. They turned into the hospital entrance as an ambulance came screaming out. 'I simply don't know.'

Forty-Two

His hand which was holding the scalpel froze. Beneath it on the slab the chest cavity of the elderly woman was already exposed. He was working very late, comparing this heart and the diseased arteries surrounding it with the fresh, healthy one of the girl. It was absorbing, fascinating.

The sudden noise of a vehicle outside shocked him. It had driven up to the unit, turned, and stopped not far away. Now, after the closing of a car door, there was silence again. It was after midnight. No one came here at this time. The security guard patrolled the main avenue of the business park and once in a while approached the turning into this side road, but he knew the sound of that van, which always reversed noisily without bothering to come to the end. He waited. The lights here could not be seen from the main avenue, or by anyone walking up the side of the building. He had gone to a lot of trouble to make absolutely sure of it. But he was disturbed and his concentration had gone.

He looked down at the cadaver, annoyed. He could return her to the drawer still opened, because he had by no means finished his work, or sew her up roughly to begin again next time he came in. He had never been interrupted in this way before. It changed things and even the smallest change troubled him.

He waited, but there were no further sounds outside, and in the end, he was able to close the chest and restore everything quite calmly and without panic.

He hung up his gown, scrubbed his hands, checked the machines, switched off the lights and locked the building. Outside, it was cold and very still with intensely bright stars.

He walked softly up the road a short way. A white van was clearly visible and there was a strip of light under the door of one of the lock-ups. So far as he knew, it was simply a store, without any office facility. He had never seen anyone there before.

He memorised the number plate of the van, which was filthy with grime and mud, and after waiting for some while in the shadows, slipped back towards his own car. He started up the engine and drove slowly past the van. He parked a block away, and then went back on foot. Nothing. No one. He had not been heard, no one had been disturbed.

He sped away from the business park, not switching on his headlights until he reached the main road. He scarcely saw another vehicle. Back at his house, he mixed himself a whisky and water, and switched on the lamp beside his chair. He would write up his notes tomorrow. Now, he wanted to think about Detective Sergeant Freya Graffham.

The weather had jerked forwards into warm spring. In CID, the sun coming through the large windows made the room hot and stuffy. DC Coates sat at his desk, computer screen in front of him, his eyes glazed over. Freya watched him for a moment, then got up and went to stand in front of him. There was no response.

'Earth to Nathan . . . are you receiving?'

His eyes refocused but he still did not respond to her.

'NATHAN.'

'What? Gawd, Sarge, you might have give me 'eart attack.'

'Anything to have you with us. Where were you, by the way?'

Nathan swivelled his chair round to face the window, screwing his eyes up against the sun. 'Wouldn't you like to be sitting by one of them swimming pools they have at the posh houses in the Flixton Road? Nice book, long cool drink.'

'It's not that warm.' She looked out at the roofs of the cars below glittering angrily in the sun. The magnolia tree in one of the opposite gardens had come into full, waxy bloom.

'I was thinking just now, Sarge – what you said the other day.'

'What?'

'Me and Em.'

'Right.'

'She's away . . . went to Carlisle yesterday for a week to see her gran. I 'ate it, by myself in the flat. I don't know how you stand living on your tod.'

'I like it. For now.'

'I was missing her half-hour after she'd gone. I don't begrudge her, like, she loves her gran and the old lady ain't been too well.'

'But you miss her all the same.'

'Yeah. So I been thinking. Maybe you had a good idea there.'

'About getting married?'

'Yeah. I quite fancy it now, you know.'

'Then do it. Don't mess about.'

'I might an' all. What sort of a ring do you think I ought to get her?'

'No sort. I think you ask her, and if she says yes, you take her to choose it for herself.'

'Yeah, right, whatever I get won't be what she wants. Do you think she'd know?'

'She could probably take you to it blindfold. Meanwhile, there's work.'

Nathan groaned. 'I 'ate it at the moment. Everything's stuck. Drugs op is bedded in sand, no news on the missing women. Any minute now they'll second me on to shoplifting.'

'Yes, I heard uniform want some surveillance in the arcade.'

'Hanging about waiting for teenagers to nick top-shelf mags. Rather get back to my database.'

Freya sat down at her own desk. Nathan was right. She knew nothing about the drugs op beyond the fact that they were waiting for the off on a raid once they had enough information, but the place was full of pent-up officers hanging round the canteen drinking too much tea. Meanwhile, her own sense of frustration had reached boiling point. The investigation into the missing women had not moved an inch further forward since the recon-struction of Debbie Parker's early-morning walk, which had elicited virtually no public response. Nathan had drawn a blank on the jeweller's list, on Starly and on the medium visited by Iris Chater. All Mrs Innes had told him was that Mrs Chater had left a seance at her house at around nine o'clock in the evening. The rest of them had remained inside. Mrs Chater had not returned home, nor apparently been seen by anyone since. Like Angela Randall and Debbie Parker, she had vanished into thin air. And any day now, Freya knew, the inquiry would be downgraded and she would be working on something else.

As if reading her thoughts, Nathan looked up from his computer screen. 'White goods for us, Sarge, just you wait.'

Freya groaned. There had been a spate of thefts of new freezers, dishwashers and washing machines a day after they had been delivered and all to empty houses waiting for new occupiers to move in. It seemed likely that there was a ring operating, with tip-offs going from delivery men to a separate set of thieves, who split the proceeds once the goods had been sold on, but so far, the police were always one step behind them. There might be less interesting jobs, but Freya was hard put to think of one.

A fly was buzzing up the side of the window and down again, up, bzzzzz, and down again, bzzzzz. She thought she might join the frustrated drugs-op team down in the tea room.

Bzzzzz.

The ringing of the phone at her elbow made her jump.

'DS Graffham.'

'Freya? Good afternoon, how nice to have got straight through to you.' The rather prissy and cultivated voice identified itself.

'Aidan . . . how are you?'

'Isn't this the most miraculous weather? Doesn't it make your heart lift?'

'It does. The whole of CID is plotting a daring breakout.'

'I can't offer an escape to the sun, I'm afraid, but I did wonder if you would have a drink with me this evening? I don't know what time you finish but I have to see a late patient. I'll be free by six thirty.'

She hesitated. This was a social invitation, and any reason she had to meet Aidan Sharpe was professional. She had no interest in forming a closer relationship. On the other hand, what else did she have on this evening? Besides, there was no reason why she shouldn't combine work and relaxation in some small measure.

'That would be very nice. Thank you. Where would you like to meet?'

'There is a very pleasant new bar in the Ross Hotel.'

'The Embassy Room? I've heard about it . . . not been though.'

'Good. Shall we meet there at six forty-five?'

Nathan was looking at her with interest as she put down the phone. Freya shook her head.

'Uh-huh. It's sort of work.'

'Yeah, right.'

'Right – it's Mr Bow Tie, Nathan.'

'Got you. Still, swish place.'

'So I'm told.'

'Sting him for one of them cocktails with little brollies.'

'OK. Right now, I'm going for a cuppa.'

'Thought you'd never ask.'

Nathan jumped up on to his desk and off the other side.

'Tell you what, Sarge – I'll take Em there and ask her.'

'Wait till I've sussed it out.'

'Yeah, if I'm going to go for it, it's got to be pukka, know what I mean?'

Nathan's monkey face was lit up with excitement. Freya felt a sudden pang of – what? Envy? Loneliness? A feeling of missing out?

'Lucky Em,' she said.

Nathan went ahead of her down the concrete stairs two at a time.

Forty-Three

The waiting room was empty, the magazines tidied up in neat piles, edge to edge, and the cover was on the receptionist's computer. Karin sat down. It was very quiet, very tidy, but for some reason, despite the pleasant if bland watercolours, the room felt lifeless rather than peaceful.

She was tense which made the pain in her back worse.

The clock was an electric one, and the windows were double-glazed, the carpet thick, so that the room was strangely silent.

Because she was Cat's patient, and because he had met Karin socially, Aidan Sharpe had given her an immediate appointment at the end of his working day, and she was grateful. But now that she was here Karin felt uneasy. She had been sailing along in such a blithe way, ignoring the facts, forcing herself into a positive frame of mind, refusing to acknowledge the existence of any shadows, let alone peer into them. It was catching up with her.

The sun had gone from the room. Karin thought she

might get up and leave. Oh, for God's sake.

'Mrs McCafferty, I'm so sorry to keep you.'

She stood up. 'Karin,' she said, though they had not managed to speak much at the Serraillers' dinner party.

'Do come through.'

Every consulting room she had been into during her weeks of exploration into complementary therapies had been warm, welcoming, informal – many of them had been what she thought of as 'real' rooms in ordinary houses, like the bright, peaceful, flower-filled living room in which her spiritual healer worked. She liked that. Hospitals and doctors' surgeries were so cold, so bleak, so bare. The scanner room, the oncologist's consulting room, the radiotherapy waiting room – she had wanted to run out of them all.

Aidan Sharpe's surgery discomfited her. Though there was nothing particularly unusual about its pastel bland-ness, it did not feel relaxing, calming at all.

She stood uncertainly.

He wore a white coat, high at the neck.

'Cat gave me your scan results. I gather you are having some back pain?'

'Yes.' No, Karin wanted to say. Her throat tightened.

'Is it painful intermittently or most of the time?'

He had a folder in his hand and glanced down at a sheet he had slipped out of it. Her scan results, pre-sumably.

'I don't get a lot of respite from it. It varies in inten-sity though, depending on what I'm doing.'

'Is it worse standing, sitting or lying? Is it worse when you're moving about or being still?'

'I can distract myself by moving about.'

'I see. Right. If you'd like to go behind that screen and

take off your things down to your underwear and slip on the robe hanging up there?'

The room had seemed to be silent but when Karin lay down on the high couch, she heard the faintest humming sound, as if the floor beneath her were charged with some high-pitched electricity.

Aidan Sharpe sat on the high stool beside her and took her hand to feel her pulse. Karin looked up. His eyes were staring not at her but into her. They were extraordinary eyes, cold, small, like little hard stones, and the lids veiled them slightly.

A terrible sensation rose up from deep in her stomach, through her chest and into her throat. It was fear, it was nausea, it was a sense of entrapment. She remembered the conversation she had had in the car with Cat. She wanted to pull herself up, throw herself off the couch on to the floor and run, now, wrench open the doors and race out into the safety and open air of the street.

The nausea was like bile in her mouth.

His gaze was absolutely steady on her face. He scarcely blinked. 'Your pulse is very unsteady.'

Her tongue was swollen like a cow's, huge in her mouth. She moved her head slightly. In the ceiling above, the fluorescent light was white-blue and pulsating gently.

She heard the sound of metal on metal. Aidan Sharpe had let her wrist go and reached out his hand to the tray of meticulously arranged small needles. He selected one and, turning back, looked down at her again. The eyes were so odd, narrowed yet staring and strangely expressionless. He smelled faintly of antiseptic, faintly of masculine soap, and yet Karin smelled nothing but the smell of death. Her head swam.

'Relax, please.'

The needle touched her temple and a hot pain shot through her back.

'Good.'

Another needle, beside her left nostril and the same back pain, lower down.

— Jesus, God, help me — Karin thought.

She realised that no one else was in the building. The receptionist had long gone home, she was the last patient of the day. She sensed the rest of Aidan Sharpe's house, empty and silent stretching back beyond the walls of the surgery.

There were more needles, carefully positioned. After a few moments, she began to feel drowsy, and light-headed, as if she had been given a hypnotic. The pain in her back had gone but her legs felt heavy and numb.

Aidan Sharpe continued to stare at her as he worked but he did not speak.

The needles seemed to be pinning her to the couch so that she was afraid to attempt the slightest movement, afraid that her flesh would be torn and the hair ripped from her scalp. She was hot and very thirsty.

She looked up. His eyes were more needles, penetrating her skull. She had lost all sense of time. Hours might have passed or only a few moments.

She wondered if anyone knew where she was. The appointment had been made over the telephone, which she had answered when alone in the house. She did not think she had even jotted a note of it down. No one else had rung, Mike was away, she was not expected any-where that evening. Why am I thinking like this? she thought, and made a tremendous effort not to sink down and down but to struggle up, towards the surface of consciousness and control. Aidan Sharpe was very still.

'You may feel a little light-headed.' His voice was soft.

Karin tried to speak.

'Don't move please.'

Something in his voice warned her to do as he asked, some cold, dry thing lacking all emotion, but infinitely powerful.

Now, her chest seemed to be cracking open as she tried to get her breath, and her lungs hurt as the air rasped quickly in and out of them, and her head was swimming and full of vapour, her limbs were losing sensation, except for her fingers which were tingling as if pricked all over by tiny pins. She became aware of Aidan Sharpe reaching down to her. She saw the pattern of small jazzy yellow commas on the navy surface of his bow tie. It confused her eyes.

'Don't try to sit up.'

His hands were on her arms and seemed to be pressing against her so that she could not move. She struggled slightly.

The navy-and-yellow pattern danced electrically in her brain. It was the last thing she was conscious of before she dropped down into swirling darkness.

Forty-Four

Freya had dithered about racing home to change, uncertain whether her work suit would fit the dress code at the Embassy Room, but when she walked in just before six forty-five, she relaxed. The place was stylish and bang up to date, which meant that absolutely anything went, from jeans and jackets to diamanté-speckled little black frocks and plain linen office suits. There was the same hum about it that she so much enjoyed in the Metro Café, where she had bumped into Cat Deerbon. Both places gave her a taste of trendy London while being firmly in Lafferton.

The Embassy was not chrome and neon, as she had expected, but pale curved wood and bright pink tweed, attractive and comfortable. It reminded her of a couple of places in Barcelona she and Don had frequented on one of their weekends there. It was also packed, the young after-work crowd jostling with couples starting on an evening out, plus a few of the older, golf and bridge set. None of them looked out of place, everyone seemed relaxed.

Aidan Sharpe had not arrived. Freya found a corner table for two, with some difficulty, and ordered a non-alcoholic cocktail called a Sunshine Moonshine, which came in a big bowl-shaped glass, with ice, straws, parasols and strawberries on sticks, and was both intensely fruity and slightly bitter.

She sat back in the curved chair and was suddenly overcome with an intense desire for Simon, to be sitting here with him, laughing, talking, enjoying, taking time before going on somewhere for dinner. It was too long since their last meeting outside the station. He had been wrapped up in masterminding the drugs op and when he had not been in meetings, was out. Several times Freya had walked past his door and hesitated, wanting to go in for no other reason than to see him, speak to him; several times she had almost picked up the phone to dial his flat number, but had always replaced the receiver. She wanted to ask him out and knew that this was one thing she must not do, that he was the kind of man who would take it amiss; she desperately wanted to get it right with him. She had waited, held back, stayed silent and so was now about to spend an hour with a prim alternative therapist in his fifties who wore a bow tie.

Whichever direction he had come from she had not seen him, so that he startled her by materialising at her side and, in a gesture that she found unnerving, kissing her hand.

'I'm so sorry . . . my last patient felt faint and I had to take her home. Do you like it here? It's rather interesting.'

Freya could have applied several adjectives to the Embassy Room bar but 'interesting' would not have been one of them. She took a silent bet that he would order gin and tonic and won.

'I suppose you're pretty booked up . . . acupuncture seems so fashionable.'

'Oh dear, I hope not. Fashionable today, out of fashion tomorrow.'

'Like this place.'

'No, my dear, I rather think the Embassy Room is here to stay and so is my profession.'

His drink arrived. The waitress, who wore bootleg jeans and boots with a white shirt, smiled coolly, before whipping off to an adjacent table. Aidan Sharpe bent down to reach for his glass. As he did so, the cuff of his jacket shot up. Freya's stomach clenched. The watch on his wrist was gold, with Roman numerals and a separate midnight-blue dial in one corner showing the phases of the moon.

She realised that she had noticed it subliminally before, on the evening of the Serraillers' dinner party but had not registered its significance.

She looked up and straight into Aidan Sharpe's odd, expressionless, intensely staring eyes.

A couple getting up to leave the adjacent table knocked over a chair which fell against Freya's, and in the apologies and general fuss, the moment was fractured, but she was in no doubt that he had seen her looking at the watch, and noticed her split second of awareness.

'This place could be in London,' Freya said. 'Lafferton is definitely coming on line.' She relaxed back and looked around, apparently at ease, thinking hard. The jeweller had said that phases-of-the-moon watches were hard to find these days – hard but not impossible, and certainly the one Angela Randall had bought was not unique. Freya had learned through years of experience that coincidence played a larger part in life than almost any other factor and probably that was what she had now – a coincidence. But she had to allow for the alternative explanation and she had also learned to listen to her instincts, though not always to follow them, and that lesson had stood her in good stead as well. Since the Serraillers' party, her instincts about Aidan Sharpe had been uneasy ones.

She turned back to him. He was sitting very upright, very still, holding his drink and looking at her, with the expression of a smile on his mouth but not on his face and certainly not in his eyes. His hands were pale, the fingers long and thin, nails neatly trimmed and oddly bloodless.

'Why did you come to Lafferton?' His voice had changed. He sounded amused.

'Personal reasons . . . and I'd had enough of London. The Met's tough and it can be shitty.'

'You may not find Lafferton a country retreat.'

'I don't want one. And you're right, it has the usual problems . . . the young, seething with frustration, petty criminals, drugs. But the whole atmosphere is a relief after London.'

'You seem to have found things to do.'

'Socially, you mean?'

Again the sliver of a smile.

'I've made some friends. Joined things.'

'I imagine house prices were a pleasant surprise.'

'Lord, yes. I bought my house for a good bit less than I got for my Ealing one. Nice to have money in the bank for once.'

'Ealing? Good gracious. I lived in Ealing when I was training. Do you know Woodfield Road?'

'Yes.'

'I imagine you've bought somewhere outside Lafferton . . . there are so many nice villages within easy reach.'

'No, the Old Town. I wanted to be in the middle of things.'

'You couldn't have done better . . . that grid of streets around the cathedral is perfect. The Apostles?'

'Sanctuary Street.'

'One of the nicest. Lafferton learned a lesson from the mistakes other places made. They slapped a conservation notice on the whole area before everyone started adding loft rooms and aluminium windows. You made a good investment. Will you stay?'

'In the Old Town?'

'In Lafferton.'

Freya shrugged non-committally. Aidan's eyes had not left her face throughout the light, easy conversation.

'Let me order you another drink. What was that decorative object called?'

'No thank you. I'm afraid I have to go.'

'Really?'

She could not read his tone. Disbelieving?

'Paperwork.'

'How many more patients I would treat, how many more crimes you would solve, if it were not for paperwork.' He picked up the bill and they made their way through the crowd to the cash desk. Freya turned as she waited for him to pay, and over the top of a group of heads saw that of Simon Serrailler, taller than most, fairer than any. He had almost certainly not noticed her.

Aidan Sharpe put his hand on her elbow and guided her to the door. His grip was strong.

'Thank you so much. Now I know what the Embassy Room is really like.'

'Fun?'

But there was no trace of fun in his voice.

'Great fun.'

She flicked the switch to unlock the doors of her car and got in quickly. It was growing dark but the lights outside the bar were brilliant, attracting the crowds to them like moths.

Freya glanced in her mirror and saw Aidan Sharpe standing, motionless, beside his own dark blue BMW staring at her, a stare she could feel long after she could see it.

She reached her house, switched on all the lamps and drew the curtains. The living room was warm. She took her post and briefcase to the table and poured herself a glass of wine. There were three messages on her machine, one from Cat inviting her to Sunday lunch, one from Sharon Medcalf, asking her if she played tennis. She took the numbers down and clicked on to the last message.

'Freya, it's Simon Serrailler. Twenty past six. I thought we might have gone for a drink but you're not there. We'll catch up another time.'

Damn. Damn, damn, damn. He had been there. She had wasted an hour in the creepy company of Bow Tie when she could have been, as she had so wanted to be, in the Embassy with Simon.

Damn. She listened to the message again to hear his voice and when she had deleted the other two, saved it.

Damn.

The house was very quiet. She took another drink of her wine, and flipped through the uninteresting-looking post. In a minute she would get a salad together.

Damn. This time she said it aloud into the silent room.

There were dark green and grey fronds twining about in front of Karin and she was trying to weave her way through them but they clung to her face and hands and pulled her back. They smelled sulphurous and foul and the water she was swimming in was murky.

Then suddenly she was clear and free. She sat up.

Her bedroom was lit by a low lamp on the dressing table and for a second she was confused by the soft glow after the slimy dimness of her dream. Karin leaned forward, knees hunched in front of her. There was a jug and glass on the bedside table and she poured out some water. It was still quite cold and she wondered how this could be so. She had no recollection of having put it there. Drinking it helped not only to ease her dry throat and mouth but somehow to clear her senses, until she remembered that she had not been here at all but on the couch in Aidan Sharpe's consulting rooms feeling sick and disorientated. His hands had been on her arms and he had been staring at her intently. Everything else was a blank. He must have driven her back and helped or even carried her up here. She was fully clothed and lying under the coverlet. The curtains had been drawn and the lamp switched on. Presumably he had also fetched the water.

She remained for a few more moments, trying to clear her head. She felt slightly odd but no longer dizzy.

Her next feeling was one of anger. She had been to the acupuncturist as a patient in good faith and the treatment had possibly caused her to feel faint and giddy. But she might have been at risk and should not have been brought home, semi-conscious, dumped on her bed and left alone. His behaviour had been strange throughout the treatment, she remembered now; she had felt uneasy and threatened, had wanted to leave, panic Red. He had neither explained anything to her nor seemed concerned about her reaction.

She drank another glass of water, got up cautiously and went to the bathroom. She felt tired, but not unsteady and when she had washed her hands and face and tied her hair back, she came back to her room, picked up the telephone and dialled Cat who answered at once.

'Have you got a minute? Something's happened.'

'Sure, but I'm cooking a lamb casserole for the freezer so I've got the receiver in the crook of my neck. What's wrong?'

Karin took a breath and began to tell her carefully and as calmly as she could manage. Cat listened as she always did, without interruption, taking in every detail of what was being said to her.

'So I'm here, I'm OK, but I'm angry. I don't know if that's unreasonable.'

'No. What else?'

'Still a bit fazed.'

'This shouldn't have happened. I don't understand Aidan, he's always been totally reliable.'

'You don't believe me.'

'Of course I do. I'm just puzzled. I'd come over but I'm here alone with the children and my car is in for service today . . . Chris isn't back till later.'

'No, it's fine, I don't need you to do that. I just needed to talk about it.'

'Do you want to come here? You're very welcome and you can stay.'

'I don't think I'm up to driving.'

'No, probably not. Acupuncture can wipe you out a bit . . . that's normal by the way, don't worry about feeling tired and light-headed.'

Karin looked round the bedroom. She didn't want to be alone here, not this evening, not for the night.

'I could get a taxi. If you wouldn't mind . . .'

'I'd ask Chris to pick you up only I've no idea how long he'll be, he's at BG.'

'If you don't mind my coming, there's a taxi in the village.'

'Come when you like. I've got to go, the onions are catching.'

By nine, the taxi had dropped Karin at the Deerbons' door. She had shovelled her night things into a holdall, locked the house and fled. Cat had put her on the sofa with her legs up and taken her blood pressure.

'It's fine . . . a bit low but that's the treatment. I prescribe peppermint tea – you'd better stay off booze tonight.'

'Peppermint tea is your cure-all.'

'Good stuff.'

'Am I being hysterical?'

'No and I'm concerned. It isn't like you . . . you faced our friend the psychic surgeon and came out of it OK.'

'How well do you know him?'

'Aidan? Not very. I refer patients to him sometimes. He's done my arthritis and he's been here to dinner and we have this informal group which he comes to . . . and talks a lot of sense. But it's really a professional acquaintance.'

'Do you find him sinister?'

Cat looked at her sharply. 'Not especially. Buttoned up. I should think he's got some repressions; he isn't married – isn't anything at all, so far as I know, and he doesn't let much slip. What do you mean by sinister?'

Karin shrugged. 'Forget it. Take no notice. I just got thoroughly wound up.'

'I think you did. It was probably a slight panic attack and when you're in the middle of one of those you can lose all sense of reality and proportion. That's one of the nastiest aspects of them. Normal things seem terrifying, ordinary people seem sinister and threatening.'

'You make it sound quite commonplace.'

'It is. None the better for that though. I can prescribe you a low dose of oxazepam for a few days. Take it at night, don't drive on it. It won't wipe you out, just ease all this. It's a phase. You've never been like it before. It's related to everything else.'

Karin sipped her tea and listened to Cat in cool, reassuring GP mode and yes, she believed her, yes, she had been worked up, yes, everything had started to get out of proportion as she faced what was going wrong with her body, probably for the first time. She felt infinitely better for being here, more in control, quite calm.

But the anger at what had happened was still there. That and the sensation of unease when she remembered Aidan Sharpe.

'What should I do?'

Cat shook her head. 'Nothing. I'll give Aidan a ring tomorrow. You're my patient and this wasn't on. I'm sure he checked that you were OK before leaving you, but the fact is, you don't remember anything, which means you were at some risk. He should have rung me.'

'Thanks. You don't think I should . . .'

Cat stood up. 'I think you should have a bath – in my bathroom, which is relatively civilised, the children aren't allowed in there. You can have a slug of the lovely smelly Jo Malone stuff Mum gave me for my birthday. Then you're going to the spare room with a soothing book, a hot-water bottle and a pill.'

The combination of them all, plus the very fact of being here in this house she always thought of as being the happiest she knew, sent Karin into a rose-pink and dreamless sleep which lasted until after eight the next morning. Whatever unease she had felt about her visit to Aidan Sharpe had been soothed away so that all she felt now was rather foolish. She had been faint which Cat said could be a normal reaction to the treatment. She had been slightly disorientated and she had panicked as a result. Sights, sounds, incidents which were ordinary had become distorted. That was all. Aidan Sharpe had driven her home and seen that she was safely in bed. She remembered none of it but that did not mean she had been unconscious, merely in some sort of fugue state or slight shock. She had cancer, she had had a stressful week because of it – was it surprising that she had reacted so violently? Probably he ought to have contacted Cat but by then it had been out of hours and clearly he had checked and not been too worried about leaving her alone. He was conscientious, he had a good reputation, Cat thought well of him.

Karin lay back and picked up the novel she had barely begun to read before falling asleep the previous night. A slant of sunlight filtered through the pretty spare-room curtains, and she heard Sam and Hannah laughing downstairs. Life seemed very good. Life was what she wanted desperately, more of this ordinary, unremarkable, miraculous life, any amount more. Courage and optimism bubbled up within her.

Forty-Five

'Where are you?'

'Hi, Sarge. The usual – hanging around.'

'Nothing gone up yet?'

'Naah. I reckon somebody's got wind of us.'

'Who's with you?'

'Dave Green, only he's just gone for a leak. I could do with a cuppa but you don't get the luxury of corner shops on the Meadow View estate.'

'Just corner dealers.'

'Ain't none of them about neither.'

'That's a triple negative, Nathan.'

'You what?'

'Scrub it. This place is like a morgue.'

'They're all out here somewhere. Word is uniform are doing a bust on the Calden Business Park later. I'm going to see if I can get to go, our brain cells are dying off here.'

'Your what?'

'Ha ha. You sound as if you survived your drink with Bow Tie, Sarge.'

'When Emma says yes, I'll take you both to the Embassy Room, it's something else.'

'You're on.'

'Why, has she said yes?'

'She ain't back till later but it's all a foregone, you see.'

'Nathan, listen – Bow Tie. He was wearing a phases-of-the-moon watch.'

'Right. Angela Randall. Might be coincidence.'

'It might.'

'Anything else?'

'No. Nothing concrete.'

'Yeah, well, that's the whole problem about these missing women, ain't it? Got to go, Sarge, something's happening. Cheers.'

The phone cut off.

Freya went down to the canteen. Four uniform were sitting together eating breakfast, but otherwise the place was empty. She got coffee and a banana and took them over to a window table.

Aidan Sharpe had come to the station, out of the blue, to report that Debbie Parker had been a patient of his, though the fact had at first slipped his mind. Why had it? And if the watch had been a gift from Angela Randall, how had he known her? As a patient? If so, why had he not said so? Why had her name rung no bells with him?

She would send Nathan to interview him. If there was anything there, he would get at it. Nathan's instincts were sound, he picked up the same vibes as she did, which was why they worked so well together. But frankly, she thought, throwing her banana skin into the bin, it was all clutching at straws.

Forty-Six

He scarcely slept and at six he was driving towards the business park. He had looked at himself in the mirror that morning and for the first time seen fear and uncertainty on his face. He had allowed things to happen that should not have happened, been careless, been impetuous, let matters slip. He had been almost uncontrollably tempted to kill Karin McCafferty. The urge had never come over him like that, unbidden and at random, and now he was terrified at how powerful the urge had been. It had also been irrational and without motive. He did not need Karin McCafferty, though possibly her condition might have been marginally interesting. He had the reports but he might have been the first actually to see the extent of the tumour, the first not to deduce but to know.

But he had not known how many people were aware of her appointment with him, he had not made careful checks and planned ahead. One impulse had been enough. He was not a risk taker and did not want to become one. That way danger, madness and detection surely lay. Risks were for the stupid.

Karin McCafferty had panicked and reacted badly to the treatment. It happened occasionally. He had driven her home in a semi-conscious state, taken her key from her bag, helped her upstairs and on to her bed and stayed with her for fifteen minutes, to see that she was safe to be left. That had been another risk, taken because he was in a hurry to meet Freya Graffham.

Then, recalling the policewoman in the Embassy Room, smart among the smart people, he smiled. She found him of interest, he could tell, she was intrigued by him. She would not have met him otherwise. It had been the right move to make, the intelligent move and he had redeemed himself in his own eyes after the mistake. There would not be any more of those.

He sped along the access road and turned into the business park. The first avenue was empty but as he reached the second, leading towards the side road in which his own unit was situated, he saw four police cars and three others, unmarked, together with a white police van whose back doors were open. Dog handlers and their dogs were climbing out and gathering on the pathway.

He turned hard left and out fast on to the south avenue. As he reached the entrance to the main road, another two police cars came screeching in.

The fact that there was clearly some kind of raid ought not to have unnerved him. They would scarcely be interested in his own unit, but he needed to find out exactly what was going on and where and for the moment had no idea how he might do so. He sat in the lay-by thinking carefully, not allowing himself to panic, holding his feelings in check as if he were muzzling a dog.

He could return to the business park and simply ask one of the policemen. He could telephone the police station. He doubted if he would be given any information in either case. He could telephone Freya Graffham, but that would give rise to inevitable questions.

He could do nothing. If in doubt do nothing had been a rule he often followed and it had stood him in good stead. They were not interested in him or his unit. How could they be? What could they know about either? He started the car and drove on to the main road.

At home he made toast and sliced an apple on to a bowl of wholegrain cereal, filled the percolator and fetched the newspapers from the doormat. He felt quite steady, quite calm, ready for a full day's appointments and for the evening to come.

But at moments in the course of the next few hours, his mind went off at a tangent of its own which he could not anticipate or control, and flashed up pictures of Karin McCafferty on the couch where a different patient now lay, and of the dogs and their handlers scrambling out of the back of the police van a hundred yards away from the unit in which he did his work.

Forty-Seven

At one o'clock, the CID room was half empty. At ten past, the doors blew open and a dozen or so people came banging in, including DC Coates, looking mutinous.

'Honest, Sarge, I'm thinking of putting in for dog-handling.' He crashed into his chair and hitched one leg up over the side. 'It's cool, that is, they've had a fantastic time this morning sniffing all over the business park and what have we been doing?'

'Sitting in a car on the Meadow Field estate.'

'Right. Now it's all called off again.'

'Did they do a bust on the business park?'

'Haven't heard. Someone said so, someone else wasn't sure, usual stuff. You don't get much out of those boys.'

'I can't see you at the other end of a lead.'

'Naw, they're all strong silent types. And that's just the dogs. You got anything for me, Sarge, only I could do with a bit of action. I've had it up to here with sitting about in cars with Dave Green. All he knows about is Bolton Wanderers and the Campaign for Real Ale.'

'Go and find DC Hardy, will you, Nathan? I want you to go and talk to Aidan Sharpe.'

Nathan Coates parked outside Aidan Sharpe's house and consulting room in Wellow Wood Drive and sat for a moment, looking at it and working out how much it would fetch. This was the bit of Lafferton he knew little of and liked even less. The detached houses with front drives and magnolia trees, wrought-iron gates and mock-Tudor gables did not fill him with envy but with a sort of bemusement that anyone could aspire to live in them. They seemed so stand-offish, so unneighbourly and closed in; people here drove smart cars and sent their children to school in panama hats and caps with crests on them and kept themselves apart, except perhaps for a few cocktail parties at Christmas.

If he and Emma got married he would like to own a cottage with a bit of ground in one of the villages outside Lafferton, or if that was beyond their reach, then one of the nice three-bedroomed houses on the private estate at St Michael's Gate. But he would never want to cut himself off in a place like this, however big the bay windows and broad the driveways, however flashy the dark blue BMWs parked there – like the one outside Aidan Sharpe's house.

He peered into it as he and DC Will Hardy went by – champagne-coloured leather seats, state-of-the-art CD player and nothing else . . . no maps, spare shoes, torn-off envelopes, spare jackets. This might have been a car fetched from the showroom that morning. He glanced over at DC Hardy, who shrugged.

Nathan rang the surgery's bell, and pushed open the front door. *Reception. Surgery. Private.*

Reception was perfectly pleasant and the receptionist looked OK too, crisp hair, fashionable oval spectacles and one of those professional smiles.

'Can I help you?'

Nathan flipped open his ID wallet. 'DC Coates, Lafferton CID. I'd like a word with Mr Sharpe.'

She looked startled, but did not lose her poise.

'Mr Sharpe has a patient with him at the moment. I'm afraid I can't interrupt.'

'That's fine. We'll hang on.'

'Yes, of course. Please take a seat and I'll tell him as soon as he's free. Can I get you a cup of tea or coffee? A glass of mineral water?'

Nathan and Will shook their heads. 'No, thanks.'

They sat down and glanced at the magazines . . . smart magazines, *Vogue, Tatler, Country Life,* the *Spectator,* all up to date. There was obviously money in this alternative-medicine lark. Nathan thought of the average GP waiting room, let alone hospital clinic . . . a few copies of *Woman's Own* and *Reader's Digest* from three years ago if you were lucky, tatty chairs, and the smell of very old people and babies with dirty nappies. This room smelled of flowers and polish and something faintly antiseptic.

'How many patients does he see in a day?'

She looked at him over her computer screen. 'Mr Sharpe has a very full appointment book.'

'Yeah. How many?'

'There are four new appointments a day . . . those last a full hour. And four half-hour appointments for ongoing treatments.'

'All sorts, are they?'

'I'm sorry?'

'Men, women, children, old, young . . . you know.'

'Mr Sharpe rarely treats children. Otherwise, I suppose you would say we have a good cross-section of the community, yes.'

'Does it hurt? I don't fancy having needles stuck all over me.'

She smiled in a patient way. 'That is a misconception a lot of people have who know nothing about acupuncture. They imagine themselves, well . . .'

'Like pincushions?'

'More or less. In fact, it's very selective . . . you may only have two or three needles, possibly a few more . . . each case is unique, each patient has a different treatment.'

Nathan decided that when he left she was going to hand him a nice leaflet. 'I should think women go for it more than men.'

'Would you?'

'Yeah, all this stuff is more in the woman's line, isn't it?'

'I wonder why you think that?'

'You get men as well then?'

'Certainly.'

The door opened, and a middle-aged woman came through. That's it, smart suit, nice hair, nice expensive handbag and shoes, she's your average patient.

'Please sit down, Mrs Savage. I'll make up your account in a moment.' She glanced across at Nathan. 'I'll have a word with Mr Sharpe.' She walked out, high heels clicking smartly.

Nathan grinned at the woman. 'Painful, is it?'

She gave him an unsmiling glance. 'No.'

'Never fancied it myself. Still, if you think it does you good . . .'

She leaned forward, picked up the shiny new copy of *Country Life*.

Nathan felt like making the sort of face he had made at passers-by over the school playground wall as a small boy, but settled for raising one eyebrow in the direction of the PC, who smiled and looked away.

The high heels came clipping back. 'Mr Sharpe asks if you could come back at five thirty. He'll have finished with patients for the day then. He has two calls to take and then his next appointment but he'll be glad to see you then.'

When Nathan and DC Hardy returned they found the door slightly ajar and the reception room empty, the cover on the computer and the magazines retidied. Nathan waited. He could find no bell to ring.

'DC Coates?'

He seemed to have materialised silently, oozing out of the walls. The bow tie was red with thin navy stripes.

'I do apologise for asking you to come back, but I was in the middle of my surgery. And this is?'

'DC Hardy.'

Aidan Sharpe nodded. 'Please come through.'

He had expected to interview Sharpe in the waiting room, but instead, Nathan was led through the door marked *Private* and along a short passage into the house.

'May I offer you a cup of tea?'

'No, thanks.'

'How can I help you? I imagine this is about that poor girl Debbie Parker. Have you news of her?'

'Afraid not, sir, though we're following some leads.'

'Ah yes. Leads.'

The room was oppressive, with a huge sideboard, dresser, desk and bookcases of heavy dark oak and a sofa and armchairs covered in brown leather. The fireplace was dark, too, and elaborately carved. There were portraits on the walls in heavy gold frames, old men in wigs and fat men on horseback, and stuffed fish in a case.

Opposite him, Aidan Sharpe sat very still in the armchair, hands together, finger to finger. His eyes stared. Surprise him, Nathan decided, no lead-up, no charm, straight in.

'Do you own a watch showing moon phases?'

Not a flicker. The eyes did not leave Nathan's face, the fingers were motionless.

'I do.'

'Are you wearing it now, sir?'

'I am.'

'I'd like to see it, please.'

'May I ask why?'

'Just take it off, Mr Sharpe.'

A thin smile, like the flick of a lizard's tongue. Gone.

'I'd like to know why you want me to do that.'

'Where did you get the watch?'

'If you mean where was it bought, I have no idea.'

'How's that then?'

'It was a gift.'

'Who from, sir?'

'That is my business.'

'We're investigating the disappearance of three women.'

Sharpe did not react.

'One of them was a Miss Angela Randall. Was she a patient of yours?'

'I have a large number of patients. I would have to check.'

'You came to tell us Debbie Parker was your patient.'

Silence. The eyes stared.

'So you'd know if Angela Randall was a patient too, wouldn't you?'

'As I say, I would have to check.'

'Would you do that?'

'Tomorrow. I'll ask my secretary. If she finds that this . . . Miss Randall has been treated here, I will contact Sergeant Graffham.'

'Did Miss Randall give you the watch, Mr Sharpe?'

A flicker. The eyes were momentarily angry.

'Mr Sharpe?'

'Why do you ask?'

'I've already said we're investigating Angela Randall's disappearance. Did you know her?'

'Not that I can recall.'

'Can I see your watch?'

He smiled, shot his cuff, slipped off the wristwatch and held it out. It was nice, thin as a wafer. The moon had little stars beside it on dark blue enamel. It was a half-moon.

Nathan handed it back. 'Thanks.'

'Is that all?'

'For the time being. But if you could check your records in the morning like you agreed?'

'By all means.'

On the way to the front door Aidan Sharpe said, 'There seemed to be something important going on early this morning . . . I happened to drive by the business park. There were police everywhere – vans, tracker dogs . . . what on earth was that all about?'

'Sorry, sir, not my department.'

'A drug raid, do you suppose?'

'For all I know, Mr Sharpe. Thanks for your help.'

*

Nathan looked back from the car. Bow Tie was still standing there, staring at him.

He stopped the car round the next corner and took out his mobile phone. 'Sarge?'

'What did he say?'

'Not a lot. I asked him if he knew Randall, asked if she'd given him the watch . . . got nowhere. Claims not to remember if she was a patient . . . said he'd ring you if he found her name in his records.'

'Me?'

'Yeah. Sergeant Graffham he said. Don't want to chat with the lowlife. He's creepy, ain't he? You been in the house?'

'No.'

'Like one of them castles they take you to from school. All big black furniture and that. Real old stuff, you know? Spooky.'

'But that was it?'

'One thing . . . just when I was leaving he asked what had been going on at the business park earlier . . . said he'd driven by and seen all the vans and tracker dogs and that. Asked if it was a drugs raid. Only, what was he doing up there at half five or six in the morning? It was all done and dusted before eight, they'd gone. And another thing was, they were up the far end; if he was just passing he couldn't have seen nothing from the end of the road.'

Forty-Eight

Chris Deerbon was on call and picked up the phone. Cat was kneeling on the floor of her office, sorting out a pile of medical journals, most of which she never had time to read. On her left were those she should keep because they contained articles she ought not to ignore, on her right were the rest. She was frustrated that the left pile was growing significantly higher. Everything was important, everything seemed to have some vital information.

'Can you take a call?' Chris tried to push open the door but was blocked by the pile of magazines.

'Who is it?'

'Hysterical woman.'

'You're on call, not me.'

'She won't talk to me, she says she can only tell you what's happened.'

'Who?'

'Mrs Marion Keith. She's my patient,' Chris said, 'but she's insisting on you.'

'What, is she embarrassed about something? If she

needs a doctor urgently, she'll have to take whichever sex is on duty.'

'So I tell her that?'

'Bloody hell. OK, OK.'

Cat pulled the door open, shoving the magazines hard until they formed a jam against the wall as Chris handed her the portable phone and fled up the stairs.

'Cat Deerbon.'

She was irritated. She was preparing her speech. By the time she had finished with this Mrs Keith, the woman would wish she'd stuck with Chris.

She heard the first few stumbling words and fell silent. Five minutes later, she was sitting on the stairs, talking quietly.

'I'll come, Mrs Keith . . . of course I understand. Of course. Is there anyone with you? Well, try and stay calm. It'll take me quarter of an hour to get to you.'

The woman was beside herself with distress and scarcely coherent but Cat had found out all she needed. She ran upstairs.

'I'll have to go. She's in a dreadful state.'

'I know. I couldn't understand much.'

Cat changed quickly from the old tracksuit she had worn to clear out the office. 'She's been to see the psychic surgeon and he assaulted her. We've got him, Chris.'

'What does she mean by assault? Rape?'

'Something sexual, but it was a bit hard to tell.'

'You'd better get the police to meet you there. You need a witness and they'll want to know about it if it is a real assault.'

'Right.' She zipped up her jeans and reached for the phone but Simon's answering machine was on. She rang off and dialled the station.

'DCI Serrailler please . . . Dr Deerbon . . . yes, I will.' She turned to Chris. 'He's out on a case but they're trying to reach him . . . Yes? Thanks. I'll hold on.'

'Serrailler.'

'Si, it's me. Listen, I'm just shooting off. 17 Bury Park, a patient of Chris's has called in a hysterical state – she's been to see this guy at Starly who calls himself a psychic surgeon and claims he assaulted her.'

'Right. I'll get the station to send a patrol.'

'Can't I have Freya Graffham?'

'No, this isn't a CID matter, you want uniform. I'm out on an op, Cat, I'll pass it on.'

'Thanks.'

Chris came down to the car with her, filling her in on his patient, Marion Keith. 'Fifties, widowed, couple of married daughters. History of gastritis, irritable bowel, done all the checks, nothing showed up but she might not have believed it. Maybe she thought he'd find something and get it out.'

He kissed Cat and closed her car door.

The police patrol car was waiting as she drew up outside the bungalow in Bury Park.

'Evening, Doc.'

'Hello, Mike.'

Cat knew many of the officers at Lafferton, not because of Simon but because the practice were police surgeons. The last time she had met Constable Mike Major had been the previous summer in a flat whose elderly tenant had been lying dead for a month. In those situations professionals relied on each other, not only to do their respective jobs but for moral and sometimes even physical support. It had not been Cat who had

had to make quickly for the fresh air on that occasion.

'You haven't been in, have you? I need to talk to her first.'

'No, seemed best to wait.'

'You know what it's about?'

'Pretty much. I read about this weirdo in the *Echo* the other week.'

'Let's hope we get enough to close him down.'

Marion Keith was wrapped in a dressing gown and blanket and propped in the corner of the sofa. She was a faded-looking woman, with pretty features, but her face was grey and her eyes shocked.

Cat put down her bag and sat beside her. 'Hello, Mrs Keith. Everything's all right.'

Marion Keith burst into tears.

'Just cry, don't worry.' Cat took her hand. 'I want you to try and tell me exactly what happened. Take your time. If necessary I'll examine you, but it may be that this is a case of criminal assault, and for that reason I've called the police. They're outside and they'll stay in the car until you're happy for them to come in and speak to you. If it does seem clear to me that you've been assaulted, they will want to hear what happened from you too. Is that all right?'

After a moment the woman nodded.

'Fine. Now, tell me.'

Falteringly at first, and at moments incoherently, Marion Keith began to talk. She had suffered from abdominal pain and discomfort since the death of her husband. As Chris had said, the investigations had shown nothing abnormal but whatever medication she had had only gave her temporary relief. The trouble always flared up again. She worked part-time as a legal secretary and a colleague had told her about the psychic surgeon.

'She said he'd cured so many people. She told me the sort of thing I suffered from was his speciality. She just convinced me to go. I was desperate, I'd have tried anything. Your husband's a good doctor, I know that, but nothing he'd given me helped for long and I wanted to have an end to all this pain and everything else. It's spoiled my life lately. I didn't see what I'd got to lose and I've started to worry they might have missed something at the hospital. You do hear stories. I had a friend die of bowel cancer, I know what all this can mean.'

'I understand. It's always a difficult area and people do worry they've got something serious when symptoms don't get better. No one's blaming you, Mrs Keith.'

She had not been afraid, she said, she had heard wonderful things about 'Dr Groatman' and even when she found that no one else was in the room with them it hadn't seemed alarming. The hands hovering above her body, the probing and twisting, the apparent incision, something dropped into a bucket beneath the couch. It had all seemed strange, Marion Keith said, but nothing had been 'wrong'. He had seemed to know what he was talking about . . . 'So confident,' she said. He had told her she had 'bad tissue', that he was having to extract a septic mass, that her stomach was seriously inflamed and her intestines both 'twisted' and infected. He would be able to cure her in one session. She would walk out of his room pain-free and the discomfort would be a thing of the past.

It had all been peculiar, incredible – yet he had prayed something, and she had believed firmly in the spirit of the doctor who worked through him. That had seemed to make it all right.

Cat kept silent, wondering at the credulity of otherwise cautious and intelligent people, and imagining their reaction if she as a qualified GP had done half the things to them that they allowed this man to do.

'Then he said there was something else. He said my stomach problems had a deeper source than he'd thought. They were centred in my female organs and this was what was causing the worst of the trouble. He said he'd need to find out more but that if I just relaxed he could cure me, he knew where the problem was. I didn't think. I just didn't think. I should have realised.'

'What happened then?'

'He muttered things . . . in some sort of foreign language. His voice went deeper and he spoke in a guttural way and then it was quite frightening. His eyes were staring. He stared right into me somehow. His eyes changed. I can't explain. They just changed.'

'Had he asked you to undress?'

'Just my skirt and blouse and he gave me a gown like a hospital gown, so that seemed all right. But now he said I'd to take off my tights and pants.'

'And did you?'

'It sounds stupid, it sounds as if I'm a halfwit, doesn't it? But there was something about him, then, his eyes and his voice. I was frightened. His eyes seemed to –'

'Hypnotise you?'

'I was going to say "cast a spell" but I suppose it was hypnotising me, yes. I can see that now. I did as he asked because I was frightened not to. I felt he had power over me.'

She had been made to lie down again, and this time

she had felt first a cold instrument of some kind and then his fingers penetrating her vagina and working about inside. He had asked her to turn over and after pressing her in the back and kidney area, he had also introduced his fingers into her anus. It took a long time for her to tell Cat everything that had happened and she needed a good deal of prompting. Cat was anxious not to put words into her mouth but the woman was filled with shame and embarrassment, mortified to have to tell even a doctor what had been done to her.

'Marion, I know how difficult this is for you but you understand that I have to make absolutely certain about everything, don't you?'

'I know.' Her voice was barely a whisper now.

'Did he rape you? Did he have full sexual intercourse with you?'

There was a long silence. Cat waited, still holding the woman's hand. Mrs Keith licked her dry lips several times and wiped her hand across her eyes. She did not look at Cat.

'He might have,' she said at last. 'I can't be sure. He might have.'

'How is it you can't be sure?'

'I don't know. I felt funny. I was frightened.'

'It's important. You know that.'

'Yes.'

'If he did rape you he can be arrested and even what you have told me constitutes criminal assault, there's no doubt about that. But if we can prove that you were raped he faces a much more serious charge. What you say could make sure he doesn't get away with this.'

'What do you want? I can't remember.' She began to cry again.

'What I need is for you to let the police talk to you, but because there's a chance you've been raped, you will have to be taken to the station and have the police doctor examine you.'

'No.'

'Marion . . .'

'I can't. I've talked to you. I said I didn't want anyone else.'

'It will be a woman doctor, and a nurse will be there. I'll come with you if it would help.'

'No.'

'Then at least will you give a statement to the police now? Tell them what you've told me.'

'Can't you do it for me?'

'I'm afraid not. They need your statement.'

'No. I didn't ask for the police, I wanted to see you. I've talked to you, I've told you what he did. I couldn't say it again.'

It was well after two before Cat got home. In the end she had persuaded Mrs Keith to make her statement and go to the police station and it felt as if she had sweated blood; she also felt guilty at persuading a woman in distress to go against her own feelings and talk about what to her were shamefully intimate things, in impersonal surroundings to complete strangers. Why should Marion Keith have to endure all of that, when she had already been traumatised by what had been done to her?

Chris woke as she switched on the lamp. As luck would have it there had been no more calls, or he would have had to get out a locum. The time when Hannah and Sam could be left alone seemed a very long way off.

'Well?'

Cat sat on the edge of the bed. Exhaustion was about to hit her but for another few moments, sheer adrenaline kept it at bay. She had been sorry for Marion Keith but at the same time she felt huge satisfaction.

'We've got him,' she said quietly. 'He's nailed. I left just as the police doctor on call got there . . . she was going to do the examination. Marion Keith's had a vile experience but some good has come out of it. This Dr Groatman alias half a dozen other names is a very nasty piece of work.'

'Marion . . . Keith . . . be all right . . . ?' Chris's voice slurred with sleep.

'Marion Keith,' Cat said, 'is a heroine.'

She was sorting out Sam's gym bag and Hannah's lunch box a few hours later when the phone rang.

'Cat Deerbon.'

'Morning, Doc. Sergeant Winder, Lafferton Police Station.'

'Morning, Sergeant. Trouble?'

'Dr Maskray asked me to call you first thing.'

'Ah – this is about the assault on Mrs Keith?'

'It is, except there wasn't.'

'Sorry?'

'No assault. Dr Maskray found no evidence of anything and Mrs Keith has withdrawn her statement.'

'Oh dear God.'

'Car took her home. She was in a bit of a state. Could be done for wasting police time but the doc recommended not.'

'All right, Sergeant, thanks for letting me know.'

She stood, holding a pot of Fun Kids Banana Yogurt in one hand and the telephone in the other. Upstairs Chris was shouting to Sam and Hannah to stop squabbling and start getting dressed.

'Bugger,' Cat said. 'Hell and damnation.'

Thinking furiously, she went across to the dresser and put the pot of banana yogurt down on the phone rest.

Forty-Nine

Angela Randall. Silly bitch. She had caused trouble from the beginning. There had been the difficult telephone calls. Letters. Cards. Twice she had simply appeared on his doorstep at night, her cow-like face full of mooning self-pity, longing to be invited in, longing for him. She had repelled him. Eventually, he had refused to treat her, and in any case she had no illnesses or physical problems to be dealt with; her problems were the distorted emotional ones of a menopausal spinster. When the first two gifts had arrived he had sent them back. They had been sent again and then others, always anonymously, always with the same ludicrous notes. After a while, he had decided to ignore them and the gifts had continued, expensive, unsuitable gifts, humiliating her. He had not cared in the slightest.

But now she was the one causing trouble. He thought of her lying in the unit, scrawny and pitiful, though he never felt pity.

Freya Graffham had noticed the watch, but how had she come to know about it in the first place? Angela

Randall must have been stupid enough to leave something lying around in her house, a receipt, his name and address. Something had alerted Graffham.

He was tired. His actions and plans were being directed from outside, by events and by other people and he had always been careful not to allow that. It set him on edge. He had not slept well. Seeing the police all over the business park had not helped.

He buttered bread and cut the plastic wrapping from around a pack of smoked mackerel. He thought he knew how to tolerate frustration, thought he had learned it years ago, but the build-up of tension in his body and mind betrayed him.

He sighed now as he mixed a salad. His hand had been forced again and there was not enough time. He knew what he must do next.

He sat down, swivelled the tuner of the radio until he came upon a programme of music by Philip Glass, and then, to its accompaniment, began to eat and think methodically.

The cathedral was full. Sitting in the middle of the rows of altos, listening to the mighty waves of sound coming from the orchestra below, Freya Graffham felt exhilarated. Singing had always raised her up to a different level of delight and fulfilment. There was a heady satisfaction in achieving notes and melodies as part of a chorus of others, and the music took on another dimension from the perspective of the performer in the midst of it. Listening was wholly inferior, a poor also-ran to this. The cathedral acoustics were not easy, and the pianissimo sections had a tendency to vanish like fine coils of candlesmoke up into the roof, but the fact that the building was so full helped and the crescendos were magnificent. She noticed Cat Deerbon, as the altos stood up, and wondered if Simon was there, but most of the audience blended back into the shadows.

As always in singing and listening, she quickly forgot everything else, as they all did. The high of the performance carried them on, long after it was over, after they had finally left the cathedral to its hollows and a silence that was somehow still full of music, after the post-performance drinks and sandwiches and mutual congratulations in St Michael's Hall. It carried each of them out into the streets, into their cars, laughing and calling, and floated them home.

Freya had walked from home tonight and only parted from half a dozen of the others on the corner of her own street. It was a mild, soft night, full of stars and sweet with the smell of freshly-cut lawns. She was tired but it would be a long time before she slept. She would have a bath, potter about, watch a late-night film and gradually, contentedly unwind.

She checked her car, as always. It was parked under the lamp a few yards from her own front door. Her name was down for one of the few garages in the Old Town but one was not likely to become vacant for years. The street was quiet, as usual, and she was never particularly worried that her car might be stolen or vandalised. Feeling safe, in her car and her house, was something she was still unused to, after the years in London.

As she closed the front door and felt the comfortable atmosphere of home settle around her, she wondered if she would ever be able to give this up again, ever want to share her space, her leisure, her waking and sleeping and daily routines even with someone she loved a great deal. Would Simon, as comfortably settled in his flat in the close as she was here, ever want to give up such independence?

For now, Freya had what she wanted in her peaceful rooms, filled with happy satisfaction at the music she had helped to make, her head still hearing the voices and instruments that had been all round her. She went into the kitchen, humming quietly.

At first, she was uncertain if there had been a sound at the front door or not. She stood still. The soft knock came again.

It was twenty minutes to midnight and all the upstairs lights in the houses of her neighbours were out. Then she remembered Simon's telephone message. She pulled a comb out of her handbag and ran it through her short hair before going quickly, heart in her mouth, to open the door.

Before she had time to take in what was happening, Aidan Sharpe had stepped quickly inside and shut and locked the door in one movement. He put the key in his pocket.

'I want to talk to you,' he said.

Instinctively, Freya turned back into the living room and went rapidly across to the table on which she had left her mobile phone. Usually it was in her bag or the pocket of her jacket but tonight because of the concert, she had left it behind here.

'We won't want to be disturbed.' He was at her elbow and his gloved hand flashed in front of her to take the handset.

'Give that back please.'

'Sit down, Miss Graffham. You're not in Lafferton station now, nor are you on duty as an officer.'

'Give –'

From the left pocket of his jacket he pulled a syringe. Freya could see that it was full of a clear liquid. She swallowed, her mouth suddenly dry.

'I said sit down.'

His voice was very soft and held a note of manic calm and sweet reason which she had heard before in dangerous men. She knew very well that for the time being she had to humour him and do as he asked. Aidan Sharpe did not take his eyes from her as he walked across the room and switched off the main light, leaving only the two lamps. Then he sat in the armchair opposite her and leaned back, the faintest of smiles on his mouth, his eyes staring. Freya began to think rapidly about the way to handle him, speak to him, change his mood, as well as about her means of escape. One door in the room led to the hall, the other to the kitchen and from there a door led to the side passage which ran between her house and the neighbouring one. At the end of the passage was a wooden door, bolted from the inside.

'I want to talk to you,' Aidan Sharpe said again.

'About Angela Randall? Or Debbie . . . or perhaps both of them?'

'Shut up.'

He was a different man from the one who had sat opposite her in the Embassy Room, different and yet recognisably the same, like so many of the psychopaths she had dealt with. She ought to have recognised the signs but then, subliminally, she knew that indeed she had.

'Angela Randall was a stupid bitch. A very tiresome stupid bitch.'

'You said "was" . . . does –?'

'I told you to shut up.'

She had to remain rational and calm and not give off the smell of fear, nor betray what she was planning by the slightest flicker.

'I loathe women, but I loathed that silly bitch more than most. She had no pride, you see, she lay at my feet like a bitch on heat, she sent me messages full of vile language, fawning and clinging and yielding. Where was the pride in all of that? She sent me cards, she sent me gifts. This . . .' He shot his cuff and displayed the watch. 'Yes, of course, and so many other things. She wasted her money, she probably got herself into debt for it and then there were always the pathetic notes. She was debasing herself. I despised her. I sold off most of the things. I didn't want them round me, contaminating me, but I kept the watch. I knew someone who had a watch like it when I was a boy. A relative I used to see. I was fond of him. I haven't seen a watch like it since.'

Now his voice had changed again, become casual in tone, as if he wanted to lull her, to make this seem like a chat between friends.

'It's typical of her, you know, that she should be the one who alerted you. It's typical that this should be her fault. None of the others would have done it.' He fell silent for a moment, sitting with one leg crossed up on the other, hand behind his head, and still staring, staring. Freya calculated how many strides she needed to make to reach the kitchen and the outside door, how easy it would be to get to the end of the passageway.

'I like my work, you know, I find it satisfying. I'm good at it. A lot of people have reason to be grateful to me. I'm sure you know that from our friend Dr Deerbon. I sacrificed a lot to qualify. I lived in a room the size of my present bathroom and scraped by for years in order to get where I am. But it was never going to be enough. I don't think I ever thought it would be, not when you consider how near I was to being a doctor. I was unjustly treated, victimised and betrayed. I had everything mapped out and they ruined it all. I discovered I didn't need them at all. The joke has been mine for years. The study of the human body, the intimate, detailed comparison between one and another. The stages of life and of death. I have come to know more about it than anyone in the world because I have had the luxury of time and been able to set up my own private place for research.'

He was silent again, this time for several minutes, and absolutely still, looking across the room at her.

The fear Freya felt was different from any she had known before. She had been confronted by angry and violent men, by men with weapons, by the deranged and the dangerous in difficult situations, and fear, even terror, had been the inevitable response; but it had never been overwhelming, there had always been a corner of herself in which she was not afraid but filled with confidence in her own skills and determination, the adrenaline racing through her, heightening her thinking and helping her to deal with the situation. Now, she could not find that corner of calm and confidence. Aidan Sharpe was mad in the most dangerous way of all, controlledly, quietly, rationally mad. His violence was not a fired-up, passionate reaction to finding himself at risk. Such a threat was alarming – but easier to deal with. This was a smiling psychopath, deluded and with all the strength and cunning of one who thinks himself omnipotent and untouchable. Faced with him holding that small, potentially deadly syringe full of who knew what, sitting in her own chair, late at night in this quiet house without her usual reliable access to help, listening to his monotonous, gloating voice, she understood the paralysis of every hunted and cornered creature.

'Wouldn't you like to hear more? I've teased you, haven't I?'

'If you feel the need to tell me, please do.'

Aidan Sharpe laughed, almost a natural-sounding laugh. 'Oh, my dear Freya, how charming! Up pops the well-trained detective sergeant who passed her practical psychology course . . . "Humour him, win him over by listening to him patiently. He will feel the need to confess so let him. This will lull him into letting his guard drop." I have no need to confess, I assure you. I enjoy my work and I will do so for many years to come. Confession is not on the agenda. I know myself, you see. I know my own psychology a good deal better than anyone else ever could. Recently, a young woman in Australia went missing for five years, did you read about that? Her family held a memorial service for her and a young man was charged with her murder. She reappeared quite suddenly. She had been in hiding quite near her home. So what is to say that these three women won't reappear too?'

'But I think you want to tell me the reason why they won't.'

'Do I? How concerned are you? How curious are you?'

'Very.'

'The knowledge will be of no use to you, of course.'

Freya felt her stomach clench. She thought she might be sick.

'You understand what I am saying.'

The walls of the room seemed very near, the air felt as if it was giving out. They might have been in some cellar or underground space where they would only have air for a little longer. Her chest hurt her as she tried to breathe normally. Wait. Remain calm and think, think. You have to get out of here and there are only two exits. He has the front-door key in his pocket so you have to get out through the kitchen. Let him talk and keep talking. Whatever he claims and however he seems, his own nerves will be strained and his blood pressure will have risen in excitement. He wants to tell you about the women. Let him. Hold his attention and then think, one move at a time. When you do move, move very fast and without warning, move from this sitting position across the room, into the kitchen, out of the door, up the passage and scream as you go and keep on screaming, scream loudly, scream, 'Police! Police! Police!' Never mind if no one is likely to hear, it will throw him. Think. Think. Is the back door bolted? Yes. Is the key in it? Jesus, she couldn't remember. If it was not, it would be on the shelf which meant another move. Was there time? As you go, look at the door, reach for the key, unlock, unbolt . . . no, he will be right behind you trying desperately to stop you and he will have greater strength than normal in his panic and because he has absolutely nothing to lose.

Think, think. If you reach the kitchen door and he is behind you, turn, swing round on him because then you'll catch him off guard and have the upper hand, you can bring him down. He is not large or very heavy. If necessary, chop him across the side of the neck and wind him, then knock him out. This is not going to be easy.

He won't give anything away. You will have to fight.

She sat without moving, looking at him, trying not to think so feverishly that her breathing quickened. He was trained. He would see it. He was watching her as intently as she had ever been watched.

'Are you going to tell me?' Freya said.

'I think I should like a drink. Shall we be companionable and have a drink?'

Don't make your move while you are getting the bottle and glasses from the cupboard. He is watching, he is expecting you to seize the moment, so don't.

She set a bottle of whisky down on the low table between them.

'If you want water, I'll have to go into the kitchen.'

'I would like water.'

She hesitated, then got up. So did he. He followed close behind her and stood watching her take the jug and fill it from the cold tap. She did not glance at the door leading to the passage, merely turned and went back into the living room. She could feel his warmth, smell his smell behind her.

'Thank you.' He gestured as she added water to his drink. 'Please join me.'

Freya shook her head.

'Something else then? I don't like drinking alone.'

She poured herself a glass of water.

Aidan Sharpe smiled. 'That's right. Humour him, don't make him angry. But my dear, I am not in the least angry.' He sipped his whisky, looking at her across the top of the glass.

She was glad of the water.

'Tell me,' he said, in a voice so pleasant and reasonable she was taken aback; they might still have been in the Embassy bar. 'What do you think motivates a serial killer? It's something I have long wondered about.'

She opened her mouth and her tongue felt sticky.

'I imagine you must have come across one or two during your time in the Met?'

'They . . . they are less common than people imagine. But yes.'

'And?'

She knew what to answer and yet could not say it, not here in her own living room sitting opposite this man. It seemed ludicrous to engage in a rational, intelligent discussion of the motives of murderers.

'For instance, Dennis Nielsen was mad but he killed for company, you know. The Wests were simply evil. Bad but never mad. Those who kill children are the scum of the earth, satanic paedophiles. But has it ever occurred to you that there may be good motives? Understandable ones?'

She swallowed more water, shaking her head. Speech was beyond her now.

'I kill in the course of my work.' He stared at her and paused.

Don't react, don't move a muscle, don't give anything away.

'The benefits will be immense. The study of the human body in its many stages will lead eventually to more knowledge about the process of ageing, the process of disease, the course taken by different ways of dying and then by the process of death, than has ever been gained before. I kill to further that work. Those I kill die to benefit mankind and, as you have discovered, they leave scarcely any behind to mourn them. I am extremely careful. Angela Randall was not missed. She is of far greater value dead than she ever was alive, you know. And she owes that to me.'

She was beyond terror. Only her mind still worked, still struggled to remember the plan of escape. Give nothing away, wait, then move, move fast, fast, fast.

Aidan Sharpe sipped his whisky. 'There are the simply mad, of course,' he said, 'those who have no motive, nor very much knowledge of what they do. They simply repeat a pattern, as children play certain games. If they have a reason for what they do it is usually a deranged, distorted one, a product of madness. Schizophrenics hear voices commanding them to kill. They deserve sympathetic treatment, do you not think?'

She wondered what his motive could be in telling her that he had killed. Pride? Boastfulness? Gloating? She glanced at him. He looked so neat, trimmed, contained, so pleasant sitting there – what her mother would have called a pernickety little man. But he was right about one thing. She did want to know. Before escaping, she needed him to tell her what he had done with the missing women and how, and whether there had been others before now, others nobody knew about.

She drank more water.

'They are perfectly safe, you know,' he said, smiling faintly again. 'I take very good care of them.'

Then she saw in his eyes not only that he was mad but the extent of his madness and the intensity of its focus.

'I plan. I go to a lot of trouble. Sometimes I wait for months. I waited a long time for poor Debbie Parker.'

'Iris Chater?' She heard her own voice, odd, distorted in her ears like a voice at the wrong end of a speaking tube.

Aidan Sharpe inclined his head. 'You're right,' he said, as if in real regret, 'of course you're right about that. There was no plan. I went against all my instincts. It was foolish. It was wrong. But I didn't kill her. She died of a heart attack and I kept the body. I took a risk and as it happens it paid off, but it might so easily not have done.'

'You mean . . . you are sorry?'

'Oh, no, not that. I regret taking a chance. But if it had not been Mrs Chater it would have had to be someone like her. An elderly woman was next on the list. I had come to exactly that stage in my work. How could I be sorry?'

Freya was dazed, with fear and with a wild sense that she herself was becoming deranged, locked with a madman in his own claustrophobic yet oddly plausible mental world. How could he possibly be sorry? How could he have been so careless as to take the chance he did? Supposing it had not worked? Think of the consequences to his life's work, think of the stupidity . . . surely she had to agree with him?

'You're very quiet, Freya? You seem unlike yourself. I expected a torrent of questions – awkward questions, perhaps, or interested questions, but not this silence. Has nothing I have said interested you? You seem somewhat detached.'

But the questions were there, like bats fluttering round inside the walls of her skull, flapping about, confusing her. She wanted to let them out, to voice them, to quieten them, but she could not open her mouth now. She simply clung on somehow to the awareness of what she must do and how and at what moment.

'Perhaps I might have a little more of your excellent whisky?'

Aidan Sharpe bent slightly forward and reached out his hand.

A light went on inside Freya's brain. Now, she said, now. Go. Go. Go.

Fifty

'Yes!' Nathan shouted. 'Yesssss!' and jumped on to the dining table.

'Get down, you idiot.' But Emma was laughing.

'Naw, I might pull you up here and we'll have a dance. I want to dance, Em. Where can we go to dance?'

'Get down – and there isn't anywhere at this time of night.'

'I feel like it. I wanna dance . . .' and he began a mock tap routine, waving his arms in the air.

Emma had said yes. He knew she would and had been terrified she wouldn't, he'd been sure she'd want nothing better than to marry him and certain she'd kick him downstairs. He would wait, he thought, he wouldn't ask her now, she'd just had a long journey, she was tired, he'd wait till the weekend. Or the one after. Or until their holiday.

She'd dropped her bag and gone straight to the shower. Ten minutes later, as she had walked into the kitchen with her damp hair tied up and wearing her old velour tracksuit, he had turned round from the sink where he was washing his hands and said, 'Em, I really, really want to marry you. Will you marry me?'

'Yes,' Em had said and gone to the fridge to get out a bottle of fizzy water.

'You what?'

She had glanced up. 'Can you open this top? I can never do them. I said yes.'

That had been a couple of hours ago and Nathan had still not come down from his high of excitement, surprise, delight and disbelief. He stood on the table and stretched out his arms. 'King,' he shouted. 'Yessss.'

'GET DOWN.'

He jumped lightly on to the floor.

'Nath, shut up, there are people below us asleep.'

'How do you know they're asleep?'

'Because they go to bed at ten o'clock and now it's after midnight.'

'Yeah, true.'

'I'm whacked as well.'

'Oh no you're not, you're going to marry me. We can't just leave it there.'

'Well, I wasn't going to just leave it there, I was going to marry you, but not tonight.'

'Let's go out and find somewhere . . . let's knock someone up.'

'Don't be daft.'

'Haven't you got any mates just coming off duty?'

'No. They're either in bed asleep or they're working. Same as your mates.'

'Yeah, we could go down to the station. Or up to the hospital.'

'They wouldn't thank us. We can tell everyone in the morning.'

'Let's just go for a drink then.'

'Where?'

'We'll find somewhere.'

'Not anywhere legal we won't.'

'Hey, I know what – there's that bottle of champagne you won in the raffle.'

'It's too late to start on that, it gives you a terrible hangover.'

'Not if we only have a bit and we'll only have a bit cos we're going to share it.'

'Who with?'

'I'll tell you who with. Do you know who pushed me into this "Will you marry me" thingy?'

'You mean it wasn't your own idea?'

'Yeah, well, I just hadn't got round to it.'

'I'd noticed.'

'I don't know when I would have, to be honest, what with this and that and you know how shy I am.'

'Hello?'

'Yes I am, I'm a very shy person actually. It was Sergeant Graffham made me think about it. I can't remember why it came up – something to do with them missing women, I think. Only she said to get on with it, kept on at me, told me how good you were for me . . . and how good a husband I'd make and all that. Honestly, you owe her, Em.'

'I'll remember to thank her.'

'You can do it now, we're going round there. We're going to dance outside her house and we're taking this bottle. Come on.'

'Nathan, don't be stupid. You can't just barge round to your sergeant's house and wake her up.'

'Oh, she won't have gone to bed, she never does till

two in the morning, she told me, and anyway, she was singing in some concert tonight in the cathedral so she'll definitely be up for a drink.'

'More likely crashed out.'

'Naw . . . come on, I'll push your bike.'

'I don't need pushing. Are you sure about this, Nath? I don't know . . .'

But Nathan had grabbed her hand and the bottle of champagne and propelled her out of the door.

The streets were empty and peaceful. Their bikes made a silky swishing sound on the dry tarmac.

'It's like when you're a kid, doing something daft like this, creeping out when your mam and dad think you're in bed.'

'You never told me you did that.'

'There's a lot of things I haven't told you. Why should I have?'

'Because I'm a copper. You'll be a copper's missus. Carries responsibilities that does.'

They swerved round the corners of the narrow streets, meeting no one, avoiding the odd cat that streaked across the road, giggling.

'Tell you what, why don't we go the long way round, on the road past the Hill?'

'What for?'

'It's real spooky round there, I fancy frightening you to death.'

'It'd take more than the Hill on a dark night to frighten me, Nathan Coates.'

'Not if I told you what had been going on there it wouldn't. Not if I told you –'

'OK, race you!'

Emma whisked off ahead, catching him out, so that he had to pedal furiously to reach her.

Freya got into the kitchen, unlocked the door and hurtled down the narrow passageway. She had managed to surprise him after all.

He did not catch her until she had her hand on the bolt of the side door into the street but then she felt a pain in the middle of her back as he put his fist into it, taking her breath away, and another as he wrenched her wrist from the door. He had not looked strong, not as strong as this.

Freya began to scream. She screamed until he put his arm across her mouth and throat, at the same time pushing her hard, back into the kitchen, back into the sitting room. She tripped and fell, hitting her face on the floor.

Remember, remember what you should be doing, don't let him surprise you, trip him up, roll over and kick him hard, don't . . .

Her arm almost came out of its socket in a wrenching pain, as he yanked her to her feet. She saw his face, intensely white with two scarlet patches on the cheekbones, and his eyes, staring insanely at her, the syringe held aloft, glinting. Somehow she had expected him to be laughing but he was not, there was a grim and dreadful concentration on his features as he faced her. Freya lashed out at him with her foot and raised her knee at the same time, trying to get to his groin, but he had her arm again and twisted it so hard behind her back she felt the bone crack. Sickness surged up.

Don't let, don't let him, don't let . . .

A split second of pain so intense that it did not feel like pain at all but was like a brilliant light boring through her skull.

Don't . . .
Then nothing.

In the end, they did not stop on the Hill road, they raced
one another, sweeping past it in the darkness and their
laughter floated up towards the Wern Stones and the
trees, dissolving the ghosts.

'Hey, hey, hey . . .' Nathan shouted, and stuck both
legs out at the sides of his bike.

Emma was still ahead of him as they swerved round
the corner of Freya's street.

'There you are, told you, her light's on,' Nathan
shouted.

They pedalled the last few yards alongside the parked
cars, past all the darkened houses to the one with a dim
light still showing. Nathan skidded off his bike and
propped it up against the low wall.

'What shall we do, sing? Let's give her a song.'

'Shut up, you'll wake the street. Just tap on the door
and if she doesn't answer –'

'Course she'll answer.' Nathan opened the gate and
marched up the drive, waving the bottle of champagne
and laughing, dragging Emma by the hand behind him.

It had been very quiet in Graffham's house. He had felt
the usual surge of power and the adrenaline had carried
him to the crest of excitement and strength. But afterwards, as he knew to expect, energy drained out of him
so fast that he had to sit and take deep, slow breaths.
His hands trembled. He knew better than to take more
alcohol but he tipped the last of the jug of water into his
glass and drained it quickly.

She lay on the floor, a few feet away from him, one

leg bent awkwardly back, her head face down on the carpet. The blood had begun to seep out from under her making a thick stain. He did not like there to be blood, not yet. He avoided blood and he was angry with himself for his own carelessness.

Things had rushed on, she had forced his hand when he was not ready. It was her fault. But she was not the one he was concerned about. *He* had to be safe. There had been very little noise, apart from the few moments in the alleyway and no one had come, no light had gone on.

He did not go near to her or touch her. He was confident he had no need to do so. In a few moments, in his own time and when he was calm and steady, he would go out of the front door and walk down the quiet, dark street to his car which was parked at the far end. He knew there would be a few moments when danger would be acute, as he carried her out of the house and put her on to the back seat, but people were asleep, no cars had come down the road for over an hour and it was too late for people walking home from the pub or the cinema.

Then he heard the noise outside. At first it was difficult to understand what was happening. There had been no car. Voices. Voices and suppressed laughter. He waited, even his breathing held in suspense. People drunk, banging on doors at random? Kids?

There was a short silence. He thought they had moved on. He would wait for ten or fifteen minutes, perhaps more. He had to be certain, had to be safe.

Someone knocked, softly at first and then a little more loudly, and after a moment, the letter-box flap went up and a voice came in a stage whisper into the hall.

'Sarge? Oy . . . Sarge . . . it's Nathan.'

The bloody little constable with the plug-ugly face. His heart began to pound very fast. He needed to think, to plan, to stay calm and he could not think, had no time to plan, was not calm.

He looked round the room quickly, then went to the back door that led from the kitchen into the alleyway. It was still unlocked so that it opened without any sound. He could hear their voices again at the front. He hesitated. If he went out of the gate into the street he would be heard and then seen. He moved backwards and looked behind him. A fence divided her house from the one next door. The garden was in darkness but the garden was his only means of escape and if he could not get out he would be able to hide there in the shadows at least for a short time.

He slipped sideways, stopped, waited. Moved again. He felt grass under his feet. It was quite a long garden and there were shrubs at the bottom and then a shed. He could see a little now. To one side the fence was lower but there was no chance that he could climb it without the possibility of its crashing down or at least creaking loudly.

He moved on. Then, at the very end of the garden, he came up against it in the dark, a low brick wall with some sort of tree beside it. From the street, he heard voices again and knocking.

Aidan Sharpe put one foot on the low wall. It did not give and he made no sound. After a second, he hauled himself up easily with the aid of a branch and then slithered down into soil at the end of the garden of the house behind.

It was easy. It was wonderfully easy, so much so that he smiled to himself in the darkness. He had been meant to get away. He had kept his head and stayed calm and now he simply walked up a long stretch of grass and slipped between two houses and into the street. It was dark here too. No lights in any of the houses. Nothing. He removed his gloves and made sure they were tucked well into his pocket.

Of course, he could not collect his car now and so he walked the two and a half miles back to his own house, steadily and calmly through the night streets of Lafferton. The only regret he had was that although Freya Graffham's death had been necessary she would now be wasted. It was a pity, he thought, remembering her as he walked. She had been killed to be silenced, but if he had been left undisturbed that would not have been the end of it. She could have been of further use.

Fifty-One

The room was full. CID and uniform sat and stood three-deep. There was a murmur but none of the usual uproar, chair-scraping, joking and laughter. As they had come in that morning they had heard, and those who had been on night duty stayed to hear more. Word had gone round but hard information was patchy.

DC Dave Pearce straddled a chair beside DC Justin Weekes. 'I just got in. They've sealed off half of the Old Town. Anything fresh?'

Justin shook his head. 'All I know is Nathan and his girl found her and went with her in the ambulance to BG. Haven't heard any more.'

'They any ideas?'

Dave inclined his head. The room went still as DCI Simon Serrailler walked in. Nathan Coates, looking shattered, followed him and slipped into a seat at the side.

'Good morning, everyone. Most of you will know what this is about, but I want to fill you all in before rumours start. Last night, DC Nathan Coates went to DS Graffham's house at approximately twelve twenty. He was accompanied by Nurse Emma Steele. They had become engaged earlier in the evening and wanted to share the good news. They cycled round to Sergeant Graffham's house on the off chance of her still being up, in order to celebrate. They found the lights on and Sergeant Graffham's car parked outside. When there was no answer to the front door or to either the house phone or Sergeant Graffham's mobile which they could hear ringing inside, they broke in and found her lying on the floor of her living room. She was unconscious and had serious injuries. There was no sign of forced entry and no sign of anything having been taken or of any damage in the house. The kitchen door which leads to a passageway at the side of the house was unlocked.

'Sergeant Graffham has been involved in Operation Osprey and also in the on-going inquiry CID have been conducting into a series of thefts of white goods. She has also been leading investigations into the disappearance of three Lafferton women, Angela Randall, Debbie Parker and Iris Chater, and I am concentrating on matters surrounding this in the search for . . .'

The door opened quietly. Everyone looked at Inspector Jenny Leadbetter, who inclined her head to Serrailler.

'Excuse me a moment.'

He went out and closed the door. People looked at one another, shuffled their feet, shifted in their chairs, but very little was said. Someone got up and opened a window.

The DCI came back. They looked at him and knew. The skin seemed to have tightened over his face and a nerve twitched beside his mouth.

He cleared his throat and looked down.

No one seemed to be breathing.

'I have just had a message from the hospital. I'm sorry
. . . Freya Graffham died fifteen minutes ago from her
injuries. She hadn't regained consciousness. This is therefore now a murder inquiry. I'll call another conference
later today. Thanks, everyone.'

He strode very fast out of the room, only pausing fractionally to beckon Nathan Coates to follow.

In his own room, the DCI poured himself coffee from a
percolator of his own. Nathan still had the polystyrene
beaker of cold tea which he had bought from the machine
before the conference and which he clutched as if it were
a lifeline. Simon Serrailler sat in his chair, drank a lot of
very black coffee very quickly and looked across at the
DC, his face still grooved and pale with the shock of the
news he had been given.

Neither wanted to speak. Nathan swirled the dregs
of his tea round. Outside in the corridor people came
and went, there were voices, the usual clatter.

Then Simon leaned forward. 'I'm taking charge of this,
Nathan. Do you feel up to being part of the team? If not,
you can stand down and go on to something routine . .
. no one's going to blame you.'

'Do I hell, guv! She was my sarge, I want me own
hands round the bugger's throat.'

'Well don't let either your anger or your distress get
the better of your judgement. I know it's difficult.'

'I owe her. It was her made me propose to Em – don't
waste it, she said, don't let her go, do it, ask her. That's
what we was going round there to tell her.'

'I know.'

'I want to arrest him.'

'Sharpe?'

'Too right.'

'Not enough evidence, Nathan . . . in fact, no evidence at all.'

'The watch.'

'Might be the one Angela Randall bought.'

'Is the one, *is*.'

'We can ask him to hand it over and the jeweller will tell us one way or the other. But even if he wears a watch given to him by Randall, it doesn't mean he had anything to do with her disappearance or with that of the other women, and it certainly doesn't mean he attacked Sergeant Graffham last night.'

'Murdered her.'

'Yes.'

'You can bring him in. Let me get him into the interview room, just –'

'No. There's a way to go yet. I'll go and talk to him though.'

'If he's bloody there, if he hasn't skipped . . . She was on to him, guv, and he knew it. When I went there yesterday he knew it. He's clever but he ain't as clever as he thinks.'

'Yes, and I'll want him taken apart and his premises too. Forensic are all over Sergeant Graffham's house now and if there's anything from him or anyone else they'll find it. Let's pray they do and we can pick him up with something solid. But if it isn't Aidan Sharpe, we have to start looking further.'

'It is. You want to look at him, you want to see his eyes. He's a psycho. What should I do now, guv?'

'Go back to the sergeant's house . . . see where they're at, give them a hard time, I want this fast-tracking. Let me know. I'm going to interview Sharpe. Is there anything in particular you think I should press him about?'

Nathan thought. The DCI wouldn't let anything get past him. He swigged the cold tea. 'There's what he said about the business park.'

Nathan looked across the desk and Simon Serrailler saw that his eyes were full of tears.

'We just wasn't there soon enough. We mucked about, rode round by the Hill for a lark . . . if we hadn't done that we'd have got there in time.'

'You don't know that.'

'I bloody do know that,' Nathan shouted, and then wiped his sleeve across his eyes. 'Sorry, guv, sorry.'

'All right, Nathan. Take it easy this morning. You're in shock.' He stood up and looked vaguely out of the window at the grey morning above the house roofs. 'We all are.'

Fifty-Two

He had slept at once and easily, and neither dreamed nor stirred, but just after five he woke, surfacing instantly, remembering everything, and then he broke into the sweat of panic, knowing that they either knew or must soon know. He had been careless at the house, getting away in a hurry, leaving her body on the floor. His car was parked on the street. Soon enough they would find it.

He got up and stood at the window. There would be no need for them to probe and pry, no need for questioning, here or at the station, no need for them to use their wits. He had given it all to them. He despised them but he despised himself more for handing them everything, making it all so easy. He felt afraid. He did not recognise the feeling. But he could still think clearly. His mind never let him down.

He knew exactly where to go and what to do.

Fifteen minutes later he was walking again, this time carrying a compact nylon holdall. No one was about yet in the avenue. He avoided the main road for as long as possible but when he had to join it there was fast traffic passing through to join the dual carriageway going towards Bevham. People were uninterested in a man walking.

The business park worried him. The police had been there very early yesterday. But his luck held. The avenues were deserted. No police. No cars. No one. No one opening up his unit early. He saw his own unit at the end of the side road with a huge relief of tension. It was all he could do to stop himself breaking into a run.

No one observed him. No one was there. He slipped up the side and undid the padlocks.

Inside, he stood shaking, sweat breaking out over his body. He went into the front office and checked that the slatted blinds were down. It was light enough for him not to need the fluorescent tubes.

He put his bag down and unzipped it, took out food, milk, a book, toothbrush and disposable razor. He had a blanket here and an old cushion, he could sleep on the carpet in this office. He could stay here a day or two and then leave at the right moment, after dark. They would be watching his house. He could not go back there so he had brought money, cards, passport, everything he could think of to give him a start.

He filled the electric kettle and set out coffee mug and milk. He drank, and ate bread and cheese and an apple from his bag. Everywhere around him was silent. He lifted up a corner of the blind. The road outside was still deserted.

He went out of the office and into the workroom. Everything was as he had last left it. No one had been here. Why would they? They might track him down here eventually but for now this was his refuge and his home, the place where he felt safe and where he felt most himself, most alive.

He unbolted the door in the back wall. In here, the machinery hummed softly, soothingly, reassuring him. He checked the dials. They were all correct, all as usual.

He could begin. He would have to work hard but that was never a difficulty for him here. He took off his jacket and hung it up, got a fresh gown from the shelf and slipped his arms into it. He smiled slightly, imagining everything that would be going on by now in the world beyond.

An hour later, he stood in the centre of the main workroom. They were all here, all round him, on trolleys. His friends. He went to each of them and touched them gently. He spoke to them. He needed them now. They were no longer just the things he worked with, they had changed. They had a value to him far beyond the original.

'Debbie,' he said, and touched her cold, stiff face, before moving to each of the others in turn. Then he fetched a stool and simply sat peacefully, surrounded by those he loved.

Just after nine thirty, DCI Simon Serrailler's car turned into the drive of Aidan Sharpe's house. As he got out, the front door opened and a middle-aged woman came quickly towards him.

'Have you come to tell me bad news?'

Serrailler flicked his ID card.

'I knew it, I knew . . . please tell me what's happened.'

'I'm sorry, you are . . . ?'

'Julie Cooper, I'm Mr Sharpe's practice manager . . . please tell me what has happened.'

'Can we go inside, Mrs Cooper?'

She hesitated, then turned, still talking, slightly hysterically, as she led him into the reception area.

'Please just tell me.'

'I've come to see Mr Aidan Sharpe. I gather he isn't here?'

'Well, no, of course, that's what I mean.'

'I don't come with any news. I want to interview Mr Sharpe.'

'When I got here, everything was just normal . . . only he's always in first, always getting ready, and he wasn't, so I went through to the house . . . he isn't there either, I don't think he's been in all night and his car isn't here. Something's wrong, he has never done anything like this.'

'When did you last see Mr Sharpe?'

'Yesterday afternoon. I left at five as usual. He was here then.'

'Did he say he was going anywhere?'

'No. Of course he didn't, I'd have remembered, wouldn't I?'

'Did he behave normally? Was there anything unusual about him that you noticed?'

'No. Nothing at all. Nothing . . . I hope you're going to find out what's happened, where Mr Sharpe is, I –'

'I'd like you to stay here please, in case Mr Sharpe comes back. I imagine you've work you can do?'

'I have to let his patients for the day know . . . I've been trying to make a start.'

'Fine, if you could get on with that. There'll be an officer here, in case Mr Sharpe returns. Don't worry about that.'

'What do you mean?'

'We need to interview him, Mrs Cooper.'

*

By the time Simon arrived, the teams who had been crawling over every inch of Freya's house were still working, turning what had been a home into a crime scene, invading, scouring, prying, fingerprinting, photographing. What the pathologist did to a body the forensic team did to a house, violating everything – it always seemed to him like this, in spite of the respectful way in which the professions were taught to go about their business.

He walked slowly into Freya Graffham's house, and at once her image was there in front of him, as it had not been until this moment. He saw her slight figure, her cap of hair, her sharp profile. The house was her, exactly her, he saw it at once. Comfortable, easy, tidy . . . he looked at the books, the sheaf of choral music left on the table – last night's concert, in which his mother had taken part too; he liked it at once here, the atmosphere was welcoming and agreeable, quite informal, very distinctive.

'Morning, sir.'

The white-overalled officer glanced up from the section of carpet beneath a low table, from which he was extracting small tufts with tweezers and dropping them into a polythene bag.

'Anything yet?'

'Lots of prints. Not necessarily his though. Some dark hairs on the back of that chair, shoe print out in the garden . . . You should have enough to go on. As long as there's a comparison of course.'

'I want it yesterday.'

'You always do.'

'This one's different.'

'I know, sir. I didn't know the sergeant myself but it's

always the worst, one of your own. Any idea what it was about?'

'Yes.'

Simon went out of the open kitchen door and looked down the narrow garden. Grass, a lilac tree, a couple of rose bushes. Wall. Fence. She wasn't a gardener then, just liked a bit of outdoor space.

He walked a few paces across the grass. Two white suits were working on their hands and knees in the soil at the far end. He left them to it. For the moment he would simply carry on, let the boys do their stuff, get Sharpe – and they would get Sharpe, that wouldn't be hard. Tie it up. Then he could go home and close the door of his flat, and try to work out what he felt about Freya Graffham.

By five, the reports had come through.

'Nathan?'

'Sir?'

'Sharpe left his car in Freya's street. He won't get far, we've got his description out. You'd better try his house. I've put a couple of uniform up there in case he turns up.'

'Which he won't.'

'Probably not. But get a photo of him, will you? Put a picture out to the press with a description. When you've done that, you might as well go home.'

'No chance. I'm here until we get him.'

'Don't be ridiculous, it might be days.'

'For tonight any road. I'm not budging, guv. I mean, are you off home to put your feet up?'

No one else but Nathan, Simon Serrailler thought as he put his phone away, could have got a smile out of him just now.

*

Aidan Sharpe had apparently been camera shy. They turned his house upside down, to the distress of Julie Cooper, and found nothing at all.

'There ain't no pictures of anyone,' Nathan said as they trawled through. 'You'd think the bleedin' camera hadn't been invented.'

'I know there was one in the paper,' the receptionist said suddenly, 'it was a while ago, at a professional dinner. I don't remember it as being much good. But if it would help you find him . . .' No one had told her why her employer was wanted. 'I hope it hasn't anything to do with those others,' she had said when Nathan had arrived. 'Those missing women. Do you think it has?'

Nathan felt sorry for her.

'Which paper was it?'

'The *Echo*, but as I said, it was a while ago.'

'Shouldn't think he's changed much.'

Nor had he. The paper scanned the image and e-mailed it through to Lafferton station. Aidan Sharpe stood, wearing a dinner jacket and holding a glass, looking faintly supercilious in a group of half a dozen other men.

Simon Serrailler stared down at the face, the small beard, the carefully combed-back hair, the black tie, the odd eyes. He had rarely felt like this. He couldn't afford to. His job was detection, not vengeance, not judgement, not even punishment, but looking at the smug image of Aidan Sharpe he felt a desire for them all which was biblical in its intensity.

He picked up the phone and called Nathan in.

'Get this copied, get them to do as good a job as they can of separating him out and making the image clearer. I want it in tomorrow morning's papers and you can go up to the business park first thing and hawk it about, see if there's anything . . .'

'Right. I suppose it's something to get on with.' He glanced directly up at Simon, his monkey face bruised-looking, his eyes red with tiredness and distress. Serrailler understood him absolutely. He needed to clutch at any straw, go hard at anything at all, to convince himself that he was helping to pin down Freya Graffham's killer. If Serrailler had told him to walk barefoot to Bevham and back again on the off chance that it might be useful, Nathan would have done it.

'You can start as early as you want,' he said now, 'but when you've sorted out the pictures, go home, eat and get some sleep. Otherwise you're no use to me and I'll sign you off. Understood?'

'Guv.'

Nathan took the print-out and left.

Half an hour later, Simon drove his own car out of the station and headed, not for Cathedral Close, but out on to the road, and his sister's farmhouse.

Fifty-Three

He waited, sitting without moving as if in meditation, until just after midnight when he heard the security patrol go round, before putting the things he had brought with him back into the holdall and stowing it away in the front-office cupboard. They would find it easily of course – he was simply being tidy. He cleared the instrument table, folded it back against the wall and swept the floor.

Then he said goodbye. He spent a few moments with each of them, touching their faces, putting his hand over theirs, speaking to them quietly. He said their names, as if giving them a blessing. He gave thanks to them and for them.

Earlier, he had read over the details of the way each of them had died, from their file.

Angela Randall – stab wounds causing fatal haemorrhage.
Debbie Parker – strangulation.
Tim Galloway – blunt trauma to the left temple.
Iris Chater – cardiac arrest.

Only the drowning of the dog was left unrecorded.

When his notes were found and the discoveries he had made understood and made public, what they had contributed would be recognised, at the same time as his own work would be hailed. People would understand then. If there was anything to forgive they would forgive him.

He hesitated before deciding to leave them here in repose together and not replace them in the inner room. It would not be for long. It would not take much cleverness to track the unit down and find them. They would come to no harm.

He glanced round, hitched on his jacket and stowed all he needed for the journey in one of the pockets. Then, for the last time, he went outside and locked the door behind him.

It was a cool night and there was a half-moon. He was surprised at how much he had enjoyed all the walking. He could have walked across England, had he needed to go so far. He counted his own paces, not striding, not going too fast, enjoying the smell of the night and the sight of the corn-coloured moon riding ahead of him, low in the sky.

Lafferton asleep. He was coming to know it almost as well as he knew it by day, though never as well as he had known it during those hours of first light. He liked to have the streets to himself, to see darkened windows, to see a mouse scuttle, a cat stare from a wall with hostile eyes.

He felt quite calm. He did not think, did not look back, did not let his mind hover over events either in triumph or regret. More than anything else, he was confident because matters had not been taken out of his hands, as he had feared. He was still his own master.

He came to the perimeter road and, for a moment,

had to press himself quickly against the elephantine trunk of a tree as a car flashed by, its headlamps on, but then there was nothing but quietness and stillness, just as he had always known it here.

He stepped on to the grass and began to climb, steadily and with a calm purpose, up the Hill.

A little after six thirty, Netty Salmon, large and stout and dressed in her usual old sheepskin, marched her Dobermanns up the Hill. It was drizzling slightly and there was a crown of low misty cloud around the trees at the summit. But weather was of little interest to Ms Salmon and had no effect on her, she merely strode on, calf muscles flexing rhythmically, up the steep path behind the dogs.

The mountain bikers were not about yet, there were no other walkers, and she had not seen the pathetic little man looking for his Yorkshire terrier for weeks.

She was not a woman who analysed her own feelings but, if she had done so, she would have said she was content. She liked her own company perfectly well and that of the Dobermanns better. She paused at the usual spot to get her breath and as she did so, the dogs began to bark. But there was nothing for them to bark at. They would pursue a rabbit or a squirrel but they did not bark in this way at either. They barked at strangers. And at anything odd or alarming.

Netty Salmon looked up. The dogs had raced to the top of the Hill and were standing at the foot of one of the trees and now their barking was furious and urgent. She was short-sighted. She had to clamber nearer before she could see. It was pointless to try and silence them. Barking like that would not be quieted.

Then she saw it, swinging from the high branch of the tree – she peered into the drizzle. Something had been put up there, some sort of figure. An effigy. Netty Salmon was puzzled. She climbed the last stretch until she was beside the hysterical dogs, immediately beneath the oak tree, and then looked up again.

No. Not an effigy. She was not a nervous woman. She did not scream when she recognised a man's body hanging from a rope. She merely turned and began to march back down the Hill, dragging the dogs, until she saw a pair of young men on mountain bikes riding towards her and held her arms out wide to stop them.

Three police cars, including that of DCI Simon Serrailler, swept up the avenue of the business park and turned left. Nathan Coates was waiting with two men outside a small green-painted unit at the far end.

'Nathan.'

'Morning, guv. This is Mr Connolly the site manager and Terry Putterby the security guard.'

'OK, what have we got?'

'Mr Connolly here recognised the press photo, like I said, only he called himself Dr Fentiman. But it's him.'

'Right.' Serrailler looked at the site manager. 'Do you have keys?'

'I do, but these units are rented in good faith, I think I should –'

'No one's blaming you for anything. I do have a warrant.'

'It was only I –'

'Right. Now, I've no idea if he's in here, but if he is he'll be dangerous. I'm going in first, uniform back-up is behind. Nathan –'

'I'm in there with you.'

Simon knew better than to argue. 'Just be careful. He's unlikely to be armed, but if he's cornered he'll think he's got nothing to lose. He'll have heard us.' He spoke briefly, bringing the others up behind him to surround the unit. 'May I have the keys please? Then you gentlemen stay right over there.'

Serrailler turned the key in the lock and stepped quickly inside, Nathan at his heels. Uniformed officers closed up behind. There was silence. Simon put his hand on the inner door that led to the office then opened it quickly.

'Sharpe?' He looked round quickly. 'No one. Doesn't look as if he did much business with his import and export. We'll get forensics in here later.' He opened a couple of drawers. 'Still nothing.'

'Here, sir.' Nathan stepped back. The holdall was on the shelf.

'Get it down,' Serrailler said.

'If he's gone away he's forgotten his overnight stuff.'

'Unless this is spare kit he keeps here for some reason.'

'Toothbrush is damp, sir.'

'OK. Leave it now.'

'Hold on . . .' Nathan took a small package from the shelf.

'Addressed to Dr Cat Deerbon, sir.'

Simon looked round sharply. The brown envelope was unsealed and Nathan tipped it up. Three tapes slid out on to the shelf.

'OK, bag them up with the rest of the stuff later. Now, there's the big storage area at the back and some sort of inner room as well. He could be in either. The side entrance is covered, he can't get past anyone this way but watch it.'

They moved forward.

'Sharpe?'

The silence was so dense they could have heard the dust seethe.

The DCI rapped on the metal door. 'Sharpe?'

'He ain't here,' Nathan said.

'Probably not, but he's as clever as paint. Right, let's go.'

He slid the bolt, put the key in the lock and turned it. Then he waited for a full minute. Behind him he felt Nathan's warmth and the young man's breath on his neck.

'We're coming in.'

He flung open the door wide and the two of them went through it almost together into what, for a split second, they thought was an empty space.

'Oh dear God.' Simon Serrailler spoke in a voice so low Nathan Coates did not catch the words but had to follow the DCI's glance across to the far end of the unit.

'Jesus Christ,' Nathan would have said, only when he opened his mouth, nothing but an odd little mewling cry came out of it.

The Tape

I have told you now. I have talked to you. I have made up for the lies and the silences. Now more than ever, when perhaps we are about to come face to face, I must tell you the truth, mustn't I?

I used to hate talking to you. I hated it when you tried to make me tell you things, tried to get under my skin, tried to live my life alongside me.

But I have come to like laying everything bare at last. I like it that you know me – what I choose to let you know. Because, in the end, I do have the choice and the power. The last word. I.

Not you.

I. I. I. I. I. I.

Fifty-Four

'Lord of all gentleness, Lord of all calm,
Whose voice is contentment, Whose presence is balm.
Be there at our sleeping and give us we pray
Your peace in our hearts, Lord, at the end of the day.'

The last verse of the hymn rang up from the full congregation, the St Michael's Singers and the choir, up to the cathedral roof. Freya Graffham's light oak coffin lay on its rests at the chancel steps. She had looked up at the roof with its gilded angels and ribs when she herself had been singing, so that Cat thought it seemed more than usually right for it to be placed there. The beautiful hymn had choked everyone.

The cathedral was full. Police from Freya's old teams in the Met sat with those from Lafferton. Gold braid gleamed. Chief constables and deputy chief constables, chief superintendents, superintendents. DCI Simon Serrailler sat at the aisle end of a pew, from which he had got up and walked to the lectern to read the Old Testament lesson. Nathan Coates sat with his fiancée in the second row, among the colleagues he had shared with Freya. In her place among the altos, Meriel Serrailler sat listening to the familiar words from the old Prayer Book and, for the first time since Freya's death, felt not only sadness, not only the loss of a new friend whom she had liked so much, but a regret for something more and which she could not articulate even to herself. She made the best of things, looked forward, worked, did not linger too long in any part of the present. It was the way she had sustained a long and bitter marriage to an angry and resentful man, but now for some reason the death of Freya brought it into acutely clear focus. The waste of time, the waste of life, the sense of things left undone, the repression of so much anger seemed to come to a head, here, in this building she loved, and she did not know how to deal with them or what her response should be. She thought of Aidan Sharpe, insane, deranged, wicked, twisted – which? From when? And why, why, why?

There was a rumble of chairs as the hymn finished. Nathan Coates got up and walked to the lectern. His face was tight with the effort of control and in his light grey suit and black tie he looked like a schoolboy. He put both hands on the lectern and cleared his throat. Emma clenched her hands in feeling for him. At first he had said he couldn't do this, that he would be afraid of weeping, as he had wept so often since his sergeant's death. Then, abruptly, he had changed his mind. 'Pulled myself together,' he'd said to her. But she knew how hard this was going to be.

'The lesson is taken from the Gospel of St Luke Chapter Ten. "A certain man went down from Jerusalem to Jericho, and fell among thieves . . ."'

His voice became stronger as he read on through the

parable of the Good Samaritan so that at the end it sounded clear and proud and vibrant through the building. As he went back to his pew he paused beside the coffin and bowed his head.

'Let us pray.'

Emma took Nathan's hand and held it pressed between both of her own to still the shaking.

Karin McCafferty felt tired. She had almost stayed at home, urged by Mike not to push herself to come, Mike who was terrified for her, terrified for himself, helpless in the face of what he now saw as her death sentence. He had not believed in the way she had taken nor understood her reasons. Now, when he seemed to be right – when everyone seemed to be right but her – he found excuses to go away so that he did not have to watch her worsen and become weaker.

But I am not worse, she said now, as they stood for the last hymn, I know. I know. For weeks past she had felt herself shielded, cocooned within the circle of some strong protective force. Slowly, gradually, she was being healed and strengthened. She was not in the least afraid, standing among them all as they began to sing.

> 'He who would true valour see
> Let him come hither.'

She wondered who had chosen 'To be a Pilgrim', whether Freya had left instructions for her own funeral. Perhaps those whose work brought them into danger often did, even just scribbled notes on a scrap of paper left in a drawer.

The moment she had heard what had happened, Karin

had closed the door in her mind which led to the room in which she had lain on a couch with Aidan Sharpe leaning over her, closed it, bolted it, locked it. She would never so much as approach it again. She had talked about everything to Cat Deerbon, had told her healer and then made the decision for herself. She could not begin to understand let alone judge. Better simply to leave it alone.

Sandy Marsh thought she might have to go out when they sang the hymn, the same one they had sung for Debbie. She sat near the back of the cathedral. Jason had come with her, though she hadn't wanted him to, but now, in the middle of it all, with the memories flooding over her again, she was glad that he had, that he was reassuringly there with his arm and his supply of large clean handkerchiefs.

Her life had turned upside down from that first night, when Debbie hadn't come home and it would never go back together properly, never be as it had been. She had not only lost her oldest friend and flatmate to a murderer, she had lost something else she couldn't define, something careless and optimistic, something that had been there since she and Debbie were children. It was gone for good.

She would leave the flat, she had decided that as soon as she had heard about Debbie, though she didn't want to leave Lafferton or her job, she needed friends and everything familiar round her, even if it was hard to bear some days when she saw the Hill or a bus going to Starly, or one of the ordinary places she and Debbie used to go to, shops, the café, the branch library.

For now she was staying with one of the girls at work whose husband was in the navy and away for long stretches. She wanted to find a new flat of her own, but finding someone to share with would not be easy and she could not afford to rent anything alone. She and Debbie had got on comfortably, known one another so well that life had been smooth even when Debbie had been so low-spirited.

They were standing for the next hymn. Jason touched her arm. Kind Jason, good, nice, friendly Jason. But she knew Jason wanted more and she had to tell him that she did not. She liked him and she was grateful. At work, he was good fun. That was it. Even if she'd been ready for a serious boyfriend, it was never going to be Jason.

'Let sense be dumb, let flesh retire
Speak through the earthquake, wind and fire
O still small voice of calm,
O still small voice of calm.'

Simon Serrailler stood in the pulpit. He had a sheet of notes on the lectern in front of him and did not refer to it once.

'We are here to say goodbye to Freya Graffham, daughter and sister and aunt, colleague and friend, and to honour her, and I know this is one of the hardest things any of us will ever have to do. Freya was with us in Lafferton CID for a short time but few people have made such a clear and impressive mark or endeared themselves to us so strongly.'

Cat's eyes did not leave her brother's face. He was a fine speaker, not showy, clear, striking and absolutely sincere. He brought Freya to life again, captured something of her vibrancy and sense of fun, her intelligence, her love of her job, her new home, her colleagues, her friends, singing – and this cathedral. He spoke movingly about her death and bitterly about the circumstances, regretted the waste and the evil, praised the bravery of his colleagues, reminded them of the risks run by police officers every day, asked them for their support and prayers for the living, even as they honoured one who was dead. It was a passionate address and it left the congregation stunned and moved once more to tears.

Then the commendation and the blessing. Suddenly, Cat's mind went to Aidan Sharpe; he was vivid before her, smug, unrepentant, smiling. It seemed that she looked evil full in the face.

The six police bearers, including Simon and Nathan Coates, stepped forward and shouldered Freya's coffin.

God help us, Cat thought, looking intently at the pale wood, at the single wreath of white roses and freesias lying on top, and the solemn faces of the bearers. She bent her head as they went past. Dear God . . .

But any more was beyond her. The funerals of Debbie Parker and Iris Chater had been smaller affairs in other places, sad, bleak occasions, full of questions left hanging in the air, and of bewilderment and rage, without any sense of resolution. Now, somehow, as the cathedral organ played Bach's great 'Sleepers Awake', there seemed to be a kind of resolution, a glimpse of rightness here. Death was a mess, a breaking apart, an ugliness, but a funeral service like this threw a shaft of light and gave comfort, gave strength.

Where would I be and how could I go on if I did not have this? Cat bent her head again.

The police guard of honour lined the cathedral path as the coffin was carried down to the hearse and silver and gilt flashed in the sunlight here and there and for a second fell on the white flowers and the pale wood, before the car moved off into shadow.

People emerging fell into pairs and groups, spoke quietly, waited for official cars or began to walk away. In the shelter of one of the huge buttresses by the side door, Nathan Coates wept without restraint in Emma's arms.

Jim Williams turned alone into the close without looking back, unsure why he had come, unsure if he was glad that he had or not, and yards behind him, Netty Salmon watched and half thought of striding off to catch him up, but somehow did not.

Gradually the area cleared. The senior officers had left first. Lafferton Police Station was open for anyone from the congregation to sign a book of condolence in Freya Graffham's memory.

'Sir.'

Simon looked round. 'Nathan.'

'That was everything . . . what you said.'

'Thank you.'

'I don't believe it though, I don't believe that was her we just carried. I can't get my head round it.'

'No.'

'Nathan . . .' Emma said gently.

Nathan wiped his eyes. 'Yeah, I know. It's only that we're getting married, guv. We was going to wait, have a proper do, but . . . we can't. Not now. We're going to the registry office Thursday morning, early. Just us and one of my brothers and Emma's mum and dad. Only . . .'

'Would you be one of our witnesses?' Emma finished for him.

'I'd be absolutely delighted to.'

'Thanks. Thanks a lot. See you back at the station then.'

They went off, getting a lift with another of the CID.

But Simon had told his driver not to wait. As the last few people left and he heard the choirboys coming out of the side door of the cathedral, he turned and went back into the great building. The air was still vibrant with the service, the notes of the organ, the voices, the prayers still hung suspended there. It was warm. There was a smell of flowers and coats. Some orders of service had been left behind on the pews.

He walked slowly up the side aisle and looked at the space at the foot of the chancel where Freya's coffin had stood. Freya. He could not picture her and he did not know for now what he felt or thought. It would come. He was a man who let such things fall as they would.

His thoughts about Aidan Sharpe were no clearer and probably never would be. Cat had said that his kind could only be left to the understanding of God. Simon wondered.

A verger was snuffing the candles, another was collecting up the hymn books and carrying them away in neat stacks. There was an abrupt squeak and then a single bass note from the organ. Simon glanced up. The organist closed the cover and switched off the light above the music rest.

Outside, it was quiet and the sun had almost slipped off the great west door.

Simon walked quickly out into the close towards his own building. He would not go back to the station. Let them think what they would. For the rest of the day he could face no one at all.

In his flat, he threw his jacket on to the sofa, then went into the kitchen and poured himself a whisky and water.

It was cool here, cool and peaceful, ordered and still.

The cathedral clock struck four.

After a moment, seeing the light blinking on his answerphone, he leaned over and clicked it on. The voice was both warm and businesslike.

'It's Diana. Haven't spoken for a bit. Miss you. Give me a call back?'

It was the only message.

Simon paused for a second, before pressing the button to erase it.

Now read the first chapter of Susan
Hill's next Simon Serrailler mystery

THE PURE
IN HEART

published by Chatto & Windus
in June 2005

VINTAGE

One

At first light the mist was soft and smoky over the lagoon and it was cold enough for Simon Serrailler to be glad of his heavy donkey jacket. He stood on the empty Fondamenta, collar turned up, waiting, cocooned in the muffled silence. Dawn on a Sunday morning in March was not a time for much activity on this side of Venice, where few tourists came; the working city was at rest and even the early churchgoers were not yet about.

He always stayed here, in the same couple of rooms he rented above an empty warehouse belonging to the friend, Ernesto, who would appear any moment to take him across the water. The rooms were comfortable and plain and filled with wonderful light from the sky and the water. They were quiet at night, and from the Fondamenta Simon could walk about among the hidden backwaters, looking out for things he wanted to draw. He had been here at least once, and usually twice a year for the last decade. It was a working place and a bolt-hole from his life as a Detective Chief Inspector, as were similar hideouts in Florence and Rome. But it was in

Venice that he felt most at home, to Venice he always returned.

The putter of an engine came just ahead of the craft itself, emerging close beside him out of the silvery mist.

'Ciao.'

'Ciao, Ernesto.'

The boat was small and workmanlike, without any of the romance or trimmings of traditional Venetian craft. Simon put his canvas bag under the seat and then stood up beside the boatman as they swung round and headed across the open water. The mist settled like cobwebs on their faces and hands and for a while Ernesto slowed right down until, suddenly, they seemed to cut a channel through the whiteness and emerge into a hazy buttery light beyond which Simon could see the island ahead.

He had been to San Michele several times before to wander about, looking, recording in his mind's eye – he never used a camera – and he knew that at this hour, with luck, he would find it deserted even of the elderly arthritic widows who came in their black to tend the family graves.

Ernesto did not chat. He was not a voluble Italian. He was a baker, still working out of the cavernous kitchen generations of his family had used, still delivering the fresh hot bread round the canals. But he would be the last, he said, every time Simon came; his sons were not interested, they were off at universities in Padua and Genoa, his daughter was married to the manager of a hotel near San Marco; when he stopped baking the ovens would go cold.

Venice was changing, Venetian trades were in decline, the young would not stay, were not interested in the hard life of daily work by boat. Venice would die soon. Simon found it impossible to believe, hard to take the prophecies of doom seriously when the ancient, magical city was still here, floating above the lagoon after thousands of years and in spite of all predictions. Somehow, somehow, it would survive, and the real Venice, too, not merely the overloaded and expensive tourist city. The people who lived and worked in the backwaters of the Zattere and the Fondamenta and the canals behind the railway station, and would still do so in a hundred years' time, propping one another up, servicing the hotels and the tourist area.

But 'Venice she dying', Ernesto said again, waving his hand at San Michele, the island of the dead; soon this was all there would be, one great graveyard.

They swung up to the landing stage and Simon climbed out with his bag.

'Lunchtime,' Ernesto said. 'Noon.'

Simon waved his hand and walked off towards the cemetery, with its well-tended paths and florid marble memorials.

The sound of the motor boat faded away almost at once, so that all he could hear were his own footsteps, some early-morning birdsong and, otherwise, the extraordinary quietness.

He had been right. No one else was here – no bowed old women with black headscarves, no families with small boys in long shorts carrying bunches of bright flowers, no workmen hoeing the weeds out of the gravel.

It was still cool, but the mist had lifted and the sun was rising.

He had first come upon the memorial a couple of years before and made a mental note about it, but he had been spending most of his time that year at all hours of the day among the market stalls, drawing the piles of fruit and fish and vegetables, the crowds, the stall holders and had not had time or energy to take in the burial island in detail.

He reached it and stopped. On top of the stone plinth was an angel with folded wings, perhaps ten feet high and flanked by three cherubs, all with bent heads and expressions of grief, all gravely, impassively beautiful. Although they were idealised, Simon was sure they had originally been taken from life. The date on the grave was 1822, and the faces of the angels were characteristically Venetian, faces you still saw today, in elderly men on the vaporetto and young men and women promenading in their designer clothes on weekend evenings along the riva degli Schiavoni. You saw the face in the great paintings in the churches, and as cherubs and saints and virgins and prelates and humble citizens gazing upwards. Simon was fascinated by it.

He found a place to sit, on a ledge of one of the adjacent monuments, and took out his drawing pads and pencils. He had also made himself a flask of coffee and brought some fruit. The light was still hazy and it was not warm. But he would be absorbed here now for the next three hours or so, only breaking off to stretch his legs occasionally by walking up and down the paths. At twelve Ernesto would return for him. He would take his things back to the flat, then go for a Campari and lunch at the trattoria he used most of the time he was here. Later, he would sleep before going out to walk into the busier parts of the city, perhaps taking a vaporetto the length of the Grand Canal and back for the delight of riding on the water between the ancient, crumbling, gilded houses, seeing the lights come on.

His days scarcely varied. He drew, walked, ate and drank, slept, looked. He did not think much about home and his other, working life.

This time, though . . .

He knew why he was drawn to San Michele and the statue of the wildly grieving angels, just as he had haunted the dark, incense-filled little churches in odd corners of the city, wandering about inside, watching the same old widows in black kneeling with their rosary beads or lighting candles at one of the stands.

The death of Freya Graffham, who had been a DS under him at Lafferton Police Station for such a short time, had affected him far more than he might have expected and for longer. It was a year since her murder and he was still haunted by the horror of it and by the fact that his emotions had been engaged by her in a way he had not admitted to himself while she had been alive.

His sister Dr. Cat Deerbon had said he was allowing himself to feel more deeply for Freya simply because she was dead and so unable to respond and therefore unthreatening.

Had he felt threatened? He understood perfectly well what his sister meant but perhaps, with Freya, it had been different.

He shifted his weight and resettled the sketch pad on his knees. He was not drawing the whole statue but the face of each angel and cherub individually; he intended to come back again to do the complete monument and then work up each drawing until he was satisfied. His next exhibition would be his first in London. Everything had to be right.

*

Half an hour later he got up to stretch his legs. The cemetery was still deserted and the sun was full out now, warming his face as he walked up and down the path between the black and white and grey gravestones. Several times on this particular visit to Venice Simon had wondered if he might even come to live here. He had always been passionate about his job – he had taken the opposite path to that of his entire family, doctors for three generations – but the pull of this other life, of drawing and perhaps living abroad to do so, had become increasingly strong since Freya's death.

He was thirty-five. He would make Superintendent before long. He wanted it.

He did not want it.

He turned back towards the grieving angels. But the path ahead was no longer empty. Ernesto was walking towards him, and when he saw Simon, he raised an arm.

'Ciao – something wrong?'

'I've come back for you. There was a phone call.'

'Work?'

'No, family. Your father. He needs you call him right back.'

Simon put sketchbook and pencils back into the canvas satchel and followed Ernesto quickly to the landing stage.

Ma, he thought, something's happened to her. His mother had had a slight stroke a couple of months previously, the result of elevated blood pressure and too much stress, but she had made a good recovery and it had apparently not left any after-effects. Cat had told him there was no need for him to cancel his trip. 'She's fine, it wasn't major, Si. There is no reason for her to have another. Anyway, if she isn't right, you can get back quickly enough.' Which was what he must do, he thought, standing beside Ernesto as they sped back across the now sunlit water.

The only surprise was that it had not been Cat but his father who had telephoned. Richard Serrailler disapproved of Simon's choice of career, of his commitment to art, of his unmarried state – of him, period.

'Did he sound worried?'

Ernesto shrugged.

'Did he mention my mother?'

'No. Just you call.'

The motor boat shot up to the Fondamenta, turned neatly and stopped.

Simon put his hand on Ernesto's arm. 'You're a good friend. Thanks for coming back.'

Ernesto merely nodded.

Simon ran up the dark staircase from the empty warehouse to the flat and threw his satchel and jacket on the floor. The telephone connection had improved since the new digital lines had come in and he heard the ringing tone in Hallam House at once.

'Serrailler.'

'It's Simon.'

'Yes.'

'Is Mother all right?'

'Yes. I rang to tell you about your sister.'

'Cat? What's happened?'

'Martha. She has bronchial pneumonia. They've taken her to Bevham General. If you want to see her alive you should come home.'

'Of course, I . . .'

But he was speaking to a dead line. Richard Serrailler wasted words on no one, least of all his policeman son.

There was an evening flight to London but it took Simon half an hour on the telephone and in the end the help of a contact in the Italian police to get himself a seat on it. The rest of the day was spent packing, sorting out the flat and arranging for Ernesto to take him to the airport, so it was not until he was on the crowded plane that he had leisure to think. And he had not thought, not until now. His father's telephone call had been an order in all but name and he had obeyed without question. His relationship with Richard Serrailler was so poor that Simon behaved towards him as towards one of his superiors in the force and with about as much emotional involvement.

His seat was over a wing so there was little chance to look down on to the lagoon when they took off, which was as well because he minded leaving Venice more than usual, leaving his refuge, his work, and his calm, private space. Walking about the city, over canal bridges, through the squares, down the little dark passageways between the tall old houses, sitting looking and drawing, talking to Ernesto and his friends over an evening drink, Simon Serrailler was a different man from the DCI at Lafferton, his life and concerns were different, his priorities changed entirely. Time on the journey was time in which he moved from one to the other, but tonight he was being hurtled back into his everyday life without the usual relaxed period of adjustment.

The sign to fasten seat belts went off and the drinks trolley was being manoeuvred up the aisle. He asked for a gin and tonic and a bottle of mineral water.

Simon Serrailler was one of triplets. His GP sister, Cat, was the second, their brother Ivo, a doctor in Australia, the third. Martha was ten years younger, born when Richard and Meriel Serrailler were in their mid-forties; she was severely mentally and physically handicapped and had lived in a special care home for most of her life. Martha might or might not recognise Simon. No one could tell.

The sight of his sister had always moved him profoundly. Sometimes she lay in bed, sometimes she was in a wheelchair, her body propped up and strapped in, her head supported. If it was fine he wheeled her into the garden and round the paths between shrubs and flower beds. Otherwise they sat in her room or in one of the lounges. There was nothing he could take her. He talked to her and held her hand and kissed her when he arrived and left.

Over the years he had come to worry less about whether she knew him or gained anything from his company; if his visits had no significance for her, they became important to him, in something of the way these visits to Italy were important. With Martha, he was someone else. The time he spent beside her, holding her hand, thinking, talking quietly, helping her to sip a drink through a straw or eat from a spoon, absorbed and calmed him and took him away from everything else in his life.

She was pitiful, ugly, drooling, unable to communicate, barely responsive and as a boy he had been embarrassed and upset by her. Martha had not changed. He had.

His parents mentioned her occasionally but her situation was never discussed in depth or detail and emotions were always kept out of such conversations. What did his mother feel about her or for her? His father went to visit her but never spoke of it.

If she was unwell her condition always became acute very rapidly yet she had survived for twenty-five years. Colds led to chest infections then pneumonia. '*If you want to see your sister alive . . .*' But it had all happened before. Was she going to die this time? Was he sorry? How could he be? How could anyone? Did he wish her dead then? Simon's mind veered away. But he needed to talk. When he got into Heathrow he would ring Cat.

He drank more of his gin. In the locker above his head were two sketchbooks full of new drawings from which he would select the best to work up into finished pieces for his exhibition. Perhaps he had got enough after all and the extra five days in Venice would simply have been spent mooching about.

He finished his drink, took out the small sketch block he always carried and began to draw the elaborately plaited and beaded hair of the young African woman in the seat opposite.

The plane droned on over the Alps.

VINTAGE

VINTAGE

BY SUSAN HILL
ALSO AVAILABLE IN VINTAGE